Caroline Bourne

# Shadow Marsh

Echelon Press

Publishing

**Shadow Marsh**
An Echelon Press Book

First Echelon Press Publication 2011

(Original publication 1985, Wild Southern Rose
ISBN 0-8217-1603-4–Zebra Books)

Echelon Press
2721 Village Pine Terrace
Orlando, FL 32833
www.echelonpress.com

ISBN 978-1-59080-852-8
(1-59080-852-5)

Published by Echelon Press LLC.

To Kristen, my daughter.
And Karen, my friend.

He caught the passing wind
And held it to his soul,
A wild, tempestuous thing
That he could not console.

A splendid garden met his path,
From which he could not part.
And from the buds
He plucked a rose
and drew it to his heart.

O, Wind!
Reclaim thy foolish son,
Upon his knees
In the morning mist,
Impaled upon the brutal thorns
Of the ruby rose he kis't.

# Prologue

A slight breeze stirred dust across the highly polished black boots of the soldiers and dragoons standing at attention. Men were solemn. Reveille had brought them to formation at half past five this Sunday morning to witness the execution of a dragoon officer, due to take place within the hour.

Rage rose in the throats of the men at Fort Marcy, who had trusted Captain Fielding with their lives in battle against the Mexicans. It was an abomination that he should die.

Fort Marcy crowned a steep hill in the heart of Santa Fe, the first United States outpost in the American Southwest. The grounds of Fort Marcy had been laid only a year ago and it was a sprawling fortification, surrounded by adobe walls rising seventeen feet from the bottom of an eight-foot ditch. Captured Mexican cannons, pointed from the parapet toward Santa Fe, could level the city at the least indication of revolt by the Mexicans.

But now, the threat of rebellion had grown into war. America's manifest destiny was to push westward toward the Pacific. The first move in this direction had been made by newly elected President James K. Polk when he had sent an army on the Santa Fee trail to seize Mexico's vast Rio Grande and Pacific territories.

The Mexican War had been the first great challenge to the skillful young officers from West Point who had joined regular Army commands. Captain Michael Fielding had been sent into Texas under command of General Stephen Watts Kearney, and he had yearned for the chance to put his military expertise to the test.

Behind the heavy wood doors of Fort Marcy's stockade,

Michael had just finished shaving. Despite the February cold, he stood, bare to the waist and the suspenders attached to his trousers hung at his sides. A Spanish priest had spent the hours of predawn with Michael, but he had heard little. Rather, he had heard, echoing softly in his head, the words of his stepbrother, Lieutenant Jarred Gunthar, who had pleaded for Michael's life before the military tribunal.

*You have heard the extenuating circumstances surrounding the death of Lieutenant John Gunthar. Yet you call this a cold-blooded act of murder. Nothing could be further from the truth. Michael, John and I were raised as brothers, and we were bound together in brotherhood for all time. When John lay mortally wounded in battle, it was Michael who expressed the greatest love. May he be blessed, even as you condemn him. He is a merciful man. Find him innocent, for God's sake, and end this travesty."*

But the tribunal had been deaf to Jarred's plea. And it had been a long, agonizing two and a half months since the sentence had echoed resoundingly in Michael's ears...death by firing squad.

Michael could not imagine life going on without him. He could not bear the thought of his mother grieving for him. Jarred had been with him these past months. He had been there on the battlefield and had seen how their brother had suffered.

A sharp rap at the door startled Michael. Greselda, the camp washwoman, brought in his freshly laundered shirt and jacket. She entered silently, carefully put his jacket across the back of the chair and his shirt across the small cot.

As she started to leave, Michael murmured, "Thank you." She grunted, put her hand on the door, and turned to bless him with a smile. Then she quickly slipped out of the door.

Michael's stomach ached with hunger and nausea. His breakfast sat, untouched, on the wooden table in the corner. He turned back to the mirror, started to sweep his long hair back from his face, but dropped his hand when it began to shake.

"Discipline," he said. "It is necessary now." He had seen death and had killed, but he could not see himself dead. Life reflected in the mirror…warm, welcome life, and a strong desire to grow old. "God, help me through this hour."

Straightening, chastising himself for his lack of self-discipline, Michael brushed back his hair, retrieved his shirt from the cot, and pulled it on. As he completed his dressing, he found himself thinking of the girl he would have married the following summer.

He remembered their pleasant walks along the Hudson River, her laughter, the way she ran with her satin skirts picked up, trying to keep several steps ahead of his playful pursuits. Oh, how long ago it now seemed!

A rooster crowed far off in the distance. Michael sat in the wooden chair beside the cot and linked his fingers together in a moment of thoughtful silence. He soon arose, made up his cot as he had every morning, and sat to write a final letter. As he wrote, he listened to the sounds of morning through the thick stone and mortar walls–the brisk winter wind whistling across the blockhouse, men's shuffling boots, the click of rifles, the commands of drill sergeants, and the mission bells ringing out the call to services. He thought that Sunday was an awful day to die.

Through the iron-barred window he saw the territorial and American flags being raised over headquarters. He took the gold watch from his waistcoat pocket and stared at it.

Then the door opened and two officers approached. Michael came immediately to his feet, just as a pain grabbed his chest: fear–his final enemy.

Captain Ward Anderssen motioned him toward the door. Michael smoothed down the front of his jacket and fastened the buttons. As he stepped into the chilling wind, he thought of his home, Tarrytown, New York. With thoughts of home crowding his mind, he paced off two hundred steps and stood in the midst of the dragoons and soldiers who had once fought at his side.

Captain Anderssen stepped forward, unrolled a document he had clutched between his sweating fingers, and began to read in a loud, clear voice. "Be it known that on the twenty-fourth day of October, 1846, Captain Michael George Fielding, under

9

the direct command of General Stephen Watts Kearney, the major command of Brevet Brigadier General Zachary Taylor, did take the life of Lieutenant John Gunthar following engaged combat with invading Mexican forces at the American position of Coballo. We, the military tribunal of the First Cavalry Division of the Southwest, impaneled under special order, do sentence Captain Michael George Fielding to death by firing squad. The sentence shall be executed at half past the hour of six on the twenty-first day of February, eighteen forty-seven." Captain Anderson looked up from the document. "Captain Fielding, do you understand that all legal delays for appeal have passed?"

Michael nodded his head imperceptibly. "I do, sir."

"Have you any issues to address to this assembly before sentence is carried out?"

"None, sir, but I wish a word in private with Lieutenant Jarred Gunthar."

Anderssen, a tyrant in the guise of officer's dress, shot back in an angry, growled whisper, "You killed the man's brother, for God's sake!"

"And my stepbrother," Michael countered softly.

Anderssen clicked his tongue as if he found the request an intolerable and unnecessary delay, and directed a hasty order to the corporal standing beside him.

Lieutenant Gunthar was immediately summoned from the Santa Fe headquarters office where he waited with his father for this grim moment to pass. The two young officers met in the bitter cold air. Michael took the letter he had written from the inner pocket of his jacket and handed it to Jarred.

"I know the general is your father and not mine, Jarred," Michael said, "but since he and my mother married and the three of us became brothers…"

"He loves you, Michael, as his own."

"Perhaps," Michael replied, putting the letter in Jarred's hand. "But right now he believes only that I murdered his son."

"I told him the circumstances. He will come to grips with it."

"Eventually," Michael conceded. "One day when he understands, give him this letter."

Jarred quickly thrust it into the pocket of his jacket. "Do you wish to send any messages for your mother when again we meet?"

"Assure her of my deepest love. Assure her that I die bravely today." Michael embraced him and whispered a final farewell.

Jarred clipped his boots and turned away, his eyes moist with tears. Before he took three steps, he pivoted back and embraced Michael once again. "The men tried hard to clear you, Michael. May God forgive this travesty." Then he turned in an abrupt military fashion and quickly put distance between them.

Captain Anderssen approached with the guards and escorted Michael to a tall, flat beam against the stone wall. Immediately, wide leather straps circled his legs just above the knees, and his shoulders, pulling them painfully back. Anderssen unbuttoned Michael's jacket and pulled it back from his chest.

Michael's eyes moved swiftly, frantically, taking everything in...the solemn faces, the immaculate formations of blue-uniformed soldiers and officers, their brass buttons and sabers gleaming in the early morning light, bayoneted rifles rigid against the gold stripes of Army trousers...above, territorial banners flapping in the wind. Michael's strength began to abandon him.

Within moments, he would feel the impact of eleven bullets in his chest. He trembled. Had his knees not been firmly strapped to the beam, they might have buckled. Tension and dreaded anticipation crawled through his shoulders. Panic blinded him. The last thing he saw before his face was covered by a blindfold was Jarred disappearing into battalion headquarters across the battery. All that was left now was the dreaded sequence of commands.

Captain Anderssen moved away from him. From another direction, he heard muted boot steps comingled with commands that seemed muffled and far away. Then all movement ceased.

The provost marshal announced, "Officer of the Day, by

11

your command, the sentence shall be..." A tremor settled in his throat, which compelled him to turn away and cough. He turned back immediately. "The sentence shall be carried out, sir."

"Carry on," Anderssen replied. He had always been a stickler for tradition and firmness among men. He was sick to the pit of his stomach that men of the United States Army were as weak and undisciplined as schoolboys. Perhaps the lot of them should take example from the condemned man, who stood motionless against the beam.

The provost marshal looked down the neat line, at twelve men whose faces seemed strangely void of emotion.

His first command, "Ready..." sent renewed nerves, and the greatest fear he had ever known, crawling through Michael's shoulders.

His throat was suddenly parched and dry. He breathed deeply. As rifles clicked in unison, behind the blindfold, the muscles of Michael's face grew taut. Sweat poured down his hairline to his collar.

"Aim..." Michael did not hear the drums roll, only the clink of weapons. The world's noises abandoned him. A second became an eternity in which a sob choked in his throat. "God," he muttered, involuntarily drawing his chest into a tight knot of muscles.

"Fire!"

# One

*Jude's Landing, Louisiana, 1857*

The weather was quite unusual for March...cold and bleak, restricting sensible people to the warmth of their parlors. Spring was overdue. Winter-stifled homes were ready to be aired, bed linens shaken, and stale air let from dreary parlors. Time was approaching for new foals and calves to begin life.

Just as all were sure the winter would be perpetually with them, spring arrived. There was no gentle transition. As the sun rose, the children of the plantation and the settlement of Jude's Landing began to wander boldly outdoors in search of mischief and adventures. Warm blue skies glowed behind puffs of gray-white clouds standing motionless for a moment, and whipping across the horizon in a burst of dying winter wind.

This night, however, gloom and imminent death veiled Shadow Marsh, the household of the St. Cyr family.

Across the folds of the bright patchwork quilt, Anna Rose searched the semi-darkness for her father's features, the once sparkling eyes now deeply embedded in furrows of pallid skin. As Anna's long, slender fingers closed over her father's mottled hand, a gleam came to his eyes. In a moment that betrayed his weakness, he turned his hand and gently squeezed Anna's fingers. His parched, dry lips parted in an almost futile effort to speak. "Come hither, lass."

She rose from her chair, continuing to hold his hand. Lightly touching her lips to his cold cheek, she whispered, "I am here, beloved Papa." She felt the gentle stirring of his fingers as they tightened on hers.

"I'll be a-dyin' tonight, sweet lass."

Yes, she knew. Bea had reported just moments ago that his flesh was blue with impending death. Anna had scarcely taken a moment to pull on her satin robe, and her dark hair was loose and disheveled from sleep. She saw death in her father's parted lips, and felt it in the fingers trying to hold hers oh, so tightly.

While death had been expected for weeks now, it still came as a terrible shock to know that tomorrow her father would be gone. She felt tears form as her forehead rested gently against the side of his face. She felt his lips brush her dark, tousled hair, and when he again spoke his voice was a dry, raspy whisper.

"Not to despair, lass. 'Tis the best of us must face it."

Something stirred in the shadows of the room. Tylas Miller, personal physician to the St. Cyr family for twenty years, moved toward the high tester bed.

Although there was nothing save a miracle that could keep Patrick St. Cyr alive this night, he felt he must make some effort, if just to check his weak, erratic pulse. But with a strength he scarcely thought Patrick still possessed in his last moments, he was waved back into the shadows.

Other members of the family, roused by the sudden emergency, drifted in and assumed their places at the deathbed. Alistair, the tall, gaunt son, leaned against the back of a chair to take the weight off his clubfoot. Violet, their cousin, sat across the room with her black Labradors, Chauncy and Bo, at her side. Bea and Mose, the house servants who were more like family, stood by the door.

Anna felt a sudden compulsion to shoo them away. She wanted to spend these last moments alone with her father, to whisper the endearments that had frequently brightened his eyes. She had visited him every day, in between keeping the financial ledgers, handling complaints that drifted in from their managers and accountants, bailing Alistair out of the constable's custody twice a week or so, and generally running the plantation, as she had been doing since her father's illness. At the age of eighteen she had taken on an onerous responsibility, very little of which Alistair had shared.

Anna's thoughts were erratic. Suddenly, the emotions of five other people in the room began to close in and smother her. Tears moistened her eyes as her lashes flicked very gently against her father's cheek, which felt like cool marble. His breathing was slow and labored, and his fingers clenched and unclenched over hers. "My Rosie–"

Only Anna heard the endearment. "Yes, Papa?" she whispered.

"Marry soon, daughter. Your future is in this land and you must hold onto it."

"There is plenty of time for that," she replied, patting his hand.

Alistair approached the bed, looked down at his father, and crossed his arms at his chest. "You're dying, Father," he said, his cold tone immediately stirring the embers of fire in Anna's emerald eyes. "It is time to put our differences behind us. Offer your forgiveness. I ask for it now." A strange expression crossed Patrick's face, and his lips parted and quivered. "Answer me," Alistair demanded.

But as Patrick St. Cyr's features relaxed in death, the secret of his answer was lost forever. In those few moments, the world was at a standstill for Anna, as if the reality of her father's death could not penetrate her foggy senses.

Was this really happening? Was Patrick Brigham St. Cyr, beloved master of Shadow Marsh and patron of the parish for many years, lying dead and helpless in the soft folds of his bedcovers? "No, no, it cannot be. It cannot be!" Anna had not realized she'd spoken in a harsh, stunned whisper until she felt Alistair's fingers tighten on her shoulder.

"I'll fetch the undertaker," he said with uncharacteristic softness.

Anna came immediately to her feet, a pained look reflected in her eyes. Moments ago, she had known her father was dying, but now, she could not believe it had actually happened. "No, he's not…he's only sleeping. He was exhausted…" Anna's words trailed off into a whisper as the terrible truth struck her. "Oh, Alistair," she whispered, sinking her face into his silk-clothed shoulder.

"I'll fetch the undertaker," he repeated, losing the softness, patting her roughly and a little impatiently as he pushed her away from him.

Anna sank into the soft down of the quilt at her father's

bedside, and her cheek touched his for the very last time. Then Violet approached and Anna stood to fold her arms very gently around her cousin's shoulders.

The funeral coach arrived from Jude's Landing shortly after midnight. Patrick's body was hastily embalmed with camphor and returned to Shadow Marsh at midmorning. He was laid in the finest casket available from the undertaker's stock–polished cherry wood with rubbed brass fittings and the best burgundy satin to be had from his dry goods supplier in New Orleans. He was attired in his black dinner suit, finery he had avoided during his lifetime.

The parlor was cleared and the casket rested on the table. Throughout the long day, as Anna sat in her somber black gown, visitors arrived from throughout the parish and from Natchitoches where Patrick had many friends and business acquaintances.

Presently, Wren Wellington, paying his respects on behalf of Hopewell Plantation, dropped to a chair beside Anna. "What will you do now that your father is gone?" he asked. "My proposal still stands."

"And what proposal is that?" Anna replied eventually, her voice brisk, almost rude.

"Now, Miss Anna..." Wren had always admired her great pride and indomitable courage, although secretly he was sure the woman in her needed a strong, masculine shoulder for support. "Whatever will you do, dear Anna? I know this is not the proper time to discuss your–our future, but–"

"You're right, Wren," she countered. "It isn't the proper time."

Briefly, she scrutinized Wren's smooth, attractive features when he looked away for a moment. There was scarcely a whisper of hair on his chin, and his rather dismal effort to grow a beard, as many of the young men were doing of late, was quite the failure. His brown eyes were his best features, drooping at the corners and giving him a slightly doleful look.

These past few years, he had been an amiable and faithful riding companion; they had teased each other, touched, caressed, their lips had occasionally met, but Anna had always drawn the line. She suspected Wren had been inclined many times to throw her to her back and ravish her in the meadows of Shadow Marsh.

Wren's image had long ago been spoiled by his compulsive need to cavort with women well suited to brothels, and to engage in gambling and cockfighting, both deplorable vices. In these days and times, to have a good, hard-working man was to have a poor man. The last of the breed that could mix both material wealth and human decency in the same cup, and not taste bitterness, was lying in the casket across the room.

Anna sighed. She wouldn't want a man like her father either. In the prime of his life he had been all business, with quick, dutiful replies that were unintentionally patronizing more often than not. She imagined spending the rest of her life with a man whose very being exuded mystery and excitement–a man who could take command with a firm hand, yet be vulnerable to tender, human emotions. Closing her eyes, Anna could almost envision him…warm, smiling eyes and strong, gentle arms. Oh, but was there such a man who could put up with her sultry moods and her frequent tendency to be a bit patronizing herself?

Again, Anna sighed. Would the day never end? Would this funeral procession march gloomily through her memories for the rest of her life? Throughout it all, Wren sat beside her. Anna vaguely remembered speaking to the present circuit judge of the parish, the elderly mayor of Alexandria, and Warren Fairgate, who had come not only to pay his respects, but also to set an appointment for the reading of Patrick's will. As Patrick's attorney, he wanted to get this task over with as quickly as possible.

As darkness fell, Bea and her daughter, Lovey, prepared *garconnieres*–bachelor chambers for several gentlemen who would stay the night–and bedchambers for the guests who had journeyed from far distances.

Anna sat alone in the casket chamber, and remained awake throughout the long night. The minister arrived from Alexandria shortly after the hour of eight. While he made preparations for the funeral service, Anna freshened up in her bedchamber.

Strangely, in her solitude she shed no tears, but whispered only once, "I will miss you, Papa." Then she sighed, a deep, weary sigh.

At the family cemetery on the high rise of the meadow far behind the Big House, a hundred parishioners listened to the minister's final prayer before Patrick Brigham St. Cyr was lowered into the ground beside his wife, Dora. Hands of comfort fell to Anna's shoulders, lips gently touched her cheek; walking, waiting, talking, leaving, shuffling feet...oh, would it *never* end? Then Bea's arm went smoothly around her shoulders.

Anna raised her head and glanced toward Shadow Marsh, the brick and cypress wood thirty-three-room structure that had housed the St. Cyr family for sixty years–the gracefully fan-lighted entrance flanked by French windows fourteen feet high, ornate metal railings, and fluted columns supporting an eighty-four-foot long second-story gallery from which four sets of French doors stood open. To the left were the coach house, stable, and blacksmith shop, and four symmetrically placed silos in the midst of what had once been tobacco fields, but were now wide, spacious meadows where the horses grazed. Only one of the silos was new; the others really needed to be torn down and replaced. The *pigeoniers*, to the right and slightly back from the recessed kitchen wing fluttered with life...Alistair's fat corn-fed pigeons residing in the larger brick and iron domed structure, and Violet's delicate doves, glistening silver in the morning light, cooing, cuddling, tranquil in the other.

A large manmade pond stocked with catfish separated the plantation house from the much smaller overseer's cottage, which was built of virgin cypress and nestled in a grove of magnolias and live oaks shrouded with Spanish moss. Named Shadow Marsh by her great-grandfather, who had built it, the plantation comprised ten thousand acres along Bayou Bouef and yielded more than a fair proportion of the cotton, sugarcane, and soybeans produced in the parish. The revenues were staggering and had brought a fortune to the family over the past eighty years.

Anna lifted her eyes. In the window of the large octagonal

cupola in the center of the hipped and dormered roof stood a solitary figure...Alistair, who had refused to attend the funeral. Anna would never forgive him for that disgrace.

Bea, dressed in her finest yellow gown, gently coaxed Anna down the hill. Tall and lithe, but unable to stand as straight as usual, Anna smiled, patting the plump hand of her old friend. As they walked slowly from the hilltop cemetery toward the house, Anna realized how lonely and empty their home would be without her father. As she reached her bedchamber, the grief she had restrained now burned rivers on her pale cheeks.

Bea's gentle hand rubbed her back, eventually coaxing her to sleep. The reading of Patrick's will and testament would be the last obligation of the day.

* * *

Warren Fairgate arrived at Shadow Marsh at precisely two o'clock. A tall, slightly graying man with deep-set brown eyes behind wire-rimmed spectacles, Warren Fairgate was, like the late Mr. St. Cyr, a pillar of the community and a staunch advocate of law and justice. But now, attempting to organize the papers he had pulled from his valise, and to still the tremble deep in his throat that had remained with him on the journey from the cemetery, he seemed uncharacteristically nervous. The room was dreadfully still. Alistair sat alone on the divan, the fingers of his right hand resting lightly over his lips.

Bea and Mose stood solemnly in the doorway, wondering why they had been summoned for the reading of the will.

"Let's get this business over with," Alistair said impatiently. "I have things to do."

The tension in the room increased. Warren gave Alistair a sharp look. "Patrick left written instructions that his last will and testament should be read within two days of his burial," Warren began, clearing his throat, something he had done several times that morning. As well as being a client, Patrick had been his very good friend. They had shared many enjoyable moments together hunting on horseback.

"Violet has not arrived," Anna announced.

Alistair flipped his wrist, drawing his fingers to his chin.

19

"Our cousin does not care to attend. She says she does not deserve to be here and has gone off walking with her mutts. I tend to agree with her."

Anna winced at the sarcasm. "But she does," she countered. "Violet was raised with us as a sister."

"We shall begin without her," Warren interceded. "The will is dated January 12, 1857."

Alistair drew a short breath. His father had recently drawn up a new will?

Warren was well aware of Alistair's fears. He made a deliberate assessment of the children of Patrick St. Cyr, his eyes lingering fondly for a moment on Anna, whose head was slightly drooped. Then he looked down at the document beneath his hand and began to read. "I, Patrick Brigham St. Cyr, being of sound mind but infirm body, do hereby ordain this to be my last will and testament, revoking all testaments made previously by me—"

In the following moments, Anna and Alistair each became the legatees of two hundred thousand dollars for their personal needs, and Violet one hundred thousand dollars. Alistair's legacy, however, was bound to a trust. Warren Fairgate would issue a draft of three hundred dollars a month until Alistair was determined to be responsible enough to handle his own affairs.

At this news, Alistair stood, his hands clenched into fists. "Damn him," he hissed. "Even in death, that bastard must taunt and humiliate me! Three hundred dollars, I'll be damned! I spend more than that at the gambling tables in one night!"

"Which is precisely why the trust was established," Warren was quick to point out.

"And in that damned bit of paper, who gets Shadow Marsh—as if I don't already know!"

Warren raised a graying eyebrow. He despised Alistair for causing the stroke that had resulted in Patrick's death at the age of fifty-four. "All in good time," he replied. "I have other bequests."

"Please, Warren, may we continue?" Anna quietly intervened, fearing an ugly scene.

Warren smoothed the document but did not continue reading until Alistair had thrown himself back to the divan. "To my trusted and faithful persons of color..." Anna cast a quick look at Bea and Mose standing back by the door, holding one another in dreaded anticipation, then drew herself to the edge of her chair, "Freedom from slavery and one hundred dollars for each man, woman and child."

Anna released a quick, involuntary cry of glee. But Bea cried painfully, "Lawd Jesus, what we do's with freedom? This be our home!" then threw herself heavily against her husband Mose.

Though Anna was anxious to assure Bea and Mose that Shadow Marsh would always be their home, she wanted the reading to be over with. "Please continue, Mr. Fairgate."

"Any child born henceforth to persons of color at Shadow Marsh shall be born free." Warren addressed Mose directly, "It was Patrick's dearest wish that your people remain at Shadow Marsh as employees of wage."

"Oh, thank you, Lord," Anna whispered, turning to smile at Bea and Mose.

But Mose's eyes were heavy with worry. "Sho' 'nuf, Mistah Fairgate?" When Warren simply nodded, Mose continued, "This be our home jes' sure as God give it to us." Then he very calmly led an emotional Bea from the room, shaking his head as if he couldn't quite believe it.

Alistair raised his hand impatiently. "Do go on, Mister Fairgate."

Their gazes clashed, although neither man would dignify their loathing for one another with words. Theirs was hatred suitable to silence.

"And lastly..." Alistair's body grew rigid with anticipation. "The managing conservatorship of Shadow Marsh, including, but not limited to, all monies not herein specifically bequeathed, all lands, movable structures, horses, livestock, crops and revenues of St. Cyr enterprises both continental and abroad, all bank bonds, mortgages and liens against property held of another, with the option to call in those mortgages at the sole discretion of the managing conservator of Shadow Marsh, and in whose name Shadow Marsh shall be governed and controlled in all matters of law and legal boundary, said managing conservatorship shall be vested in the name of the child who has been the bread of my life and the nectar of my happiness...my beloved daughter, Anna Rose St. Cyr."

Anna was speechless. Her sea-green eyes were fixed on Alistair, and his look of loathing was more than she could bear. She quickly turned away, slowly aware of Warren's voice, which lowered somewhat strangely as he continued.

"Managing conservatorship in the name of Anna Rose St. Cyr shall terminate and full ownership of Shadow Marsh, less and except those individual bequests herein made, shall be assumed by the first of my two children who shall sire or give birth to a legitimate son."

Alistair sat forward in silence, seeing hope where it had all but been lost to him. Despite his father's hatred of him, he was giving him an equal chance to own Shadow Marsh. Frankly, Alistair was surprised. But—he stopped to think about it. He really shouldn't be. Patrick St. Cyr had been an honorable man, and Alistair remembered the last words his father had said to him before their final confrontation. "You're a disappointment to me, son, but I'll treat you fairly..."

Alistair departed to the liquor cabinet and a goblet of whiskey. Anna heard him mumbling to himself as she watched Warren collect his papers and the will he would probate later in the week. When Warren turned and eyed her critically, Anna hesitated for a moment, her thoughts scattered and irrational. Warren bowed imperceptibly and started to leave.

"Mr. Fairgate." He turned back when Anna spoke. "Did you not try to discourage my father from attempting to control his children from the grave? He had no right to direct when I would marry and bear children."

"I did try to discourage him, Anna Rose. But he was insistent on including the language. I believe he felt you were too stubborn and independent to win a husband, and this stipulation would give you incentive."

"Incentive... Bah! I am much too busy to entertain amorous attentions, sir!" Then, "Did my father believe the plantation too much for me, so wanted to give Alistair a chance to own it?"

"You have managed it these past three years, since you turned eighteen."

"Yes, I have managed it...but it has been difficult."

"You have more than managed it," he replied. "You have proven you can handle the plantation. And I would suggest..." He had been about to remind her that she should be thinking about marriage, and the man she would marry. Despite her disappointment in her father's provisions, he knew that she was an ambitious woman and would do what was necessary to fulfill those ambitions.

Anna needed Warren's assurances. She had relied on him heavily—and often—these past three years. "I may continue to consult you in business matters?"

"I would expect it."

"Is our overseer, Mr. Brady, under contract?"

"He is not," Warren replied.

"It is within my power to dismiss him?"

Warren hesitated. "You may, if you wish, though I would caution you to go about it with tact. Mr. Brady has been with Shadow Marsh for a number of years."

Anna's lips pressed into a thin line. "He is dull-witted, incompetent, and a sot. I kept him on only because my father felt sorry for him." She rose and offered her hand to Warren Fairgate. "Good day."

Anna wanted Shadow Marsh more than anything in the world, but she was not ready for marriage. Was this her father's way of putting her obsession for Shadow Marsh to the test, and accomplishing his own desire to see her married and a mother...even from the grave?

Anna stood at the window for a moment, gazing across the meadows. She did not remain long in solitude. Alistair returned, his clubfoot heavy and dragging, the aura of his loathing drifting toward her. His eyes were cold and narrow, his jaw taut, and his lips pressed into a thin, sneering line.

Unconsciously, Anna's eyes lowered to the ugly black boot custom made and a bit wider to accommodate his clubfoot. "Well, you finally got what you wanted, dear Rosie?

Her eyes lifted. "For the time being," she replied quietly. She wondered if there was anything she could say to salve the pain of Alistair's wounded pride. It didn't seem to matter to him that he had never helped her manage the plantation, not even to write out a single invoice or meet with a creditor. He had always been gallivanting. As the silence between them grew, she blurted out, "It was your fault Papa slighted you. Your laziness and...and...what you did to Paddy!"

"It had nothing to do with Paddy! I gave him a little whipping! He was none the worse for it!" Alistair closed the distance between them, took her by the shoulders, and pulled her forward. Anna was startled and tried to break away. "It's because I'm a clumsy, clubfooted clod dragging around like a one-man freak show!"

"That's not true," she shot back, stunned by his self-hatred. "Papa loved you, even after you whipped Paddy!"

Alistair released his grip and turned slightly away. He remembered only too well that the whipping had driven the final wedge between him and his father, because Paddy had been his favorite among all the slave children. "You will rub Paddy in my face until I draw my last breath, won't you?"

"If you hadn't whipped him, he wouldn't have run away and drowned in the creek."

In a moment that seemed like a thousand hours, Alistair relived the encounter with his father that resulted in Patrick's illness and death. He remembered being pinned against the door of the coach house by an incredibly strong hand, his father's ravings pounding in his ears and the riding crop slashing back and forth, leaving thin rivers of blood through Alistair's white shirt.

But worse than the physical pain had been Patrick's ravings, which suddenly ceased, and the dark flush of his face as he had crumbled in a convulsive heap at Alistair's feet, clutching at his chest. Alistair had wished a thousand times these past three years that it had never happened. He had prayed that Patrick would not change his will, but he had underestimated his father's loathing for him…a loathing that had given him strength to summon his attorney when he knew the end was nearing.

Only now succumbing to the tensions of the last two days, Anna dropped to the divan and wept quietly against her sleeve.

"To hell with you," Alistair spat at his sister. "I'll own Shadow Marsh. I'll marry any damn woman, plant the seed of the St. Cyrs in her gut and Shadow Marsh will be mine!" Before he walked away, he threw the crystal goblet from which he had been drinking against the red Italian marble hearth, where it shattered into pieces.

# Two

This early Sunday morning the sun had not yet penetrated the dawn mist or cast its shimmering rays across the gentle ripples of Bayou Bouef. In the meadows beyond Shadow Marsh, four mares nibbled at summer-green grass as their frisky colts raced along the wood fence. From another direction came the laughter of children, followed by an older voice calling them home. The bell would soon ring for morning church services. Anna wanted only to enjoy the warm summer day and forget for a moment the worries of managing Shadow Marsh alone. The problem of finding another overseer to replace Mr. Brady, who had finally left, quite hostile and making threats, was still unresolved.

Three houses in Cabin Row were left vacant by families who had collected their hundred-dollar legacy and decided to begin the journey north. Alistair was drinking more than usual and becoming more belligerent. "Heaven help me," Anna said as she stood in a grove of magnolia in the quiet of the family cemetery. Her dark hair was loosened from riding her sorrel mare fast along the bayou. Her wide green almond-shaped eyes moved fluidly over her father's monument, then paused for a moment to read the inscription. Memories of her father dulled the sparkle in her eyes. But her thoughts were diverted by a rabbit scurrying between two gravestones, and disappearing beyond the peach tree planted by her mother's grave seven years before.

Anna's thick, raven-colored hair fell in cascades over her slender shoulders, sparkling in the morning sun. Her eyes swept over the bayou and the plantation house just beyond. The wide green lawns of the house had been freshly trimmed. The aviary and summerhouse had received their annual whitewashing and had lost the look of winter's neglect.

Patrick St. Cyr's thoroughbred horses grazed down the

meadow. Once raised for profits, the horses would be sold at the New Orleans auction late next week. Anna felt that she defiled her father's memory by selling the horses he loved, but by the provisions of his will, she had to do what she felt was best for Shadow Marsh. The horses were too fine to be used for work and wagon, and the racetrack her father had once loved was overgrown with weeds now.

"Business, posh," Anna said aloud, drawing her lips into an unattractive frown. She hadn't ridden out here today to think about business. A light breeze rustled her gown. She looked down, to be sure everything was in order, and that she was presentable for Sunday services. She would attend the baptism of Bea's new grandson, the first St. Cyr child born free under the provisions of her father's will. On a whim Anna had donned a new emerald satin gown, with tiny silk roses in a shade of green so light as to appear white, scattered thickly over the lace neckline. She sighed deeply as she pulled her shawl closer around her shoulders, covering her smooth, ivory skin which lay exposed through the lace above the satin bodice. The tightness of her gown, outlining small, firm breasts and a tiny waist, was now decently covered for Sunday services.

Down the bayou toward Cabin Row, the residents were filing toward their clapboard church, accompanied by the haunting melody of voices rising in gentle song, and hands clapping to the rhythm of gospel lamentations. The music helped Anna forget that several members of the Rapides Organization of Planters, which she dearly wanted to join, would convene at Shadow Marsh that afternoon. Not only would Anna have to face the staunch old guards, but also Wren Wellington would attend with his father. Anna had applied for the organization chair vacated by her father, and the matter would go to vote for the third time that afternoon.

Anna dreaded the outcome. The men considered her a mere girl, without brains and business logic. Anna wanted the opportunity to prove them wrong. The past few months had taken their toll, and Anna's nerves were brittle, yielding to the slightest pressure. Tears came to her as she gazed over the bayou, where soft, swaying masses of Spanish moss glistened silver in the early dawn light; the mist swirled in hypnotic motion from the damp ground, and the herons floated to their roosts along the shore.

Anna breathed the fresh, clean breeze whipping up from the bayou, and allowed herself a final moment to gather her thoughts. Absently smoothing down the folds of her satin skirts, she wanted to lose herself in the mesmerizing warmth of the day, and in comforting reminiscences. But past and present were interwoven and inseparable. What had begun on a chilly March night, a strange legacy that pushed marriage and motherhood upon her, left Anna no true peace.

"Apple blossom?" Bea stood beside her, wearing the yellow scarf Anna had given her for her birthday. "The Lawd an' the new black young'un, they's be waitin' on you, chile."

* * *

Baptism was a joyous occasion for the God-fearing, and a traumatic one for the baptizee. The child bellowed at the top of his lungs as the cold bayou water enveloped him, and drifted off to sleep in the crook of his mother's arm during the ensuing church services. Afterwards, contented by the morning service among her friends, Anna rode her mare over the plantation grounds, reluctant to return to the tension of the main house. Her satin gown sparkled like green fire beneath the summer sun as she inspected the cotton fields and the lower pasturelands, where the cows and their new calves were separated from the herd.

Then she sought out her favorite spot at the bend in the bayou, and had just settled in when Wren Wellington approached, riding his father's prize black stallion. Wren dismounted and dropped to the ground beside Anna. She had picked up a small twig and began stabbing at the dirt, dismayed at his intrusion. More annoyingly, she felt the gaze of his brown eyes drop and linger too long on her bodice.

Anna was in no mood for his amorous attentions. "For a *gentleman*," she said in her softest, most patient voice, "you can be such a beast, Wren."

"You make me *feel* like a beast, Anna," he responded after

28

a moment, and hoping to ease the tension he sensed in her, touched his lips to the back of her neck, lingering for a moment on her soft black hair and the ribbons gently pulling it back. "Marry me, Anna."

Anna flicked her wrist close enough that Wren felt the breeze of her fingers against his cheek. "You're such a child, Wren."

"And you, dear girl, are a shrew and a cruel tease," he countered politely, drawing his knees up. "Yet I am deeply fond of you."

Despite his tendency to be a bore, Anna was fond of Wren as well. It had always been her father's wish that she and Wren would marry. But she did not love Wren, he knew that, and she felt the matter should have been settled by now. They were friends…nothing more. "Why have you ridden to Shadow Marsh this morning, Wren?"

"To see you, of course," he replied, removing the stick Anna fumbled nervously between her fingers. He knew she was troubled. "It's the organization, isn't it?" he questioned, lifting her chin.

"The organization," she echoed, her look momentarily rebellious, then anxious again. "I deserve my father's chair in the organization…as managing conservator of Shadow Marsh. I have so many good ideas, and they won't listen to me, Wren. It is because I'm a woman, and for no other reason."

Wren drew closer, feeling the soft satin of her gown against his sleeve. Again, he lifted her chin and forced her stormy gaze to meet his own. "You don't have to plead your case to me, Anna."

"It is because I'm a woman," she repeated, suddenly very vexed. "But this afternoon you shall see me have the last laugh on the whole lot!"

Wren stood, flicked dust from his boots, and put his hand out to assist Anna up. "My father has asked that I accompany him to New Orleans. We depart in an hour's time."

"But I need his vote–"

Wren caressed Anna's hand very softly. "And if I relay his

full support, and his vote, will you kiss me as you never have before?"

Anticipation, not for the kiss but for Rodney Wellington's vote, rose in Anna's heart. "If I have his vote—if I truly do—then I shall most surely kiss you," she replied. Their gazes met and held in playful anticipation. "Don't tease me, Wren. You scoundrel! Have I your father's vote?"

"You do."

Anna's arms circled his neck. "Oh, you are a scoundrel, Wren! Thank him for me, won't you?"

"Anna, Anna… Wren's palms cupped her face and gently rocked it. His voice was soft and comforting. "You have his vote only because he expects you to be his daughter-in-law one day. Now! My kiss. I demand my kiss!"

Anna's soft lips puckered and lightly touched the dimple at the side of his mouth. "There is your kiss."

Immediately, Wren's arms circled her waist and drew her close, betraying the hardness of his body. "This is a kiss," he replied firmly, his hand rising, gripping her chin, and drawing her face nearer to him. Then his lips parted and closed over hers, caressing them, bruising her mouth which rebelled by drawing tightly against his.

The forced kiss startled Anna, and the woman within fought to penetrate the barrier of cold detachment. She attempted to break the kiss before it overpowered her, but he was strong, easing her back onto the cool grass. The weight of Wren's long, lean body pressed against hers, and his lips caressed her eyelids, her ears, and the small of her neck. His right hand at the hem of her gown began to slowly ease upward.

Anna had gathered her determination, and she rolled out from under him, quickly rising. The rapid rise and fall of her chest strained against the stays of her gown. Silently, quickly, she began straightening her disheveled appearance.

"Anna, you're a damned tease!"

Anna's cheeks burned with embarrassment and confusion. She would not be compromised, even though her body flamed inside. She approached her horse and mounted. "You think that just because we cuddled as silly children and stole a few kisses behind our fathers' backs that I'm going to let you make love to me, Wren? Indeed not!" Anna nudged the sorrel mare into a canter.

"Crazy woman," Wren mumbled as she disappeared through the orchard. He picked up a small stone and angrily tossed it into the bayou.

Then, from the corner of his eye he saw movement. Violent stood in the shadows of a sweet gum tree, the black Labradors protectively by her side. She was looking fondly at him as she clapped her hands and the dogs, obedient to her unspoken command, turned and ambled slowly back toward Shadow Marsh.

While Violet was not conventionally pretty, there was something compelling in her bearing. Her thin form was hidden beneath a plain brown muslin skirt and tan blouse with the sleeves rolled to her elbows. Her stays were unfastened, but failed to reveal the slightest hint of cleavage.

Wren was strangely enchanted by her silence and her almost ghostly movement through the ground mist that had risen from the bayou. She dropped to her knees before him. Her gaze moved over Wren's square jaw and his face, to the sandy brown hair which, softly swept by the breeze, lay untidy across his forehead.

"I have always loved you," she said after a moment, "but your eyes only beheld Anna. Had you looked my way, just once, you'd have seen long ago the love and adoration I bear for you." While Wren sat unmoving, Violet's hands moved to the back of his neck and caressed his hair and shoulders. She eased to the ground, bringing the weight of his body down with her. "Oh, Wren, look at me as a woman, not as a child. I do so adore you."

She had taken him quite by surprise...Anna's tragically orphaned cousin, two years younger than she, who had managed always to slip between them when they sat on the garden swing or walked along the bayou. But now, a woman sat before him, tender, gentle, her wide, lavender eyes beholding him with a woman's passion, imploring him to love her as deeply as she loved him. Violet's lips covered his in hot yearning.

He caressed Violet's lips and pretended it was Anna responding with such passion. He tore at her clothing, imagining it was Anna's gown giving beneath his hands. He wanted to touch her flesh. Frantically, his hands slipped beneath her skirts, traveled the length of her silken legs, and to the warm of her thighs. The draws of her pantalets easily gave, allowing Wren to expose her most intimate flesh. As her long, lean legs eased apart, his trembling hands moved to the burning flesh of her inner thighs. He was in agony with desire.

"Wren...dear, Wren," Violet whispered, "Haven't you known all these years how much I have wanted you?" As his hips and his manliness were exposed, Violet's soft breathing became a broken, erratic vow of love as he joined to her without the prelude of foreplay.

* * *

Anna rode through the stone archway of Shadow Marsh, slowed the mare to a halt, and dismounted. She walked toward the house, allowing herself a moment to halfway straighten her appearance. Bea met her on the porch and reminded her that the organization members would arrive shortly. Anna closed her chamber door and leaned heavily against it. She realized only then that she was still trembling, and wondered if Bea had noticed. The experience with Wren had unnerved her; he had awakened her passion, and she found it both confusing and frightening. She and Wren were no longer naughty children sneaking kisses behind the oak tree. They were man and woman, with powerful wants and desires. This afternoon, Anna's body had felt the first pain of desire and she wondered if, perhaps, she should marry him. He was of a good bloodline, and male children predominated in his family.

Anna changed into a blue gown with matching embroidered jacket more suited to an afternoon meeting with male organization members. Through her chamber window she watched the men arrive–a silent procession that ended, eventually, with Bea's knock at her chamber door.

Moments later, Anna greeted the men in the parlor. They

seemed as morose as at the last two elections. Mr. Hayson started to speak, but Anna quickly cut him off. "Gentlemen, before we begin, may I report that just this morning I have received confirmation of Squire Wellington's favorable vote? There are only your five votes remaining–"

"Yes, we heard...Miss St. Cyr." The greeting was that of Peter Reynaud. "The Board of the Organization is no place for a...what I mean to say is that you have no experience in these matters."

"I have the experience," she replied, slightly lifting her bellowing skirt and moving into the midst of the men. "For the past three years I have cast my father's votes on behalf of Shadow Marsh, and he left it up to me what those votes would be. I have made his decisions and recommendations on all matters before the board. And not once has there been a complaint. Should you give me an opportunity I intend to be as active a member of the organization as my father had been. I ask only the chance to prove myself worthy."

Hayson outstretched his hands. "It would be a more appropriate move for your brother to make, Miss St. Cyr."

Anna paused. "Oh, I see. It does not matter that I have made my father's decisions for the past three years and have efficiently represented Shadow Marsh in the organization. You would prefer a man, no matter his character." She turned among them for a moment, studying each of their solemn faces. "Gentlemen, let me put a proposition to you. Give me half a year to prove that I can carry my weight in the organization. If at the end of that time you are not pleased with me, I will step down." Turning toward the door, she added, "Enjoy the tea Lovey will bring to you. I will be nearby when you have made your decision." Favoring each with a parting smile, Anna quietly closed the door.

Anna went no farther than the foyer, where she paced back and forth for what seemed like hours. Then Lovey broke her concentration with an announcement, "Massa Edwards say the votes be cast. You come quick."

When Anna looked into the men's faces she felt that she

knew their answer. Reynaud was the only one who really looked dour, but his loose, flaccid features tended to set naturally in a frown. "You shall assume your father's seat," he informed her, "on the terms you proposed. For the next six months, your vote shall have equal bearing in all matters decided by the Organization."

Anna scarcely contained her delight, but she knew it was wise to be calm. Moving among the men, she briefly held each of their hands and favored them with a very personal word of thanks.

# Three

Violet sat alone on the veranda this early Monday morning, sipping freshly squeezed orange juice and watching Cabin Row stir into life as the wagons were loaded with provisions for a long day in the fields. Thinking about Wren and their first moments together–and now a proposal of marriage–she absently watched a stranger delay the departure of the wagons, possibly making inquiries, and approach the veranda where Violet sat. His dusty attire consisted of a loose, striped garment over his shirt, tan trousers, fringed leather boots, and a wide-brimmed hat pulled low on his forehead. When he dismounted his painted stallion, Violet's eyes fell to the richly tooled leather saddle and martingale. It was, perhaps, the richness of the horse beneath a man who scarcely seemed deserving of it that compelled Violet to rise, open her parasol, and start toward the steps.

The shadows of Morgan York's face, created by his wide-brimmed hat, guarded his first impression of her...wealth evident in her style of dress, and the way she sauntered slowly and deliberately toward him, curious, yet held aloof by inbred southern inhibitions. She was quite plain, actually, except for her eyes, which were the color of amethyst. Her tight purple velvet bodice was a pleasant contrast to the rich plaid of her skirts billowing from a tiny waist.

Morgan could not prevent his bold, assessing look. But he became cautious when he saw the two black dogs with teeth bared, and heard a low growl churning from the larger one. He removed his wide-brimmed hat, revealing golden hair, a strong, unshaven jaw, and vivid amber eyes. "Good day, Madame. I wish to speak to the master of the house."

Violet was caught off guard by his well-mannered, educated voice, when she had expected an uncouth western-raised cowboy that had never seen the inside of a schoolroom. She raised her parasol, framing her head against its soft, lined interior. "What do you want here?" she asked abruptly.

He pulled his foot up to the bottom step, rested his right hand on his knee, and gave her a cool look. "I came about this." He removed one of the familiar bills Anna had posted throughout the parish, advertising for an overseer–a man of exceptional business logic and intelligence, who possessed a high degree of humanity and compassion. "I wish to apply for this position."

"Do you have references?" Violet asked.

"No," he replied.

"I am sorry...references are required."

"It does not state on the bill that references are required."

Violet shrugged. "Accidentally omitted, I am sure. But references are most certainly required. We cannot have just any old vagabond hanging around here."

"Then this old vagabond will waste no more of your time." He returned the hat to his head. "Thank you for seeing me." Morgan York mounted his horse and lightly tipped his hat as he departed.

\* \* \*

Lovey had just put a plate of freshly baked biscuits and a pot of tea on the breakfast table when Anna entered the veranda. She was wide-awake and glad to be away from the ledgers she had been working on. "Have you seen Alistair this morning?" she asked.

"Half hour or so ago, he went out to see Joby Cade 'bout the trip to N'Awleans with them horses." Lovey started toward the kitchen, but soon turned back. "Stranger, he rode in this morn'. Missy Violet, she 'changed words with him an' he rode off. What you reckon that all about?"

Anna absently stirred the cream into her tea. She wanted to remind Lovey she was much too nosey, a trait she had inherited from her mammy, Bea. But if she told the gumbo pot it was much too black, it wouldn't listen either. Thus, Anna replied nonchalantly, "An old friend perhaps?"

"*Harrumph*! Missy Violet, she ain't got no friends, not with a nasty nature like she got!" Lovey returned to the kitchen just as footfalls echoed from the south stairs.

Alistair entered the veranda, still buttoning his jacket. He said nothing, but sat at the breakfast table, poured tea, and spread butter on a warm biscuit, which he then left untouched.

"Are you ready for the trip to New Orleans tomorrow?" Anna asked.

"I am." Alistair sat back, flaring his coat away from his chest.

"You'll get top price, won't you?"

"I always do," he replied shortly. "Joby and Mose will accompany me also—"

"Not Mose. Take one of the younger men."

"Why not Mose?"

Anna gave her brother an intense look. "He's been feeling under the weather...and he serves the house now. Putting him on horseback for a two hundred mile trip would be unfair to his position and his health."

"Position!" Alistair muttered obscenities beneath his breath. "You put him in a fancy black suit to answer the front door and call it position. It's a wonder the darkies work at all the way you mollycoddle them!"

"I won't argue with you, Alistair."

"Since when?" he countered sarcastically.

Silently, Anna stood, leaving Alistair alone on the veranda. Her very presence always reminded him of the unfairness of their father's will. His sullenness quickly became anger. Tension crawled through his shoulders and neck. Alistair left the veranda and ordered Joby, whom he saw approaching the stables, to ready his horse. He needed to get away from Shadow Marsh.

* * *

Tense encounters with Alistair had become a way of life. Anna wished at times she could involve him more in managing the plantation, but his irresponsibility would ruin Shadow Marsh in two years' time. He would throw their cash funds to the wind, neglect to purchase seed for spring planting, and watch the cattle die of starvation and disease. Anna could not sacrifice Shadow Marsh. She wished that Alistair, who would soon be twenty-six years old, would become a responsible adult. But he seemed to have no interest in doing so.

She set herself to domestic chores during the day, and spent an hour engaged in needlepoint with Violet. Later, she took warm broth to Bea's little granddaughter, who had been snake bitten.

The fallen condition of Cabin Row brought shame to Anna. She immediately put in an order for quicklime, gravel, and shovels. The men could do the work improving the sanitation facilities as they had time.

Alistair did not return home by twilight, and the following morning Anna was roused early by Bea. She sat up in bed, feeling the beginnings of a sick headache at the base of her skull. She drew her knees up, and dropped her forehead heavily against them.

Bea started to open the drapery. "Please, don't," Anna asked quietly.

"Another headache, chile? Should Bea fetch you a powder?"

"I'll wait a bit," she replied. "They make me feel so sluggish." Then she looked up, wondering why she'd been awakened so early.

"The men–they's outside with the horses for N'Awleans, and yo' brother, he didn't come home last night."

"But Alistair was looking forward to the trip. He loves every chance to go to New Orleans."

"Well, he ain't lovin' it now."

Anna stood and grabbed her velvet robe from the open door of the chifferobe and moved into the hallway. She rushed Bea to the coach house to send Joby Cade into Jude's Landing to make inquiries, and sat at the veranda table to await his return. An hour later, Joby Cade rode up to the veranda. "He's in Pop Gunter's jail...ag'in. Pop, he say fifty dollars get him out, along with fifty dollars fo' the other man..."

"What other man?"

"The other man what yo' brother pop over the head with a two by fo'."

38

There were times when Anna was sure Alistair enjoyed being her nemesis. By half-past eight she was pulling on her wrist gloves and positioning her silk bonnet carefully on her head, so as not to disturb her ringlets. She was just about to call to Bea when Wren Wellington appeared at the front foyer, nervously holding his hat.

"Anna, I wish a word with you."

"Not now, Wren," she replied hastily. "I'm just on my way out for the morning."

"Now," he insisted. "It is important."

Having never before heard Wren sound so aggressive, she was quite taken aback. "Very well, Wren. What is so important?"

Wren took her hand and held it very gently. His own hands were cool and slightly trembling. "As you know, Anna, both our fathers had assumed you and I would one day marry–"

Anna clicked her tongue, quickly withdrawing her hand. She had tolerated his nonsense since childhood, and today she was in a hurry. "I told you, Wren, that I am not ready for marriage. Why must you persist along these lines?" She called out to Bea, "I'm leaving, dear," and gave Wren an irritated look. As she started toward the carriage where Joby awaited her, Wren stepped in her way.

"Forgive me, Anna, I do apologize for any misunderstanding. I have not come to Shadow Marsh to ask for your hand in marriage." Silently, she awaited his explanation. Wren turned away from her, his shoulders drooped. "It is Violet I wish to marry."

Anna's eyes grew wide, her lips parted, trembling involuntarily. "But you've never so much as exchanged a kind word with Violet. You have always thought her a bit of a pest." Anna's surprise had become a breathless accusation.

"That is in the past, Anna. She and I now wish to be married. Since you are the mistress of Shadow Marsh and, as such, the head of the family, I thought it proper that I mention it to you before we begin our plans. Of course, Violet will reside at Hopewell with me."

Anna had begun to feel the impact of his words. Her dumbfounded look became almost pained. "Of course, Wren," she softly replied, "and I do appreciate your approaching me on the matter." As an afterthought, she asked, "When do you plan to be married?"

"In the spring of next year, when the azaleas are in bloom." Wren bowed stiffly, took Anna's hand, and briefly brought it to his lips. She sensed his regret as he said, "Good day, Anna."

Anna stood in the foyer until Wren was far away from Shadow Marsh. When she eventually settled into the carriage, Joby asked, "What Mistah Wellington be troublin' you about?"

"It's nothing," she replied. "He wishes to marry Violet."

\* \* \*

The four-mile trip along the bayou to Jude's Landing was little more than a blur to Anna. Only the noise of the Jenkins Mercantile just inside the village brought her back to her senses. Jude's Landing, comprised mainly of the mercantile, tavern, railroad depot, and bayou docks, had acquired possession of the stone smokehouse, which served as a jail after it had failed to burn to the ground, along with Widow Prynne's house.

Anna stood outside while the door was being unlocked, and looked from one man to the other on the dirt floor. Unrecognizable, and coated in thick, dried mud, neither man moved so much as a muscle as she stood looking at them in disgust. Anna was able to distinguish Alistair's identity only by their father's gold pocket watch dangling from the fob attached to his jacket pocket. At least it appeared to be a jacket. So coated in muck, it could easily have been an old rag.

Alistair was dragged out to the carriage and thrown into the baggage compartment. Anna stood by, tapping her toe and rolling her eyes as Pop Gunter completed the latest of many, many lectures on the lamentable after-effects of Alistair's nocturnal habits. As the carriage entered the road along the bayou, Joby pointed out the black and white stallion trailing some distance behind the carriage. Anna took her white handkerchief from her handbag and flicked it impatiently, but the animal merely drew back, throwing up its magnificent head to look at Anna as if one or the other of them had lost their senses.

Thereafter, he kept at a steady pace with the carriage and would not be frightened off by her handkerchief. He remained with them as the carriage pulled up to the common of Cabin Row. Alistair had stirred only enough to betray that he was still alive.

Joby alighted, offering his assistance to Anna. "Let's dump our naughty boy in the trough," she said, accepting his hand.

Joby pointed toward the stallion. "With that devil a-standin' there?" he responded, pointing to the stallion. "Not on yo' life!"

Again, Anna's handkerchief came up, and she flicked it at the big horse. "I don't know who you belong to," she remarked, exasperated, drawing her hands to her hips, "but if you were mine, I'd come looking for you." Anna had a keen eye for a good horse, and this one was a champion.

Meanwhile, Joby laid Alistair in the trough while Anna entered the cabin. Bea passed her on the way out, impatiently clicking her tongue and mumbling to herself. Joby entered the cabin, and Bea went to the washboard for her brush and lye soap. When she returned, she pushed Alistair's head beneath the water several times and held it there. "What wrong with you, boy?" she asked, dragging him up by his hair. "You done got the spirit o' the devil in yo' veins, goin' off an' drinkin' an' gamblin' an' brawlin' like po' white trash!"

But the man who emerged from the grime had strong features in no way resembling Alistair St. Cyr. Bea screamed, let go of the man, and her scrub brush and soap flew into the air. Meanwhile, the stranger slipped unconsciously beneath the water's surface.

Anna had just poured cups of strong chicory coffee for herself and Joby when she heard Bea's heavy footsteps scramble across the porch. Her arms flailed, lowered to her apron as she despairingly wrung her hands, and flailed again.

"They's a devil out yonder in the trough done consumed Massa Alistair, body and soul!" At the same time, the stallion's powerful hooves pushed at the trough until it tipped over, spilling its unconscious master onto the ground.

# Four

Despite a deathly pallor, life began to stir in the stranger tucked beneath Bea's quilt The shoulder-length hair that had appeared light brown when Joby had pulled him from the trough was drying in pale golden waves. The man might be in his mid-thirties, though it was hard to tell. There was a smoothness of youth in his features, yet a certain wisdom that came with age.

Now recovered from the shock of discovering a stranger beneath her scrubbing brush, Bea was fussing beneath her breath and rubbing his strong, muscular arms to revive his circulation. Anna stood by, drawn to his masculine beauty. This man, even unconscious, reflected strength and a very strange sort of gentleness. His partially exposed chest rippled with well-nourished muscles, though there were the telltale signs of a cracked rib beneath bruised flesh. Bea had also mentioned that he had the scars of a whipping across his back, though they were years old.

Anna wondered briefly what had caused his trouble with Alistair, and she wanted to know more about him. After she had searched through his jacket, which had yielded only a few dollars, her father's pocket watch, and a bill advertising the overseer position at Shadow Marsh, she cautiously approached his horse. The beast allowed her to go through its saddle bags, which contained a strap and straight razor, several small books, military medallions, a pair of matched dueling pistols, a mahogany chess set enclosed in a small leather case, and a portfolio bulging with personal papers. The most important thing she gleaned from her snooping was his name: Morgan York. She was about to go through the remainder of his papers when Bea called to her.

Bea was looking curiously at the still face slightly drooped to the side on the soft down of the pillow. "I believe his eyes—they snuck open a tad," she whispered, "but can't be sure."

Anna approached the bed. The left side of his face was bruised and swollen. Cautiously, she sat by his side and her face eased toward his. "I don't think…" Without warning, a strong, muscular arm darted out, slipped around her neck, and pulled her close. Anna felt the coolness of his lips touch hers. She immediately drew back and broke free of his grasp. She stood away from the bed and smoothed down the wrinkles in her skirt. "I think he's delirious and–despicable."

Yet, unconsciously, her fingers rose to her lips, to the warmth that had replaced the coolness of his kiss. For the first time, Anna felt a sensation she had never felt before. As she settled the tremor rising within her, she pondered if he were truly unconscious or. He looked terribly innocent, his copper eyelashes unmoving against his high cheekbones. "Do either of you know him?" she asked.

"Not me," Joby replied. "Stranger to these parts, sho' 'nuf."

Moser approached from behind them, looked down at the man and quietly said, "That be the man Miss Violet speak to yesterday. Yas'sum, that be him."

"He looks like a kind man," Bea reflected thoughtfully.

"He looks like a rogue and a rabble rouser," Anna countered at once.

"But look here at his hands. Jus' li'l ol' calluses…sho' not like Massa Brady or any overseers in these here parts."

"He probably wears work gloves," Anna remarked absently. She sat on the small stool beside the bed and picked up his hand. It had long, slim fingers, which lay cool and unmoving in the palm of her hand. A strange sensation overcame her, and she quickly dropped his hand back on the quilt to stand away from him.

* * *

Anna sank herself into her chores for the following two days, during which she received daily reports on Morgan York. Early in the morning of the third day Bea announced that he had come around and had spoken his first sensible words since his arrival: "Where's my horse?"

Later in the afternoon, Anna enjoyed a leisurely ride alone, surveyed the fields, and upon her return decided the time was right to make her presence known to Morgan York. She dismounted her horse at the porch of Bea's cabin, and saw him through the narrow window, sitting up in bed with his white shirt unbuttoned, drinking warm broth from a spoon Bea held for him.

Anna drew back a little, shielding herself, watching for a moment in silence. He had received a very serious head wound in the fight with Alistair, and Bea had reported that he'd become delirious that first night, mumbling things that made no sense at all. But as she watched him now, weakly sipping the broth, allowing Bea to scold him when he refused to take another spoonful, he hardly seemed to be in any danger of dying.

Hesitantly, Anna knocked. "May I come in?" she asked, slowly opening the door. She was wearing a dark green satin riding dress and black boots, and on entering the cabin smoothed down her skirts, which had become creased in her long ride along the bayou and through the fields. Anna did not look directly at Morgan, but felt his gaze following her. When she looked up, for a moment her gaze met and held his, transfixed. Her full, moist lips turned up in a smile. "How are we feeling today?"

Morgan didn't reply right away, but continued to hold her gaze. "I don't know about you," he replied eventually, "but I feel like hell."

Anna looked to Bea, who stood, placed her hand briefly on Anna's arm, and returned the bowl to the washtub. Presently, the cabin door silently closed. Anna walked around the bed, absently flicked her gloved hand over the metal post, and held it there for a moment. "Well, Mr. York, you're more than welcome to stay at Shadow Marsh until you feel better."

"Thank you," he replied. "That's quite generous, considering it was your brother–I understand– who bashed me in the head with a two-by-four. Is he always so friendly?"

"Always…I would imagine, since you're still alive, he was in one of his better moods when you two had your little difference." Anna's eyes turned directly to him, assessing him boldly. The way he looked at her, Anna was both flattered and embarrassed. She wondered what he was thinking.

He was at the moment racing back through his memories to recall whether he had ever seen such a beautiful, albeit very youthful, woman. He saw before him a tall, lithe, graceful woman with a straight, classic nose, smiling green eyes, and full, moist lips slightly turned down in a pout. Her raven-black hair cascaded in full rich waves to her tiny waist. He imagined her to be warm and sensual and soft.

Since Morgan had made no reply to her observation, Anna continued, "I am quite at odds, Mr. York, trying to rationalize how you could possibly have taken possession of my father's gold watch–"

"At the gambling table," he replied.

"Is that what caused the dissension between you and my brother?"

"Not actually. The dissension arose when I tried to give the watch back to him."

"Indeed?" Anna straightened her skirts, sitting in the chair Bea had vacated. "Why would you give it back to him if you had won it fairly?" She watched Morgan cross his arms. The right side of his head was still encrusted with blood where he had been hit, but the wound did not detract from his masculine good looks. Anna had never seen hair so golden, and eyes so amber. Despite his wound and his obvious pain, there was the tiniest light of a smile in those eyes.

"Because," he replied after a bit, "I could see that it was a family heirloom, and I didn't feel right taking it. He said offering it back in front of the other men at the table made him look like a fool."

"My brother *is* a fool," she reflected, then, "A conscience, Mr. York?" Anna sat forward and clasped her hands, favoring him with a smile.

Morgan made a move, which instantly brought pain to his cracked and bruised rib. "Hand me my jacket, will you?" Anna brought the jacket to him, and from the inside pocket he removed the gold pocket watch. Holding it out to her, he asked, "Since your brother would not take it, will you? On one condition?"

She hesitantly took the watch her father had carried for thirty-five years, unwilling to believe that Alistair had been so careless with it. Despite the differences between them, Patrick's watch should have been special to him. "And what condition is that, Mr. York?"

"That *you* keep it for your firstborn son...whenever that may happen."

Flustered, Anna stood and turned slightly away from him. "Is there any reason you have made this request?" She wondered if Alistair had boasted of the provisions of their father's will, by which he planned to take control of Shadow Marsh. Her retort must have momentarily taken Morgan off his guard, for he did not answer. So she asked again. "Well, is there?"

"Yes, ma'am," he replied softly. "I didn't know how else to ask you if there was a husband somewhere in the woodshed."

"No, there isn't." Anna felt relieved and somehow happy that he was concerned with her state of wedded bliss, or lack thereof. "Now...I have come to you because you are interested in the position of overseer. Am I correct in this assumption?"

"You are. But I would prefer to be referred to as a foreman instead."

"I have no problem with a change in title, but I must know something about you." She paused. "Most important, Mr. York, is that you're a man of high moral character, honesty, and integrity." Then she remembered the whip scars Bea had mentioned to her. A man of high moral character does not get whipped without cause. For some reason, though, she could not bring it up to him.

"I can pass on those points," he replied, "if you can take into consideration that I am human and capable of making mistakes."

She smiled briefly, but turned away so that he would not see it. "And your reason for wanting this position?"

"I've been traveling a very long time, Miss St. Cyr. I'm tired. I'd like to put down roots for a while."

"Will you work hard?" she asked, turning back. "Even

47

mundane labor? Your hands are hardly calloused for a working man."

"I always work hard, and I always wear gloves to do that work. No sense in having rough hands that might one day want to hold a beautiful woman." Only now did a smile turn up his mouth.

Anna felt there was something compelling about him, gentle and kind, yet hard and aloof. "Will you take the position?"

"Are you offering it?"

"I am." Anna surprised herself by offering such an important position to a man with no experience. But she really wanted him to stay.

"May I think about it for a while?"

"For a few days," she replied, a little disappointed that he should feel the need. "I don't want to wait very long, as the position needs to be filled." A moment of silence fell between them before she spoke again. "I am in charge here, Mr. York. I do hope that my being a woman won't hinder your decision or your performance should you decide to accept the position. I can be as demanding as any man you may have worked for in the past."

"How old are you?"

Anna was a bit flustered by the inquiry. "What does it matter how old I am?"

"It doesn't. I would just like to know."

"I am twenty-one, but don't let my age fool you. I can be tough as leather when the need arises."

"Yes, I'm sure you can be," he replied, unable to mask the humor reflected in his golden eyes. "I won't let it bother me, if you won't let it bother you."

"Since you've been so personal with me, how old are you?"

"Thirty-two."

"Well, Morgan York–thirty-two–I would eventually like to know more about your past."

"My past does not matter. *Now* is what matters."

Ann felt strangely drawn to him, to the mystery of a past

48

that was clearly a secret.

* * *

In the days that followed, Anna rode frequently through Cabin Row and past the Overseer's Cottage, hoping for a glimpse of Morgan. He had stirred an alien sensation in her and color rose in her cheeks at the very sight of him. He was gentle, yet strong and demanding, and those eyes…she loved the way they looked at her. She wondered how soft his hair would be beneath her fingers, how gentle his body would be pressed closely to hers. Indeed, something warm and wonderful was happening to Anna.

When Alistair learned of the proposed hiring he, of course, turned sullen. And the more he thought about it, the angrier he became. The angrier he became the more he wanted to be as far from Shadow Marsh as he could get. Early Friday morning, he gathered his men, and by ten o'clock had begun the two hundred mile trip to New Orleans to sell the St. Cyr thoroughbreds at auction.

Anna was almost relieved by his absent remark that he might be gone two months or more. She was also relieved that one of the men would take charge of the profits from selling the horses and make sure it arrived at Shadow Marsh and not the gambling tables of New Orleans.

Alistair was still her brother, and she supposed she would miss him. However, things would be quiet and tolerable during his absence. Anna couldn't imagine the dawning of a boring day with Morgan York in residence at Shadow Marsh. "Oh, please stay, Morgan," echoed softly in her heart.

* * *

Morgan walked out to the small porch of Bea's cabin where he had sought a cup of her good chicory coffee. He looked around. The men were in the fields, and a pleasant-faced nanny supervised the play of children too young to work. The cabins were of whitewashed cypress wood, arranged in rows fronting a narrow red dirt and gravel road, and shaded by a fine row of cone-shaped cottonwood and China trees. The peaceful, domestic scene was marred only by the stench of improper sanitation drainage from the several community outhouses beyond the cabins. If Morgan stayed on, as he was inclined to do, he would set about improving conditions for the people he would work with.

The chapel, set in a grove of willow oaks, reminded Morgan how many years had passed since he and his brothers had sat quietly in a church pew, listening in awe as hellfire and damnation spewed from the lips of their Methodist minister. Memories of his childhood came rushing back, staying just long enough to open painful wounds. Shaking himself free of his memories, Morgan looked across to the small cabin porch opposite him, where the nanny, whom he'd heard called Auntie Goose, was deeply engaged in her knitting. Off to the left, in a large clearing, were stacks of newly cut and planed oak and pine, and handmade bricks in various shades of red and gray. Morgan was startled by the approach of Mose, who served the Big House and whose bed Morgan had occupied for the past few nights while Mose slept on a cot in another room. He recalled how timidly Anna had asked him, just yesterday, if he would be more comfortable at the Big House. Perhaps he should have accepted her offer.

"Up and about, huh, massa?" Mose asked, removing the black tie he was required to wear at the house.

"Don't call me *massa*," Morgan replied, his tolerance for the title, which he'd heard only too often these past few days, wearing thin. "Morgan will do. Or York, if you prefer."

"Ain't proper," the old man replied, shaking his head. "But if that's what you be wantin', Mistah Morgan."

He could accept the compromise. Morgan pointed across the clearing, at the stacks of new lumber. "Why is that out in the open like that?"

"What, mass–uh, Mistah Morgan?"

"The brick and lumber."

"Fo' the market. The young fellas, they be cuttin' all summer, to be sellin' at the market. Ever' Saturday night, they's be a market at Jude's Landin'. Black folk sells their wares, chickens and lumber and cypress, and eggs a'plenty. You be stayin' on as overseer–you be stayin', mass–uh, Mistah Morgan?"

"I don't know yet," Morgan replied truthfully. "If I stay, I won't be overseer. I'll be foreman. If I stay, make sure everyone knows that." Then, "Does the money from this labor go to the plantation or to your people?"

"It our money, Mistah Morgan. Miss Anna, she insist on it ever' year. Now–if you be stayin'," Mose continued, rubbing his graying head, "Miss Anna, she be wantin' you to come to market with us. They's be trouble from Massa Brady–what used to be overseer here. An' he got fo' mean boys. It'll be yo' place to be gettin' the pass from the Big House, or Pop Gunter–he won't be lettin' us set up our wares."

"This Brady…what kind of man was he?"

Mose propped his foot on the narrow porch and again scratched at his head. "Massa Brady tip the bottle ever' day, an' he get real mean. Miss Anna–she be tellin' him he don't straighten up, she be dischargin' him. But he hired by Massa Patrick, and Miss Anna don't be feelin' right firin' him. But when Massa Patrick go to his Makah, she tell Brady to be packin' his bags."

Mention of Anna made Morgan smile. He could well imagine the youthful woman approaching a ruthless drunk and telling him to get out. "If I stay, this Brady won't be causing any more trouble for your people."

Mose stepped up to the porch, preparing to enter the cabin. "Got to be changin' my clothes," he explained. "Missy, she be wantin' the overseer's–uh, the fo'man's–place fixed up and cleaned right proper." He grinned widely. "She be thinkin' maybe you stay. An' she don't be likin' to be wrong."

Morgan truly wanted to stay, but he disliked the idea of being in charge of people who had no legal rights. He stood on the porch for a long while, exchanged a few words with Mose when he left the cabin, and allowed his thoughts to return to the decision he would have to make very soon. He wasn't sure what held him back. He needed the job and was tired of drifting. And the lovely, emerald-eyed woman who would be his employer had somehow reached into his heart. She was fiercely independent–he liked that rarely seen quality in a woman.

Morgan might have continued deep in thought if Lovey had not entered Cabin Row with his breakfast plate. The cooked ham steamed through the delicate embroidered cloth napkin personally placed there by Anna, or so Lovey would tell him with a note of pride. When Lovey saw Morgan standing at the porch, his tall, slim build leaning lightly against the support post, she clicked her tongue in gentle chastisement. "Get on in, Mistah Morgan. They's mighty weak legs a-holdin' you up. An' Missy Anna, she say men stubborn as jackasses in a burnin' barn!" Lovey preceded him into her mother's cabin and put the plate on the table. "You sit down and eat this here breakfast Miss Anna sent you. She say, you don't make up yo' mind 'bout stayin', you get ready to saddle yo' devil hoss and ride out! Can't be wastin' victuals feedin' you, you be leavin' soon!"

Morgan sat at the table where Lovey had set his plate and removed the napkin. "She said all that?" he replied in a rich, fluid tone, fighting the hint of a smile. "You like her, don't you?"

"Like Missy Anna?" Astonishment rose in Lovey's voice, followed immediately by a stern, yet waving, look. "Don't jus' like her. Love her, mo'n like it. Her heart's as big as a mountain in Tenn'see."

"You ever been to Tennessee?"

"Well…no."

"You say her heart's big, but she keeps your people in chains."

"Chains! What's this 'bout chains?" Lovey drew her hands to her hips. "You bad-mouthin' Miss Anna what been feedin' you good victuals fo' the past week? Why she placed that napkin on yo' victuals with her own purty hands!"

Morgan gave her an apologetic look. "I meant only that your people are in bondage–slavery."

"Slavery?" That what been troublin' you? Why, they's no slaves at Shadow Marsh. Massa Patrick, he done give us our freedom papers when he meet the Lawd." Lovey, snickering quietly to herself, set about straightening dishes in her mother's

52

wash bin and hanging dishtowels over the cupboard door. "Now!" Lovey continued, getting back to Morgan's proposed employment as overseer, "She says you work fo' seventy-five dollars a month, and in three months, she pay you eighty-five dollars."

"Are you hiring me, Lovey?" Morgan asked with a hint of humor.

Guilt settled on Lovey's smooth, pleasant features. "Lawd, no! That be's Miss Anna's job. Why, Lovey, she peel her ear to the do', and she hear ever'thang. Anna tell her brother she invite you to stay. Massa Alistair real quiet at first, then he scream an' rave and threaten to dig yo' eyes out with a pitchfork. But Miss Anna—she run things here. Now, what you say, white man? You stay? You ain't got no whip, huh?"

"No whip," he replied nonchalantly. "You tell Miss St. Cyr I'll stay for a while."

\* \* \*

Morgan had planned to go about his business, settling into the overseer's cottage and assuming his duties with little fuss. Anna, however, was not content to watch him from a distance and wonder from day to day if he was properly learning the job, and whether he was aware that he would be required to keep daily accounts of the plantation's expenditures for supplies. But who was Anna trying to fool? She was so strongly attracted to the very secretive Morgan that she had scarcely given his duties a second thought. She simply wanted to be with him. Thus, she abandoned her reserve and summoned him to the house.

She was in the morning room, a warm, pleasant alcove at the east side of the house, surrounded by wide, spotless windows, dainty pink chintz curtains, and carefully tended plants in iron pots. She was sipping tea and reading over her domestic expenditures for the month and did not look up as a sharp rap sounded at the morning room door. She knew who her visitor was and felt the need to be nonchalant—even a bit indifferent. "Come in."

Masculine boot steps approached, halted, and stood slightly apart. At last, compelled by the silence, Anna looked up from her tea to find steely amber eyes watching her intently. His masculine strength overwhelmed her. He was so tall and broad-shouldered, his tan jacket flaring back with his thumbs tucked into his beltline, his dark brown trousers neatly pressed, and knee-high riding boots polished to a military gleam. His blond, wavy hair had been freshly washed and shone like glass in the morning sun. But his look was critical, and it momentarily flustered Anna.

Morgan wondered why they were engaged in this childish contest to see who could outstare whom. He was also a little angry that she had summoned him from the fields.

Anna had worn her white gown–the one that hugged her body closely–in hopes that he would notice. She could tell as his eyes slowly lowered that he had indeed. She had taken special care with her hair and had pulled it back with ivory combs. She smiled, revealing straight white teeth and the tiny dimple at her chin. "Mr. York, please have a chair. I hope I haven't summoned you at a bad time?"

"It was a very bad time," he replied. "I was in the east fields with the men."

Anna gave him a cool look, which turned cold as humor gleamed in his lean features. "Would you care for tea?" she asked, quickly recovering her good mood.

"I would," he replied shortly, sitting across the table from her.

Anna handed him the delicate china cup. "Sugar?"

"Rots the teeth."

"Cream?"

"Makes you fat."

"Indeed." Anna smiled. "I do apologize for taking you from the fields, Mr. York. I thought perhaps we should discuss any problems you may already have encountered. I did want to go over the finances."

"I have read over the ledgers, Miss St. Cyr. Since they are in a deplorable state, it will take a little work to get them straightened out."

"I am sorry...Brady was lazy with the ledgers." Then, "And

your duties?"

"I am aware of my duties and the hours I am required to put in for Shadow Marsh. I am aware that I am on call in case of emergencies twenty-four hours a day and that I am responsible for summoning medical help for the people here. Now, Miss St. Cyr..." He couldn't prevent his bold, assessing look, or his quick smile as he added, "I found the neatly written list of instructions you left for me in the cottage. You have a nice hand, by the way." He settled back and looked at her more critically. "I'll enjoy the tea and be back to my work. You would not have hired me had you not felt confident that I could handle the job."

Anna, too, settled back, and her look became as intense as his was critical. "Aren't we a little testy this morning, Mr. York?"

"Are we?" he replied seriously, sipping his tea.

Anna felt color rise in her cheeks. She was at a loss for words. Perhaps he thought her–the very young mistress of a large plantation–merely something to amuse himself with. "Since you're here, perhaps you can tell me a little about yourself. I've assigned you a very large responsibility and I know so little of your background."

The coolness of his look sharpened into anger. "I was born in Tarrytown, New York. I am thirty-two years old–as I told you before–and for the past few years I've done nothing worth a damn for anyone, including myself. I gamble, I drink, and I often cuss like a pirate. I've stayed in no one place longer than a few months and I will stay on here only as long as it suits me...and I'm not smothered by curiosity."

Morgan quickly drank his tea and stood. Anna was not aware that she had made him feel taunting and sarcastic. At the moment he was wondering if there was something he could say to rile her, to keep her alert and on her toes. "You know, Miss St. Cyr," he began thoughtfully, "this is my first position as an overseer. I've heard ugly stories of life on the southern plantations and, frankly, I'm surprised that not one single sweating back in your cotton fields bears the marks of a whip."

Anna stood up from her chair. She was not angry. Rather,

55

he had humored her. She thought about what he had said for a moment, and replied, "Like yours, Mr. York?" He was visibly surprised. His teeth gritted, sharpening the line of his jaw. When he did not reply, Anna continued in haste, "People talk, Mr. York, especially of a white man bearing the marks of a whip." She paused, immediately regretting that she'd created tension between them by bringing up a subject that was obviously painful to him. But it was out now, spoiling whatever could have been salvaged of their meeting this morning. "And for what reason were you so brutally mistreated?"

"Stealing a horse," he replied shortly, favoring her with another of his cool, intimidating looks.

Anna resumed her chair. "Well..." The softness of her voice hid her disdain. "I trust you learned your lesson." When he did not immediately reply, Anna looked up. Strangely, a smile turned up his perfect masculine lips.

"I did," he replied. "The next night I crawled back on my belly and stole the damn horse again. The lessons I learned, Miss St. Cyr, were patience, not to trust anybody, and how not to get caught." He didn't like the way she returned his look, silently appraising his character. "And if you make moral judgments of me because of an incident that occurred years ago, may I add that I put in six months on a cattle drive for the man whose horse I stole and who, outraged by a fight I'd had with his spoiled son, refused to pay me for my work. Now—good day, Miss St. Cyr."

"Wait... Mr. York, this purloined property? The painted stallion?" He nodded imperceptibly. "You enjoy the thrill of a spirited horse, do you not?"

"I certainly wouldn't have risked my hide for a plow nag," he replied, returning his hat to his head, and flipping it back from his eyebrows. "Good day."

With his back turned to her, Anna blurted out, "Will you ride with me on Sunday?" When he again faced her, she saw the faint glimmer of a smile in his golden eyes and hastily added, "I wish to view the condition of the fields and point out those requiring special fertilizers in the fall."

"Of course," he replied, adjusting his hat. "I'm at your

56

service."

As Anna watched him walk away, she felt her nerves dance with excitement, wild and uncontrolled, like the desire that grabbed at her flesh.

She counted on her fingers the number of days until Sunday came around once again.

# Five

This dark, moonless September evening, Morgan stood at the open parlor window of the cottage, where a lovely magnolia tree grew. Its fragrance drifted into his senses, reminding him of Anna, whose pride and rebellion had stirred the embers of desire in him. During the past four weeks they had taken frequent horseback rides together, and a terrible toll was taken on Morgan's stance as a gentleman. He wanted her, and she knew it.

Yet she had conducted herself with discretion, and hid her intelligence behind small talk and her feelings behind a polite exterior. Since the morning she had been with him in her pleasant little alcove, surrounded by her plants and flowers and chintz curtains, Morgan had become an obsession with her.

She had also noticed these past few weeks that he was terribly cautious. He tried very hard–too hard at times–to hide his feelings. Several times he had started to tell her something about himself, but he had always changed the subject to something noncommittal. Although it irritated her that he closed her out of his most intimate thoughts, she admired his quiet enthusiasm as he buried himself in the duties of his new position.

Lovey's husband, Joby Cade, assisted Morgan where he was able. Joby suggested to Morgan that the wetland fields, comprising some nine hundred acres, be cleared for rice and readied for spring planting. Morgan broached the subject to Anna who, despite her late father's opposition to the planting of rice–an opposition she had once gone against–she viewed the proposition enthusiastically and gave her permission for the planting. At the bottom of her reply to Morgan, she hastily scribbled, "Will I see you on Sunday for a ride?"

He had just read her note when she rode through Cabin Row without glancing his way, and dismounted at the Shadow Marsh stables. He had lit his pipe, an infrequent habit he'd been weaning himself from, and now he set it on the porch rail. He wanted to see Anna before the wagons left for the fields. On the short walk around the catfish pond to the stables, Wren Wellington rode past on a fine black Thoroughbred, stirring up dust that immediately settled on Morgan's polished boots. Wren dismounted at the stables, and disappeared into the dark interior where Anna had just entered.

Anna had ridden her horse hard this morning, and the animal stood hot and lathered outside the stable door. She had risen early, saddled the horse herself, and had watched dawn break the timberline from her favorite spot at the bend of the bayou. Morgan York filled her thoughts. Her flesh heated with desire every time she saw him. She had hoped an early morning ride, sitting quietly in the shade of the cypress, would quell her infatuation with him. But he was also a man with a past veiled in a mystery that had become as great an obsession with her as her desire for him. It alarmed her that, in the chill of the late evenings, she could actually be warmed by her thoughts of him.

Anna entered the dark barn and found the groom was nowhere to be seen. She began to unsaddle and brush her horse, but a low whimper drew her to the far corner of the stable. There, an old dog belonging to Quash, the blacksmith, nursed nine new pups. She wagged her tail as Anna dropped to her knees, drawing the nearest of the pups fondly to her. "Well, girl, you've got quite a bunch there." Anna held the pup to her cheek, immediately assailed by its sweet, milky smell. "You are a fine one." She was still kneeling in the hay when Wren saw her. She gave a small gasp as he approached in silence, speaking only when he was within touching distance of her. "Wren, you did startle me."

"Anna, I've got to explain about Violet…"

Anna stiffened. "You've waited quite a few weeks to do that." She returned the pup to its place with the others. "There is nothing to explain, Wren."

Wren dropped to his knees beside her. He was quite handsome this morning, in dark brown corduroy trousers tucked into highly polished brown boots. The lapels of his tan riding jacket were embroidered in a floral pattern matching the color of his trousers.

"I don't want bad feelings between us. And I must know–I simply must," he stated emphatically. "Would you ever have married me?" Anna eased herself to a sitting position and looked directly into Wren's soft brown eyes. When she did not immediately reply, Wren closed the distance between them, the sweetness of a mint julep he'd had that morning overwhelming her. "Oh, Anna, Anna–I love you so!"

"Wren!" Exasperation smothered her voice. "You're my cousin's fiancé!" His arms darted to her back, drew her close, and his lips touched hers. The stable door creaked. Anna pulled quickly away. "For mercy's sake, Wren. Someone will see. Oh, please–won't you leave?"

"Tell me, Anna! Would you ever have married me?"

Anna studied Wren for a moment, during which she very carefully composed her reply. "I've always been especially fond of you. We were good friends as children. I hope we remain good friends in the future. But..." Her eyes lowered. "I would never have married you, Wren. We just aren't right for each other."

He drew back now, his face betraying both pain and relief. He couldn't bear the thought of marrying Violet if there was even the smallest chance with Anna. He picked up a bit of straw and flicked it back and forth across his boot. "I'll marry Violet and be a good husband to her."

"Do you love her, Wren?"

He looked to her now. "I hope she's a kind-hearted person. I should grow to love her, surely." But Wren knew Violet could be, and was often, venomous, and that he could only love Anna. She was in his blood. "Now, what have you got there?" he continued with a bit more inflection, "a fine lot of pups?"

\* \* \*

Morgan knew he had no right to feel as he did. Seeing Anna in Wren Wellington's embrace had stirred jealousy in him. But in all his years of travel he had not met a woman who so thoroughly captivated him. He desired Anna Rose so much that breathing had become a chore. Her soft glances and graceful movements had overcome the discipline he had nurtured in eleven years of aimless wandering. At the moment he felt that the image of her in Wren Wellington's arms would stay with him forever.

That evening Morgan tried to soothe his nerves at the piano in the cottage. Bea explained it had been stored there after Luther Brady's dismissal. But music was no balm, so he took a bottle of whiskey from the cupboard, strolled down to the peaceful little clearing by the bayou, and simply waited. He knew it was Anna's favorite spot, and she usually visited it at least once a day, often late in the evening.

The call of a night bird drifted hauntingly through the night, quelling Morgan's anger. He rested lazily against the trunk of an ancient oak, closed his eyes, and allowed the cool breeze drifting up from the bayou to calm his nerves. Nearly asleep when the rustle of crinoline skirts slipped past him in the dark, Morgan dreamily watched Anna Rose's lithe form drop to the ground. She was weeping.

A woman's tears always had a strange effect on Morgan. Rising, he moved quietly through the evening mist, dropped to his knees, and very gently drew Anna into his arms. When her trembling hands moved beneath his coat, it seemed a natural thing. It seemed, too, that she could not stop crying, and Morgan was rapidly forgetting his earlier qualms about Wren.

Anna became lost in the strength of the male body pressed so closely to hers, the hand moving gently over her back, comforting, expressing concern, and asking nothing in return. When she shivered, he drew her into the warm folds of his jacket and sat, unmoving, allowing her to vent her hurt against his chest.

"You're a strange man, Morgan."

It was the first time she had called him Morgan. It had always been Mr. York. Morgan was pleased. "Of course I am," he replied after a moment. "Now–tell me what has broken your heart?"

Anna shrugged weakly. Rather than respond, she asked in a

trembling voice, "Do you think I conduct myself as ruthlessly as Attila the Hun?" Then she drew back, her eyes brimming with yet unshed tears.

Morgan rested his hand over his drawn-up knee. With his left hand, he gently swept the dark, loose hair back from her cheek, allowing his fingers to linger there for a moment. He wanted very much to touch his lips to hers. "Attila the Hun?" he echoed with a slight smile. "Would it help you a little to know that the ancient gentleman wasn't half as ruthless as historians have made him out to be?"

"Not really," she replied, managing a smile of her own.

Morgan sighed. "Sounds like a spat with your brother," he surmised, favoring her again with a comforting smile.

Anna drew her knees up, straightening her wide skirts, and picking up a small stick to stab aimlessly into a dead oak leaf. "Whatever will I do with Alistair? He returned from New Orleans with an absolutely dreadful woman named Sudie…Sudie, of all things!–whom he said is his new wife. Every other word she utters is either 'bloody' or–or 'damn.' And she wears red trimmed in black lace. This is not the only horror for today." She drew back, so that she might see his face. "I have the auction bill, which shows that Alistair received sixteen thousand dollars for the horses. I had specifically requested that Joby Cade take charge of the funds, but he said that Alistair refused to turn them over. Now he has returned to the plantation without a single dollar of the auction funds."

"Sixteen thousand will break the plantation?" he asked.

"Well, no, but that's not the issue. He refuses to tell me what happened to the money. I should not have trusted him, and I will never trust him again." She looked to him somewhat shamefully. "He's my brother. What must you think of me disparaging him like this?" When he did not reply, Anna quickly changed the subject. "My great-grandfather, Patrick St. Cyr, was standing right here when he named this land Shadow Marsh. He looked out over the bayou, cool in the shadows of the hanging moss, and the name came to him, like a gift from God he said. It's a beautiful name, isn't it?"

"A beautiful name," Morgan replied. "And you're a beautiful woman. Let me add that you have every right to be disappointed in your brother." His hand rose, absently, to the dampness of her cheek. Although the tender move flustered Anna, she did not withdraw, even as his hand slipped to the back of her head and entwined in her thick hair. She felt his grip tighten.

His breathing, moments ago soft and even, now quickened. His eyes became liquid gold and penetrated the very core of her heart. Timidly, she met his gaze, the desire stirring within her new and alien and wonderful. And his lips claimed hers, sweetly and gently. Anna knew she had trembled as she'd responded to his kiss, and her hand eased to his back beneath his jacket, but recoiled just for a moment when she felt the scars. But if Morgan had noticed, it did not prevent him from easing her to her back. His iron-hard body met her gentle one in an embrace such as she had only dreamed of.

Morgan took her wrists and rubbed them very softly. His mouth caressed hers, and his hands slipped beneath her, to lift her body against his own. "Anna...Anna..." Morgan whispered against her cheek. "What is it that draws me to you?" When he released her wrists, her hands slipped round his shoulders to hold him very close.

"I must be mad," she replied, trembling. "But–I have dreamed of this moment when you would hold me. Were death to be awaiting me this very minute, I would meet it willingly, knowing I spent my last moments with you." Tenderly, Anna's fingers rose to his golden hair, to feel its softness, and to his jaw, to feel its strength. Their eyes met. His lips moved to the smooth, ivory flesh exposed above her bodice and she did nothing to prevent it. As he caressed her gently, Anna took a sharp, pained breath.

Desire overwhelmed her. Morgan was no longer an overseer–or foreman, as he preferred–but a man...strong and virile, gentle and exciting. She wanted him, his intimacy and passion. She wanted to know how it felt to be with a man–but with Morgan, not just any man. She didn't want to be an

63

emotionless machine that would rust with age and neglect.

The heat of passion flowed painfully through her. She had never felt like this. It was wonderful—more wonderful than she had ever imagined. Morgan caressed her, and his lips moved to her neck, and to her firm, ivory breasts, which he exposed and kissed tenderly. This gentle man, turning cold flesh into a rapid river of fire, was the man she had waited for all her life. She was delirious with passion as Morgan eased her satin skirts upwards and touched her smooth flesh beneath…and yet she was afraid. "I–I want this–don't I?" she stammered, fear crisp and undeniable in her breathless words.

Only now did Morgan stop to think about what they were doing. He did not want to damage the respect and trust they had patiently nurtured for one another these past few weeks. The consummation of their love now, at this very moment—and in a bayou clearing—would be a travesty. Hating himself for what he was doing, Morgan pulled the stays of her dress together and refastened them. "No…it is not the right moment."

Anna's arms slipped round his neck, and her cheek drew close, to rest against his own. "When it is right, it will happen," she whispered.

They held one another silently, neither counting the minutes that passed. Then Morgan drew away from her and straightened his disheveled clothing. When he sat with his back to her and his silence deepened, Anna rose hastily to her feet. She was hurt and confused by his sudden detachment, and wondered if he regretted their moments together.

But before she could move out of his reach, he took her hand and held it gently to his cheek, which was warm and flushed. "Forgive me, Anna, there are things about me–"

Anna dropped to her knees, her gaze moving imploringly over his strong features. "I want you, Morgan, and I believe you want me. I am willing to wait as long as you are, as long as it takes to break the barrier separating you from the rest of the world. These…things about you–they will not matter to me. I see the man you are now, and that is what matters to me."

Morgan drew her into his arms, and they held one another

for another long, silent moment. "Twelve years ago I killed a man," he quietly confessed.

Anna drew close to him and her dark hair touched his strong shoulder. "If you killed someone, there must have been justification in it. I've seen in you only a kind, sincere man."

"I wonder if there is ever justification to taking a human life. As for sincerity, hell...I haven't even told you my true name."

"But you will, in time. For now, Morgan is nice enough."

Morgan stood and helped her up, and they walked toward the Big House. At the veranda, Anna turned, lifting her chin. "I'll never forgive you, Morgan, if I awaken one morning and find you gone. I'll just never forgive you." She could have left this unsaid. Her eyes were the mirrors of her heart and soul, baring her feelings for all to see...for Morgan to see.

His jaw hardened. "I'll see you tomorrow, Anna," he muttered, feeling somehow trapped by his desire for Anna. At other times like this, he *had* moved on.

# Six

Lovey was clearing the dishes from the breakfast table when she pointed out Morgan York climbing the hill toward Shadow Marsh. Since he had kept himself deliberately aloof these past few weeks, Anna wondered what he had on his mind. Her eyes lowered to the newspaper she pretended to be reading, although she watched his slow approach. His golden hair shone as brilliantly as his polished boots did in the morning sun. She could not see his expression because he kept his eyes concealed beneath the brim of his hat, but she could see that his jaw was clenched tightly.

These past few weeks, Morgan had found various weak excuses not to ride with Anna on Sundays. It had embarrassed her, and she had wondered over and over if he regretted their moments together at the bayou. As Morgan reached the steps, he tucked his thumbs into the waist of his breeches. Anna looked up only when he stopped before her. "Good morning," he said in his most pleasant voice.

"And to you, Morgan," she replied a bit stiffly, motioning to the chair across the table from her. She was determined to treat him as he had treated her these past few weeks—with noncommittal indifference. "Won't you be seated?"

"Umm, no, I have only a moment before the wagons head out. Anna..." His arms were loosely crossed. "I've treated you badly these past few weeks. I wish to apologize."

Their eyes met. Anna wanted to ask him why, when their last moments together had been so beautiful and intimate. The gaze seemed to go on forever. Morgan's eyes, deep and golden beneath thick blond eyebrows, could look rather devilish, as they did now. Finally, Anna replied, "Apology accepted, Morgan. Whatever it was that didn't set well with you, I, too, apologize."

"There's no need, Anna. It's me, not you. I've got a lot of problems to work out." He tipped his hat, took two steps backward before turning away from her, and turned back, favoring her with a long, thoughtful look. "I was wondering...umm, never mind." Again, he tipped his hat. "Good day."

"Morgan?" Anna's velvety voice compelled him to turn back. "This Sunday afternoon, would you find time to ride with me?"

A smiled turned up his lips. "I'll show you the work we're doing."

Only when he disappeared into Cabin Row did Anna's gaze leave him. Lovey was giving her a broad, knowing smile. "There's a real purty pink done rose in yo' cheeks."

"Hush, Lovey," Anna replied without feeling, returning to the newspaper she had only half-heartedly been reading earlier.

* * *

By Saturday, Anna wanted to ride and wanted Morgan with her. He would, she reasoned, have plenty of time before departing for the market at Jude's Landing, and she hoped he might be just as anxious to be with her. Eagerly dismounting from her mare at the porch of his cottage, she knocked at the door. There was no answer, and one of the children told her Mr. York had taken his horse down to the bayou for a bath and would be back in a while. Anna would not deprive horse and rider of their time together, so chose to await him inside the cottage, in the foyer she herself had decorated several years ago. She wanted to see how Morgan lived. The ravages of Luther Brady's wild lot had taken its toll on the heavy mahogany furniture, and the rugs were worn thin throughout the walk areas. Otherwise, the room was clean and neat.

On a small table in the corner lay an antique chess and Tric Trac board, walnut inlaid with copper gilt, ivory, and mother-of-pearl. The chess pieces were silver, except for a crudely carved wooden queen. Anna was intrigued by the piece, strangely out of place among her silver counterparts. Somewhere in his travel, Morgan must have lost–or perhaps gambled away–the silver queen. Now anxious for Morgan's return, she stood and strolled casually around the small parlor, flicking her gloved fingers impatiently over the furniture. She saw her mother's piano, kept out of sight for many years in the farthest corner of the storage house, but stored here after Luther's departure. It had been a painful reminder of Dora St. Cyr in the Big House, and Anna's father had ordered its removal from the house after her death. So–here was the source of the haunting music she had thought part of her dreams at night.

What kind of man confessed to drinking and gambling and cursing, yet spoke well-educated English, played the piano, and, from the looks of the board, a skillful game of chess? Anna returned to her chair and sat down. She absently fingered a bit of paper on the table beside Morgan's portfolio, noticing it was a clipping from a newspaper, crisp and brown with age. Bored, waiting for Morgan, she began to read it:

> The New York Times reports the execution by military firing squad of Captain Michael George Fielding, a native son of Tarrytown. A West Point honor graduate of 1845 and aide-de-camp to General Curtis Lee of Washington D.C. prior to his service on the western front against hostile Mexican forces, Captain Fielding was court-martialed in the latter part of 1846 for the murder of Lieutenant John Gunthar. Captain Fielding is survived in life by his mother, also of Tarrytown.

Anna did not hear the door softly close. Morgan stood in the doorway, his arms crossed, and his feet slightly apart. Anna smiled, but the smile faded at once when she met his eyes, narrowed and strangely expressionless. Her hand dropped as he approached her. Very gently, he took the newspaper clipping from her hand and returned it to the portfolio.

"One of the boys said you were waiting here for me," Morgan said dryly. "What can I do for you?"

"I had hoped you would ride with me this afternoon."

"I may have earlier…not now."

"Why not now?" When he did not reply, she continued with haste, "You didn't think I was–oh, for heaven's sake, Morgan, how could you think I was prying? It was just lying there and I read it."

"It was with my personal papers."

"It was on the table," she argued. "Why are you acting like this? I don't care about this...this Michael Fielding! I care about you! I have grown to love you!"

*Don't you care about Michael?* he thought, the painful memory of Fort Marcy clouding his thoughts. He simply stood there, looking at her as if she were so much rubbish.

Anna was suddenly quite furious. "You're such a strange man, Morgan! Why ever did I think I could fall in love with you?" Her eyes moved slowly over his rigid form, her gaze dropping. Despite her anger, she felt the pain of desire pulling at her. She wanted to be in Morgan's arms, not standing back from him like this. "Morgan, why must we argue?"

Morgan crossed his arms. He wanted to be stubborn and belligerent, to express his fullest disdain. He wanted to put an end to her outrageous prying, once and for all, but he knew the only solution to that was to divulge his past, fully and completely, to her. She had just hinted that she could love him. But could she if she knew his past? He could not tell her. She would never understand. So he dropped into an armchair and brought his thumb and forefinger to his closed eyes. He lowered his hand, and his eyes slowly came open as he reminded himself in silence who he really was. *Morgan York* was a fiction, a name chosen from a tombstone somewhere in West Texas.

He looked to Anna, who had backed toward the door and stood there in utter silence. He wanted to form his thoughts into words and tell her about his past. He wanted her to know everything, because he was tired of his past standing constantly between them. Morgan turned his eyes toward her, rose, approached the window, and stood with his back to her. A moment of silence passed between them. "Anna, there is so much I want–need–to tell you, but I cannot...not yet."

"You told me once you had killed a man. If it has anything to do with that..."

Turning swiftly toward her, he warned, "Right now, Anna, I will stand for no more of your prying." But even as he spoke, he knew she had not really pried. He vaguely recalled taking the clipping out of his portfolio to read it, something he often did simply to remind himself who he really was.

"I was not prying!" She quickly closed the distance between them, tears of anger flooding her eyes. Her hands clenched into fists, she wanted so much to strike him. Rather, her cheek touched his strong chest and her hands circled his waist beneath his jacket. "I would rather my love fill your heart than your brutal memories, Morgan, so that one day you might love me. Please—one day, let there be no secrets between us."

Morgan gently held her. "Right this moment, Anna, what do you want of me?"

She held him tightly, possessively. "You, Morgan. Just to know that you will always stay at Shadow Marsh...my courage and my strength. Oh, how very fond of you I am...dare I say that I love you and you will have no doubt of that?" Her gaze lifted and moved over his taut features. "I want to lie in your arms, Morgan, to love you, and be loved by you."

Could he believe her? He had seen women like her before, strong, yet vulnerable, wealthy, egotistical bullies in satin skirts, who maneuvered men toward their own selfish ends. What was it she wanted of him, when she could have any man?

At the moment, Anna wanted only to lie in his arms in the gentlest of raptures, in the wildest of passions. Their common destiny was to love each other to the fullest.

A thought suddenly came to Morgan; he stepped away, took her arms just above the elbows, and held them tightly for a moment. She winced from the pain traveling to her fingers, making it impossible for her to reach up and break his hold. His eyes had suddenly become dark, glowing embers of rage.

She had often seen him angry, but not like this...looking at her as if he might suddenly spring and kill. She became frightened. When his grip loosened a little, she raised her hand to break his grip on her left arm. But his grip tightened instead. Driven only by her fear of his strange, uncharacteristic mood, her right hand drew briskly back to strike him. But he caught her hand mere inches from his cheek.

His hands fell, and in the same moment the strangeness left his features. "Why would you want to strike me, Anna?"

Tears fell over the smooth contours of her cheeks. "You frightened me, Morgan." Turning away, her shoulders drooped. "Perhaps I don't know you as well as I thought. Perhaps I don't know you at all."

He did not seem angry that she had raised her hand against him, just a bit bewildered by it. His arms slipped around her waist and held her close. "You're right, Anna. You don't know me. You may never know me."

The muskiness of him sifted into her senses. Vexed, she pulled away as if to leave, and pivoted swiftly to face him "And whose fault is that?" she asked, her arms flailing wildly. "You keep your secrets and hold me constantly at arm's length." The color rose in her cheeks as she threw herself into his arms. "Do you even believe that I care so deeply for you…that I am growing to love you?"

"Yes," he replied quietly. "It is the one thing I do believe…and I am not sure how I feel about that. You deserve better than me, and I–rogue that I am with his blasted secrets–do not deserve a woman such as you."

Anna could be content to feel his arms around her shoulders, if that was all he was offering. But she wanted more from him. He brought out desire in her that she had never before imagined. She wanted to feel the strength of his body beside hers, through all the days and months and years lying in their future. "Say that you love me, Morgan?"

He hesitated only slightly. "I do love you, Anna–and that is your misfortune."

She lifted her mouth to his, to possess and be possessed. They had learned to trust to a certain degree, to understand; she had only to be patient and he would share all of his secrets with her. They had learned to care. These past few weeks, they had learned to love and desire, to put aside convention and meet each other on mutual ground. It seemed natural that they should be together. That was the only thought stirring in Anna right now.

The look in her lovely, almond-shaped eyes, her lips

seductively parted, awaiting the tenderness of his touch, hinted that the moment was right. Morgan lifted her into his arms and moved toward the bed where he had rested for a few moments that afternoon. He stood beside the bed, where the quilt was folded neatly along the bottom, then dropped gently with her.

Morgan made her feel bold and seductive. His gentleness calmed the fear rising within her, turning it into a desire that was her only motivation at the moment. She was lost in the tender strength of his arms and wanted only to lie beside him, to experience the sweet, grabbing pain that could only be quelled by the union of their willing bodies. His flesh excited her and she felt her cheeks glow crimson among the loose, disheveled tresses of her hair. In the impatient, angry fling of her arms some moments ago, the stays of her blouse had loosened, revealing to him the ivory flesh hidden only by the lace of her undergarment.

Morgan responded to her willingness in splendid agony, his body hardening against the soft contours of hers. The heavy masculine draperies had been drawn earlier and the room was semi-dark and cooled by the late evening. Alone in her prim, proper bedchamber at Shadow Marsh Anna had often dreamed of this wonderful moment with Morgan.

He entwined his fingers through her disheveled hair and firmly lifted her face and her lips to his own. She could tell by the way he quickly accepted her kisses that he wanted her as badly, and that he might find the necessary foreplay burdensome at the moment. She couldn't have been more wrong. In the following moments, as all reason was abandoned, Morgan touched her in places that had never before been touched, his lips moving to her neck and the pink buds of her breasts.

Anna's body went rigid with desire and anticipation. She wanted to be free of her clothing, and for him to be free of his, so that their flesh could meet in the icy heat of desire. Moments later, her clothing lay crumpled at the foot of the bed. Morgan had removed his shirt and wide leather belt as casually as he might prepare for bed alone. Then Anna felt the thick hair of his chest gently touched her breasts, and his musky, manly aroma filled her senses.

She loved the way he looked at her fully exposed body in the semi-darkness. His eyes glazed with desire, yet behind the desire there was a hesitation, even as he turned, sat on the edge of the bed, and began removing his clothing. Then he was fully exposed to her, and she thought his body exquisite in every way. She held her arms out to him.

Morgan turned and his body fell gently across hers. "Do not be afraid, Anna—"

"I am not afraid," she responded quietly.

"The bodies of man and woman are made to be together." But even as he spoke, he remembered seeing her and Wren Wellington in the stable—both kneeling in the hay looking at each other—and he wondered just for a moment if any explanations were necessary. He had heard that Wren and Violet would be married, so he was still confused by the intimacy between Wren and Anna he had witnessed in the barn.

No matter what, she was here now, with him, and his lips lightly brushed her cheek, her eyelids, which closed gently against his touch. Foremost in his mind was his desire to believe that she had not been with a man before him. Yet, he couldn't help wondering, as her legs gently eased apart to allow for him, if she was much too comfortable right now to actually be pure.

When Morgan's hands moved from her flat stomach to the warmth of her silken thighs, then slipped beneath her buttocks, she lifted herself to him. She knew only that she wanted this moment, and her movements became erotic, almost wild against his sweating flesh.

Although Morgan was ready, even now, to take her, his lips and his hands explored every part of her warm body, tingling, exciting, fanning the flame of her desire. She drew her legs firmly against his and, unable to bear the pain of his desire, he began to enter her.

Anna closed her eyes tightly, in the same moment drawing her arms firmly around his shoulders. As his penetration deepened, the pain brought moisture to her eyes. Dropping her hands, clutching the quilt, her fists tightly balled, she might have cried out if his lips had not closed over her mouth. Instantly, the pain was gone, and her hips moved instinctively, matching his rhythm and pace.

She could never have faked such a reaction, and Morgan knew she had never been with a man before. "I am sorry," he whispered, hating that he had hurt her. "I'll never hurt you again."

"I–I know," she whispered in reply. Anna had never imagined that being with a man could be like this, that her body could be warm and wild against strong, masculine flesh. Trembling, her hands drew around his shoulders to close the distance between them.

His thrusts grew in intensity, like nothing she had ever conceived of. She wanted their union never to end, to lie forever with this powerful man who had awakened the woman within her. Then his movements ceased and although he remained joined to her, his palms again cupped her face. His lips nipped playfully at her willing ones, and her closed eyelids.

"Morgan?"

"Yes, love? he whispered against her hairline.

"There's something wrong with me."

His head lifted, his brows pinching in a frown. "What is wrong?" He looked very worried.

"Women are not supposed to enjoy this," she replied, her hands slipping down the length of him, and gently resting on his narrow hips. "Bea said it is a duty to be gotten over with quickly. But I enjoyed it. Am I a wanton woman?"

Morgan laughed. "Don't listen to Bea. If you didn't enjoy it, there would be something wrong with me!" Morgan slowly broke their union, eased to her side, and propped himself on his elbow. A gentle laugh remained in his eyes.

"You're making fun of me.," she accused with a pretty pout.

"No, my love," he replied. "Your naïve innocence thrills me." He was suddenly ashamed that he had thought she'd been with Wren Wellington that morning in the stable. He took her hand and held it to his chest. He watched her eyes shyly turn to him and slowly move down the length of his body. Then they made love again, his hard, masculine strength becoming one

74

with her softness.

Anna's heart quickened, and as his movements grew in intensity, the end came only too soon. The agonizing explosion of ecstasy deep within her, simultaneous with his, drew her closer to him in these final, beautiful moments.

Morgan's cheek rested lightly against hers. His breathing, quick and erratic just moments ago, now became soft and even. He did not immediately withdraw from her, but eased his hands beneath her shoulders to lift her against his body. His fingers again entwined through her thick, damp hair, and he touched his lips briefly to her cheek before dropping his face to the pillow beside hers.

"It was the right moment, wasn't it, Morgan?"

He eased to her side, pulling the sheet across both their bodies. "It certainly was," he replied, drawing her close to him.

She sighed deeply, feeling safe and secure beside him. She hadn't realized how lonely she had been until now—how sterile and empty her life had been. And she knew one other thing—it was a good time to ask a very important question. "Morgan?" She felt a gentle pressure on her shoulder. "You're Michael Fielding, aren't you?"

His breath caught, but only for a moment. "Yes."

Her fingers moved absently through the hair of his muscular chest. "When you killed John Gunthar, was it an accident?"

"No." He might have left it at that, but her hand ceased to move and her body instinctively recoiled. He sensed her fear. "It was war. John was mortally wounded. For an hour he writhed in his own guts after being disemboweled by cannon shrapnel. I put a bullet through his head to end his suffering." He paused. "He was my stepbrother, Anna. I couldn't watch him suffer. I couldn't–"

Anna placed her fingers to his lips to quiet him. Tears moistened her eyes. "And who am I to love? Morgan York or Michael Fielding?"

"The Army would shoot Michael Fielding."

"And who would shoot Morgan York?"

Morgan shrugged. "A few husbands, I suppose," he replied in a weak attempt at humor. "I cannot tell you which man to love, Anna. The choice is yours."

"Then I have made my choice," she replied. "I love you, Morgan."

# Seven

*Tarrytown, New York, November 1857*

Jarred Gunthar sat quietly in the velvet armchair, staring into the orange and yellow flames lapping at logs in the hearth. His children, George, aged eight, and Selma, aged seven, were asleep in their trundle beds beneath their heavy quilts on this cold pre-winter eve. Jarred's wife, Rebecca, sat across from him, putting the finishing touches on a needlepoint chair cover that had taken the better part of two months to complete. She looked up occasionally and smiled for her husband.

Jarred's dark moods had troubled her of late. He awaited word, which was long overdue, from President Buchanan, and had not really enjoyed his first two-week furlough home in over a year.

Jarred gazed at the portrait of a young West Point officer—his stepbrother, Michael. The amber eyes looked back at him hypnotically, softly smiling. The artist had captured well the pride of this beloved brother, whose fate these past eleven years, and the injustice inflicted on him, had instilled an obsession in Jarred to remove the stain that had tarnished both Michael's name and his military career. He dreamed of nothing else.

"You're thinking of him again, aren't you?" Rebecca asked, dropping her needlepoint, her look hard and unyielding. She had never known Michael, and resented the hold he had over Jarred.

Jarred brought his fingers up to his clean-shaven chin in a moment of thoughtful silence. He knew how Rebecca felt, though she'd only spoken the words once. But he had often seen it in her eyes—the hard hatred—for this man she had never known. She was a pretty woman, with soft brown hair pulled back and held by a velvet ribbon. But her hatred of Michael often made her ugly. "Yes," he admitted momentarily. He approached, dropped to one knee, and clasped her hands. "I know how you feel, Rebecca, but if I only knew...if I only knew if he was dead or alive–"

"It wouldn't make any difference," she replied, the bitterness evident in her voice. "It wouldn't make any difference at all to this obsessive campaign you started eleven years ago, before we were married. There are times that..." Rebecca stopped short, unable to say that she felt Michael had damaged their relationship as husband and wife. She could not admit her jealousy toward a stepbrother she knew only as the smiling amber eyes over their parlor hearth. She had never been able to see him as a flesh and blood human being. She could not admit that she hated him. Jarred would merely think her selfish and childish.

Rebecca picked up the needlepoint again to resume her trim work, but her fingers closed tightly over the fabric. Although she had never known her husband's stepbrother, his presence had hovered over her household since she and Jarred had married, as well as the household of his father and stepmother. Mr. Gunthar would not allow Michael's name spoken in his presence. Mrs. Gunthar, after reading a false report of her son's death in the *New York Times* written by an overzealous reporter, had suffered a stroke. Several years of recuperation had followed. Her speech remained affected, and she had regained only partial use of her left arm. Her illness had merely added fuel to the fire that had stirred bitterly in the elder Gunthar's heart.

Rebecca knew only that Michael had killed their mortally wounded brother, John, and had been sentenced to death–a sentence that, through the grace of God alone–had never been carried out.

She was only too aware of the pain that had torn at Jarred for eleven years. She remembered the many appeals he had made in Michael's behalf, commencing in the lower military courts, each appeal dashed to the ground with the reaffirmation of Michael's sentence. But Jarred had refused to give up.

Eighteen months ago, he had taken his appeal directly to the White House, an appeal that was now in the hands of the new president, James Buchanan.

Rebecca looked up at the lean, handsome face of Michael

George Fielding, and she silently cursed him once more. Her mouth pressed into a thin line of bitterness for this man who filled the spaces in Jarred's heart that should have been reserved for her and their children.

A loud rap sounded at the foyer door. Jarred lurched, startled, and came immediately to his feet. "Who could that be at this hour of night?" he asked, smoothing down the front of his robe. "I hope I have not been recalled to Washington."

Rebecca heard the deep, graveled voice of a man at the door greeting Jarred as "Colonel Gunthar." Muted conversation followed, and the door closed. Jarred returned to the parlor and resumed his chair. His fingers were closed tightly over something that Rebecca could not see.

"Who was it?" she asked, alarmed by the ashen cast of his features.

Jarred's hands were trembling, his eyes lingering for a moment on the large document bearing the seal of the President of the United States. "It is from President Buchanan," Jarred replied softly. He felt pain grab at his chest, and the gnarled, twisted fingers of anticipation drove the breath from his body. This was Michael's last chance...and if it—no, he could not bear to think that.

Rebecca put her needlepoint aside, arose, and dropped to her knees beside Jarred. "Before it is opened," she said. "I want you to know that my prayers are with you...and with Michael." She forced herself to add Michael's name, for Jarred's sake.

Jarred placed his hand lightly on Rebecca's. "Thank you," he replied, unable to disguise the emotion rising in his voice. "I know how difficult this has been for you all these years."

As he stared quietly at the folded document, his fingers, as if possessing a mind of their own, hesitated to break the seal. Jarred's mind wandered back, through the long, troubled years, back through the pain and disappointment of appeal after appeal—back to the day that had burned its memory into his heart.

* * *

It was a cold, brisk February morning. Jarred had seen

Michael for a few minutes on the parade ground. He would never forget Michael's bravery, the strength of his arms around his shoulders in their final embrace. Unconsciously, Jarred brought his hand up to the pocket of his military coat, to feel the bulge of Michael's letter, which he had pressed into his hand just moments ago.

In the small office of HQ, his father sat quietly, unmoving, his features cold. Jarred almost hated him for feeling nothing for the man who had been like a son to him.

The thick walls of battalion HQ reverberated with sound from the parade ground. Jarred was sick at heart, nausea eating at his stomach, and nerves crawling through his neck and shoulders. Outside, a deathly calm silenced the February wind. It seemed a thousand hours of that unnerving silence passed before the dreaded sequence of commands began. "Ready...aim..."

"God! Get it over with," Jarred heard himself mumble frantically. At the sound of twelve simultaneously exploding rifles, Jarred dropped his head into his hands and wept. The horror of imminent death was over for Michael.

Then Jarred heard the rush of booted feet, sharp, shocked voices, Ward Anderssen's outraged screams, and the loud, boisterous cheers of a thousand men. Jarred rose and moved toward the small window of headquarters. Across the parade ground, Anderssen's arms flailed like those of a madman as he moved swiftly down the neat line of the firing squad. Jarred looked beyond Anderssen to the wood beam against which Michael stood. There was no bloody mass where his chest might once have been, no limply hanging head—no aura of death. The men of the firing squad had refused to execute Michael.

"Michael is alive," Jarred muttered in disbelief. "My God! Michael is alive!" He moved quickly into the bitter cold of the battalion parade ground. Anderssen had now ordered the men to reload their weapons, and simultaneously threatened to shoot the lot of them if they refused his orders again.

But Anderssen's fiery, red-faced threat did not move the men to action. Total disorder erupted and General McManus was forced to intervene. He ordered Michael removed to his cell and a full investigation made of the incident. Thereafter, the sentence was reaffirmed, and Michael, due to immense popularity among the troops at Fort Marcy, and another officer–also a captain–court-martialed on a lesser crime, were ordered transferred to Fort Scott in Kansas territory. Michael's execution was rescheduled for April 7th.

But the trip was ill-fated from the outset. One of the horses drawing the prison wagon had collapsed a few miles from Fort Marcy and a detour was made off the Santa Fe Trail because of Indian trouble. The convoy never reached Fort Scott. An exhaustive three-month search ended when the convoy was found beneath the buttes forty miles from Fort Marcy…five dead horses, four dead guards, and only one manacled corpse reduced to a skeleton in the prison wagon, whose door had been pried open. There were no signs of attack and the investigating team reported the cause of death as "exposure to the harsh elements."

Identification of the one prisoner was impossible. For that reason both prisoners were listed as fugitives with the War Department in Washington. But Jarred would never believe that Michael was dead. The West Point officer was alive somewhere–his brother, running from "justice" and his past.

\* \* \*

"Jarred?" Rebecca lightly shook his arm. "Aren't you going to open it?"

Only now did Jarred shake away his memories of that time so long ago. His trembling fingers slowly broke the seal and unfolded the document.

"Dear Colonel Gunthar," he read. His eyes became liquid silver as they flew over the words in silence. When he had finished reading, he turned to Rebecca, drew her into his arms, and held her very gently. "Dearest Rebecca, my darling, patient wife." A tremble settled in Jarred's normally stern, unwavering voice.

The past ten years had hardened the dedicated Army officer and had instilled resentment in him that the love of his family had not been able to touch. Nothing had been as important to him since that February morning so many years ago as had the injustice suffered by Michael. Jarred had been a man possessed, and here before him, in the neat, legible hand of President Buchanan's secretary, the long, arduous trial was ended.

Jarred patted Rebecca's thin shoulder. He wondered at times why she had remained with him all these years. He had been unfair to her, and had closed her out of his most intimate thoughts. He thought now that she must love him very much. Their life could begin afresh now. A tremendous weight had been lifted from his shoulders.

Jarred whispered softly, "Be he dead or alive, Michael had been granted a full pardon."

# Eight

Morgan had politely declined Anna's invitations to two house parties hosted by Alistair, the first to introduce his voluptuous new wife, Sudie Redding to southern society, and the second to announce formally that she carried their first child.

Morgan thought that southerners spent too much money on frivolous entertainment, and the disregard by the wealthy for their fellow man was, in his view, typical of southern priorities. For Anna's sake, he tried not to involve Shadow Marsh in the turmoil plaguing the South. The rancor and frustration in politics was quickly filling the newspapers. The newly elected president, James Buchanan, faced his greatest challenge in the opposition between North and South over the issue of slavery. While Buchanan personally opposed slavery, he had gained the favor of the South by denouncing abolitionists as troublemakers, and by standing on the side of the South in the outcome of the Dread Scott decision. Buchanan's political career was destined for ruin, just as surely as were excesses of southern living. The southern planters, trapped in their dependency on slavery, walked a deadly path toward self-destruction.

As the oil in his lamp burned low, Morgan's forehead fell against his palms. His golden eyes picked lazily over the chess pieces scattered in skilled maneuvers that had filled many lonely hours. He had carved the wooden queen sitting among her silver counterparts himself. He still did not know what had happened to the original piece, possibly bounced out of his saddlebags when he was making a hasty retreat from somewhere–God only knew where.

The overseer's cottage was too quiet, allowing for all sounds of the night to sift in and aggravate him. Many of the Cabin Row inhabitants were serving at the house party. Across the darkness, feminine laughter and the boasts of men with too much liquor beneath their belts drifted out toward Cabin Row.

Late guests were arriving in carriages, which clattered noisily and stirred Morgan's nerves. Tension crawled through his shoulders. His look was diverted to the open parlor window, to the sheen of moonlight casting a silver glimmer on the timberline.

Then his attention turned to the Big House...the definable Shadow Marsh perched on its hill and taking up the sky. Twilight was illuminated by a hundred candles on the wide verandas. Morgan could imagine the belles demurely accepting admiring glances from stumbling courtiers and dance partners as antique matrons in delicate satin gowns looked on in silent approval.

Music drifted toward Morgan, stirring the embers of his anger into a fire. The mood at the house was festive and gay. The music swelled in volume, then ended abruptly, its rhythm instantly replaced by the laughter and chatter of small groups filling the ballroom. The outrage continued to rise in Morgan, a result, in part, of too much whiskey beneath his belt.

Beyond all hope of reviving his prior good mood–if he even had one–he turned the half-empty bottle up to his lips and drank again. He stood, pulled on a clean tan jacket, and moved toward the cottage porch. Standing for a moment, feeling the cool of the early November evening, he stared up at Shadow Marsh, watching the shadows of dancers flit across the lighted windows. Then he began to move slowly through the willows, toward the bend in the bayou that was the one place able to soothe his senses.

* * *

Anna Rose was not enjoying herself. The music was too loud, the laughter unnerving, and Alistair's quickly mounting state of intoxication embarrassing. Wren had chosen Anna for the new dances once too often, and Violet had fled upstairs in tears. The red-haired Sudie, though, bubbled with gaiety, and took great pleasure in displaying the roundness of her abdomen where Alistair's child grew.

She looked down at the tight bodice of her own gown, a cascade of white chiffon with delicate yellow jonquils spilling thickly across its front. But her corset was too tight and she felt ill. The circlet of matching silk jonquils in her hair kept slipping to one side. Thus, she made her excuses to Tylas Miller, with whom she'd been talking at length, and eased toward the wide veranda. She was bored with false smiles and being polite when all she wanted was to be with Morgan.

Why did he have to be so stubborn? Why couldn't he just once do something she wanted him to do? Being here with her tonight might have made the event somewhat pleasant rather than a tedious bore. Despite the November chill and the fact that she had not brought her shawl with her, Anna began to move toward the fishpond and the bend in the bayou. Through the darkness of the bayou clearing, she saw Morgan's dark form slumped lazily against a tree. Her nerves danced with raw excitement. She was not surprised to see him there and had even hoped that he might be.

Morgan made no visible move as she approached, although she was sure his eyes had followed her movements. The ground was soft and damp, covered by a thin layer of oak leaves felled by last evening's rain. Morgan said nothing as she slightly lifted her skirts and dropped to the ground beside him, then eased her body toward his, to lie very quietly against his strong chest, bare beneath his unbuttoned shirt.

The golden glimmer of the bayou reflected in his eyes, his hand, lying limply over his knee just moments before, now moved to her back, to rest there very gently. "Why have you left the party?" he asked quietly.

"Because you were not there," she responded, her hand instinctively rising to the thick blond hair of his chest. The musky aroma of him permeated her senses, his silence compelling her to study his profile—the straight, narrow nose, his warm golden eyes, his lips—yes, the sweet, warm, wonderful lips that often possessed hers. She enjoyed the comforting touch of his hand at her back, his chest pulsating gently against hers, and his masculinity hardening against the soft contours of her body.

"It's beautiful, isn't it?" he asked softly. "The moon casts its hues across the blackness of the water, the moss drapes its tentacles hauntingly over the fallen logs and the bayou, and the sounds of night soothe the heart and soul. Tell me, Anna, if you had one wish this night, what would it be?"

Not a single breath of space separated their bodies. Moisture coated Anna's emerald eyes, even as she drew as close as she possibly could and her hands darted to his back to hold him possessively. "I would wish to be with you forever, Morgan," she replied, breathless in her desire. "And if you were to leave Shadow Marsh, I would wish to go with you."

Although this was what Morgan had hoped to hear, he felt isolated. He was a fugitive, not only from the military, but also from his conscience. He could not ensnare her in the shame that was his and his alone. He felt undeserving of the woman who lay tenderly in his arms, expressing her love for him without inhibitions.

Anna wanted only him. They had shared their desires and their bodies, and she wanted something more permanent. She wanted to be assured that whatever happened, he would always be with her. Enjoying these moments in his arms, her fingers brushed back a lock of hair fallen across his forehead.

All around them a breeze flowed gently through the willows. An owl screeched far off in the woods and storm clouds moved swiftly across the skies, blocking out the golden haze of moonlight that had shimmered on them just moments ago.

Morgan and Anna were lost in the peace of the late hour…a peace that could not be violated by daily domesticities, duties, and sensible thought. Anna was irrational in her love for him. Lifting her slightly flushed face so that it was just oh, so close to his, she whispered, "I have confessed my wishes, Morgan. Won't you tell me yours?" She felt the slight, reassuring pressure of his hand at her back as he started to speak.

"I would wish you to be with me forever, Anna. Should I ever have to leave Shadow Marsh, I would want you by my side." His tall frame surged from its slumped position against the tree. Anna drew slightly back from him, her eyes darting over his features and the thin line of his mouth. Her eyes alone implored an explanation for his sudden move. "We are dreamers,

Anna," he continued, his tone sharp, yet tinged with regret. "I'm a fugitive. For eleven years I have watched constantly over my shoulders."

"Yes, my love," she reminded him, "and for eleven years you've seen nothing over that shoulder but your own fears. Stop running, Morgan, entrust your heart to the woman who so dearly loves you." Defiance sparkled in her eyes. "I did not enjoy my life until you entered it. My early life was constantly being chased by Wren Wellington, and then I had to work so hard to keep the plantation running when my father became ill. How blessed I am now that fate has thrown us together. Let us not exchange harsh words, but enjoy one another."

Morgan studied her youthful features in the shadows of the night. Every time he saw her she was more beautiful; her wide emerald eyes capable of so much meaning, the smooth, ivory features partially hidden in the shadows, the thick cascades of raven-colored hair falling across small, firm breasts. But what he had found even more remarkable was her intelligence, her wit, and her ability to run a plantation that would prove an insurmountable chore to the strongest of men. He had never encountered so much determination.

"Besides having me stay here at Shadow Marsh, what do you want of me, Anna?" Morgan asked after a moment.

Again, Anna's eyes danced imploringly. "I don't care who you are—Morgan York or Michael Fielding. I care only that I enjoy lying beside you, and I love you. I love a man who might suddenly drift into the wind. You are all I have ever wanted in a man."

"I'm an old geezer...eleven years your senior."

Snuggling against him, she replied, "I love old geezers!"

He laughed as his hand came under her chin. "I prayed you would love me as I have grown to love you." A soft kiss touched her mouth, trembling with desire. "Marry me, Anna," he whispered. "Though I have nothing to offer you but my love...and some damned hard work on this plantation, I will be a good, faithful husband. As long as you want me, I will be with you." But even as he spoke, the past and painful memories grabbed at him.

Anna felt his hand, which had rested gently against her back, now ball into a fist. "I never thought love could happen to me, Morgan." Lifting her face so that her smooth, slightly flushed cheek rested gently against his unshaven jaw, she whispered, "Before you change your mind about this proposal, yes, I will marry you. I will be a good, faithful wife and will be with you as long as you want me." Drawing slightly back, a small hand hit his chest. "And that had better be forever."

Touching her lips sweetly to his, they were swept along helplessly in their desire for one another, to fulfillment and love that could not be spoiled by the foe following constantly at Morgan's back. Before either could prevent it, the heat of their desires stirred to life in the late autumn evening. Anna did not feel the brittle twigs beneath her tender back. She felt only–wanted only–the strong, warm hands stroking her silken thighs, and the powerful movements that filled her, thrusting, rhythmic, moving swiftly in the throes of primal passion that joined their bodies as one beneath the late November moon.

# Nine

Anna awoke in an exuberant mood. She had promised Morgan she would keep their plans to marry a secret for a while, but she accidentally let it slip to Bea, and insisted on her confidence. She knew from past experience that Bea was the one person at Shadow Marsh who would take a secret to the grave with her. To celebrate the good news, Bea had Lovey add perfumed oils to Anna's bath and lay her day's attire on the satin day bed, although this was something Anna always did herself. Lovey wanted to know what was going on with all this attention.

Last night, after they had made love by the bayou, she and Morgan had gone to his cottage and had slept together into the wee hours of the morning. The wonderful night Anna had spent with him was still with her, cloaking her in the warmth of his love and adoration. She hadn't wanted to leave his bed in the overseer's cottage and had done so only at his insistence. He had lightly hinted at the scandal their affair might cause, but she loved him too much to worry long about it.

Perhaps she had known from the very start that Morgan would have this power over her–the power to bring forth the woman hidden beneath the icy exterior, denied, and abused by the thirst for power bred into her by the ambitions of the St. Cyrs. But was it truly a thirst for power, or something that simply had to be done when she took over the management of Shadow Marsh? She would much rather not have had to take on the responsibility, and did it only because there was no other choice. She loved Shadow Marsh and would not see it fall to ruin. She knew, though–now–that Shadow Marsh could never hold a place as strong in her heart as Morgan York.

After breakfasting alone on the veranda, Anna sat for a few moments to catch up on her ledgers. The November air was chilly, and she drew her shawl closer around her shoulders. She laid her pen aside when a shadow darkened the veranda. Alistair gave her a long, thoughtful look that frightened her a bit.

"Alistair, would you care for tea?"

"I heard Mose and Lovey talking in the kitchens. Lovey said she overheard you tell Bea that you're marrying York. Is it true?"

Dread filled Anna. Lovey must have been lurking nearby–a very bad habit–when she'd told Bea her plans. "Yes," she replied quietly. "I'm going to marry him."

"Anna, the overseer? You'll marry the overseer? It's indecent...it's scandalous!"

"I love him," she replied, refusing to be intimidated. "I have every right to marry the man of my choice. He is that man."

"He only wants the wealth of this plantation!"

She was immediately angry. "He does not! He will marry me because he loves me!"

"We have a reputation to uphold...have you thought of that?"

"Morgan is a decent man. He doesn't drink, cavort, or gamble!" She ended on a deliberately cruel note. Alistair did both–plus other deplorable vices that often drifted back to Shadow Marsh.

Alistair, tottering even this morning from too much whiskey, hardly needed to be reminded of his vices. He had even brought a drink out to the veranda this morning. "He's a drifter, Anna. You don't know where he came from or what he's done. You're drawn to his fine face and–God only knows what else!" Alistair turned, preparing to depart as quickly as possible. But a thought came to him and he turned back, a rather cynical look marring his thin features. "Or is it the will, Anna? You want a son and Shadow Marsh that badly, do you? What is it...hoping that my child will be female...or if a son, that he will die at birth?"

Anna's head snapped up, dislodging the ringlets she had been so careful with this morning. An ivory comb clattered to the veranda floor. Her hands clenched in the pink folds of her gown. "I would never hope such a horrible thing, Alistair! And I have not given father's will a second thought. You are the one who is obsessed with that!" The thought that Alistair might run to Morgan about the will filled her with dread. She did not want him to think anything but that she loved him, for that was the sole reason she wanted to marry him. She would leave Shadow Marsh, as much as she loved it, if that was what he wanted to do. "Run to him, Alistair," she goaded snidely. "Run and tell him something he already knows. Make a fool of yourself again."

Alistair thought that, by the crimson rising in her cheeks, Morgan York knew nothing of their father's will. Anna was fooling no one but herself. Alistair had been swirling whiskey in the goblet, but now set it on the table with certain deliberateness and walked off.

Dread and uncertainty filled Anna. Only now could she face the repercussions sure to rise because of the will and her failure to communicate its contents to Morgan. But what was she to say? *Oh, by the way, Morgan, I must have a legitimate son before my brother does in order to maintain my control of Shadow Marsh?* What would Morgan think?

Despite their mutual confessions of love, Morgan might assume their marriage was for the sole purpose of providing a male heir for Shadow Marsh. "Oh, what should I do?" Anna uttered dismally. But as quickly as the question softly left her tongue, the answer came to her. She must tell Morgan about the will, and pray that he would believe only in her love.

* * *

Morgan had risen early. Despite the evening he had spent with Anna, and their commitment to one another, he felt tired and irritable. Anna was everything in the world he wanted, but with the fresh dawn came sensible thought. The past was an ugly, black wound festering in his heart.

Thus, he worked doubly hard in the fields. He was deep in thought and did not joke pleasantly with the men as usual. He closed himself off in his own private world and did not see Anna halt her horse on the hilltop overlooking the fields.

Anna wanted only to talk to Morgan alone, to inform him of the provisions of the will before Alistair had the chance. But she was too late. From the timberline to the right Alistair's gray gelding appeared, momentarily pulling to a halt a few feet from Morgan. He dismounted; the two men exchanged words, and walked a few feet away from the working men.

Anna's heart fell; she could almost feel it striking the barren ground under her mare's hooves. Alistair was gesturing dramatically with his hands and Morgan, his head lowered, appeared to be listening without making a comment. Only when Alistair returned to his horse did Morgan's gaze lift, drawn to the timberline where Anna sat astride her horse. As Alistair mounted and rode away, Morgan returned to his work in the field.

Anna was at odds wondering what to do. She watched the golden-haired man she loved sweating profusely, straining his bare muscles against the large boulder he and the men were attempting to dislodge from the ground. With her mare nibbling tidbits of grass, Anna continued to watch in silence. She hated to think that Alistair had cast doubt in Morgan's mind about her love for him.

Morgan wanted to ignore her, but even with his heart pounding with rage, he felt compelled to lift his eyes and watch her every once in a while. How could she look back at him with such innocence, merely a ploy beneath the conniving surface of her? Her waist length hair was loose and gently fluttered in the breeze, catching the glimmer of dawn.

Even through the bitter gall of his rage, Morgan imagined the sweetness of last night's kisses, and felt the softness of her body against the hard ripples of his muscles. But she had deceived him, and had callously used him toward her own ultimate end. It was in his mind to pack what few belongings he had to his name and move on. Only when the boulder had been dislodged and the men were moving it toward the wagon did Morgan feel the cool of the early November morning. He pulled on his shirt, tucked it into his trousers, and took his coat from the back of the wagon. He had tied a bandanna around his forehead, but now removed it to wipe sweat from his brow. He slowly began to climb the hill toward Anna.

She had brought a canteen filled with warm coffee, black and unsweetened the way he liked it. She untied it and handed it to him. "You're out early, Anna. Couldn't sleep?"

"I wanted to talk to you, Morgan," she replied.

"About what?" he questioned. He drank from the canteen, recapped and handed it back to her. "Thanks." He started back down the hill, his manner still a bit cool.

There was no reason to wonder what Alistair had told him. It was only too evident. "Morgan, we must talk."

He turned back now, his mouth quirked into a sarcastic line. "About what, Anna? Your tremendous love for me? How much you want me in your life?" A short brittle laugh erupted. "Or is it merely my seed planted in your belly so this damned plantation will be yours?"

Anna quickly dropped down from her horse and flung herself into Morgan's arms. "Don't accuse me so indecently, Morgan. It's not what you think. I never thought about the will when I fell in love with you. If it were only a son..." She moved away from him and her chin lifted defiantly. "If I only wanted a son, I'd have married Wren. He pursued me for years."

"Why didn't you marry him?"

"Because I didn't love him!"

Again, Morgan laughed sarcastically. "And you do love me?" He turned slightly away, his palm lifting to his forehead to sweep back his hair. "Damn, but you frustrate me!"

Immediately Anna was in his arms. "Look at me, Morgan." When he did not, she demanded, "Look at me!" His narrowed eyes turned to meet her wide, tear-dampened ones. "Tell me you don't believe I love you. Tell me, if you dare!" She knew that, right now, he hated her almost as much as he loved her. She felt his gentleness as he drew her close and his hand rose to the dark tresses disheveled in her ride from Shadow Marsh.

"I don't know what to believe, Anna. I love you. God knows I love you, but–I hadn't planned to be your pawn. I have feelings, and they're crawling across my skin like prickly heat!"

Anna's hands traveled the length of his chest, resting lightly on his strong shoulders. "How can I prove my love, Morgan...that I would follow you to the ends of the earth and ask for nothing but your love in return? I would leave Shadow

Marsh tomorrow if you asked me to. No greater love can I show for you—no greater love..." Although his eyes burned through her like hot pokers, Anna lifted her chin, touching her lips to his. They were warm and moist, trembling with the rage that he still felt above all other emotions.

"Last evening I worried that people might say I'm a worthless drifter," he began in a tightly controlled voice, "a glory-seeker, marrying the riches of the plantation rather than the woman. This morning I wondered why you wanted me when you could have any man. But—now I know."

"Do you?" Impudence touched her voice, then caustic accusation. "What are you saying, Morgan?"

"You want a son, Anna...not me."

She pulled away, her unshed tears replaced by vexation. "You truly think I would marry you because of the will? Damn you, Morgan...damn you!" Anna balled her fists but relaxed them and sat on a large rock. "I think I hate you...why do you deliberately hurt me?" Resting her forehead on her palm, she sat there, unmoving, too angry to speak, and too hurt for tears.

Morgan approached and dropped to one knee before her. "I love you, Anna, I always will." Anna sighed, a deep, pensive sound, lifting her head so that he would not see the tears now moistening her eyes. Morgan took her hands and enveloped them fondly. "And because I love you—love you with every fiber of my being, if it's a legitimate son you want, Anna, I will be honored to be his father."

Life stirred in Anna. Without warning, her open palm struck out at his face, sending him staggering from his kneeling position. She rose and hurried toward her horse. But through her tears she scarcely saw the stirrup and her foot kept slipping. When Morgan caught up to her, she flailed her hands madly at him when he took her wrists and attempted to pull her around to face him. When she beat savagely at his chest, he merely pulled her close until she had calmed somewhat.

"I hate you, Morgan. I–I hate you–I hate–I–I love you too much to take your abuses." Although she was furious with him, she wanted to feel the hard muscles of his body against her soft one. Thus, she drew close, her mouth partly open, breath sweet and quick against his cheek. Their bodies were as one, molded by the hot, liquid flame of their shared passions. Morgan dropped to his knees, bringing the weight of her body down with him. His arms folded gently around her shoulders.

"I want you," he whispered against her tousled hair. "I want you right now. Please trust, Anna, that I would rather feel again the raw edges of a whip than to be parted from you."

As he spoke his lips moved soothingly across her cheek and her closed eyelids. He felt the gentle touch of her eyelashes wet with tears, and her full, moist lips part and await the intimacy of his own.

Anna took short, pained gasps, overcome by the virility of his body against hers, penetrating the very core of her existence with its warmth and desire.

"I should take you, here and now," he threatened hoarsely. "There is not a soul within shouting distance–no one would know but Anna and her prince." The warmth of her body and his own unsated passion drove the breath from his body.

"Then take me...if you dare," she replied breathlessly, wrapping her arms possessively around his shoulders and drawing him close. "I wouldn't care if an audience surrounded us–watching us as you make love to me, Morgan." She felt wild and reckless, like the delicate primrose growing along the highest bows of a great oak. Her trembling fingers rose and unfastened his shirt buttons, slipping beneath the sweat-dampened fabric.

She wanted only to touch him, to gain the intimacy that had been theirs last evening and so many evenings before. She wouldn't care if the world were watching them. She wouldn't care if she were branded a harlot, as long as this strange, wonderful man who had reached into her heart with his gentleness continued to love her. She cared not a whit who he was or what he had done. She knew only that she loved him and wanted to feel the weight of his strong body claiming her for his own.

Anna hungered for the gentle caresses that reawakened her

passion. She felt his warm breath against her cheek, soft and pleasant, quickening in pace as his hands moved to the warmth of her hips and thighs beneath the crimson satin of her riding gown. Her right hand lowered to the firmness of his narrow hips and the muscles growing taught as he exposed her most intimate flesh and prepared to enter her, the preliminaries merely a burden in their moment of overwhelming passion.

As she was filled with him, Anna drew her long, lean thighs against his hips. Simultaneously, her fingers caressed his strong features as obsessively as his mouth closed over the bared pink buds of her breasts. Pain grabbed at her stomach as her hips rose to meet his. How wonderful it was to make love in the soft, cool grass, with the live oaks shrouding their intimately intertwined bodies like a warm, downy blanket.

"Stay with me forever, Morgan–"

Immediately, his movements ceased, and although his body remained one with hers, he propped himself on his elbow and gaze into her lovely green eyes. Taking her wrists, he pulled them gently over her head and pinned them to the ground. "Is it love that keeps us together, or this damned, despicable lust?"

Anna was confused. Moments ago, Morgan had said he loved her and would give her a son, if that was what she wanted. Was he now telling her that he did not love her, but merely lusted for her body? Despite the angry frown that had settled on his bronze features, her mouth rose to his, to capture the tiniest of kisses. Only then did his hips resume their gentle rhythm, filling her with his manliness.

The explosion of ecstasy drove them together in the final moments of their mutual desire. When Anna tried to draw him close, he pulled away from her and quickly straightened his clothing. He stood and looked down at her with such a cruel, cynical smirk that she could scarcely believe they had just made love.

"Make your wedding plans, Anna, if it's that important to you. I'll marry you. Like I've told you before, I am always happy to oblige."

His willful, calculated cruelty stirred wild fire in Anna's

eyes, which lifted defiantly to his. She threw her skirts down over her legs and rose quickly to her knees. "I wouldn't marry you if you were the last man on earth, Morgan York! You're smug and arrogant. You–you're a..." A lump rose in her throat. "I could dispose of you in a moment, without blinking an eye!"

Morgan tipped his hat. "*El hombre propone y Dios dispone*," he said in pedantic Spanish that could not successfully hide the sarcasm in his voice.

Anna became wild in her rage. Coming immediately to her feet, her fists balled and she screamed at him, "You think you're so damned smart, Morgan! If you have anything to say to me, you could have the decency to say it in English!"

Morgan had never seen her so angry. Humored by her melodrama, he caught her wildly flailing wrists, to keep them from striking out at him. "All I said, little *chica*, was 'Man proposes, God disposes.' Nothing more insulting than that." His mouth moved toward the dark crimson of her high cheekbones. "My wild southern rose, I have never seen you as lovely as now, with fury beaming in your warm cheeks."

He was taunting her. Anna tried to free her wrists, but managed only to bruise her flesh between his unyielding fingers. When he kissed her lips, taut with rage and rebellion, his hand slipped to her back, taking one of her wrists with him. Anna felt she would smother. His hard body was pressed so closely to hers she could not even kick him, as she felt inclined to do. She fought the intimacy of his kiss, so possessive upon her mouth, teasing, taunt, caressing, toying with her rage.

She truly wanted to hate him, but felt the flood of desire force her body against his own. What a cruel, despicable...warm, loving, passionate and desirous man he was! His very being exuded the power necessary to conquer the darkest of her moods.

"Let's go away, Morgan," Anna suddenly suggested. "Our petty bickering is the product of boredom and always worrying about Shadow Marsh. Christmas is only a few weeks away." Before he could have the chance to say no, she continued breathlessly, "We can visit New Orleans before Christmas. I'll send a telegraph message to my aunt at the St. Charles..."

Morgan drew back, a little humored. "One minute you fight me, and the next minute you ask me to go away with you. Do you even know what you want, Anna?"

"Don't tease me, Morgan. Please, let's go away."

"Leave the plantation? To whose trust, I might ask?" He stood tall and erect, his arms straight, with his hands firm around her small waist.

Although his look was slightly intimidating, Anna merely bubbled forth, "Do say it's a good idea, Morgan. My dear Aunt Louvenia Etienne is a wealthy, eccentric old girl, disowned by the family years ago. You will like her."

He drew back now, putting a good bit of space between them. "I love eccentric old girls, but...I asked you, Anna, who will manage the plantation? With us both gone..."

Anna pulled away now, a little vexed that he should worry about it. After all, if she could commit herself to leave for a few weeks, especially during the winter months, so could he. "I'll give Alistair another chance," she said, turning back to give him a reassuring look. "After all, Sudie might have a boy, and the plantation will be out of my hands. She turned to give him a reassuring look, but questions lingered in his shadowed features. "Joby Cade can keep an eye on him. You said you trust Joby, and I'll make sure all expenses are paid directly by our accountant." When the questions seemed to linger, Anna stomped her foot. "All right, Morgan! Make me say it. I want to be alone with you. Is that so wicked?"

Humored again by her melodrama, Morgan approached and drew her into his arms. "So much anger and frustration, little *chica*. You didn't give me a chance to say that I would enjoy the trip with you–but I will go on only one condition."

"Don't make it too difficult. I want to be free. I want to enjoy time with you, away from Shadow Marsh, and not have to worry about one damn little thing."

"My condition is..." Again he drew slightly away, to meet her waiting look. He imagined that she wondered what his condition was that it should be such a mystery. "My condition is that this trip be our honeymoon, Anna. Marry me soon. Our hearts, our bodies, and our souls are destined for unity. My love and passion is yours for all time, if only you will accept it."

"But you were so angry...you believed Alistair."

"I had my doubts at first, yes, but I have never questioned your love for me, Anna."

Her arms darted to his back to hold him possessively. "I wonder that you should want to marry me, Morgan. I slapped you quite viciously. I'm ill-tempered and a bit of a tart at times. Could you put up with me forever? I love you almost too much to ask it."

His hand rose, to feel the coolness of her thick, rich hair, his fingers entwining in the tangled tresses and pulling her head back firmly. His mouth covered hers, possessing, conquering, filling her with the heat of his passion and his love. "Marry me," he repeated with more firmness, the two short words more an order than a request.

"But...Alistair. The will—my father's provisions—"

"You could just as easily believe I was marrying you for your wealth." Drawing back slightly, an eyebrow arched. "You don't, do you?"

"Of course not, Morgan." Anna suddenly felt the need to reassure herself—and him—that it wasn't just a child, a male heir for Shadow Marsh that drove her into his arms. "I won't agree to marry you until I am sure you trust me, Morgan."

He straightened and looked rather menacingly into her captivatingly narrowed eyes. "Is it so important?"

"Right now, it is the most important issue between us."

He half smiled. "We'll see if it is *that* important," he replied huskily, turning toward the field where the men awaited him. He tipped his hat in that outrageously sarcastic fashion and walked away from her.

# Ten

The lovely, large Gothic structure was deserted this brisk December morning. Situated to the south of Lafayette Square on South Street, the tower and steeple of The First Presbyterian Church, from foundation to pinnacle, measured nearly 220 feet. The lofty, commodious galleries on the level with the organ loft echoed the hushed tones of the kind-faced preacher, whose eyes appeared tired and drawn beneath shaggy white, overbearing eyebrows.

Before him stood a woman whose grace and beauty were enhanced by the gleam of happiness in her startling green eyes. A gentleman stood beside her, tall, reserved, immaculate in black coattails and high, ruffled jabot beneath a strong, clean-shaven chin. Yet, the preacher's first impression was that he was a remote, troubled young man.

The wedding guests were sparse in the large alcove where the marriage was taking place. Madame Louvenia Etienne leaned heavily on thin, gaunt Mr. Pettigrew, her latest of many paramours. Cable, her nephew, the son of the brother of her second or third husband, tottered from the effects of too much whiskey last evening. He had firmly attached himself to the generous wealth of the aging Madame Etienne.

The decision to marry had been an impulsive one for Anna. She had hoped to restore Morgan's trust in her and assure him that her love had no ulterior motives. But she wanted to be his wife, and she didn't want to wait any longer.

These past two weeks, they had shared their intimacies through the cold, bleak winter days and enchanting New Orleans evenings, nudged indelicately and breathlessly from one glittering banquet or ball to another. It had been impossible to say no to Morgan. They had both been swept along helplessly in the contagious gaiety of insouciant New Orleans society.

Anna watched his strong profile, his warm, masculine lips parted ever so slightly. Only when the minister began to speak did she avert her stare from the man standing beside her, the man who would soon be her husband.

And thus, wide-eyed, half-existing in a wonderful dream, Anna was married to Morgan in the simple Lutheran ceremony. The only thing she really remembered was the way Morgan's hands had trembled as he'd placed the wedding band, purchased only yesterday, on the ring finger of her left hand.

Anna felt that she looked nice for her wedding day–Aunt Louvenia had said she looked like a princess–startling white chiffon over satin, with a lace bodice thickly scattered with tiny peach rosebuds, her veil held to her raven-colored hair by a circle of twisted satin and tiny sprays of baby's breath.

She could not remember ever having been as happy as she was right now standing beside the man she loved. Proudly, she looked up to his handsome features as the final prayers were being said. And in the same moment, she was suddenly afraid, her knees weakened, and Morgan's cool, moist lips touched her own. Her trembling fingers met and twisted the cold band of gold, even as Morgan pulled her close in a warm, gentle embrace and whispered, so that only she could hear, "I love you, my darling wife."

Thereafter, Anna was lost in fond wishes and rough hugs, in parodies of wisdom and suggestions for an everlasting marriage. Some of those suggestions were so naughty that they left her speechless.

Morgan, drawn among the men, appeared to be graciously accepting their good wishes and gentle chiding. But Anna felt a lump rise in her throat, choking her, forcing her to press her lips into a thin line to still her tremble. She forced a smile and sniffed back the tears resting on her eyelids.

"Always a fear to tug at your heart, Dearie, at the very last minute," Aunt Louvenia said reassuringly, giving her a loving squeeze. "A natural thing. Look at me–married seven times! And never once did I snatch up a fine man such as you've got there."

"Thank you," Anna replied, taking her aunt's thin, dry hand.

The despair that had suddenly rushed upon her could not be hidden. Morgan's attention was being monopolized by the loud, boisterous Cable, whose last name Anna could never remember, yet above his voice, she heard the mystery and the secrets of Morgan's life. They screamed, like a high, piercing wind.

Morgan's slim frame towered over the shorter men, the reflection of morning through the stained glass windows casting brilliant hues across his golden hair. Anna's fingers closed firmly over Louvenia's wrist.

"I don't really know him, Aunt Louvenia. He's so secretive." Why was she having doubts now? It was, perhaps, his mystery, combined with the gift of loving that was undeniably his, that had so thoroughly compelled her to desire him and to love him in return. Perhaps she knew him as well now as she would ever know him. And her love for him–oh, so blinding, constantly filling her with the chilling heat of desire. She would rather share him with his secrets than live without him. "He's a kind, gentle-hearted man," Anna conceded, managing a warm smile. "I am, indeed, a fortunate woman."

Only when she and Morgan had settled, together and alone, in the plush leather seat of their rented carriage, did the little voice inside Anna's head, filling her with fears and doubts, slowly drift away.

Louvenia, Cable, and Mr. Pettigrew stood on the wide brick steps sheltering themselves from a sudden drizzle of cold rain. Anna returned their smiles, waved back at them, and again settled comfortably against Morgan. They had no firm destination, and their only goal was to be alone, perhaps ride along Canal Street and listen to the drizzle of rain become freezing droplets of ice on the waxed canvas roof of the carriage. They would dine in the evening with Louvenia and Cable, and attend the Cordon Bleu ball at the St. Louis Hotel. Lovely quadroon women, splendid dancers and finished dressers, would entertain the gentlemen of New Orleans.

Before the carriage lurched ahead, a group of street children, huddled in a small alcove nestled among the gravestones beside the church, caught and held Morgan's attention.

Anna had never seen such a look as was now reflected in Morgan's features, slightly flushed by the brisk wind. The children, three boys and two girls, were singing a song in low, hushed tones, in the pidgin French of the bayou people:

*Si to te 'tit zozo*
*Et moi-meme mo te fusil,*
*Mo sre tchoue toi–Boum!*
*Ah, cher bijou*
*D'acajou,*
*Mo l'aimin vous*
*Comme cochon aimiu la boue!*

Morgan continued to watch the children, whose small forms were bundled beneath thick woolen rags that scarcely resembled clothing? "A Christmas song?" he asked, his eyes only now returning to Anna.

She laughed sweetly, her dark, tousled hair falling against his strong shoulder. Her arm linked through his. "Hardly a Christmas song, Morgan," she replied. "It is supposed to be a love song. '*If thou wert a little bird, and I were a little gun, I would shoot thee–bang! Ah dear little mahogany jewel, I love thee as a little pig loves the mud!*' It is one of the many songs Bea sang to us when we were children. Morgan–the way you looked at the children..." She did not finish her statement. This was her first indication that Morgan would be a wonderful father. It was the first time she had ever looked at him in any light except as a lover, and a husband. She was suddenly very proud–very proud indeed that she was the woman he had chosen to spend his life with.

The carriage lurched ahead and the waving hands and good wishes of friends were lost in the morning mist. Anna looked to Morgan, who was silent, and as she dropped her head again to his shoulder, he tenderly caressed the dark, soft tresses now disheveled beneath the circle of twisted satin.

"Do you like me, Morgan?"

"What kind of question is that, Anna?" he replied, more abruptly than he had intended. "I love you."

"I know that you love me but–do you like me? There is a difference, you know."

"I love you," he offered reassuringly, stifling a small laugh. "And I like you, too. Now, hush, and tell me where you want to go. Are you hungry?"

"I need to change from my wedding clothes," she replied. "Let's return to our hotel room." She drew closer, lest their driver overhear. "Morgan, what better time, with the winter wind whistling, singing its song through the barren trees and gray overcast skies, than to be alone and–and cuddle."

Morgan's eyebrows arched, a conscious reaction to the humor he felt turning up the corners of his mouth. "What have I married?" he asked in a low whisper. "A little vixen who wishes to fan her fire beneath silk sheets?" Then, pulling her to him, he rapped his knuckles firmly against the carriage top. "To the St. Charles, driver–and be quick about it…please."

Anna nestled protectively against him, removing her headpiece and veil as she did so. "There…" she ended, tossing it to the seat across from them. She did not bother to catch up her long, dark tresses, which fell loose when she removed her veil.

There was a dash of excitement and bohemianism in New Orleans hotel life that made it especially attractive to visitors. The hotels were the centers of gaiety. The immense dome and Corinthian portico of the St. Charles Hotel were among the finest architecture on the American continent. With the exception of the cupola, it was of the same style as the old St. Charles, which had been destroyed by fire in 1851, along with Dr. Clapp's Church, the First Methodist Church on Poydras, and the Pelican House.

Anna had been a sixteen-year-old debutante attending her first Cordon Bleu ball with her third cousin, Trevor. She recalled the helter-skelter of firefighters and victims, and the mighty crash of the front portico of the St. Charles as it fell into the street, crushing the noble marble statue of Washington. It had been hours before she and her father, across town on business, had been reunited. Then they had returned home, to find her mother lying ashen and still in the soft folds of funeral satin...

"Anna?"

She startled, her body becoming rigid against Morgan's. "I was shamelessly daydreaming."

"We're at the hotel," Morgan said, brushing a strand of hair back from her crimson cheek.

While Anna waited on the walkway outside the St. Charles, Morgan spoke to the driver and slipped some money into his hand. They entered the St. Charles, hurried through the large, ornate lobby where they immediately became the center of attraction. The elderly tenant of the suite across from theirs on the second floor stopped to offer congratulations. Morgan was brief, but courteous, and within moments they had climbed the stairs and were at the door of their suite. Morgan fumbled with the key, cursed good-naturedly beneath his breath, and summoned some degree of control that allowed him to open the door. As he stepped aside, he stretched out his hand so that Anna could enter before him.

Anna lifted her pert nose and did not enter. "It is customary, dear husband, that the bride be carried across the threshold."

Morgan immediately swept her into his strong arms. "I'm getting old, wife. My back isn't what it used to be."

Anna smiled sweetly, dropping her head to his strong shoulder. "There is nothing wrong with your back or the rest of you. And you are not old. You, kind sir, are in a gentleman's prime."

Morgan closed the door with his boot and before he released her kissed her tenderly. His lips were still cool from the outdoors, but warmed quickly against hers. His hair was slightly tousled and, for some reason, it made her remember that she had tossed her satin headpiece to the carriage seat, where it apparently still remained.

When Anna's feet eventually touched the floor, Morgan pulled her close for a longer kiss. His hand was firmly at her back, and it momentarily took her breath away. It certainly wasn't the right moment, with his iron-hard body against her soft one a ready indication that he wanted her, and wanted her soon, to suddenly whisper against his lips, "I'm hungry...aren't you?"

He immediately pulled back and looked at her incredulously. "Of course I'm hungry...for you, little *chica*." Without hesitation, he eased the bouffant sleeves of her gown down her slender arms and kissed her warm, white shoulder. Lifting her again in his arms he moved toward the large tester bed, and very soon they were both free of clothing.

As they lay together, his hard body against her soft one, Anna was so very happy that they would be together for all time. She wanted him, to know that whenever she looked around for support, he would be there. She wanted to feel the wonderful craving in her body for him, to become a wild, untamed thing beneath him, its only purpose to be satisfied by him, to explode in gentle, wonderful ecstasy. As their bodies entwined in the rhapsody of their love, Anna held him as if there would be no tomorrow. She ached for the sinewy muscles hardening above her, and the sweet, warm breath upon her cheek as their mutual desires moved quickly toward its peak.

She whispered his name, over and over, her mouth rising to meet his, her slim, white hips matching his rhythm and pace. She was delirious, enflamed by her intense desire for him. Anna's fingers moved over every tight muscle of his back and shoulders, and over his hips. She was in awe of the beauty of their limbs entwined like the wisteria that grew amongst the highest bows of the pine.

When Morgan's breath slowed enough that he could speak sensibly, he whispered," Now you can be hungry, little *chica*."

Anna laughed, gently patting his cheek. "Hungry! Only for you, my loving rogue. Only for you."

"Now that I'm an old married man, I'm not sure I can keep up this pace with a very young woman."

Anna snuggled against him, absently smoothing her fingers through the coarse hair of his chest. "You'll do just fine...old man. Isn't it wonderful...so wonderful...Mr. and Mrs. Morgan York." There was no response, and the lack of one surprised Anna. She looked up at Morgan's handsome, bronze features, at his brows pinched with worry. "Morgan?"

His senses snapped back. "Sorry love. I guess I was remembering who I really am–and who you really are."

"And that is?"

"Michael George Fielding, a condemned fugitive, and his innocent wife. God! I don't want to ever hurt you, Anna, and being married to me can only lead to hurt."

"Nonsense!" Anna snuggled possessively against him. "I don't want to talk about this, Morgan. Please–I am Mrs. Morgan York, and I am a very happy wife." Suddenly pulling away from him, she sat up in bed. She did not want their wedding day spoiled by speculations that, inevitably, Morgan's thoughts would lead to. He was her husband. For eleven years he had been a free man, and she had no reason to believe that circumstances would change any time in the near future. He had covered his tracks well, and they were happy.

Because their wonderful moments together had taken a depressing turn, Anna wanted to recapture the gaiety, the happiness of their wedding day. She wanted to be with people– to lose her grim thoughts in the delights of old New Orleans. "I'm very hungry," she announced somewhat pertly, turning to him. "Shall we dine at Crescent Hall? Aunt Louvenia and that horrid Cable seldom dine there, and I really don't want to run into him again today–at least not until we have to meet them for dinner this evening. I wish my aunt would boot the freeloader out on the streets."

"We'll dine wherever you wish." Morgan sat forward and swung his feet to the edge of the bed. "I'll beat you dressing, little *chica*."

"Not if I don't put on a corset," she said, laughing, rising to rush for the chifferobe.

* * *

Only when they had nestled again in the carriage did Anna's mood pick up. She began to chat incessantly, scarcely aware of Morgan's short, dutiful replies. She pointed out the sights along the way, and when they arrived, scarcely allowed Morgan a moment to wrap the white fur cape around her shoulders before preparing to exit the carriage. The driver, a rather somber-faced man, did not manage the horses well, and when the carriage jolted a little Anna almost fell. But she steadied herself right away, laughing, turning and slipping her hand into Morgan's.

They were soon seated in the elegant dining room of Crescent Hall and the waiter approached."

"Shall I order for us both, Morgan?" Anna offered, opening the large, gold-lettered menu.

"If you wish, Mrs. York."

She smiled. "Let's see...umm, we'll begin with green turtle soul, then *filet de poularde* and asparagus with drawn butter. Then we shall have woodcocks with watercress, and for salad, *cresson de fontaine.* Oh, bring a bottle of claret, and for dessert we shall have *pyramide de crème-a-la-glace.*"

Morgan sat back in his chair, humored, waving his hand rather absently when the waiter looked to him, anticipating some change in the order. He departed, and Anna rested her chin on the back of her linked fingers, looking a bit satisfied with herself.

\* \* \*

"You know, Morgan, I'm not sure how we'll enjoy dinner with Aunt Louvenia and her guests this evening, after consuming all this food for our lunch," Anna said later, as they were finishing their dessert.

"We may not join Aunt Louvenia for dinner," he replied, somewhat nonchalantly.

"But we must," Anna countered. "We promised." Cocking her dark head sweetly to the side she awaited his further argument, but it did not appear to be forthcoming. She was not aware of the other patrons, whispering among themselves, occasionally glancing at her as she gazed at the tall, thoughtful young man across the table from her.

But Morgan had noticed. He took her hand and held it fondly. "We'll discuss it later," he replied.

"There is nothing to discuss. We *will* dine with Louvenia this evening." Anna was prepared to argue further when an intoxicated patron bumped into Morgan's chair, forcing him to raise his hand to steady him.

The flushed, flaccid face scowled, followed by fat, sickly white fingers rudely slapping Morgan's hand away. "You son-of-a-bitch," he growled at Morgan, "Get your hands off me!"

Morgan slowly stood from his chair. "I don't know what your problem is, Mister, but your belligerence is an insult to my wife."

"To hell with your wife," suddenly reverberated back at Morgan.

As the patrons looked on in awe, and waiters, fearing a scene, frantically summoned their supervisors, Morgan drew the fat little man up by the collar and dragged him toward the entrance. The manager rushed to the scene of the altercation, but Morgan said nothing to him. Only when he had reached the outside, and the man was stumbling to maintain his footing, did Morgan release him.

He did not raise his voice as he stated, "Do yourself and everyone else a favor and go for a swim in the Mississippi undercurrents." Rubbing his hands down the front of his black tailored jacket, Morgan returned to the dining room and resumed his seat as if nothing had happened. He ordered coffee, for both he and Anna, which was immediately brought. "If this had happened yesterday," he said eventually to Anna, "I'd have whipped the hell out of that man."

"And what is different about today?" Anna asked, awed by the cool manner in which he had handled himself.

"Yesterday I was just a man. Today I am a husband, and I will conduct myself as one. Now—let us drink up our coffee and get out of here. I am as stuffed as a Christmas goose."

In the carriage moments later Morgan unfastened the buttons of his jacket and leaned back in thoughtful silence. He allowed Anna to tuck herself under his arm.

Everything Morgan did was all the reason for Anna to love him more. She knew nothing, save death, would ever come between them. They took a detour down Chartres Street, where the oddly furnished galleries looked as if the rooms had come out to see what the neighbors were doing. The carriage occasionally halted for the throngs of Christmas shoppers rushing to and fro, and Anna saw into the long, dark tunneled entrances and paved courtyards that looked sterile and barren in the coolness of winter.

They passed a kindly-faced black woman, who wore the white snows of time wreathed on her gentle features. A great sadness filled Anna, and she was suddenly very lonely for Shadow Marsh. She wanted to leave the sterile gaiety of New Orleans. She wanted to see familiar faces, and the familiar house where all her fondest memories were. She wanted to ride along the bayou and wish for the coming of spring. In these final days of 1857, she wanted only to look forward to the New Year and the wonderful days and months and years ahead that she would spend as Morgan's wife.

Anna eased close to him in the shade of the carriage, hearing again the drizzle of rain become tiny beads of ice. When her face lifted to Morgan's strong, clean-shaven jaw, she felt his gentle move, and his lips touched and lingered on hers. His fingers closed firmly over her delicate shoulder and drew her close in a hard, uncontrolled embrace that forced the billows of desire to drive the breath from her body. It was as if they had yet to make love and their bodies craved it above all other treasures.

The carriage halted at the wide entrance of the St. Charles Hotel where their rooms awaited them. Morgan pulled quickly away from her, fell back rather lazily in the thick, padded cushion of the carriage and began tapping his knee. He sat for a moment, unmoving, appearing to be deep in thought. It troubled Anna. She was afraid that he now regretted their rash decision to marry.

Morgan lifted his slightly crooked finger to his chin and made no indication that he was even aware they had arrived at the St. Charles. "Let's return to Shadow Marsh."

"When?

"Now."

"Now?" she echoed. "What about the Cordon Bleu ball this evening? Aunt Louvenia will be so disappointed. She has invited guests from Plaquemines to meet you."

Morgan said nothing for a moment. "There'll be other trips to New Orleans and other balls. I just want to go home to Shadow Marsh."

Smiling briefly, warmly, bringing her hand up to Morgan's strong, gently pulsating chest, Anna relaxed again. "Tomorrow morning, Morgan...please. Aunt Louvenia is two years older than God and may not be around next year or the year after." She was prepared to argue further, but Morgan had hopped down from the carriage and put his arms around Anna's waist to assist her down.

He tossed a twenty dollar gold piece up to the driver. "Will that cover the last two weeks, including taking us to the train station at about six this evening?"

"Well ," Anna said, a bit miffed, "I guess we will not be staying."

An elderly gentleman, an employee of the hotel, approached. "Miss St. Cyr?"

Anna started to answer *Yes* but instead, "Mrs. York now. I was married this morning."

"Congratulations," the man said in his deep monotone. "A message has arrived for you."

Anna took the bit of paper and unfolded it. As her eyes darted over the words, she felt a sudden dread and her hands began to tremble. She turned, dropped her hand to her side, and returned to the street, where Morgan stood, talking to Mr. Pittman, a gentleman from St. Louis they had met earlier in the week.

"Morgan?" His head slightly turned. When he saw the ashen cast of her features, he put his arm out to her. "Yes, we must go home immediately. A telegraph message has arrived from Alistair. There is trouble at Shadow Marsh."

Morgan took the folded bit of paper and read: *You are urgently needed at Shadow Marsh. Please return posthaste.* It was signed, simply, *A. St. C.* "Yes, we will make immediate arrangements."

"What could have happened, Morgan?"

"Let's not speculate, or think the worse. It is probably

nothing. Alistair can't bear the thought that you may be having a good time...with me."

Still, the whirlwind of her worst speculations made her dizzy. Tears moistened her eyes. She hadn't imagined their wedding day would end on such a sour note.

# Eleven

"It takes a cold, cruel, heartless man to kill another man."
Anna had spoken the words impulsively, without thinking. One
of the many explanations she and Morgan had discussed for
Alistair summoning them home was the possibility that, in one
of his drunken rages, he may have killed another man.

Anna shuddered to remember the way the color had drained
from Morgan's face, and the way his shoulders had
unconsciously dropped from the weight of her thoughtless
statement. She wished her anatomy were so situated that she
could kick herself in the butt.

Anna was half reclining, feeling a bit sorry for herself
because their wedding day had been spoiled. Louvenia had not
taken the news well of their immediate departure for Shadow
Marsh, and had said she probably wouldn't be around for their
next visit. That had smothered Anna Rose in guilt, because she
truly loved Louvenia.

Morgan sat beside her, his arms crossed, his head slightly
fallen against the leather cushion of the train coach. She averted
her gaze to the window where the blackness of the winter
countryside rolled slowly by them. She was anxious to be home
and see to this thing requiring her attention.

Morgan had now closed his eyes. If Anna's rash statement
this afternoon had hurt him, it was not reflected in his tired,
blank features. Yet, he had been quiet these past few hours–too
quiet–and had scarcely spoken a word. She feared that her words
had, indeed, silenced him.

*Posh and begone!* Anna pouted silently, crossing her arms
and dropping her head to the cushion. If she had to guard against
every word she said in Morgan's presence, lest something strike
too close to home, what kind of marriage would they have?

And what kind of wedding day was this? To be cramped on
a train, traveling home to Shadow Marsh like thieves in the

night, to be denied warm greetings as Mr. and Mrs. York and the affectionate fussing of doting friends?

Indeed! First on the agenda was to learn what this *tragedy* was. Why couldn't Alistair have gone into further detail? Anna couldn't bear this waiting and wondering. She would rather have known what she would have to face when they arrived home.

Without warning Morgan lurched forward, straightened his shoulders, and stretched them back. Anna watched him quietly, expecting him to depart to the smoking section again and leave her alone to think about what she had said. She had noticed these past few months that he only smoked when something troubled him.

Rather, he draped his hands across his knees and sat for a moment in brooding silence. When he looked to her, he favored her with a smile. "What do you say we request sleeping compartments and get a little shut-eye?"

Anna felt relief at the lightness of his voice. "I am a little tired," she confessed, then with more haste, "This has been quite a day and..." When she paused, Morgan lifted his eyes to her, "Morgan, this afternoon–I didn't mean..."

His hand, warmed by the creases of his jacket sleeves where he had tucked them, closed gently over Anna's. He caressed her hand for a few moments. "I know you didn't, Anna– and please, don't think you have to be careful what you say around me. I'm a tough old bird, and I can distinguish between an insult and a statement. Now–let's see to those sleeping compartments."

Moments later, with their bags firmly under Morgan's arms, they were escorted to small, cramped sleeping quarters several cars to the rear. The old black gentleman waited patiently for the coins Morgan pressed into his hand.

Anna took the compartment on top, Morgan the one on bottom. She felt the discomfort of changing into her sleeping clothes as she maneuvered in the limited space of the cubicle. As she prepared to whisper good night to Morgan, she heard his gentle snoring.

Resting for a moment in silence, her lips pressed into a line,

Anna felt the effects of loneliness on a night that should have been special for them. She had imagined their wedding night as more glamorous. They should be together in the big, comfortable Tester bed, their lips meeting in the darkness, touching, caressing each other into blissful awakening. She had not imagined this cold, bleak, rumbling night, tossed about in a four-by-six cubicle barely suitable for one person, listening to steaming train wheels clatter on poorly maintained tracks. Still, she fell quickly asleep.

Between midnight and dawn she crawled down from the cramped space of her sleeping cubicle, and awoke in the morning lying against Morgan, his arm wrapped lightly around her shoulders.

They arrived home in the late evening of the following day. Anna was glad to have the long, cold journey behind them and to see the familiar lights of Shadow Marsh come into view through the thin row of pines separating the public road from the wide, barren meadows.

The trip by train had, at the least, been cramped and uncomfortable. The second leg of the trip to Jude's Landing, locked in a public coach with a foul-smelling trapper whose last bath had surely preceded puberty, had been quite nauseating. She had not felt any discomfort traveling to New Orleans. She had felt only happiness.

Both Bea and Lovey met them at the veranda. Hugs were exchanged, and Mose exited the house to help Morgan with the bags and boxes of gifts Anna had purchased in New Orleans. Joby Cade, who had been chopping firewood behind his cabin, now walked briskly up the lawn, hugging his thick woolen jacket firmly about him. He greeted Morgan with a handshake; they exchanged words, and Joby Cade took the carriage to the barn. He would return it to the livery in Alexandria in the morning. Presently, a lantern cast a wide golden glow through the open doors of the barn, and Joby Cade was heard singing a ballad.

Anna felt totally confused, and could scarcely catch her breath. From the beaming faces and wide smiles, it hardly

115

seemed that anything was amiss. "What happened, Bea? We rushed right home."

Bea gave Anna a quiet, quizzical look. "What you talkin' 'bout, girl?"

"Alistair." Anna hastily adjusted her gloves and turned slightly to see where Morgan was standing. "Alistair sent a message that I was needed at home. I thought perhaps something terrible had happened."

Bea drew her hands to her wide hips. "If it did, it sho' is news to me!" Then she clucked her tongue. "Only thing diff'rent happened here is that Massa Alistair didn't fall down the stairs when he loaded his gut with the juice, like he usually do's."

At that moment, Alistair appeared, his tall, gaunt frame a dark shadow against the light spilling from the doorway, his shirt unbuttoned, and the ever present goblet of whiskey swirling between his fingers. "Well, dear sister, you have returned." He stood with his feet slightly apart, his arrogance only too evident in the twist of his mouth.

"Alistair...I don't understand." Anna felt, suddenly, that if she didn't sit, she would fall. Morgan immediately put his hand under her arm for support.

With a clumsy, yet self-assured stride, Alistair slowly descended the stairs. He raised the goblet to his lips and emptied it. "Whatever are you babbling about, dear sister?"

"Anna received a telegraph message from you that she was needed. We rushed right home," Morgan said.

Alistair threw his head back and laughed. "Got you here, did it, old boy?" The laugh instantly became a rude smirk. "I'll talk to my sister alone. You can go on about your business...as the overseer."

"Git on," Bea ordered brusquely, "and stop ridin' yo' sister an' Mr. Morgan."

"One day, old darkie, that smart mouth of yours..." Alistair did not finish the threat. "Come, sister, we need to talk."

When Morgan too moved toward the house, Alistair took his arm and halted him. "Where do you think you're going, York? Mose has my sister's belongings. You just need to scat."

116

Their eyes clashed like opposing armies. Morgan roughly pulled his arm loose. He half-expected Anna to speak up, to tell Alistair they were married, but she seemed hesitant to do so. She had dropped her eyes. "If Anna doesn't want me to accompany her, she will tell me."

Alistair was obviously drunk; otherwise, he would not have sidled up to Morgan the way he had. He was afraid of any man larger than he was. Then Anna was standing between them. "Please, Alistair–Morgan, don't start a fight."

"I'll talk to you inside, little sister. He can go about his business." To Morgan, he said, "You escorted my sister on her trip and took care of her. Your duty in that respect is fulfilled. I would suggest you resume your duties as overseer–or foreman, whatever the hell you want to call yourself. There are still two-hundred acres of land that must be cleared before spring planting. Do you understand, *Mr.* York?" Alistair ended sarcastically.

Morgan's jaw hardened into a knot of muscles. Alistair always had that effect on him. They stood for a moment, hatred clashing between them.

Anna had decided it was not the proper time to tell Alistair about their marriage. He had something on his mind, something that had made him arrogant and cocky. "Morgan, perhaps you'd better retire for the night. I will speak to my brother and, hopefully, calm down his mood somewhat."

Anna wanted to joyously share the news of their marriage with the ones she loved. She wanted to feel Morgan's arms around her and hear his words of understanding. But he did not understand–it reflected in the dark glow of his eyes. She watched him walk briskly away without even a polite *good night*, his hurt evidence in the way he deliberately threw his shoulders back. She would go to him later and soothe away the hurt.

"Let's don't stand around catching our death," Anna replied quietly, and to Alistair, "Why are you so hateful to him? He has done nothing to you."

"He's the overseer, for chrissakes!"

Anna wanted to scream, *He's my husband!* But she could not say the words until she knew why he had called her back to Shadow Marsh.

A bright fire burned in the parlor hearth, and Anna quickly removed her wrap. A little of her confusion had settled; she wondered what Alistair had on his mind as he threw himself lazily onto the divan after refilling his goblet. He seemed terribly satisfied with himself, and she wondered what was on his mind.

He had no intentions of keeping her in the dark. "Captain Michael George Fielding—native son of Tarrytown, murderer of his own stepbrother. Twelve rifles...bang...bang...bang!" Throwing his head back, he laughed, that wicked, heinous laugh he had nurtured to perfection.

So! This was his ammunition. Slowly, Anna sank into the armchair beside the hearth and brought her trembling fingers to her chin. A sinking feeling hit her inside her chest, clawing viciously at her hopes and her dreams for the future she would share with Morgan. "How did you find out, Alistair?"

"How do–I learn–everything," he asked in between sips from the goblet. "By prying into the dossier our overseer has kept over the years. He is either proud of the heinous act of murder he committed back in '46, or he needs reminders when he tends to get a little careless...as he has these past few months."

"It wasn't murder," Anna replied quietly, the sinking feeling inside her producing nausea. "It was an act of mercy."

"Mercy in a bloody pig's eye!" Alistair rose clumsily to his feet. "He's a damn fugitive, Anna!"

"He's not!" Despair settled in her throat. "All right, so he is," she conceded reluctantly. "What are you going to do about it?"

"Nothing," he replied, turning to her, swirling the whiskey remaining in the goblet. "Nothing–as long as you don't marry him. If you do..." A smirk touched his thin mouth. "I'll send a telegraph message to the War Department and–bang, bang, bang!"

Anna dropped her forehead into her palm. "Are you saying

he can stay on as overseer as long as we do not marry?" She looked to him now, hatred hard in her heart. "Why would you do this? If you have this ammunition, why not use it to be rid of him once and for all? They could have been waiting for him when we returned."

Alistair fell silent for a moment. He had no intentions of telling Anna that he had already sent a telegraph message to Washington, that he had received a reply just three days ago, advising him that Morgan York–or Captain Michael George Fielding–had been granted a full pardon by the President of the United States.

"Because I can see that you truly care for him, dear sister, and I am aware that you often go to him for your nightly pleasures. As long as he is here, you will not allow yourself the chance to meet another man, marry and bear a legitimate son that will rob me of Shadow Marsh."

"Your wife is with child," she shot at him. "You may yet have the first son."

"Ah, but with my rotten luck, it may be a blasted girl. I can't take that chance." She gave him a look that could only be interpreted as hatred. "I don't give a damn what you and York do," he continued cruelly. "As long as you don't marry. He can stay on as overseer. It's good business. Besides, I'll rather enjoy watching the two of you together, and knowing you can never be married." Alistair paused, finished the last dregs of whiskey, and walked casually around the divan toward the chair where Anna sat. "Tell me, little sister, do you enjoy fornication with this murderer?"

"State your terms, Alistair! But what I do or do not enjoy is none of your affair!" Suddenly she was very frightened. Suppose Alistair were to learn of their marriage? Would he send the message? *Merciful heavens, what am I to do?* Anna thought desperately. "Have I your word, Alistair, that you will be no threat to him?"

"My word as a gentleman." Alistair laughed heartily. "You do hate me, don't you, little sister."

"You are hardly a gentlemen and–yes, I do hate you, with

all my heart and all my soul. I wouldn't spit on you if you were on fire. Not even if you paid me for the spit!"

"You may depart from me now. Run to your overseer," Alistair replied mockingly. "And keep that killer in line, will you? We wouldn't want Alistair to waste any part of his monthly allowance on telegraph messages to Washington, now would we?"

"You're a ruthless, conniving bastard, Alistair—"

"Perhaps—but keep in mind that any brat conceived of your fornication with the overseer will be a bastard as well. You remember that, Anna, when you flop in his bed and spread your pretty white legs." Alistair was trembling, shaking his finger, and glaring down the length of his arm at her.

Anna saw madness in his eyes.

Frightened, she dropped her head and did not look up as he slowly left the room. Tears fell gently to her flushed cheeks. She didn't know what to do. She could not admit that she and Morgan were married without jeopardizing his life. And she could not tell Morgan what Alistair had learned. She could not take the chance that he would leave her, that he would keep running from his past—always running, always watching across his shoulder.

She knew only that she had to be with him. Her knees trembling as she left the parlor, she rushed quickly through the foyer and past an astonished Bea, who had been bringing a tray of hot lemon tea. Anna ran out into the cold night air without her wrap, refusing to hear Bea's gentle entreaties that she return to the warmth of the house. She rushed across the lawns, scarcely able to see through the rush of tears filling her very soul.

When she reached the overseer's cottage, she caught herself from falling against one of the porch columns. Collecting herself valiantly, she burst into the cottage. A lamp had been lit, but the hearth was black and cold. She ran frantically from one room to the next in search of him. "Morgan? Morgan?" She saw his canvas bag where he had dropped it beside his bed, but he was nowhere to be found. She felt weak and sick and dizzy. "Morgan...where are you?"

Then, across the coolness of the wind against the parlor window, she heard the dull, rhythmic swing of the axe and logs splitting and falling to the ground. She ran outside and to the side of the cottage. Morgan, naked to his waist in this dreadful cold, was chopping wood. She remembered once that he said it was his chosen activity when he was trying to settle his anger. She saw the sharp line of his jaw and the dark anger flashing from his eyes. He had just raised the axe when she threw herself into his arms and touched her face to his chest. Despite the cold, he was sweating. He dropped the axe and, slowly, his arms went around her shoulders. But they dropped at once, and hung limply at his sides.

"Morgan, please, hold me...hold me." The musky smell of him filled her senses. She felt the thick ripples of his muscles and the hardness of his body against hers. "Please, don't be angry with me," she whispered. "I couldn't bear it."

Only now did Morgan feel the evening chill. "You didn't tell him, did you?"

"No...please understand...I would rather wait a bit. He's so cruel. He might–do something awful to cause you harm."

Morgan took her arms just below the shoulders and put her away from him. Daggers shot from his narrowed eyes. "What could he possibly do? You're in charge here. Your brother has no control over you! He certainly has no control over me! He can do nothing to hurt either of us!"

*But he can hurt you*, echoed softly through Anna's head. She wanted to tell him about the conversation she'd had with Alistair in the parlor and the terrible power he now wielded over her. She wanted to tell him that keeping their marriage a secret was for his own good.

When she said nothing, Morgan again pushed her away from him. "Go on back to your comfortable house, Anna. I am the overseer. I must get up early in the morning and work the fields with the men." He started to walk off, but turned briefly back. "And please, do ride out to the fields to check our progress. I wouldn't want you to think I had gotten lazy...just because I'm your husband."

She hesitated to say, "You must not tell anyone we're married...no one can know."

"Fine! Your reputation will not be tarnished."

Anna did not want to hear his mockery. She wanted only the strength of his arms around her, to lie with him and be loved by him.

"May I come to you tonight?"

He stood there, his eyes flinging daggers at her as he prepared to leave her alone in the darkness. "No...I need to get some sleep."

Anger flooded Anna–anger and indomitable pride. With the agility of a cat, she threw herself into his path of retreat and hit against his arm. "I'm your wife," she slung at him with each painful hit of her fist. "Regardless of whether I'm too cowardly to tell my brother, I am still your wife! You can't just ride off from me now, not like you might have before." Again, a painful lump rose in her throat. "You're a coward, Morgan, running from your past." As Morgan stood looking at her with a cold blankness, the blood boiled in Anna's veins. She released a half-growled "Ohh," turned and stormed away from him.

She wasn't really sure how it happened, but she suddenly found herself waist deep in the catfish pond. Engulfed by the cold water, she cried out, and when the icy water poured into her bodice, she began to thrash and cry, both in her anger and her fear as she slipped on the slimy rocks beneath her feet.

Just as her face hit the water, strong arms darted beneath her and lifted her from the water. She felt the coarse fur of Morgan's powerful chest. But when she met the humor in his eyes, which were darkened in the moonlight, she began to thrash clumsily at him with her fists.

"Put me down! Put me down, you big bully!"

Her rage instantly became a choking sob, and as he carried her out of the water, she sank against his chest. Morgan carried her into the front room of the cottage and dropped her to the divan. He disappeared into the bedchamber and returned with a thick woolen blanket.

"Get out of those wet clothes before you catch your death.

I'll bring in the firewood."

His voice was sharp, an order rather than a suggestion, born of his concern for her. She did not protest. Only when he had left the room did Anna begin to unfasten the stays of her bodice. She was soaked through to her skin as she stepped out of her dress and under-things as if they were all one garment.

When she stood naked in the golden glow of the oil lamp, she quickly dried off with the articles of her clothing that were still somewhat dry. When Morgan returned, she had wrapped herself in the blanket, and was huddled in the corner of the divan. He held a clean dry towel from a kitchen rack out to her, but she hesitated to take it. She was so angry with him.

A fire soon crackled in the hearth and Morgan's strong muscles were a warm, golden glow in the light of the hearth. He put out his hand. "Come here."

Anna rose from the divan, only because there was affection in his voice. She continued to hold the blanket to her. When she stood before him, his hands went to her shoulders and removed the blanket. It fell to the floor. As they stood for a moment in the glow of the hearth, Anna still felt the sob of anger in her throat. She almost burst out crying, both in humiliation for walking into the pond, and for the fear she would now have to carry inside her for Morgan.

"I don't know why you wish to keep our marriage a secret—and yes, I am very angry about that—but I will not question you." He whispered the words softly against her hairline. "I know that you love me, Anna. A man can make no mistake about that."

His hands moved, gently touched the small of her back, and lowered to the smooth roundness of her buttocks. He loved her nakedness against him. As mad as he was with her, he could not deny the desire surging through his veins.

Morgan raised her chin and touched his lips to hers. His tongue explored the hollow of her slim neck and the crevice between her youthful breasts. Dropping to his knees, his lips moved fluidly over her tight, flat stomach, lower...lower...

Anna gasped. She felt the tightness of her body, and the heat surge through her veins as his thumbs gently coaxed her thighs apart. And for a few wonderful moments that seemed like a thousand hours, his hands, his mouth, his tongue explored the very depths of her body.

Her moment of shock became ecstasy. She released a small, involuntary groan as her fingers closed tightly over the muscles of his shoulders. The spasms that shook her body forced her back to arch violently. She gritted her teeth, unable to bear the wondrous excitement he had created in her.

Then Morgan's lips moved upward and his hands rose to her waist, to bring her down to the bearskin rug with him. A radiant glow surrounded her as Morgan's hard, lean body covered hers like a warm downy blanket. He quickly shed himself of his boots and trousers.

"When a man loves a woman," he said, cupping her face between his strong hands. "He will do the most amazing things for her."

"That was certainly amazing–"

He slipped between her parted thighs, and she was filled with the gentleness of him. She rocked with him and clung to his shoulders as their mutual needs moved swiftly toward fulfillment and the simultaneous expression of their love for one another. Their rapid breathing slowed in gentle harmony, their bodies stilling, their cheeks resting lightly against each other's.

Morgan rolled to his side and brought the weight of her body against his own. Her eyes, caught in the glow of the hearth, became emerald fire, and the raven sheen of her magnificent tresses lay softly against his chest.

"I will confess Anna that I was angry enough at you tonight to collect my belongings and head out of here. But–I do not flee from my obligations."

"You consider me an obligation?"

"A wife is always an obligation to her husband. As a husband is to his wife. I also did not flee because I love you...I cannot imagine my life without you."

"Promise you will never leave me."

"That is an easy promise. I will never leave you...unless you ask me to."

"That will never happen."

"Good."

With the blanket lying across their bodies, Morgan quickly fell asleep, his arms holding Anna lovingly to him.

But Anna could not sleep. In the still of the night, the horrible threat made by her brother filled her with fear. She wept, very gently, flicking away the tears before they might touch Morgan's chest and awaken him. She didn't want to imagine life without him. She would play Alistair's game–on his terms. She would humble herself...belittle herself if she had to. She would grovel, if that was what Alistair wanted of her.

She would do anything–anything rather than risk losing Morgan. They belonged together. They were man and wife.

# Twelve

Christmas was Anna's favorite time of year. A huge tree was erected on the front lawn and decorated with pine cones painted bright colors, and with fabric bows, hundreds of tiny candles, garlands, holly, mistletoe, and sugar mice for the children of Shadow Marsh. Traditionally, the candles were not lit until Christmas Eve.

The families of Cabin Row gathered on the lawns to celebrate with dance and song, and the men, because the weather was warmer than usual and suitable for it, to engage in contests of strength. Instinctively, Anna's eyes moved toward the clearing in which the men were wrestling–where Morgan and Joby Cade, both bare to the waist, were locked in combat. The crowd cheered when Morgan took a fall, and popped back up, his eyes daring Joby Cade to lunge for him again.

It was all Anna could do to restrain her enthusiasm. She wanted to be right there, boosting Morgan on, watching his muscles become iron-hard against Joby Cade's. They both seemed determined to win the round, as though a prize awaited the one who triumphed.

Anna was so proud of Morgan. She wanted to brag about him, show him off as her new husband, and express her love openly and freely. But mistresses of large plantations were not expected to blush with pride when the overseer was nearby. Everyone on the plantation knew she often went to him in the night, and the only one who had dared mention it–besides Alistair–was Violet. She thought it was *simply sinful*. She was playing the part of the chaste virgin, and would do so right up to her wedding day, which would take place in April when the azaleas were in bloom.

Later in the evening, with the assistance of the eager children, Anna passed out the gifts she had purchased in New Orleans–shirts, pipes and tobacco for the men, yard goods and lilac water for the women, and rag dolls and brightly colored wooden soldiers for the children. Anna had purchased special gifts for Mose and Bea, which she had given them earlier in the evening.

Two dozen stuffed turkey hens were carved and eaten, along with hot, buttered corn, cranberry, sausage stuffed with rice, chopped chicken livers, spices and peppers and sweet cinnamon puddings and honey cakes smothered in dewberry jam.

After a second match with Joby Cade to work off some of the food he'd eaten, Morgan pulled on his shirt and sat quietly at the edge of the veranda, resting against a marble column with his leg drawn up. Mose sat beside him, offering his condolences for Joby Cade winning both matches. Invariably, though, their conversation drifted to Anna. Mose noticed the gleam in Morgan's eyes at the very mention of her name.

"She's a real fine lady," Mose stated emphatically, looking toward Anna. She sat on the lawn with the children, her features golden in the light of the candles each child held. They sang Christmas songs in the Creole French of the Louisiana people.

"She is, indeed," Morgan replied.

"Mr. Morgan?"

"Umm?"

"You like her a lot?"

"A lot," he replied shortly.

Mose softly chuckled. "Why, Miss Anna, she lights up jus' like that decorated tree when you comes 'round."

"I'm the one who lights up," Morgan laughed, patting the old man lightly on the shoulder. Tonight, he'd tried to forget that their marriage was being kept a secret for reasons he had yet to understand. It mattered only that he loved her, and she him, and it was Christmas Eve, a time for celebration and joy.

"Mr. Morgan?" He turned his head slightly. "I worry about the missy," Mose continued. "You reckon y'all be stayin' fo' a while at Shadow Marsh?"

"I reckon I will," he replied. "For as long as she'll have me." If Mose knew they were married, he'd have no reason to ask. Morgan gritted his teeth in a moment of ire.

"Y'all be watchin' out fo' the missy?" Mose continued. "Don't be lettin' her take no huff off'n her brother. An' you be–" Again Mose chuckled. "Lawd, y'all be thinkin' Mose touched in the head."

Morgan couldn't help noticing that something troubled Mose–something that even the mood of merrymaking could not hide. Morgan was about to question him in depth, but Anna approached and stood quietly by, watching the children happily disperse with their gifts. "When Morgan's hand slipped round her shoulders, she shivered a little.

"Are you cold?" he asked, rubbing her arm.

"A little," she replied. When Mose started to leave, Anna's fingers closed on his sleeve. "Merry Christmas, Mose."

Mose smiled widely. "An' to y'all, Missy...an' Mr. Morgan." Then he quietly disappeared into the darkness toward Cabin Row.

Anna leaned close and whispered to Morgan, "Merry Christmas, my husband."

Morgan's touch, gentle just moments ago, became a firm embrace. There was no denying what he wanted, and from the look in her upturned eyes and the slight tremble of her moist, parted mouth, she wanted the same thing. But there was a time and place for everything. Along with the gay festivities of Christmas Eve, there were duties to attend. Anna could scarcely restrain her passion as the evening wore on and parents began carrying sleepy children clinging to Christmas treasures to their warm, comfortable beds.

Because Wren had not made an appearance this evening as he had promised to do, Violet had retired to bed hours ago. Sudie had complained so bitterly about *her condition* that she had not attended the festivities. Alistair, as usual, was off on a drunken binge, and characteristically would not return for a week or more. Thus, the burden fell to the shoulders of Morgan and Anna, who both stayed up well into the predawn hours and assisted in the clean-up of Christmas leftovers.

In the quiet of the overseer's cottage a little later they

exchanged their gifts. Anna gave Morgan a gold pocket watch she'd purchased on a shopping excursion with Louvenia, in which was inscribed: *To my beloved husband, with undying love–Anna.* Morgan's gift to Anna was a silk scarf from the Orient, in which he'd wrapped a small velvet box containing a locket. Its ivory cameo was surrounded by three dozen square-cut diamonds.

"How on God's green earth did you afford this, husband?"

"Every penny of my wages for two months," he replied, turning her so that he could put it around her neck. "And it'll look much better on you than it did on the ledgers." He folded her into his arms and kissed her warmly.

Anna was content to be held by him, to feel the surging strength of his body against hers and to know that for all time he would be with her. As the passion burned brightly between them, Anna wondered how she had come into this happiness. What could she possibly have done to deserve this proud, gentle man? She prayed she would have a lifetime with him to learn all the answers.

Morgan lifted her chin and kissed her. His lips were cool against hers and his breathing soft and even. But there was an unspoken question in the way he held her and absently smoothed the silken tresses fallen across her shoulder.

"You are troubled, husband?"

"Yes. How much longer must our marriage be kept a secret?" Caught up in the Christmas festivities earlier in the evening, he had thought it didn't really matter. But it did. It mattered very much and had troubled him greatly. When he felt her tremble, he asked, "Are you ashamed for people to know I am your husband?"

"I am very proud of you, Morgan," she replied quietly. "Were I to search every corner of this world I would not find a more suitable husband. You are all I have ever wanted. But–"

Despite her firm resolution to reflect only strength, her eyes dropped, and a lump rose in her throat. She didn't want to think about Alistair, armed with his terrible weapon, waiting–just waiting to spoil her happiness and threaten the life of the one man in all the world she had ever–or could ever–love.

"Come now," Morgan gently coaxed, resting his hands across her shoulders. "Something is on your mind."

Oh, how much she loved him–how much it pained her to know he was plagued by these doubts. She eased into his arms and said, "It is Christmas morning, Morgan. The children will arise early for church services and we must get some sleep."

"You were going to say something," he reminded her, lifting her chin when she refused to look at him.

Her shoulders shrugged. "My husband, I was going to say that..." Anna touched her cheek to his chest and felt the warmth of his skin through his shirt. Her thoughts swirled. If she kept quiet and allowed Alistair to blackmail her, Morgan, none the wiser, would stay with her. If she confessed all, fearing for his life, he might leave and she would never see him again.

Yet, it could very well be that she had underestimated Morgan. Perhaps he would have a sensible solution. He would, at least, understand why their marriage must be kept a secret. They would no longer find themselves trapped by these moments that invariably produced distrust and doubt.

It was Christmas Day. What better time than now to make things right between them, once and for all. Anna pulled slightly back, favoring him with a small smile. She slipped her hands into his. "Yes, Morgan we must talk."

But as she turned so that they might sit together on the divan, a series of sharp raps broke the stillness of the early morning. Bea desperately called, "Mr. Morgan, Mr. Morgan." He was immediately at the door. "Come quick, Mose, he real sick...can't get up."

All else was forgotten as Morgan rushed past her, arriving at the cabin first. He picked Mose up from the floor where he had collapsed. His skin was cool and his eyes dull and lifeless. As Morgan put him on the bed, he noticed the dark, circular marks resembling bruises down his arms. "What happened, old fellow?" Morgan asked, taking the cold, dry hand and settling his fingers over his weak, erratic pulse.

"Don't rightly know, Mr. Morgan," Mose replied weakly.

"Jus' standin' there talkin' to Bea an' the flo' come up and hit Mose in the face." When Anna and Bea entered, Mose clicked his tongue and fussed at Bea. "Foolish ol' woman, botherin' Mr. Morgan and the Missy with this ol' man's ails."

Morgan saw the question in Anna's eyes. "Rouse Joby Cade and have him fetch Dr. Miller in Jude's Landing."

Bea sank quietly into the chair beside Mose's bed. "An' you a silly ol' man," she scolded, "Scarin' yo' Bea like that." But the underlying softness was there, and the affection of forty years together as man and wife.

When Anna departed, Morgan motioned to Bea to come into the front room. She sat across the table from him. "Tell me what happened, Bea."

The happiness so usual with her was missing. There was a silent despair in the way she looked at Morgan. "He ain't been feelin' good fo' a long time, Mr. Morgan. Jus' drags around sometimes, and he gets real bad pains in his arms an' legs. Real weak. An' them ugly black marks, they jus' pop up from nowhere. He been tellin' me he feels like somebody poked a knife in his veins and let all his blood leak out." Bea sighed, a deep, weary sigh. "An' I been tellin' him to quit bein' a sissified ol' man and do his work. Lawd, Jesus, if my man dies–"

Morgan's hand covered her arm in comfort. He felt her despair, deep and penetrating, as he recalled the many long conversations he'd had with the likeable old gentleman. He was about to offer words of encouragement when Lovey entered.

"What's wrong with my daddy?" she asked. Without awaiting a reply, she entered the small room and knelt beside her father's bed.

It was just breaking dawn when Joby Cade returned with Tylas Miller. He spoke a moment with Bea and made a mental note of Mose's symptoms. Then he spent an hour with him with the curtain drawn across the door. When he returned to the family, he sat for a moment in thoughtful silence, drawing toward himself the cup of hot coffee Bea handed him. He ran his fingers lightly around the rim for a moment. He had known Bea for a good many years–a stout woman, but emotionally fragile–

131

and he didn't believe she would be able to handle the news he had to give. Thus, he spoke to Morgan, "Could I speak to you alone?"

Bea visibly trembled. "Oh, Lawd!"

"Don't worry." Tylas patted her arm. "You just make your man comfortable and have Joby Cade bring in more firewood. Keep him warm."

Morgan silently accompanied Tylas out of doors. "It's serious, isn't it, Dr. Miller?"

"Very serious," he replied glumly. "I've seen it a few times before–a blood disorder seldom seen outside Mose's race. No research that I know of has been done on it."

"What are you telling me?"

"It's an anemia, with many other symptoms, that has no cure. From speaking to Bea, I have learned it's been coming for a long time. Lately, he's had excruciating pain in his legs and arms. I would suggest you make the old man as comfortable as possible."

Dr. Miller's buggy had drawn the curiosity of the people of Cabin Row. Morgan slightly raised his fingers from the porch rail, to acknowledge the field hand, Ossie, who had waved to him.

"How long will it take him to recover on his own?"

"You impress me as an intelligent man, Mr. York. I don't think I have to tell you the old gentleman is dying."

Morgan really wasn't sure what to say. "How long does he have?"

"Hours, days, a week, a month, perhaps longer. I'll leave laudanum for his pain with instructions for its use."

"There is nothing more you can do?"

"There is nothing more anyone can do. I would suggest you keep him comfortable. I'll come out in the morning to see him." Tylas dropped to a wooden bench against the porch wall. "My father sold Mose's family to the St. Cyrs when we were just boys. He was a friend then, and he's a friend now. I feel so helpless."

Morgan drew his foot up to a small stool. He bent forward,

with his hands resting across his knee. "I'm not a born Southerner, Tylas. I abhor slavery. I consider it an insult to man. But–you're not interested in what I think on the subject, are you?"

"Slavery is a way of life, Mr. York. One accepts." Tylas slapped his knees as he rose. "It is Christmas morning. I'd like to spend it with my wife and family. Come out to the buggy. I'll leave a good portion of that laudanum for Mose. And I may have a tonic for the blood." Only when Tylas was seated in the buggy and ready to depart did he offer Morgan a bit of advice. "Mr. York, I would warn you to keep your views on slavery to yourself. God knows I would never own a human being, but southern planters do–and depend on them. You could cause trouble for Shadow Marsh. There were a good many planters angry when Patrick St. Cyr freed his slaves on his death bed." Then he flicked the reins at his horse and the carriage wheels stirred dust as he disappeared onto the roadway along Bayou Bouef.

Morgan hadn't heard her approach, but suddenly, Anna's fingers closed over his arm. "He's dying, isn't he, Morgan?"

"Yes." Morgan felt an emptiness of heart. He wanted to crawl off somewhere and spend a few minutes alone. Rather, he gave Anna a weak smile and gently patted her fingers. "We'll take care of the old gentleman."

\* \* \*

While Christmas Eve was customarily a private affair at Shadow Marsh, the fireworks and festivities of New Year's Eve always drew a great throng of people from throughout the parish. Wives and sweethearts were bundled in expensive furs and gallant young masters vied for the attention of blushing belles by racing their prized thoroughbreds. It was the one day of the year on which the slaves of the neighboring plantations gathered together at Shadow Marsh for a celebration of their own.

After the fireworks display there was the usual wrestling among the strongest of the slaves, dancing and singing among the women, and games among the children. Anna wondered if

Morgan would dare challenge Joby Cade to a rematch of their Christmas Eve bouts. The men had chided him indelicately this past week. She stood back and watched a wild, gypsy-like dance being performed by the Mulatto slave girl from Hopewell Plantation. She was a favorite among the young masters, who often sent brightly colored dancing gowns to her from the places they had visited. Tonight she wore a blue and green tiered gown that bared her knees and, when she whirled, her straight golden thighs. The young masters had gathered around and were clapping their hands to the rhythm of her dance.

Marigold began to move erotically, her body bending and swaying, baring her midriff beneath the short blouse she wore. She had stirred the men to excitement with the seductive poses of her long, agile body, which glistened gold through the perspiration that had broken out in the heat of her dance. She was a beauty and she knew it. Wren Wellington's father had recently received a twenty thousand dollar offer for her from a plantation in Plaquemines, but he had refused to sell.

Anna sighed pensively as she dropped her head. She was in no mood for merrymaking. There were too many things on her mind. Alistair's binge was into its third week, Sudie was ill, Violet, saddened by the death of one of her dogs, had chosen to mourn rather than join the festivities, and Mose was slowly dying. Yet, he had insisted on serving the house yesterday when guests arrived for the noonday meal.

Anna was content to stand alone on the veranda, hugging her shawl to her and watching Marigold dance. But from the corner of her eyes she saw Wren's young sister, Sarah, saunter slowly toward her. Occasionally, she would flick her fingers at a gentleman she knew, or flutter her eyelashes and favor a special one with a knowing smile.

Presently, Sarah's sleeve brushed lightly against Anna's. "Why, dear Anna, you do look lovely tonight," she said in her high-pitched voice that naturally bordered on sarcasm. "That shade of green does you such favor. It's no wonder the men are watching you."

"They are watching Marigold," Anna countered.

Sarah Wellington looked distastefully at her father's favorite slave girl. "She is a bold creature, is she not? I would like nothing more than to see whip weals on that shiny golden skin!" When Anna made no comment, Sarah continued with haste, "What is that fabric you're wearing? Homespun wool?"

Bea had made the dress for her as a Christmas gift, and Anna was proud to wear it. That Sarah spoke sarcastically of it annoyed Anna. She took a moment to study Sarah Wellington, short, petite, overdressed as usual, her waist-length cape and riding hat trimmed in startling white fur. Like Wren's, Sarah's eyes tended to look doleful and empty.

When Anna did not reply to her insult, Sarah continued, "Where is your handsome overseer? Oh, there he is, talking to Mr. Reynaud. What a splendid specimen!" Sarah drew her gloved hand to her lips, and began fidgeting with her pearl necklace. "If one is to believe the rumors, I simply must know how your handsome overseer is beneath the sheets."

In the same mocking tone, Anna replied, "And if I am to believe the rumors, I'm surprised you haven't already tried to find out."

"Such a cat," Sarah shot back. "You'll never change, Anna St. Cyr! Thank goodness my dear brother won't be marrying you!"

Anna looked up, crossing her arms. "Thank goodness!"

Sarah Wellington lifted her nose and quickly walked away. Marigold's dance had suddenly ended and Anna's gaze moved over the lawns, which teemed with activity and the loud boasts of young masters betting on their prize wrestlers. Then Anna saw Morgan moving slowly through the crowd toward her.

He propped himself against the veranda support and started to whisper some endearment to her. But Otis Hayson approached and gave Morgan a critical, unyielding look before directing his attentions to Anna. "May I have a word with you in private, Miss St. Cyr?"

"Business on New Year's Eve?" she asked, arching a well-groomed brow. Deliberately, she closed the breath of space separating her from Morgan. She had heard the women–the wives of these sanctimonious do-gooders–talking loudly enough behind her back that she would surely hear.

"Why, umm, yes," Hayson replied after a moment. "It is rather important."

"The Organization?"

Hayson was reluctant to speak of the Organization in the presence of Morgan York, a mere overseer.

Morgan gave Anna's arm a gentle squeeze. "Take care of your business...Miss St. Cyr. I have some of my own that cannot wait."

* * *

Anna wanted only to be outside and found the parlor unusually stuffy. New logs had been added to the fire some time ago and the room was uncomfortably warm.

"Would you care for a sherry, Mr. Hayson?"

"No, Miss St. Cyr." Hayson was nervously fingering the rim of his hat. "I'll get right to the point, and please forgive me for being blunt."

Despite the gloom settling on her and her suspicions as to the source of the discontent, Anna smiled. "Mr. Hayson, is it too warm for you? Your face is terribly flushed."

"I am fine," he snapped, tugging at his collar to loosen his tie. "The Organization has asked for your resignation."

This news took Anna quite by surprise. Just a month ago, she had received a letter of commendation signed by all members of the Organization stating that she was doing an excellent job. "My six months are not yet up, Mr. Hayson. Is there a problem with my performance?"

"It has nothing to do with your performance."

Pretty eyes narrowed, becoming slithers of emerald glass. "Then what, Mr. Hayson?"

"It is your intimate association with your overseer. It has caused a great deal of embarrassment to the Organization."

"The overseer happens to be my..." The fact that he was her husband had almost come out in her moment of ire. Instantly, Anna pivoted away and her balled hands slowly sank into the pockets of her *panier*. "The overseer is my employee," she

136

continued on a quieter note. "Our relationship has nothing to do with the Organization. Now..." She spun back, forcing a smile. "You will not have my resignation."

"We must insist, Miss St. Cyr."

"It will *not* be forthcoming."

"You are powerless..."

"Am I, Mr. Hayson?" Anna's lips cracked into a cynical, knowing smile. "I'll make a proposal to you, Mr. Hayson. You resign for immoral reasons, and I shall do likewise."

"Im-immoral reasons?" he stammered "You have no proof!"

"Don't I now? Do you deny you sired the child recently born to Squire Wellington's fourteen-year-old slave girl? Now—what would the good Mrs. Hayson think about that, being the mother of your seven legitimate children?" When he did not answer, she demanded, "Well, do you?" The look in his eyes was all the answer she needed. "I suggest that you clean the skeletons out of your own closet before you start cleaning out mine!"

Otis Hayson had never seen such fury. The usually smiling eyes had become steel daggers. She was right, of course, about skeletons in the closets, and he wondered if she knew about the others in his. This was the first time his skeletons had been dragged out in his presence, and by a woman at that.

Hayson said nothing, but rather, turned to leave. When Anna heard the foyer door close, tears moistened her eyes. She didn't want to show emotion. She was angrier than she had just about ever been as she stormed out of the house, past an astonished Bea, and out to the lawn where the last of the fireworks were being lit. Through the crowd of people on the front lawn, Anna moved confidently toward Morgan. When she reached him, she threw herself into his arms and kissed him as though it would be their last kiss ever.

He was quite taken off his guard, both by the unexpected kiss and the defiance sparkling in her eyes. It was the first time in a long, long while he could remember feeling that he was violently blushing. "What are you doing?" he asked, taking her aside.

A sob collected in her throat. "I wanted to kiss you," she said, the defiance flickered back to life by her anger. "And because no one, not Otis Hayson or the Organization, has the right to tell me I can't be with you. He had the audacity to ask for my resignation!"

"I see," he replied, slipping his arms around her waist to pull her close. "Not because you love me, but because it's against every moral fiber of the Organization for you to fraternize with the overseer. And you wanted to prove that you could damned well do anything you wished."

Quickly, Anna drew away from his angry gaze. "Don't you dare start anything with me, Morgan," she threatened. "I have had just about enough!" But her rage was quickly replaced by hurt. He could have the decency to understand, rather than sling a few accusations himself.

"And why this melodrama, Anna? You've told me yourself that people will find out. Why are you so shocked now that Hayson has asked for your resignation?" Then he bent close and whispered, "If you had told them I was your husband...for God's sake!"

Her rebellion stirred to life, Anna turned and fled through the crowd toward the sanctuary of her bayou clearing. She refused to hear Morgan's gentle, compassionate call above the drone of voices and fireworks fading into gentle colors far above the timberline.

But she had scarcely gone a hundred feet when he caught up to her. She felt the strength of his fingers close around her wrist, forcing her back against the great oak that separated the overseer's cottage from the catfish pond. Her surprised gasp immediately became an angry cry. Then she balled her fist and hit him very hard in his chest. He took her wrists, pulled them above her head and, displaying the same degree of stubbornness he had often seen in her, pressed his body firmly to hers, making it impossible for her to escape.

"What a child you can be," he whispered against the disheveled tresses of her raven hair. "Sometimes I wonder if you're not two instead of nearly twenty-two. Act your age, Anna...I want to talk to you, and I don't want to waste my words on an angry child." His body became hard, yet gentle, against hers, allowing a breath of space in which she could maneuver, should she wish to flee from him. His grip on her wrists became gentle, caressing, easing her hands down to his shoulders. "I did not mean to hurt your feelings. I just don't understand. But– foolish me," he continued more lightly, "perhaps I am being a child, too."

Anna wanted to tell him everything. She wanted to erase all the tension between them, so that they might go on with their lives. But they were prisoners–distinct, separated by circumstance–he by the past that had followed constantly after him, and she by the great power Alistair held over her. Timidly, Anna's hands fell from his shoulders, tucking around his waist beneath his jacket. She felt secure with him and safe from all the terrible injustices being dealt to them.

"Morgan...suppose someone were to find out about you– who you really are. What would you do?"

He pulled slightly back, his eyes narrowing. "Has someone found out?" His voice was guarded, fearful.

"No, I was just wondering."

"Well..." His arm went firmly around her waist, pulling her close. "Nothing will keep me from you. Should I be faced by twelve guns right here at Shadow Marsh, I would meet them willingly, as long as your lovely face was the last thing I saw. I love you, Anna. My past will never part us."

Anna would rather have heard anything but this. It confirmed her worst fears, that Morgan would jeopardize his life to stay with her.

Morgan did not sense the despair that had settled on her. He knew only that she was his wife. All day long Shadow Marsh had been deluged by people, and he wanted to be alone with her. "Come, little *chica*," he coaxed, taking her hand. "We shall greet the New Year with fireworks of our own."

She did not move, but squeezed his hand, holding him back for the moment. She was only now feeling the chill of the late night. But when his eyes turned questioningly toward her, she was at a loss for words. She wanted to confirm her love and to solicit his sworn promise that he would never jeopardize his life to be with her. But that would only entail explanations, and explanations could lead to losing him.

Thus, she pushed herself from her slumped position and into his gentle arms. She was prisoner to the love she had for him–a love she feared might one day cost him his life.

# Thirteen

Morgan had a special way of making things all right. He was tender and commanding, caring, loving...Anna felt as though she were the only woman in the world and it was his primary function to dote over her, protect her and cherish her. As she slipped between new silk sheets, Anna realized she had so casually forgotten her guests, who were drifting away for lack of attention as quickly as the fireworks were dwindling. She cared only that Morgan filled her with the wonderful ecstasy of his love and his passion.

Being with him was all that was important in the world. 1858 had just arrived, and she prayed it would be as wonderful a year for her and Morgan as their first months together had been. In the cool of the evening, with the wind gently whistling against the window panes, the intense fire of his body met hers. Her legs entwined about him, and the sinewy muscles of his chest met her soft, supple one just for a moment before his mouth explored every warm, ivory inch of her slim neck and the delicate hollow where the tiny, throbbing pulse increased in intensity, then lowered and captured one pink bud of her breast, then the other. Their lips searched frantically in the heat of passion and found each other, seizing the moment to caress and possess, while their bodies molded together as one and moved toward the beautiful moment that had become an obsession to Anna. Their love culminated in liquid-hot ecstasy, and Anna's fingers closed tightly over Morgan's shoulders.

Their rapid breathing slowed simultaneously and her fingers relaxed. She was content to have him lie gently atop her, his body still one with hers, and to feel the flicker of his eyelashes against her hairline. She was warmed by his love, secure and happy in his arms. She would not think about his past, or Alistair's vicious threat.

Oh, but she would think about it. It would be the reason for her every action; the cause of her every fear; and part of the reason she would love Morgan totally every chance she had. She would cherish the time she had with him. He was her every reason for being alive.

As he moved to her side and slept in the aftermath of their love, tears moistened Anna's eyes. In the pale moonlight streaking through the parted draperies, she studied his handsome profile, the straight, narrow nose and slightly full lips, long golden lashes that would have looked more in their proper place on a pretty woman. Instinctively, Anna's hand moved to the soft, matted fur of his chest to feel his soft breathing. In his sleep, his hand rose and closed over hers.

It wasn't fair that this dark, vicious cloud hovered constantly over them.

* * *

In March, 1858, on the anniversary of Patrick St. Cyr's death–and directly in the middle of preparations for Violet's wedding to Wren due to take place the following month–Alistair's wife gave birth to her child. Anna assisted Dr. Miller in the delivery, made unnecessarily difficult by Sudie's crude curses at Alistair, the child, Shadow Marsh, and at life in general. In the course of an event that should have been among the most wonderful in a woman's life, she made an embarrassing spectacle of herself, screaming hysterically and thrashing about so that Dr. Miller was forced to tie her to the bed.

Her loose red hair tossed madly as she spat at Tylas, "You old bastard! Get your hands off me! Take these ties off. So help me God–"

While Tylas patiently restrained verbal abuses of his own against this coarse repugnant creature, Anna bathed the newborn infant. Wrapping him in a blanket, she walked into the corridor where Alistair awaited.

Only now, holding this precious little one, did Anna realize how completely Morgan had taken over her heart. In the glazed, dark eyes of this new St. Cyr son, she saw, not an unwary thief who had taken a fortune from her, but the blessing that had lifted a great weight from her shoulders. True, she feared for the future of Shadow Marsh in Alistair's hands, but she and Morgan were free of the terrible control he had over them. They were free to tell the world of their marriage and their love. It no longer mattered. Shadow Marsh would soon belong to Alistair, lock, stock, and barrel.

She and Morgan could begin afresh, as husband and wife. They could go away together and build a life of their own. Still, it was all Anna could do to restrain tears as she approached Alistair. Anna couldn't look into her brother's cold, cruel eyes, the features sharp with dreaded anticipation as he awaited news of the child's gender.

When she stood beside Alistair, she folded the blanket back to show him the robust, pink babe, his gentle cries lulled into short, broken grunts by the exhaustion of the birth process.

"Is it a boy?" Alistair asked cautiously. A moment of silence passed. "Is the blasted thing a boy?"

Anna lifted her eyes and studied the thin, hard features of her brother. He cared not that the child was healthy, or whether his wife had survived the birth. He cared only whether the child was a boy. "Yes," Anna replied quietly. "You have a son, Alistair."

"Hot damn!" Startled by Alistair's jubilant cry, the baby jerked in Anna's arms. "Shadow Marsh is mine! Mine!" He looked at the child and a cynical smirk twisted his mouth. "Thanks, you ugly little bugger."

"He's a beautiful boy," she countered, attempting to keep a tight rein on the anger building inside her. "What will you name him?" A lump rose in Anna's throat. This dear child had merely been a tool by which Alistair would assume ownership of Shadow Marsh.

Alistair turned away, in need of a goblet of whiskey to celebrate this good news. "You may have the privilege of naming it."

"And what about Sudie's right?"

Alistair laughed maniacally. "Sudie? She doesn't want it!"

"Him," Anna snapped. "Not it..." But Anna was in no mood to argue with Alistair. Something much more important was on her mind. "Alistair." He turned slightly back, thinking, perhaps from the tone of Anna's voice as she'd spoken his name, that she would beg to remain at Shadow Marsh. It had, after all, been her lifelong home. "You have your baby son, Alistair. Shadow Marsh is yours now."

"I told you I would have it," he replied triumphantly.

Frankly, Anna was surprised at how well she was taking the loss of Shadow Marsh. "So you did," she replied calmly. "And now is the perfect time to advise you that Morgan–"

"You still want him?" he asked incredulously. "The overseer? Even knowing you have lost Shadow Marsh?" When she did not reply, he continued in haste, "Frankly, dear sister, I couldn't give a damn. You marry the bastard, if that is what you wish–"

Morgan was safe now. Alistair had Shadow Marsh and there was no reason left for him to be a threat to Morgan. "He is already my husband."

At first Alistair was surprised by the news. Then his features darkened into anger...just before he realized that it no longer mattered whether Anna was married. He had the first son and he had Shadow Marsh. "Indeed, sister? Well, so much the better." Alistair sauntered slowly toward her, his hands half tucked into his trouser pockets. "I'll petition the probate courts to transfer Shadow Marsh into my name. Until such time as a judgment is signed, your...husband may stay on as overseer. After that, you may remain if you so wish, but he goes." Alistair couldn't help but notice the question in her eyes, the fear–it pleased him that he wielded so much power over her. If their father could only see them now...the strong, unyielding Anna at the mercy of the unfavored brother. "I will not turn him in to the federal authorities, if that is what you fear. With that creature..." He pointed toward his child, "I have no need to snuff out the life of the man who beds you, and beds you often."

"I will go wherever he goes...I will not remain without him."

"As you wish. You shouldn't do too badly with the large sum of money Father left you in his will. The overseer has probably never been so well off."

"Morgan will provide for us. I have no need of Father's money." Even as she spoke, her fingers lifted to the locket Morgan had given her for Christmas. She recalled that he'd said he spent the last of his wages on it. Indeed...how would they live without Father's money?

"The little martyr!" Alistair laughed again. "You'll sacrifice the luxuries of rich living and exist in poverty because of love? How quaint! Frankly, dear sister, I had expected you to have higher ambitions." With something of a crude grunt, Alistair walked off. Momentarily, his uneven footsteps disappeared down the carpeted steps.

Anna drew the new babe close to her cheek, to feel the softness of his skin against her own. She sighed deeply and returned to the birthing chamber, where Dr. Miller was scrubbing his hands and arms at the wash stand. Sudie's face was turned away from the doctor, and Anna saw the way her mouth was pressed into a hard, bitter line.

Despite her exhaustion, Sudie had heard everything of the conversation in the corridor. She had not yet seen the child, but imagined his red, pinched features and tiny form curled up against this strange, new life thrust upon him. Sudie shuddered, remembering the nights she had slept with the repulsive Alistair in order to conceive this child. But the reward Alistair had promised her–sixteen-thousand dollars deposited in a New Orleans bank–made the terrible year she had spent with him worthwhile. She certainly expected to have the last laugh once she returned to New Orleans, to her friends, and to the money awaiting her.

Anna approached the bed, started to put the babe in the crook of Sudie's arms, but thought better about it. "Do you wish to hold your son?"

Sudie's head snapped around as she said harshly, "Get that disgusting thing away from me!"

There was a maniacal hatred in her features, sharpening unnaturally beneath the makeup caked in small masses by the hours of sweat and exhaustion. Anna could not prevent her tears.

She stood for a moment, looking first at the tiny babe, then at Tylas Miller. The old gentleman merely shook his head in disgust.

Anna felt as helpless as this new life sleeping peacefully in her arms. Alistair couldn't care less about the child, and Sudie hadn't hesitated to express her hatred for him. Anna returned to the corridor and dropped into a large chair. A very tearful Bea was putting a vase of early spring roses on the trestle table, and their sweet aroma physically renewed Anna.

Anna wondered how the child could sleep so peacefully amid the mixed, emotional mutterings of the servants as they hurried from the house to spread the word of the birth. Bea approached and stood off a few feet, watching Anna tenderly hold the boy child, the newest St. Cyr in the family. Bea wept, not only for the child who would have no loving parents, but for Anna and her own people, their futures uncertain now that Alistair would take control. It was frightening to imagine the changes he would make, frightening to imagine Shadow Marsh, one of the richest plantations in Louisiana, sinking slowly into ruin.

Anna was determined that the uncertainties of the future would not despair her, nor would the despair of the father ever touch this dear child. If she and Morgan had to leave Shadow Marsh, she would take him with her. "Isn't he beautiful, Bea?"

"Sho' is, Missy," Bea replied quietly. "A fine li'l man."

Anna looked at the boy child with the greatest love and softly said, "How cruelly life has begun for you." Her lips touched his plump cheek and his little forehead. He smelled so fresh, so new. "Look at your little red nose..." she continued, touching it. "Like your Grandpa St. Cyr's." Gently, she began to rock him, as proud of him as if he were her own. "Patrick...that is a good, strong name. You shall be named after your grandpa." Anna lifted him to her cheek and whispered, "Welcome to my heart, little Patrick. I will love and cherish you, I will care for you, and if I must leave Shadow Marsh, you will go with me as my son. I will never let you stand alone. I will never leave you to bear the tyranny of your father."

Morgan was away, and she felt that this was a terrible time to be alone, with new decisions and new worries brought on by the birth of this innocent child. She recalled early last week, the tenderness of his arms folded round her, and his easily spoken confession that he wished he did not have to leave her, even for a little while.

The trip to Natchez he and Joby Cade had planned couldn't have been put off. They had to buy grain for the spring planting, which was overdue, and good breeding stock for the dwindling herd of cattle. They'd been gone ten days now, and every day had seemed longer. Anna wanted him home, especially today–so that she could explain everything to him, unburden her heart, and relieve all his doubts of her love for him.

"Looks like that li'l man be needin' a mammy," Bea said.

Anna did not look up, but continued to look fondly at little Patrick. "I'll be his mama, but he'll need someone else to wet nurse him. Do you know of someone?"

"Lizzie, wife of Shuckin' Sam–she be pappin' a young'un. Plenty milk for this li'l soul." Though Bea roughly patted Anna's shoulder, Anna felt the gentleness beneath her heavy hand.

Lovey and Violet approached, both looking over Anna's shoulder to smile dubiously into the baby's sleeping face. The smiles, without feeling, did not linger. Violet asked, "Anna, what will happen to Shadow Marsh?"

"We mustn't worry about that now, Violet. We'll have to wait and–"

Anna suddenly felt dizzy, the excitement of the morning, the worry and the confrontation with Alistair had been too much for her. She quickly handed Patrick to Lovey, who stood closest to her. She stood, but her body trembled and she put her hand out to Bea. "Bea–I..." Everything whirled around her and her body became limp and lifeless. She would have fallen if Bea's arms hadn't come firmly around her.

Violet brought her fingers to her mouth in fear for Anna, then cried out, "Dr. Tylas, Dr. Tylas, come quickly...it's Anna!"

"I'm sorry, Bea..." Anna's words were drowned out in the sea of darkness gently enveloping her.

When she came to on her bed sometime later, Tylas was sitting beside her. Bea and Lovey stood behind him, their features pinched and worried. A cool cloth rested on her forehead. She felt terribly foolish and tried to smile. Tylas roughly patted her hand and when Violet approached with a cup of water, coaxed Anna to take a sip. The worried looks of the women only brought tears to Anna.

"You know me," she said quietly, flicking away the tears with her fingertips. "I've always got to be the center of attention." Anna removed the cloth from her forehead and tried to rise, but Tylas Miller's hand came down to her shoulder. "You just lie right there and rest a bit."

"It was just the excitement...I'm fine now."

"Excitement, bull!" Tylas laughed. "Young lady, you're with child."

Anna's stupefied look was followed by stunned silence. It took a moment to collect her thoughts. "But–but I–oh, Tylas," she stammered, "I can't–are you sure?"

Violet dropped to a chair and painfully droned, "Oh, the disgrace–the disgrace..."

Tylas had overheard Anna's conversation with Alistair in the corridor. While he certainly would not have condemned her had she not been married, he was quite pleased that she was. "You may consider me an old horse doctor, young lady, but–no, I wouldn't make a mistake about that. Give yourself about seven months and you'll be holding a little one of your own in your arms."

Anna's strength was fueled by overwhelming joy. She threw herself gracefully into Tylas Miller's arms and hugged him. "Oh, thank you–"

"I had nothing to do with it," he laughed again, affectionately tousling her hair. "I'd take that up with your husband!"

"You–you're married? The words slid from Violet's tongue in a stunned whisper. "To the overseer? My God! Have you no shame?"

Anna chose to ignore Violet's note of doom. She was so

happy–so happy to be pregnant with Morgan's baby–that she was bursting inside. "I can't wait to tell him," she confessed. Morgan filled her thoughts. With her eyes closed against Tylas Miler's shirt, she imagined the look in Morgan's eyes when she told him. *A look of pride and joy–oh, please let him be as happy as I am.*

Bea had put her hand to her mouth to suppress her surprise, not only at the news of the forthcoming birth, but at the even more wonderful news that Morgan was her husband and the father of her child. Bea had always hoped that Anna would find a kind, gentle man–a man such as Morgan York. Tears moistened her eyes as Anna's hand went timidly out, inviting Bea to her.

Anna had never been so happy. She wanted Morgan, his arms, his warm embrace, his softly whispered endearments assuring her of his joy. She wanted to share her happiness with the man she loved. She didn't want to think about Shadow Marsh and the future.

\* \* \*

But the future of Shadow Marsh was all that concerned the devious Alistair. He wasted no time initiating the steps that would put the plantation in his possession. He rose before dawn the following morning, saddled his horse, and began the fourteen-mile trip to Alexandria.

Warrant Fairgate had opened his office early. The March air was cool and an arid wind stirred from the open window, temporarily easing the mustiness of the long weekend and hundreds of dusty law books. Many were stacked on the floor for lack of shelf space.

Tylas Miller had paid Warren a visit late last evening, so he knew about the birth of Alistair's son. Warren did not look up from his reading when the door opened at mid-morning and a man stood before him. His trousers were dusty from his long ride, and a short riding crop gently rapped against his right leg. "Congratulations," Warren said dryly.

"Mr. Fairgate, you have already heard?" Alistair's greeting was cocky, at best. "My, but news does travel fast...especially good news."

Only now did Warren look up and assess this brash, overly thin man with his thin face and his thin nose. The only physical thing of substance about him was the overly wide boot hiding his deformed foot. He leaned back, cupping his hands behind his head, and met Alistair's sarcastic, gloating look.

"You're here, I suppose, to change your will, to name your new son as sole heir of your monthly stipend?"

"Don't be an ass, Fairgate." Alistair half turned and impatiently began flicking a gloved finger over dusty books. He had so looked forward to this moment. "I have the firstborn son. By the terms of my father's will, Shadow Marsh is mine."

"Is it?"

Alistair's cocky countenance faded into confusion. "Yes, it is," he replied hesitantly. "I'll expect you to file the necessary documents."

Warren rose, arched his back to relieve the stiffness of two hours behind the desk. He removed his spectacles and set them atop his papers. The very presence of Alistair St. Cyr consumed him with hatred, because he blamed him for Patrick St. Cyr's death. He wouldn't trade this moment for the world—this moment in which he expected to triumph over the evil, conniving man standing before him with outrageous arrogance. He had looked forward to this moment as enthusiastically as had Alistair.

"As the attorney for your father's estate," he began, "I have certain duties, one of which was to document your marriage to this, umm, lady you met in a New Orleans brothel. I certainly wanted that documentation in my hands in the event you slid into my office like scum to claim what you felt was rightfully yours."

"How dare you insult me! I could ruin you, Fairgate!"

"Could you, indeed?" Warren countered. "Enough of insults and ruination. Actually, I am quite pleased you have paid me this visit so soon after the birth of your heir."

Alistair's eyes widened; unconsciously, he gritted his teeth. "What are you insinuating?"

"Look at my hands," Warren ordered politely. When

Alistair continued to hold his look, transfixed, Warren repeated more firmly, "Look at my hands!" Alistair's eyes slowly lowered. "What do you see?"

"Hands," Alistair spat back.

"To be more precise...empty hands," Warren replied indulgently. "Hands that cannot file the necessary documentation and supporting evidence with the courts, namely a certified copy of your matrimonial license, which will prove a legitimate issue...because it does not exist!"

"You're a liar!"

"The woman put one over on you, St. Cyr," Warren laughed. "The minister who married you was a tavern keeper, and this..." His hands lowered and a large piece of paper slid across the desk toward Alistair, the writings on it scarcely legible through dark, almost black stains. "This is your marriage license. A cleverly lettered document on the back of a slave auction bill that ended up, eventually, beneath the head of a man the tavern keeper had shot between the eyes. You may recognize your own signature, you fool!"

"You're a liar," Alistair repeated in a softer tone.

"Your heir is a bastard. You have not met the provisions of your father's will. Anna remains managing conservator until such time as a legitimate offspring is born. As for the sixteen thousand you deposited in the Bank of New Orleans in payment of the—your wife's services—I have had it declared stolen property and returned it to the working account of Shadow Marsh."

Somewhere in the past few moments, the life had drained from Alistair. A sick, sinking feeling forced him down into the nearest chair. "I don't believe you."

"My affidavit has already been filed in the probate records. You may check with the parish clerk yourself."

Alistair was too stunned to feel rage. He came to his feet with perfect grace and calmness, his hands clenched so tightly around the handle of the horse whip that his knuckles paled beneath the strain. Hatred emanated from his eyes as they glared across the desk at the gloating Warren Fairgate. His voice remained deceptively calm. "You seem to have been armed with this deception for quite a while," he accused. "Why have you not exposed Sudie's little prank before?"

Warren could see no need to keep his reasons a secret. He was more than willing to divulge them now that no more harm could be done. "So that Shadow Marsh could remain in the hands of the person who truly deserves it, without threat from you. Your sister, Anna Rose...the woman who lovingly cared for Patrick in the last years of his life."

Alistair drew back a little, his mouth twisting into a wry smile. "So that's it. You blame me for Father's death." When Warren did not answer, Alistair continued spitefully, "Or is it my sister, Fairgate? Has she seduced you with those lovely eyes as she has the overseer?"

The overseer! God, even as he spoke, Alistair's devious mind planned revenge. Morgan York, or Michael Fielding, was no longer a fugitive, but Anna was not aware of it. This was the control Alistair had over her. Perhaps he would not yet take possession of Shadow Marsh, but he would certainly be rid of Morgan York and break dear Anna's heart. If these vicious circumstances resulted in Shadow Marsh going to Anna, he would make sure she didn't share the wealth with Morgan York, a damned rogue.

With a twisted, knowing smile such as only he could accomplish, Alistair pivoted on his heel and walked away. The door to Warren Fairgate's office slammed soundly behind him.

\* \* \*

Anna was not at all surprised when Sudie donned her fanciest traveling gown, packed her clothes, and requested that a carriage be brought around to take her to the train station in Jude's Landing for the first leg of her trip back to New Orleans. Her son was not yet two days old.

Anna was rocking little Patrick when the carriage pulled away from the veranda. Sudie had not spoken; rather, she had looked down her nose at Anna and the child and grunted rather rudely. Anna was glad to be rid of her.

Lizzie had fed Patrick to fulfillment just minutes ago, while her baby girl slept in a cradle beside her, and had returned to Cabin Row. Anna enjoyed holding Patrick; it would give her the experience she needed to care for her own baby in a few months' time. She hadn't imagined herself a mother, but thinking about it now brought joy and great anticipation. She wanted to share something with Morgan as precious as their love–a product of their love–a dear child.

Twilight cast a warm, golden glow over the horizon and filtered pale light through the trellis overlooking the veranda. Anna drew the babe more securely in her arms. She rocked him for a few minutes and might have fallen asleep if Bea had not put her hand gently to her shoulder. Startled, Anna's eyes came open and she looked to Bea for a moment, bewildered and disoriented.

Bea sat beside her in silence. There was a hesitation in the way she looked at Anna. "Don't normally be askin' the white folk to come see the black folk, Miss Anna, but Mose, he down sick an' he be wantin' to see you an' the little 'un. Jus' this once, do you think y'all might come to see Mose?"

Anna's hand fell gently to Bea's. "I wasn't sure if Mose was up to visitors or I would already have been there. If you'll fetch an extra blanket for Patrick, we'll go right over."

As they walked together across the lawn a few minutes later, and around the fish pond, several of the children rushed up, begging to see the baby. Anna took a moment to let them gaze into his tiny, sleeping face.

Mose was sitting in the rocking chair by the window, watching their slow approach. He'd seen Anna grow from a gangly, rebellious young girl, who'd taken every opportunity to ruffle her father's feathers, to the beauty he now heard laughing as she walked with Bea. He remembered how patiently she'd taught Lovey to read and write and sing the songs of the white folks. He remembered the pride in Patrick St. Cyr's eyes when she'd entered a room and the stammered excuses when she said something naughty and embarrassed him in the company of their friends and neighbors.

Mose smiled widely when Anna entered the cabin,

followed closely by Bea. Anna dropped to her knees beside his chair and laid the baby in his arms. The old man held him as gently as he would a butterfly that had just escaped its cocoon. "My, what a fine, healthy boy," Mose remarked. His smile faded, and though he said nothing as he looked to Anna, she knew what was going through his mind. They had all been happy at Shadow Marsh, and he feared that would change now that Alistair was taking control.

"Don't worry, Mose," Anna said assuredly. "We'll take care and everything will be all right. Nothing will change for you and your people, I assure you of that."

"Not worried about me, Missy...gwine meet my maker soon." His hand came from under the blanket. "Better take the young'un, Missy. Ole' Mose, he been real clumsy lately."

"I'll take him for a bit," Bea offered. Anna watched in silence as she held Patrick close, entering the small bedroom parted from the front room only by a drab brown curtain. She heard Bea talking to the baby as she put him on the bed to sleep.

Anna eased to a sitting position on the floor beside Mose's chair. She was glad to be here with him. His bright, smiling eyes always made her feel secure. She had been especially fond of him as a child–a fondness that had been deepened by his tenderness, and his tendency to give unselfishly of his time and care. His had been the shoulder she'd cried on when her father had been away. She had never told him how she felt about him, but she was sure he knew.

"Thank you, Mose."

"Fo' what, Miss Anna?"

Anna sighed pensively. "For taking me fishing when I was a wee bit of a girl and always putting the worms on my hooks. For telling my papa I'd been with you when I'd snuck off somewhere to be with Wren. For teaching me to ride my very first pony and for being the best friend a girl could have."

Mose laughed very weakly. "It be Mose what should thank you, Missy, fo' lettin' him put them squiggly worms on yo' hook, and fo' givin' Mose that purty smile when his spirits was real low. Why, chile, ol Mose, he be the one what blessed, what with you an' my fine family an' this freedom yo' daddy give us. Mose, he don't have no complaints. An' if he did, why, I feel sho' the Lawd be mighty displeased with Mose."

He looked out the window now, at the white-washed cabins stirring to life, where he'd been happy these long years, at Miss Violet slowly approaching for her morning visit, one arm securely holding a pot of her good stew and the other holding together a bouquet of freshly gathered early spring flowers. He looked fondly at Anna sitting beside him, tucking the blanket around his thin form.

Then his dark eyes moved slowly to Bea, putting the finishing touches on a piece of crochet she was making for the big House, and to Lovey, his daughter, rocking his first granddaughter to sleep, and his grandson, playing quietly at her mother's skirt.

He had no complaints and no regrets. His life had been fulfilling. He just wished he could have seen Mr. Morgan and Joby Cade one more time.

A smile, too weak to touch his lips, glowed brightly in his heart. He'd had a good life and now he was tired. He closed his eyes and his chin sank slowly to the soft blanket Anna had tucked about him.

A radiant, yet tranquil light glowed around him just as the voices and all the worldly noises–the laughter of the children, the faraway, haunting echoes of the bayou creatures, the escape of steam from Bea's old black pot crackling in the hearth–they all drifted off into the wind.

And his life gently ceased.

# Fourteen

The mourners had just left the cemetery when Alistair rode up to the gates and dismounted from his horse. Anna had lingered at Mose's gravesite a while longer, to pay special homage to her friend. She was slowly walking from the cemetery when Alistair intercepted her. His gait, as usual, was more unsteady from drink than from his deformity, and the smell of liquor left the air foul around her. His eyes, narrow and glazed, cause fear to leap within her.

She had seen Warren Fairgate yesterday evening and knew the reason for Alistair's silent hostility. Because he was her brother, she felt sorry for him, and felt that Sudie's trickery was evil and unforgiveable. Sadly, Alistair had gotten what he deserved. He had never been able to rise above his own shortcomings and patiently work toward earning his goals and dreams. He had sought them only through greed and lust, and using other people to his own selfish ends. He had used Sudie, which had resulted in the birth of an illegitimate son for Alistair. If Alistair had only disliked his son before, he would certainly hate him now.

If nothing else, Anna swore that little Patrick would never know he was illegitimate. She had years to come up with an explanation.

Alistair fell into pace beside Anna and another fear came to her. Alistair's competition for Shadow Marsh would begin anew, and he would again view Morgan as a threat. A sick, sinking feeling hit her. Alistair knew of their marriage...how foolish she had been to tell him about it.

"Well, little sister, I imagine you've heard what Sudie did."

Anna halted. Alistair took a few more steps and turned to face her. His hands went steadily to his back.

"I am sorry, Alistair. I would never have wished that. You know that she left Shadow Marsh, don't you?"

"Yes...too bad. I was going to kill her," he replied tonelessly. "But should we meet again..." He left yet another threat hanging.

A cool, refreshing breeze whipped across the meadow, carrying the fragrance of wild flowers mingled with the muskiness of mares grazing nearby. New foals basked in the security of their shadows. Shadow Marsh stood bold against the timberline, the azaleas in profuse, multicolored bloom taking away the desolation of the barren winter months. She only hoped there would be late bloomers for Violet's wedding next month. Like the wave of a magic wand, green had crept across the countryside as far as the eye could see. But Alistair stood beside her, casting a dark, threatening shadow across her line of vision.

"You know that Mose died?" Anna questioned.

"Quash told me. Sorry...I know you liked the old gentleman."

Alistair was being uncharacteristically amiable, except in his threat to kill Sudie. Anna was surprised and wary. His mouth was pressed into a thin line and, as they continued to walk, his eyes lowered. His mind appeared to be a hundred miles away.

"Alistair, I truly am sorry. About Patrick–"

"Who?"

"Your son...for heaven's sake, Alistair! We named him Patrick. Do you approve?"

"Couldn't give a damn. The little bastard is yours, if you want him." Bitterness sharpened his voice. "You wouldn't know a woman willing to marry me, would you? Someone blind, perhaps, who won't have to look at my ugliness as I lie with her?"

As Anna again halted, she took his arm and swung him around. "Alistair, you are not ugly! Why do you persist in this...this self-hatred?"

"Why not?" he shot back contemptuously, pulling his arm free. "Look at me."

Her hand went tenderly out, but he would not allow her to touch him. "Despite your shortcomings, Alistair, you are my brother. I don't like you at all, but I do love you, and it still hurts me to see you punish yourself like this."

"I don't need your sympathy!" He continued to walk, crossing his arms again at his back. "Don't you think I would rather reap the rewards than the punishments? Damn it all to hell, I want Shadow Marsh! And..." He stepped into her path, halting her. "I won't have it if you conceive a male child by that bastard overseer you say is your husband. I want him to leave...today."

Desolation emptied the life from Anna. She felt her breathing become shallow, almost nonexistent. "Please, Alistair, I love him. I'll go away with him and leave Shadow Marsh to you."

"It wouldn't matter if you were three thousand miles away, Anna. If you bear a legitimate son, Shadow Marsh will go to you, as your property and yours alone. I want you to be rid of him before that happens. But..." he continued, glaring scornfully. "I want you to remain married to him, so that you cannot marry another."

"You cannot ask me to separate from my husband!"

"I don't ask it...I command it."

"I beg of you..."

Alistair grabbed her arm and squeezed it tightly. "St. Cyrs do not beg!" Only now did he notice how beautiful his sister looked in her black tiered gown and wide-brimmed hat, her remarkable beauty shaded behind the veil tucked beneath her chin. Her smooth, opaque skin was a lovely contrast against the somber black, and her eyes, oh, so filled with pain. He realized only then how tightly he was holding her.

Releasing her, he groaned with frustration. Not only was she beautiful, but she was gentle, kind and remarkably intelligent. She had a good head for business, and the enthusiasm and skill of a thousand men. She was everything Alistair was not. He had never questioned their father favoring her the way he did.

Anna was at odds. She felt she would rather die than lose Morgan. "I'll relinquish my right to Shadow Marsh," she quietly offered, hoping beyond all hope that he would withdraw his cruel order that she send Morgan away. Perhaps if she told him that she was already pregnant with his child–

"Don't you think I've already thought of that, Anna? I took a copy of Father's will to Baton Rouge, to another solicitor. Where do you think I've been for the past three days? You cannot relinquish your right! It is prohibited by further provisions of that damned will."

A deep, desolate pain born of the prospect of losing Morgan rose in Anna's heart. "Please, Alistair–if you have any mercy at all–don't make me send him away. I love him dearly. I'm his wife–he's my husband."

"If you don't send him away," he threatened flatly, "I'll send the telegraph message to the War Department...bang, bang bang!"

"I just don't believe you'd do that, Alistair."

"Don't doubt it for a second." He scowled contemptibly. "It won't bother me a bit to see him dragged away...to see your heart broken."

"Let him stay on as overseer. I won't go near him. I swear this to you."

"I'm not stupid, Anna! I've watched you, for God's sake, sneaking out there to spend nights with him! Giving less than a damn what anybody thought about it."

Anna balled her fist, her despair deepening into anger. Why was she humoring him with alternatives? Why was she pleading with him? Had her love for Morgan sunk her to these depths that she would grovel at the feet of her brother? How dare he try to control her life like this! How dare he order her to send her husband away! She was about to tell Alistair that she would not do it when one of the children from Cabin Row ran toward them.

"Joby Cade and Mistah Morgan, they's comin' up the road with the wagons."

Anna's heart leaped, both in joy and in despair. Morgan was so close–just a few hundred yards away, but Alistair was right beside her, ripping away her happiness. She started quickly down the hill, wanting only to feel the warmth, the strength of Morgan's arms about her.

"Heed my words, Anna..." echoed threateningly over her shoulder.

Morgan had just jumped down from the wagon when Anna threw herself into his arms. Tears welled in her eyes and immediately touched his shirt. Her black attire and veil told him that something was very wrong at Shadow Marsh.

"Mose passed away?" he questioned.

"Yes...we buried him this morning."

"I am so sorry. He was a great old fellow." Putting her away from him he remarked, "I smell like a horse."

On hearing the news about his father-in-law, Joby Cade quickly climbed down from the second wagon and disappeared into Bea's cabin.

Anna couldn't tell Morgan that the tears she shed now were for him, and not for Mose. The threat that Alistair dangled over them was as lethal as an arrow shot straight into her heart. She felt the pain and she sensed—oh, God, how she sensed—that the time she had remaining with Morgan was so brief.

Morgan's lips softly, gently touched hers and, despite the fact that he hadn't bathed in three days—and did, indeed, smell like a horse—he pulled her close into his arms. Her lilac perfume flooded his senses. But as he realized they were not alone, he quickly released her and turned toward the men who had gathered. "Let's get these wagons unloaded," he ordered briskly.

Anna saw that the long trip had exhausted Morgan, that he would want to bathe and rest a while. But she felt selfish. She wanted to lie beside him and feel his protective warmth. Would he be too tired to bother with her today? She looked deeply into his golden eyes, hoping, perhaps, that she could see his thoughts there. She wanted to know if he had dreamed as obsessively of her these past three weeks as she had dreamed of him.

As the wagons were being unloaded, they walked slowly toward the overseer's cottage. "Sudie gave birth to the baby four days ago," Anna announced somberly.

"A fine, healthy child, I hope," he replied tiredly.

"Yes—and a boy."

"How do you feel about it?"

"I felt relieved," she admitted, shrugging against him, entwining her fingers through his resting across her shoulder. "But the baby is illegitimate. There is no documented marriage between Alistair and Sudie."

Morgan paused, accusation easing into his tone. "And you found this out how?"

"I didn't find out, Morgan...I knew nothing about it. Warren Fairgate has known for months. He told no one until after the child was born. I'm afraid he greatly favors my inheritance of Shadow Marsh."

They were on the veranda of the overseer's cottage. Morgan took a handkerchief from his pocket and wiped his face. Then he sat down for a moment. "I go away for a few weeks and when I return, a child has been born and a kindly old man dies. What else has happened that I should know about?"

Anna's fingers rose to her slightly round abdomen. It was too soon to see the child growing inside her, but she felt crimson rise in her cheeks, as if she was sure he knew. As she met Morgan's silent gaze, she quickly flew back through the past few moments and remembered what he had asked her. She wanted to tell him about her pregnancy, but she was apprehensive, not of his reaction, but of Alistair's, should he find out. In his present mood, he could do anything.

"Nothing, Morgan. That's enough, don't you think?"

Morgan rested his ankle on his knee, removed one boot and then the other. He had seen one of the younger women enter his cottage when he was out at the wagon and was sure he'd have a warm bath awaiting him. He put his hand out to Anna. "Stay with me while I freshen up?"

"Of course...I haven't seen you in weeks."

There was, indeed, a bath awaiting him, with soap and clean towels neatly laid out on the chair beside the tub. Anna removed her hat and veils and slumped lazily across the bottom of the bed, watching Morgan undress. Each discarded item of dusty clothing revealed a masculinity she had missed terribly these past weeks. He moved immodestly from the spot where he had dropped his clothing and entered the tub.

"How was Natchez?" she asked, rolling to her stomach and tucking her hands under her chin.

"Busy," he replied working up a lather of soap on his chest and shoulders. "Lots of planters and buyers attending the slave auctions." She was looking away thoughtfully. "Why don't you get out of that drab dress and scrub my back for me."

She rolled over absently, drew her knees up and slowly unfastened the front stays of her bodice. Presently she stepped out of the dress and her slip-on shoes as if they were all one garment.

Morgan watched her from across the room, so flawlessly exquisite that she took away his breath. But there was beneath her beauty blankness in her expression as she approached him, dropped to her knees and picked up the soft brush.

"Did you miss me...really?" he asked, resting his hands lazily on the side of the tub.

Anna seemed to be deliberately avoiding his gaze. "Missed you something fierce," she responded. "Did you bring the rose bushes I asked for?"

"Four dozen or so. Joby Cade will unload them at the house. You show him where you want them and he'll make sure they're in the ground before the warm weather."

"And well fertilized," she reflected thoughtfully. "You know how moody roses can be."

"And well fertilized," he echoed. Her mood troubled him. She had been absently rubbing soap on the scrub brush for two minutes; he had timed her in his mind. "Anna, something has happened that you're not telling me."

It didn't matter that he was covered in soap. She knew only that if she didn't feel his arms around her this very minute she would surely go mad. Dropping the brush, her arms slid around his neck. "Morgan...hold me, please."

"You're upset," he replied, returning her embrace. "Is it Mose?"

"Partly." Anna quickly pulled away, betraying to him the deepest despair he had ever seen in her. When she rose and fled toward the bed in tears, he hastily rinsed off the soap and wrapped himself in a towel. He fell to the bed beside her and put his hand on her back.

"I am here for you, little *chica*. You're my woman. If you cannot tell me what troubles you..." The despair, the sadness, he couldn't bear it. He drew her into his arms and his hands went tenderly to the back of her head. It had been weeks since he'd felt her sensual softness, or touched the loose, raven waves now shrouding his shoulders. He wanted to be with Anna this very minute.

Anna wanted to be cruel and indifferent, to build the courage it would take to end their love. But could it ever be ended, even if she sent him far, far away?

A mutual, very intense need inflamed them, coursing through their bodies. Tossing off the towel, and pulling her undergarments away, Morgan gained the intimacy of her flesh, his mouth seeking her trembling one, wetting his lips with her tears. Touching her, caressing her, was like discovering a new treasure. As he rocked her gently against him, overwhelmed by the liquid fire molding them together, he whispered her name over and over..."Anna...Anna..."

Anna knew the smoldering flame created by the touch of their bodies could not now be extinguished, that it was beyond all control. She ached for the touch of his hands awakening, creating the ecstasy, the beauty, the unselfish capacity for love he had restrained all these years, waiting for her. She felt the pain of want grab her, travel across the plane of her abdomen, her long, lean thighs, and the very depth of her that throbbed in anticipation of their union.

She felt the steely hardness of his body, saw, in the low shadows of the early morning, the ripples of his muscles, his strong, hard chest beneath the matted fur, the way his jaw clenched tightly and his eyes closed as his searching lips again found hers. Oh, that it would never end was her dream; that reality would never come back and strike her with its brutal force.

"I have wanted you, little *chica*," Morgan whispered, "All the way home I imagined you like this, against me..." As he almost impatiently eased her legs apart and pushed into the warm, moist depths of her, he again whispered, "little *chica,"* and their bodies moved quickly toward fulfillment.

Anna remembered the very first time they had made love, his look of embarrassment as her fingers had absently traced the patterns of the scars across his back. He no longer seemed bothered by it. Her hands caressed him, his flesh, his being–not his past.

The heat of their passion raised them to heights Anna had only experienced in his arms. Her body was a hard, tight knot of desire begging to be satisfied. Filled with the power of Morgan's love, she knew she could never be parted from him. She loved him too much. The rapture–the unfettered rapture that was hers for the taking–she had never imagined it could be so deliriously wonderful...her euphoria, her paradise. It destroyed logic, consumed everything but the lust, the need, the fulfillment of her physical being. As the ultimate joy of fulfillment came, Anna cried out in wonderment, in beautiful, explosive satisfaction, and drove her body hard against his, to savor the liquid fire of his strength to the very end.

As he locked her in the iron grip of his embrace, his body trembled in the aftermath of their love. For a long, silent moment, he remained joined to her, breathing heavily. As his breathing became a slow, gentle rhythm, he eased to her side.

"You are my woman," he said quietly. "My wife...my whole purpose in being." His hand touched and remained gently resting on her abdomen.

Panicked by this sudden touch, Anna swept his hand from her abdomen, lest he notice that it was slightly rounded with the child growing within her. Because surprise lit his golden eyes, she lifted his hand and held it in the slight valley between her breasts.

He gave her a deep, penetrating look, again lowering his hand to her abdomen. "Don't worry, I won't tell you you're getting a bit plump. Bea has fed you well since I've been away?"

Nothing could have prevented her tears as she whispered, "Oh, Morgan..."

His eyebrows met in a confused frown. "What troubles you, Anna? I was only teasing." Quickly his eyes lowered to her hand, which had again indelicately flicked his away. "A baby, Anna, are you carrying my baby?"

She pressed her trembling lips for a moment before lying, "I don't know."

His voice broke with excitement. "But are there any signs? Haven't you any idea? Women can generally tell these things. We shouldn't make love if you're..."

Anna quickly sat forward, clutching the sheet to her nakedness. "Don't jump to conclusions, Morgan." Her voice was brisk, almost rude. "It is possible that I am...there are signs." When she turned and looked at him, she had never seen such pride, such joy. She had never before seen a light such as now shone in his eyes. She died a little inside. The horrible thing she must do, because of her intense love for him, was becoming harder and harder. Easing into his arms, she said, "You're tired...get some sleep. We'll continue this discussion later."

Yes, he was tired, but he didn't think he would be able to sleep now. If Anna carried his child, he would be a father, and he could think of nothing he wanted more in the world...a precious little one to scamper among the hedgerow and the azaleas. A precious little daughter or son he could teach to ride a pony and love and cherish to the end of time.

Eventually he fell asleep and bathed in the beauty of a deliriously happy dream—a dream of becoming a father. He was only now beginning to realize what a treasure life truly was. He had a sweet, warm, loving wife, and soon, perhaps, a child of his own

Anna couldn't sleep. Alistair had devastated her happiness and her world. She couldn't sit back and watch harm come to Morgan. She couldn't see him chained like an animal and dragged away to die. There was only one thing she could do, and she wondered—dear God—she wondered where she would get the strength to do it.

For a little while, she watched Morgan sleep. How contented he looked, his eyes, which seemed to be closed in deep sleep, his features relaxed, healthy, bronzed by the past three weeks of traveling and being out-of-doors. His hair was drying in pale, golden waves; she touched it, enjoyed the silky coolness of it beneath her fingers. Her hand lowered to his gently pulsating chest, and in the next moment, his hand rose and fell to hers.

"You have been watching me," he said quietly.

"Yes...you're beautiful."

His laugh was gentle; he turned his head that he might look at her, at the innocent beauty beneath which lurked something terribly frustrating to her. He had sensed it since his return this afternoon. He sensed regret, yet he knew she loved him. He sensed melancholy, yet he knew she was happy. Was it the possibility of her pregnancy? Was this the deep sense of regret casting its shadow over their embracing bodies? Morgan didn't want to think so.

"Morgan?" He slightly moved against her. "I know you've politely declined in the past and you've always had your reasons, but will you take supper with us at the Big House this evening?"

"Anna..."

"Please...it will mean so much to me."

"Darling—I really don't care to be in the company of your brother. There is no purpose to be served in deliberately antagonizing him."

Anna's voice became ruefully quiet. "I say what goes on at Shadow Marsh—not Alistair—and if I want you to come to supper, then I should be able to extend that invitation."

Morgan's hand went to her back and simply rested there. "If it is important to you, I will take supper at the house."

She turned into his arms. "They already know, but I'm going to make it clear to the family that you are my husband."

Morgan quickly sat up and swung his feet to the floor. "What is the significance of this particular night?"

"I want them to know, there is no particular significance. Now...I'll have Lovey bring you lunch in a little while. You must be famished and I have things to attend this afternoon."

"What time should I show up for dinner?"

"Seven, will that be suitable?"

She seemed terribly stiff and unwilling to talk. Morgan thought she was annoyed with him, though he didn't know why. Moments ago they had been lost in the wonders of their passion. Now, it was almost as if they were strangers.

\* \* \*

Alistair was lounging in the parlor with a goblet of whiskey pressed tightly between his fingers. He heard the front door slam, and presently his sister entered the parlor, still attired in her somber black gown and dragging the wide-brimmed hat lazily at her side. He managed to favor her with a smile that was lewd, at best.

Anna knew he'd been drinking all afternoon. "What are you doing here, Alistair?"

"I live here," he reminded her. "So...how was your reunion with the overseer...your dear, dear husband? Hasn't forgotten how to satisfy you, eh, little sister?"

"You're a pig, Alistair." She had been determined to be resolute and firm, but now, facing him, she felt her chin slowly sink and weakness ease into her very being from head to toe. "We must talk."

Alistair slowly swirled the whiskey, watching the delicate waves barely skim the top of the glass. "Alistair is listening."

"When Morgan goes, I will go with him."

Immediately, Alistair was on his feet. "No, you won't, Anna. You'll stay right here where you belong, play the part of the jilted wife and play it well."

"I will go with Morgan," she insisted, tossing the hat to the divan. "You can't stop me."

Alistair pulled a small pouch containing several gold coins from his waistcoat pocket. He dropped it to the side table. "Be sensible, Anna. When you tell him to leave, you may give him this. From your ledgers, it appears he has not drawn his wages since December. We don't want to be in debt to our former overseer."

"How dare you pry into my personal ledgers!"

"Get rid of him today, Anna."

"No," she stated flatly. "If I cannot go with him, then he stays here."

Alistair thought she seemed resolute, as if she knew he was bluffing. There was nothing he could do to cause harm to Morgan York, except to put a bullet in his forehead...and he had certainly thought of that. But...perhaps Anna was the one bluffing? Perhaps she was playing that same game they had played as children–the game of war–the game of victory.

"You have waited too late to get rid of him," Anna whispered, keeping her eyes turned from him. "I carry his child."

Alistair's goblet fell to the floor, smashing, wetting the oriental carpet with the whiskey. Contempt glared in his eyes, but that contempt instantly became a rude snort. "Nice try, Anna. All you ever knew how to do was tend the old man's business and run this damned private empire of yours! Frankly, I wouldn't be surprised if you're bloody well barren!"

His words were cruel, and although they came from a man of Alistair's character, they still hurt. "No–it's true–Dr. Miller confirmed it. I carry Morgan's child."

She hadn't heard Alistair move, but she was suddenly being dragged by her arms toward him. She cried out from the firmness of his grip. "You get rid of that bastard York! Do you hear me? As for this–baby!–I don't believe you are capable of carrying a new life...you bloody cold bitch!" He turned away from her now, so that she would not see his eyes. Even as children, she had always been able to tell when he was lying, and he had vital lying to be doing right now. "Do you know where I went this afternoon, sister?"

"You've been right here...drinking."

"Wrong. I went into Jude's Landing. Telegraph messages are getting quite expensive–especially messages to Washington."

A sick, sinking feeling forced Anna to sit. "Tell me you did not send a telegram, Alistair. Tell me you didn't."

"Oh, but I did. I plan to be here when they come for him. By damn, but I'll get a great pleasure out of seeing him torn from your arms."

Tears filled Anna's eyes...the horrible picture formed again in her mind of a firing squad, Morgan's tender, loving eyes brutally covered by a blindfold...the horrible picture of his death. "You know that I love him. You know I'll send him away to protect him...may you be forever damned, Alistair. One day–one day–I'll get even with you for this!" She had screamed that last sentiment with frustration and rage. She knew that if she had a gun in her hand this very moment, she would kill him. There would be no remorse–no familial loyalty to twist her insides with guilt and regret. She hated her brother...she had never hated so deeply before.

A cynical smile twisted Alistair's face into more ugliness than it usually was. He walked out, and Anna heard the pounding of horse's hooves across the lawns. He was probably riding into Jude's Landing to see if an answer to his telegram had arrived.

She sat for a moment, tears streaming down her cheeks, her fingers digging madly into her temples. "Morgan...Morgan, what am I to do?" she whispered softly. Then she gallantly composed herself, rose from the divan and approached the window where Joby Cade was unloading the rose bushes.

"Joby, could you ask Mr. York to see me?"

Joby tipped his hat respectfully. "Right away, Missy."

Anna rushed to her bedchamber and freshened up, changed into a cooler gown and swept her hair back in ivory combs. Trembling, she touched the locket Morgan had given her and felt its coolness between her fingers. What could she do but send him away? If she told him the truth–everything–he would stay with her until the end. She remembered only too well the words he had spoken: *I will gladly face twelve rifles, as long as your lovely face is the last thing I see.* No–the truth would not make him see reason.

With Morgan far, far away from Shadow Marsh, Alistair's threats would be empty and he would no longer wield such control over her. Morgan would be safe, and Anna–she placed her hand lightly to her abdomen–oh, the baby, the dear little one. The prospect of its birth had so pleased Morgan. Now she would have to raise their child alone, a small, beautiful reminder of

Morgan for all the years to come. She *had* to send him away. With him gone, Alistair would merely be a wolf with its fangs removed.

When she returned to the parlor, she saw through the open window Morgan approaching the veranda on the painted stallion. The spirit of the beast, penned and without rider for three weeks, could scarcely be controlled, the quiver of its powerful muscles aching to break into a run. Morgan dismounted and his boot steps echoed across the veranda toward the door. Presently, Anna heard a short, pleasant exchange of words between Morgan and Bea, and he soon stood in the parlor entrance. He said nothing, but looked steadily at her, waiting for her to speak.

Anna was turned away from him. But she knew what had to be done could not be put off, not if she was to save his life. Gathering all the strength she had in the world, she turned to face him. A strange, sarcastic smile turned up the corners of her mouth. "You do answer a summons as dutifully as a spaniel, don't you, Morgan?" Her tone was cold, controlled; it took Morgan aback. "I'm tired of the game...*husband*," she continued, forcing a yawn. "I want you off Shadow Marsh land before nightfall."

"What the hell are you talking about, Anna? Just this morning you invited me to supper–now you want me to leave?"

Anna leaned against the trestle table, supporting her weight by placing her palms on the flat surface. "You asked me earlier if I was with child...yes, I am with child, and since I have a valid marriage certificate in hand that will validate the child, I no longer need you."

He said nothing at first; simply looked at her with a world of confusion and hurt reflecting in his eyes. "Anna..."

"Your days of milk and honey are over, Mr. York," she hissed, walking slowly and deliberately toward him. "A child grows within me. I have as good a chance of giving birth to a boy as a girl. I want you to leave. I no longer need you...hell, fire and damnation...if I have a damned girl, I'll just drag some fellow off the roadway, marry him and flop in his bed...no sense

170

in you hanging around and getting in my way every day."

His tone was measured and controlled. "I don't know what brought this on...but for God's sake, stop it! If this is a game, I am *not* laughing." He approached her, gripped her shoulders firmly and touched his lips briefly to hers. "Is Alistair making you do this?" She did not reply, but pressed her mouth into a thin line. "Deny that you want me, Anna...if you think you have something to prove..."

Unyielding as he again started to kiss her, she drew back and completely broke his grip. "Are you deaf? I want you to leave! Can't you understand what I'm saying? I am tired of you!"

"Anna, our love..."

"Our love was a joke from the beginning," she flung mockingly at him, her eyes brimming with tears. "You fool! You stupid, ignorant, blind fool! Why do you think I kept this marriage–this farce–a secret? Do you think I wanted people to know I married an overseer? An overseer, for heaven's sake! You're a servant...and worse than that–a murderer!"

The words flowed uncontrollably, feeding all the love she had for him into her heart and spewing it back in a flood of lies and degradations, like a vicious metamorphosis.

"Don't do this, Anna..." His stunned shock instantly became doubt, confusion...the greatest hurt he had ever felt "If it's because of Alistair..."

Anna knew if she did not continue, if she did not get this over with quickly, she would break down and tell him how much she loved him and why–God, why–it was necessary to drive him from Shadow Marsh.

"Look at you," she continued, wringing her hands. "Look at who you are, and look at me! All I ever wanted from you was a son to ensure Shadow Marsh for me! And you..." She flung her wrist at him. "You think I actually loved you? You can get out of my life and stop lapping at the wealth attached to Shadow Marsh–and my skirts! You're a gold digger...you make me sick!" Somewhere during her last harsh words, her hand had fallen to the small pouch of gold coins Alistair had dropped to the table just moments earlier. Her fingers closing tightly over it, she slung it out at Morgan. He did not try to catch it, but let it hit the floor at his feet. "Take that and go...payment in full for your stud service. And thank you for the jolly good times while we were getting the job done!" When he did not move to pick it up, but stood looking at her with a world of hurt in his eyes, she screamed, "Take it! Then get out of my sight! You have served your purpose here!"

Oh, his look...those eyes slowly hardening. She felt his hatred burn into her flesh as deeply as his love had warmed her just this morning. She loved him more than life itself, but right this minute a telegraph message was finding its way into hands that would began a terrible chain of events. She was prepared to lose him...she was not prepared to see him die.

Pain grabbed at Anna. She imagined an escort of federal troops riding up from Baton Rouge, chaining him like an animal and dragging him away. She imagined men in uniforms putting to death this kind, considerate man who had loved her, who had so generously filled the empty void in her life. He had taught her the wonderful passion she had thought would bind them together for all time. But she had never seen such hatred as she saw now. She had never even imagined him capable of it.

She would rather he hated her for all time, as long as he was safe, and far, far away from Shadow Marsh and Alistair St. Cyr's cruel vengeance. Only her love for him gave her the strength to remain quiet as he walked away without picking up the coin purse. Only her love kept her from flinging herself into his path and confessing this horrible deception.

As he quickly walked out to the veranda, mounted his horse and rode away, Anna knew that everything in the world she had lived for was gone. He rode straight through Cabin Row without speaking to a single person, and the timberline beyond the meadows soon swallowed him whole.

She would never forget the look in his eyes, the pain in her heart, or the tears that burned like fire on her cheeks as she sank slowly to the divan, overwhelmed by the love she had for Morgan—a love she had denied, and a love that would never again be returned to her.

Trembling, consciousness clinging to her by a thin thread, she touched her fingers to her lips and felt the warmth of his kisses lingering from their morning mingle with the bitter salt of her tears. His last kisses would have to last a lifetime.

Then she saw the angry set of Bea's features as she stood quietly in the frame of the doorway, and knew she had heard every word. Shamed...so very shamed...and knowing she would never see her beloved husband again, the darkness came, like a great billowing fog.

# Fifteen

*Tarrytown, New York, November, 1858*

The wheels of the coach clattered noisily on the cobblestones. The crisp, clean smell of winter was in the air. Multicolored leaves of greens and golds and browns drifted from the sycamores lining the avenue, cushioning the ground with a soft blanket.

Jarred Gunthar drew his fingers to his chin and settled back in the carriage. Rebecca sat beside him, silent for the first time since they'd left ship in New York Harbor. They were both tired and anxious to get back to the children and to the drudgeries of household and daily obligations and duties. Jarred, especially, was anxious to return to his post as a senior officer in the War Department.

Rebecca's gloved hand closed tenderly over Jarred's. "I know I've thanked you a thousand and one times, husband, but thank you again. It was a splendid trip. I will never, ever forget it."

Asking for a year's leave of absence, so that he and his wife might go on their first trip together since their marriage, had been the hardest thing Jarred had ever done. Since leaving West Point, he hadn't taken more than a few days' absence at any one time. He was a military man, and the Army was his life. He had never been able to put anything else first, including his family. They had even taken a back seat to his quests on behalf of Michael.

He had thrown his career to the wind, to devote a year to being a good husband to Rebecca and fulfill her greatest wish–to visit Europe. They had visited London, Versailles, Rome, Paris– had traveled from one exotic, enchanting European capital to another. And he had enjoyed every minute. He had, however, missed the children, who had remained at home with their grandparents.

174

"And I should thank you," he replied eventually, affectionately patting her hand, "for putting up with my sultry moods for twelve years and not divorcing me."

Rebecca gently touched her lips to his cheek, and dropped her head to his shoulder. "If a woman cannot stand with her husband through thick and thin, good and bad, then she should not plan to marry. You know, husband, this trip would never have been possible had it not been for Michael...and President Buchanan."

Jarred could think of Michael now, without the terrible, empty feeling. "I wouldn't go so far as to say that," he argued lightly.

"But it's true. When the President pardoned Michael your heart was set free to enjoy life. I should love him for it..."

"The President?"

"No, my foolish husband," she chided. "Your stepbrother, Michael."

Reminiscences flooded Jarred, but he shook them away before they might gain clarity and become a threat to his moment of happiness. He would not–could not–admit to Rebecca that, even this past year, accompanying her throughout Europe, not a day had passed that he hadn't thought of Michael.

At once, Jarred saw the large, rambling stone house of his parents come into view on the quiet little street of Tarrytown, his stepmother's immaculate gardens showing signs of the approaching winter. Jarred tapped his cane on the top of the coach, attracting the driver's attention. "Here, driver."

The coach pulled into a short circular drive and halted. Immediately, the quiet was replaced by the high-pitched, gleeful squeals of their eight-year-old daughter, Selma. He climbed down from the coach, and Selma threw herself into his arms. His son, George, who had left the house with her, bowed lightly in greeting and offered his hand to his mother, who was just climbing down from the coach. He seemed terribly grown up. Jarred was surprised. Just a year ago he had been a pouting, irritable, argumentative boy who had been a frustration to him.

The driver threw the bags down to Jarred one at a time, and

Jarred dropped them to the ground in a pile. He placed several coins in the driver's hand, and the coach slowly pulled away.

"Papa, I have so missed you," Selma cried in her smallest voice. She was wearing a new, crisp blue dress and white pinafore that Grandma must have made, and her loose, straight hair was pulled back in matching blue ribbons. When Selma saw his eyes dart over her small, immaculate form, she readily offered, "Grandma made it just for your homecoming, and fixed my hair, too."

Jarred knelt and embraced his daughter, and when George approached, drew him to his other shoulder. "And were my children good for Grandma and Grandpa?"

"I was very good," Selma replied in a small, serious voice. "But George was quite bad. He pushed my friend Victoria down in the street and skinned both her knees."

"I was trying to kiss her," George replied indulgently, rolling his eyes. "And that was six months ago." Jarred just smiled; indeed, his boy was growing up.

Hester Gunthar had given the children a few minutes alone with their parents, but could no longer restrain her enthusiasm and joy at seeing them. She walked briskly down the walkway, without her cane, hugging her shawl to her, and Jarred at once noticed that she appeared to have fully recovered from her stroke. The children must have been a healing balm for her.

Jarred hugged her tightly. "How happy I am to see you...and you looking so well!" He stepped back and favored her with a smile. "They said they were, but now you tell me the truth—were the children good?"

"They were angels," Hester replied.

Her speech, Jarred noticed, that had been affected by her stroke so many years ago, had greatly improved. "Where is Father?"

"He was called away to the city this morning due to vandalism at the shipping docks. He should return late this evening. We weren't sure just when you'd arrive. He'll be so disappointed that he wasn't here to greet you." When Rebecca approached and stood beside her, Hester embraced her stiffly, in her usual fashion. "Good to have you back, Becky."

She was the only person to ever call her *Becky,* and Rebecca felt she did it only because it displeased her immeasurably.

George helped his father with their bags, and Selma took her father's free hand as they walked toward the house. "Did you bring me something pretty from Europe, Papa?" Selma asked expectantly.

"Lots of pretty things."

"Oh..." Selma's small, rather tight features beamed. "When may I see them?"

"All in good time."

"We have new kittens, Papa," Selma announced.

"Do you?" Jarred hadn't remembered Selma being so talkative. She was usually a glum child and seldom made friends with other children. Today was the first Jarred had heard of a friend named Victoria. Perhaps Rebecca kept too tight a rein on the children when he was away. "Grandma's old cat had kittens?" he questioned absently. "This late in the year?"

"Four of them, Papa. Grandpa said they would make a tasty stew, but," she shook her head. "I think he was teasing me. Grandma said I could take one home. Oh, can I, Papa–maybe two of them?"

"We'll see," Jarred laughed quietly. "We'll have to talk to your Mama about that."

"Mama's crotchety," Selma whispered up to him.

"And where, young lady, did you hear that?"

"Don't you remember, Papa? You said so yourself."

Laughing again, Jarred's finger came up to his lips. "Shh–mustn't tell your mama I said that."

They were in the parlor where a bright fire burned in the hearth. Jarred looked around, at the massive mahogany secretary where he and his brothers had once hidden their small treasures from one another, at the Chippendale side chair his father had burned many years ago with the droppings from his pipe, at the French rococo fire screen set off to the side, at warm gray carpets and crocheted doilies beneath every porcelain ornament

177

and silver bowl. How he'd missed this handsome old house where memories flowed like wine.

Jarred picked up a familiar scent, his stepmother's clam pie baking in the oven. It was good being home in Tarrytown again. Tomorrow morning they would return to their own modest house on the Hudson.

Then he saw the letter addressed to Colonel Jarred Gunthar, dated several months ago, from his aide, Captain Hundley. He picked it up, but sat it back down at once. "Whatever this is, it can't be important after all this time." He began unfastening the buttons of his coat.

"Aren't you going to open it?" Rebecca questioned.

"Later," Jarred replied. "Right now..." He dropped his coat and opened his arms. "I am going to get reacquainted with my children."

Selma threw herself into his arms, but George, at nine, considered himself a little man and approached with dignity. Jarred saw a lot of his father in the boy, aloof, somewhat withdrawn–secretive. Then Selma drew away and begged excitedly, "Can I bring the kittens, Papa?"

"You bring the kittens."

Pride swelled in his heart as he watched Selma bounce away. She was his daughter, and he thought her pretty, but her mother's plainness was evident in her features and the limp, brown hair that even Grandma's curling iron couldn't improve.

Throughout the afternoon, Selma chatted incessantly while George constantly chastised her for it. But both children asked a multitude of questions about Europe and seemed to be satisfied with the answers given by their parents. Selma, because her mother had said she couldn't have a kitten, much less two, spent the afternoon selling her on their virtues. Finally, in desperation, she reminded her mother about the mice in the pantry.

"She's got you there, Rebecca," Jarred interjected with a humorous chuckle. "It might be nice to have a cat–or two– around."

Rebecca had always believed in firmness with the children, and didn't want to give in. But there were times her determination melted a little–and there were, indeed, mice in the pantry. "Oh, very well–a male kitten. It must be a male."

"There are two males, Mama–a matching pair," she announced, holding up the two white kittens.

"Very well–you may have the two of them."

Selma leaped for joy, rushing to her grandmother to whisper something in her ear. A smile touched Hester's face as she put her arms around Selma and sealed their secret with a kiss on her forehead.

While Rebecca and Hester prepared the evening meal, the children played in the back pantry with the kittens. Jarred sat for a moment in silence and read the paper. He had kept abreast of the news, even while he was in Europe. The daily accounts of the tensions between the North and South over the issue of slavery troubled him. Neither was willing to give an inch and he wondered where it would lead. Considering the passions of the South, war was certainly a possibility, and probably inevitable. Hotheaded northern abolitionists, like John Brown, who pillaged and murdered in the name of God, only added fuel to the flames.

Jarred was very tired. He rested his head back against the soft cushion of the chair and closed his eyes for a moment. These past ten months of traveling, two of which had been spent aboard ship, had been very exhausting.

"Jarred! Jarred, boy!" The front door slammed soundly, and the voice of his father echoed through the parlor. Jarred lurched forward, coming to his feet just as his father entered from the foyer. The elder Gunthar removed his coat while he crossed the room and threw it to a chair. He roughly embraced his son. "Good to have you home, boy!"

He had always called him *boy*, and Jarred thought that, perhaps, it was no longer appropriate. But he wouldn't hurt his father's feelings for anything. "Good to be home, Father," he replied fondly, returning the firm embrace.

Hester and Rebecca entered from the kitchen, fond greetings were shared, and Hester announced that dinner was being put on the table. During the course of the meal, Mr. Gunthar asked as many questions as had the children earlier in the day. Jarred was glad of the three weeks he still had to spend with his family before he would report to Washington.

After dinner, when the children were tucked into their beds, the four of them gathered in the parlor to share Mr. Gunthar's nightly sherry. They lifted their glasses in a toast to good tidings. Then Jarred's father noticed the unopened letter on the mantel. "You haven't opened that, son?"

"After this length of time, Father, it cannot be that important."

Its contents had been a source of curiosity to the Gunthars since its arrival, but at Hester's insistence he had left it alone. Jarred readily saw his father's disappointment. "Very well, Father. I'll open it now." Jarred took the letter and returned to his chair. He sat down and got comfortable before breaking the seal put there months ago by his aide. His eyes moved dutifully over the words and with his brows pinched worriedly, sat forward in his chair and continued to read. His hands began to tremble; a lump caught in his throat like a cannon, smothering him, compelling him to raise his hand and force it down that he might breathe again. He stood and silently approached the mantel. When he turned back to his Father, there was a strange calmness in his features as he looked at them.

"This message is from my aide, Captain Hundley," he quietly began. "I would like to read it to you, if you don't mind. Please...call in the family." The elder Gunthar did so, and soon, Hester, Rebecca and the children joined them. "Father...Mother...Rebecca and children, just sit for a moment and indulge me." When they had seated, the children on the floor at their mother's feet, Jarred began to read:

*Colonel Gunthar: May this short message reach you before you sail for Europe. I am informed this day that on December fourteenth, a telegraph message was received at the War Department from a gentleman in the state of Louisiana, attempting to collect a reward for the capture of your stepbrother, Captain Michael George Fielding. The War Department was advised that Captain Fielding, under the assumed name of Morgan York, was working as an overseer on a plantation called Shadow Marsh. Knowing of your interest, I attempted to delay a return reply until you could be contacted. I was, however, too late. The sender was informed that Captain Fielding was no longer a fugitive and had been granted a full pardon by the President. I attempted to obtain a copy of the original telegraph message, but to this date it has not been located. You might wish to see me for further information.*

When Jarred dropped the message to the mantel, the elder Gunthar, without speaking or betraying his feelings about the news, arose and left the room. He hadn't mentioned Michael in years, and Jarred knew he had never forgiven him for killing John. He had relayed the horrid details to him one day a few years ago, when he had finally been in a mood to hear it, but still, he was angry and unforgiving of Michael. John kept the hope alive that one day he would understand that Michael did what the rest of them were too cowardly to do...that day he had shown the greatest love a brother could have for another.

Michael's mother, Hester, put her hand to her mouth and her eyes filled with tears. Rebecca's arm went around her shoulders, and she touched the tiniest kiss to the elder woman's temple. Rebecca was a little angry with Jarred for ruining their day with this new information, and irritated with Michael for continuing to pop into their lives.

"I knew he was alive," Hester said quietly. "I always knew my dear son was alive."

Jarred said nothing, but merely dropped his eyes. He, too, had known it...in his heart. He looked up at Rebecca, giving him a strange, questioning look. "No, Rebecca," he assured in a soft voice. "I will not let Michael ruin our lives...not any longer. Not as I did in the past. I am happy he is alive, and I hope he is content. I hope this mysterious bounty collector, this *gentleman*, had the good graces to inform him of his pardon." Jarred drew himself up firmly. "I'll see Hundley soon. Perhaps he will have obtained more information, and I. . ." He'd been about to say that he might contact Michael, but Rebecca would not want to hear it.

Memories rushed through Jarred's mind–the happiness of

their brotherhood–he, John and Michael, brothers who loved each other. He wanted to know more about Michael, how long he'd been an overseer, wielding authority over people deprived of their rights as human beings. He wondered where he'd been all these years, or had he been there, on this Shadow Marsh Plantation all along? If only he could be assured that he knew about his pardon, so that he could stop running, perhaps return home to Tarrytown...be Michael George Fielding again...

Had he made a good life for himself in Louisiana? Was he happy? Married? Jarred felt the obsession filling him once again. Did Michael have children of his own?

* * *

Yes, Michael had a son–a strong, healthy son whose mother was too exhausted to hold him in her arms. He had been born shortly after the midnight hour on the 16th of November, following a long labor. Right now, because of her own self-neglect these past few months, Anna's life held on by a very fine thread.

She had made up her mind the moment Morgan had ridden away that there was no more purpose to her life. Even the child growing inside her had not been able to replace the happiness she had lost. Through the months of her pregnancy she had grown listless, had ignored her ledgers and her duties to Shadow Marsh, and had scarcely eaten enough to maintain life. Every day she had watched out the parlor window, waiting for the blue-uniformed soldiers to come and take Morgan away. But they had never arrived.

Now, Morgan was gone. All that stood before her was a vacant future, and a child who would be better off without her. Even Alistair's vicious slurs and insults, which had begun the moment her pregnancy could no longer be hidden, had not been able to move her. She was emotionless. She hadn't wept since the day Morgan had left.

She'd tried not to think about him, or to remember the hurt flooding his golden eyes as she had viciously attacked him with lies and degradations. But she could not forget their love, and the warm embrace of his arms.

Bea had been cool to her these many months, because she was the only one who had heard what she said to Morgan that day he had left. She hadn't asked for explanations, and Anna hadn't offered any. She hardly even smiled for Anna, and in her sorrow, Anna had scarcely noticed. But now, Bea, holding her newborn son, approached the bed where she lay. Her words were soft and affectionate. "What you goin' to name him, precious?"

"Michael," Anna responded weakly. "His name is Michael George."

"Mighty purty 'nough," Bea replied. She had avoided questioning Anna's actions these past few months but now, looking down at her pale, translucent skin, her eyes almost devoid of life–eyes that had once been vivid, round and beautiful–all the questions rose like a tidal wave. But only one stood foremost in her mind. "Lawd, Jesus, Miss Anna, when Bea knowed you loved him with all yo' heart and all yo' soul–why'd you send yo' man away?"

Anna drew a weak, trembling breath, her eyes shutting briefly. When she again looked to Bea, she replied quietly, "It was because I love him–with all my heart and all my soul. She attempted to close her eyes against the rush of tears flooding them, the first she had shed since that horrible day. "Because I will always love him, Bea...he was my every reason for living."

"This li'l fella...he needs to be yo' reason now." As for Anna's confession, Bea mumbled her lack of understanding. As she moved away from the bed, carrying Michael close to her bosom, she hoped that Anna would drift off to sleep and dream away her sadness.

For Anna, the voices slowly drifted away, like a gentle wind through the timberline far, far away. A deep silence surrounded her, and she felt her mind become an empty, void nothingness–a swirling black vortex in which the only sound was her faintly thumping heartbeat, slowly, slowly becoming fainter. She waited for it to cease, but it refused, like a naughty, defiant child.

Then in the swirling darkness a form began to take shape–misshapen at first, but slowly gaining depth and dimension. A man stood there, his hair pale and golden, his eyes about to burst into flame. She felt her body rise, weightless, an empty shell, drawn like a magnet toward him, toward the intense heat of his very being and the amber fire in his eyes that slowly turned to ice. She reached out to embrace him, to draw strength from his love and adoration and renew her own deteriorating strength, but her arms met only space–empty, sterile space–and she awoke screaming.

Hours had passed in those few moments of dreaming. Bea drew her tightly into her arms. Sweat streamed from Anna's face, plastering listless black hair to her neck and shoulders. "Bea–Bea–I don't want to live without him."

Anna sobbed brokenly against the shoulder of her dear friend. Bea gently rocked her, as she had so many times in Anna's childhood. Bea saw that Anna was killing herself with grief...a grief she kept bottled up inside her, a lethal poison that drew the strength from her body as viciously as bloodsucking leeches.

* * *

Tylas Miller had chosen to stay following the birth to be sure that Anna would be all right. He slumped lazily in a chair before the hearth, his hand drawn and pressed firmly against his cheek. He was too exhausted to think about returning to Jude's Landing. He had done everything possible for Anna; he had brought a strong, healthy boy into the world, but he was at a loss as to how to help Anna. She had survived the birth, and he felt sure that, under different circumstances, she would completely recover. But he could not give her a reason to live. That, alone, left her a shell, dying just as surely as if a dagger had been driven deeply into her heart.

"You're worried that she might die, aren't you?"

Startled, Tylas Miller looked around at Violet, her hands folded gently in front of her. Since her marriage to Wren Wellington in April–a fine affair held on the grounds of Shadow Marsh with the backdrop of azaleas and blooming dogwoods–Violet had gained a few pounds, not one of which was a son or daughter for Wren Wellington. Even being a doctor and knowing better, Tylas often wondered if nasty, disagreeable personalities had the tendency to make a woman barren.

"No–I hope not," Tylas eventually replied.

Violet approached, sitting in the chair beside Tylas. She stared ahead and her eyes followed the dance of the flames in the hearth. "She's grieving for him–her husband," Violet said. "And I know where he is." No emotion moved Violet and her tone did not change. "I even know why Anna sent him away. Alistair told me last night when he'd had too much to drink. He came to Hopewell asking for money."

"Where is Mr. York, Violet?" Tylas asked.

Violet shrugged her shoulders. "I won't tell you, of course. I love Anna, really I do, but if she dies..." Violet's mouth pressed into a thin, hard line. "If she dies, my husband will stop loving her."

Tylas rose, disgusted, turning to the fireplace and keeping his voice calm. "You would see her die? Your own cousin whose family took you in when your parents died?"

"Of course...I love my husband–and one day he will love me as he has loved Anna. So, I will not tell you were her husband is."

"But you *will* tell *me*!" The sharp voice reverberated from the parlor entrance. Violet rose quickly to face Wren. "You will tell me where he is, and you will tell me now!"

Violet thought Wren had gone upstairs to see Anna, and was shocked to see him standing there. Her hands clenched into fists and anger rose, quickening her heartbeat. "Why? So you can rush after him, bring him home and pray to God that Anna will live? You will sacrifice her to another man, just so long as she lives?"

"Yes," he replied, approaching a wife he had never loved, and probably never would.

"You could have the decency to deny that you love her," Violet cried. "I am your wife, Wren!"

Wren bowed stiffly to Tylas Miller, standing uncomfortably nearby and unaware how to exit the room gracefully. He was glad to leave now. When he had departed,

Wren continued, "I will not deny that I love Anna, Violet, that I have always loved her. When you and I married, you knew that I loved her. Still, I vowed to be a good, faithful husband. I could never have Anna–she made that perfectly clear–and you are my wife now. Don't force me to change that."

Violet gasped in horror. "You–you would divorce me?"

The threat had the impact he had hoped for. "Will you tell me where Morgan York is?"

"Yes, of course I will."

"Then the answer to your question is, no. I will not divorce you. But I will tell you this now, Violet, that I will never forgive you for this."

Violet sank deeply into the plush cushions of a chair.

# Sixteen

No place on earth matched the squalor of the half-mile stretch from the Natchez docks along the Mississippi, where barges joined by half-rotted wood planks, shacks and lean-to's a couple of hundred yards beneath the bluffs overlooked the Mighty Mississippi River. The criminal element of Natchez, a quaint little city of beautiful mansions and splendid architecture, conducted all manners of abomination in hundreds of taverns, whore-barges, dog pits, and gambling houses that were the scourge of humanity and the sewer of the South. The police had long ago ceased to investigate the crimes and depravities in this dangerous, repulsive place.

Natchez-Under-The-Hill bred the vermin of the human race, and destroyed it just as quickly.

Even with a knife in his boot, a pistol in his holster, and a rifle slung over his shoulder, Morgan York walked cautiously along the narrow walkway. Hearing a sound from the darkness between two shacks, Morgan instinctively walked faster, the click of his boots scarcely heard above the noise of the whore-barges, the thick, masculine laughter, and the music one might expect to hear in the most elegant of Natchez ballrooms.

Morgan turned left, crossed a narrow plank, and stood on the deck of a red painted whore-barge lit by a hundred oriental lanterns. A black waiter standing at the entrance took his weapons–with the exceptions of a knife and small derringer Morgan didn't admit he carried–and allowed him to enter. He was scarcely able to see through the pipe smoke of a dozen men lounging on red satin couches, attended by immaculately dressed black waiters with trays of champagne and delicate crystal goblets. Around him, voluptuous women with painted eyes, their bodies scarcely covered by scant chemises in varying colors, met every need and fancy of the men of Natchez. Some of those men undoubtedly had journeyed upriver from New Orleans to buy the sexual services of the women whose reputations were known from the Gulf to St. Louis.

A sultry woman approached, put her arms around Morgan's neck and attempted to pull his mouth down to hers. Politely, he removed her arms. "I wish to speak to the barge *madame*."

"Don't you like me, pretty boy?"

Instinctively, drawn to her comely, feminine face, he started to smile, but caught himself. He had sworn six months ago, with the wound inside still festering, that he would never again leave himself vulnerable to a beautiful woman. "The barge madame, if you don't mind."

Sulking, the dark-haired woman turned and shouted, "Minette, he wishes to see you," then threw herself heavily onto a black velvet divan, pouting prettily as she watched Morgan.

The thin, dark-clad woman who approached might have been forty, and she scarcely fit the image of her occupation. Until she spoke, Morgan almost envisioned her as someone's mother. "What do you want?" she asked in a coarse, husky, noticeably male voice.

It was the first time Morgan had ever seen a man dressed as a woman, and dressed as one very convincingly so. Though it tickled at the side of his mouth, he forced himself not to smile. "I wish to see a man named Graz–a black man who I understand lives aboard your barge."

"About what?"

"Personal business."

The coarse *woman* laughed. "Sure–personal business," and called out, "Graz...Graz, there is a gentleman to see you."

Within moments, a bare-chested man wearing loose silk trousers gathered at his ankles exited a small, dark gaming room at the rear of the barge. He was bald and wore a gold loop in his left ear. As he approached in the half light of the red and gold parlor, Morgan noticed his eyes, one remarkably blue, and the other white and obviously sightless.

He stood before Morgan with his arms crossed and his feet slightly apart. "You want to see me?"

"If you're Graz, yes, I do." Morgan, at six feet-two inches, was seldom intimidated by the size of a man. But he felt intimidated by this one. If he'd been a slave, he'd have brought a fetching price, regardless of the missing eye. He was indomitable...frightening.

"I am Graz. What do you want?"

"May we speak alone?"

Graz's large, burly hand went out with unexpected grace, motioning Morgan to a table off in a corner. When they were seated, Graz snapped his fingers and one of the black waiters brought a tray with champagne. A glass was poured for both of them. "Now, you have sought out Graz. He wishes to know what you want?"

"I work for a man named Pettigrew–owns a line of riverboats–"

"I know of him. Even here..." Graze motioned with his right hand. "This Pettigrew is spoken highly of. He treats all men–black and white–as equals. That is a good trait in a man, is it not?" He smiled, revealing straight white teeth. "So what does the good Mr. Pettigrew want of Graz?"

"He is in need of a dealer in the game room aboard the *Gulf Princess*. He has heard you're the best."

Graz laughed heartily, an act that made the blood vessels rise on his thick forehead. "Mr. Pettigrew is right–I am the best. But I deal here, and I am paid ten percent of the take of the table."

"Pettigrew will pay you fifteen percent."

"Will he indeed?"

Morgan saw by the humor in the black man's good eye that a session of bargaining was inevitable. He was sure Graz would want to find out how badly Pettigrew wanted him. Morgan kicked back and rested his booted foot across his knee. He would have to be patient–he had promised Pettigrew he would employ every possible tactic to hire Graz away from the barge.

"Do you arm wrestle?" Graz asked.

Pettigrew had warned Morgan to expect a challenge of some sort, and to consider it a compliment. "I've engaged in a few bouts in the past," he confessed.

"Tell you what, Mr....?"

"Morgan will do."

"Okay, Mr. *Morgan-will-do*...one bout. You win, Graz goes to work for your Mr. Pettigrew for fifteen percent of the table's take. In addition..." His face lowered to his hand and came back up, proudly displaying the empty socket that had held the glass eye now rolling across the table toward Morgan. "You may have this–it is very valuable." Morgan kept it from rolling off the table. "If I win, I will go to work for your Mr. Pettigrew for twenty percent of the table's take, keep my glass eye, and you will personally polish my boots for a month."

A smile turned up the corners of Morgan's mouth. Casually he stood, removed his coat, and dropped it across the back of the chair. "You've got a deal. Only..." Either way, Graz would hire on board the *Gulf Princess*. Morgan had nothing to lose in accepting his challenge except, perhaps, his pride. He returned to his seat and rolled the glass eye back across the table. "You keep this and, instead, I'll take ten minutes alone with a woman of my choice–at your expense–and with your personal assurance that I won't end up with a knife in my back."

"Ten minutes! That is hardly enough time to drop your britches!" Graz laughed again and popped the eye back into the socket. "Very well. Ten minutes, your choice, no knife."

Morgan rolled his shirt sleeve up to his elbow. Graz leaned toward him, to meet Morgan's arm, which was taking its position on the table. Their hands entwined in an iron grip and their eyes met across the table.

"You ready, Mr. Morgan-will-do?"

His amber eyes narrow and unblinking, Morgan nodded. Simultaneously, their arms hardened into tight knots of muscles. Their eyes continued to hold one another across their tightly joined hands. The black man was strong. Morgan wanted to prove he was stronger, but he knew immediately that this would be a match such as he had never before faced. Graz grunted, trying to dislodge the iron hardness of Morgan's elbow joint. The grunt drew the attention of a young dandy nearby.

"Hey, boys and girls...we're missing a battle!"

His voice was high-pitched and feminine. Beyond the bald head of the man named Graz, Morgan watched his approach, his short, effeminate footsteps and the fluttering of sickly white hands. He'd heard of men like this...ah! Graz almost caught him off guard. Morgan's forearm jerked in Graz's direction. He would have to be more alert and concentrate on the match. Pettigrew would not be happy having to pay him twenty percent of the table's take.

With a small grunt of his own, Morgan's forearm again went tight and straight. Sweat broke out on his forehead. He gritted his teeth. Around them, the half-naked women and immaculately dressed gentlemen urged them on. But Morgan would not allow his gaze to move from the sharp, humored face across from him.

For half an hour neither man gave an inch. Morgan's elbow hurt so badly he could scarcely bear the pain, and he was sure Graz was feeling the same effects. The strain showed in both their faces–the blood vessels in Graz's forehead looked as though they'd explode. Morgan could hardly see through the sweat streaming across his eyes.

Graz had never faced such a fierce opponent...especially in a white man. As he stared across their tightly locked fists and felt the brutal ache in his arm and shoulder that made defeat inevitable, he knew he would walk away with tremendous respect for this white man. He would, after all, bear the distinction of being the only man to beat him at this contest of strength. His victory was inevitable. Graz didn't think he could hold out much longer.

His thoughts had taken him off guard. With a mighty grunt, Morgan gathered an army of strength, and it was enough to send Graz's knuckles painfully into the table. With a loud, boisterous cheer and firm pats on the back, the crowd quickly dwindled away.

Graz rubbed the soreness out of his hand and arm. "For a white man, you're not half bad," Graz said evenly, and even with a tinge of respect. He outstretched his hand, which Morgan took

191

at once. "I keep my promise. Take any woman you want–my courtesies." Graz threw him a gold coin. "That should be enough."

Morgan leaned back for a moment and his amber eyes scrutinized the parlor where the men and their whores were resuming their positions on the couches. Waiters were returning to the duties they had left to watch the arm wrestling. Morgan spied the dark-haired woman who had initially greeted him, sitting alone, the only one who had not watched the match. She had pulled her red and black gown up to her thighs and sat with her legs apart, one bare foot across her knee. She was trying very hard–too hard, in fact–to look bored.

Approaching her, Morgan threw the five-dollar gold piece to her. "You'll do...that man," he motioned toward Graz, "has paid you."

"I heard," she replied indulgently, rising, slipping the coin into the bodice of her gown. "I'm surprised you would ask for me–since I am not the barge *madame*," she added mockingly. She moved toward a back room that was large enough only for the bed it contained. When Morgan entered, she pulled the curtain, to allow them some degree of privacy. "My name is Sugar," she said, unfastening the stays of her bodice. "But you can call me Sug."

He did not acknowledge her introduction. "Don't bother with the gown. Just remove anything you're wearing beneath your skirts and bend over the bed."

With an intolerant look, she obeyed his command. She had met all kinds of men in the four months she'd been on Minette Boudreau's whore-barge, and she had learned to expect anything. Men who did not want to be face to face during sex were usually pining for a lost–or dead–wife or lover.

Morgan approached and unbuckled his trousers and slid them down just enough to expose his groin. He quickly prepared to enter her. "Animal," Sugar growled. "Why do men want to make love so quickly?"

"I am not making love to you...Sugar. I am having sex with you. That is what I paid you for." Morgan gritted his teeth, sharpening the line of his jaw. Aboard the *Gulf Princess*, he had kept to himself, unlike the polite, well-mannered man Mr. Pettigrew had met in New Orleans, whose wedding he had attended with Louvenia Etienne. Morgan worked daily on the riverboat account ledgers, filed receipts, ran errands, and stayed away from the gaming rooms and riverboat guests. It had been seven months since he'd been with a woman, and he felt the ache of abstinence in his groin.

He pushed hard, plunging into Sugar's moist warmth. She felt good after so long without feeling the heat of a woman's body. Pulling her tight against his hips, he kept a rhythm that would bring him to fulfillment at his pace—and, he imagined, with time to spare in those ten minutes.

Sugar had been with many men—wealthy, slobbering, conventionally boring men, but she had never felt like this. This man treated her as commonly as a bitch dog, yet she did not find it distasteful. Morgan's pace became aggressive, and tears moistened her eyes—tears caused by this cruel, detached and enjoyable violation of her body. She did not like emotional attachments of any kind—especially to the men who paid for her body—but she would love to be facing this very unhappy man when he possessed her, fully and completely. Perhaps it was just that he was tall and slim and oh, so handsome—not like the dottering pigs who customarily paid for her services.

When he had satisfied himself, Morgan hastily withdrew from her, slapped her firmly on her thigh and pulled her skirts down over her body. Without giving her a second glance, he pulled up his trousers, righted his appearance and prepared to leave.

"Mister..." He paused, half turned toward the feminine voice attempting to disguise delight behind loathing and disgust. "You must have loved her very much—the woman who left you cruel and bitter and hating all women?"

"Why do you say that? Did I hurt you?"

"No—a woman just knows these things."

Slowly, Morgan eased his hat to his head, flipping it back from his forehead. He didn't need any reminders from a whore.

"If you expected thanks, then...thanks. But you didn't seem to be in any pain, so I don't know why you would think I am cruel and bitter. Not that I care what you think–Sugar."

Morgan's smile wasn't really a smile as he backed into the red and gold parlor. Graz awaited him. When Morgan approached, Graz grinned widely and slapped him on the shoulder. "You did not take your full ten minutes. I should collect a refund from our Miss Sugar."

"Forget it," Morgan replied tonelessly. "Let's get out of here."

The woman had awakened a flood of memories in Morgan. It was the first time he'd stopped to realize that he did, indeed, find women–all women–intolerable, self-serving beasts, their cruelty and greed sickening, the way they used men to satisfy their own wants and desires, then cast off the men like so much rubbish. Morgan had made up his mind to use all women as he had been used, with complete, unadulterated abandon. They would get the respect from him that he had gotten from women like Anna Rose St. Cyr. She had done this to him. How proud she would be if she knew.

Still, Morgan felt a little guilty that he hadn't been nicer to Sugar. It wasn't her fault his wife was a conniving bitch.

He sat at a table and waited for Graz to pack his few personal belongings into a satchel. Graz had pulled on a white long-sleeved shirt, leather vest, and black boots into which he'd tucked the silk pants. It was a strange combination of attire, but Morgan couldn't imagine any sensible man pointing it out to him.

When they had stepped outside where Morgan collected his weapons, the barge *madame*, Minette, leaning heavily on a wealthy, bearded patron, drew bony male hands to her hips and, with a smile, said to Graz, "Finally got a better offer, did you–you ungrateful heathen?" There was no anger behind the husky voice.

Graz, too, smiled. "Did," he replied shortly.

"Put the octoroon on the gaming table?"

"Did," Graz again replied.

"Good luck to you then." When Graz turned away, Minette called to him, "My friend—you know where I am when you need me."

Returning to the arms of the fat man, Minette drew her leg up tight against his thigh. As Morgan and Graz crossed the plank to the walkway, the nervous patron was emptying a small brown purse into Minette's waiting hand.

"I have been with Minette a long time," Graz volunteered the information to Morgan. "Even when she was trying to be a man." When Morgan did not reply, he asked, "Are you not curious as to how long?"

"No."

"Graz will tell you anyway. I have been with Minette since she bought me from my master—when she was a he-and gave me my freedom." Graz sighed. "You do not talk much, do you, Mr. Morgan-will-do?"

"No."

"Graz will talk to you then. Know what happened to Graz's eye?"

"No, and don't care."

"My master dug it out with a knife. He was my father and could not bear the reminder in my blue eyes every time he looked at me. He was drunk and passed out, leaving one good eye with which I could continue to view the cruelties of the world. I was only eight years old at the time...now tell me, Mr. Morgan-will-do, why a man as well spoken as you keeps ledgers aboard a riverboat?"

"It's an honest living."

As they reached the mud path leading up to the bluffs, Morgan paused and lit a cigarette he'd rolled earlier and stuck into his jacket pocket. He had rested his rifle against a boulder. As cigarette smoke dissipated in the darkness of the midnight hour, he picked up the rifle and started up the steep path, slicked by a light rain earlier in the evening. He said nothing to Graz, who walked closely behind him. Halfway up the path, they passed a man and woman, hidden back in the shadows, their presence betrayed only by the rustle of skirts and slobbering masculine grunts.

At the top of the bluffs, Morgan again paused, crushed the cigarette butt into the mud with his heel, and slowly started in the opposite direction from the shipping docks where the *Gulf Princess* was moored. "Where you going?" Graz queried.

"To visit a friend."

"Nothing this way but a livery and whore houses. Your friend live in one of them?"

"One of them," Morgan replied noncommittally. "You go on to the *Gulf Princess* and make yourself known to Mr. Pettigrew."

"Think I will come with you to visit this friend. Do you mind?"

"Come on then." Morgan continued his walk, his rifle resting lazily on his shoulder, past the shanty houses adjoining a large livery. He and Graz entered the stable, lit only by a lantern hanging from a hook in the rafters. Through the semi-darkness, Amigo, his stallion, watched the slow approach of two men, his head lifted, and his nostrils flaring as he cautiously sniffed the air. Off in a corner the sleeping livery boy stirred, but Morgan said, "It's only me, Adam. Go back to sleep."

Immediate recognition calmed the big horse. Morgan approached and firmly patted the diamond of white hair between his dark eyes. "So, Amigo, you have missed me, eh? The lad gave you some oats?"

"Sho' did, Massa Morgan," drifted sleepily from the dark corner.

Graz approached. Again, the stallion drew back cautiously. "Fine animal. Where'd you get him?"

"Stole him."

"Horse thieves are generally hung."

"I got worse than hanged," Morgan replied absently, giving the horse a final pat. "Now–let's see Pettigrew before he thinks I've failed at my mission."

Graz fell into step beside Morgan. "I think I'm going to like you, white man."

"Why?" The tone of Morgan's voice did not change.

"Do not rightly know. You are a strange one, not much taken to words. Maybe that's what I like. And—hell-any man beat me in arm wrestling and steal a horse—a fine horse at that—I reckon I can stand to know him."

Morgan half smiled, continuing to walk beside Graz in the direction of the Natchez docks. The *Gulf Princess* would depart in three days' time for St. Louis, Missouri. Morgan looked forward to the trip—and the extra distance he would be from the woman at Shadow Marsh who was, unfortunately, his *loving* wife.

For a little while, as they walked along the bluffs toward the docks, the dark night bathed in the warm, golden glow of lanterns on ramshackle porches, Morgan thought back over the past seven months. He had left Shadow Marsh stunned, hurt—full of anger and resentment. But today, he felt only pity for Anna Rose. Sensibly, he should hate her; he had even tried to convince himself that he did. But his thoughts of her brought the ache of desire. She held on to him with her vicious pincers just as surely as if she stood beside him, branding his flesh with the searing passion that had been his for the taking. He wanted to hate her, yet he knew that if she stood before him, this very minute, he would not hesitate to take him in his arms and possess her.

Frustrated with himself, Morgan drew a long, deep breath of the rancid smell of the Mississippi River caught on the passing wind. He heard laughter aboard the riverboat, growing in intensity as they approached and stepped onto the cluttered docks.

"How long have you worked for Pettigrew?"

Graz's question snapped Morgan from his thoughts. "Half a year, give or take." Morgan paused, pulling his hat down on his forehead. "You may be bloody damned good at the gaming tables, but you bloody damned well talk too much."

Graz laughed. "My sire removed my eye, not my tongue." Curiosity about the man who walked beside him filled Graz. "A woman made you like this, eh?"

"What the hell are you talking about?"

"Your faraway look—a look that lingers between hatred and

fond memories–only a woman can give a man this look."

Morgan halted, turned toward Graz, and lowered his rifle from his shoulder. His eyes narrowed. "You have been prying into my life ever since we left the barge," Morgan said in a husky voice laced with anger. "I don't like answering questions."

Graz shrugged carelessly, as if it didn't matter one way or another. "But Graz likes asking them, even when it stirs a man to anger."

Morgan tried to keep a good head on that anger, but Graz's wide smile erased his moment of disdain.

* * *

Pettigrew stood at the stern, watching Morgan and the black man. He liked Morgan. Running into him here in Natchez had been a strange quirk of fate. He had readily hired him on board the *Gulf Princess*, and opened his private livery to his beloved horse without charge. He'd asked no questions about why he left Shadow Marsh and his new wife. But he'd gotten all the answers from Louvenia Etienne, in whom Morgan had confided a few weeks ago. Hiram Pettigrew still could not believe that Etienne's beloved Anna Rose was capable of such deception. She had seemed a kind, sensitive young woman, and had gazed at Morgan with love and adoration during their wedding ceremony. What an actress she must have been. This soft-spoken man slowly approaching him could hardly have deserved her deception and cruelty.

Pettigrew knew only that Morgan wanted to be informed when Anna's baby–his baby–was born. If he harbored resentment, and he surely must, he had kept it very well hidden. Pettigrew had noticed, in Morgan's conversations with Louvenia Etienne, he had spoken fondly of Anna, without malice. Pettigrew knew that Morgan wished Louvenia did not keep in contact with Violet, who was a notorious gossip and troublemaker. He wasn't sure what Louvenia might tell her, but he did hope she would be discreet.

When Morgan was within ear range, Pettigrew called out, "You convinced the blighter, did you, lad?"

Graz laughed. "You might say he won me, Mr. Pettigrew."

198

Morgan crossed the narrow plank, followed closely by Graz. Pettigrew took his hand, shook it firmly, then Graz's. "Good to have you aboard, Graz. I've had my old eyes on you for quite some time."

"It will be my pleasure to work for you," Graz answered, "For fifteen percent of the table's take."

Pettigrew released his hand, smiling, glad that it wasn't going to be twenty-percent, which was the cap he had placed on the hiring. Morgan had done a fine job in the bargaining process. "Come, gentleman, I have a good bottle of port I've been saving for just such an occasion."

Morgan stepped back. "I'll retire for the evening if you don't mind, sir."

Pettigrew had learned not to argue. These past six months, Morgan York had spent his time alone, as he seemed to prefer. "Get some sleep. You've done enough work for the day."

Morgan disappeared into the darkness toward his cabin.

"You know, Mr. Pettigrew," Graz said, "I haven't seen so much bitterness since my mule got into the ragweed."

Pettigrew patted his shoulder. Yes, I know...now, come, we'll work out the details of your contract.

* * *

Morgan's short walk to Natchez-Under-The-Hill was the farthest he'd ventured from the *Gulf Princess* in six months. The change had done him some good, for when he returned to the small cabin below the galley deck he didn't feel the ache of boredom in his shoulders. He was two weeks behind on the gaming room ledgers, but wasn't in a mood to resume his work this evening. He looked at his watch–the same watch Anna had given him for Christmas last year. It was ten past midnight.

Tossing his jacket across the back of a chair, Morgan unbuttoned his shirt and flexed his shoulders, to relieve the ache of tension. He was tired, yet he knew he would be unable to sleep. He lay on the long, narrow cot and brought his arms up to cover his eyes. Because he hadn't eaten supper, and had very little lunch, he felt the gnawing pains of hunger in his stomach. His eyelashes flickered nervously.

Invariably, his solitary moments produced memories of Anna. He imagined how she must look now, her slender frame great with child–her raven-colored hair wind-tossed, and her emerald eyes–the mirrors of her heart.

A stupid, romantic notion! Such women had no heart. Women like Anna Rose St. Cyr were cold and sterile and empty. It wasn't the anticipation of motherhood that filled her with joy, but her cruel, despicable quest for power...and her ownership of Shadow Marsh.

God! How he wished he could hate her–

Yet, he would never forget his last afternoon with Anna. The memory of it was forever branded into his soul. He couldn't bear to remember the wonderful, intimate moments they had spent together–the happiness, the laughter–the love they had shared, and then, all Anna's vicious lies and deceptions. But he had to believe it–he had heard those horrifying words spew uncontrollably from her trembling mouth, as deadly as snake's venom. He had heard the mocking growl of laughter as she had thrown his love back in his face. The pain lingered and festered, like a raw wound. His heart was ripped apart every time he thought of her...those cold, mocking green eyes–

Eventually, he fell asleep, but his sleep was filled with visions of Anna. Her smile possessed him; her wide almond-shaped eyes mesmerized him. He felt her body, warm and soft, as if she were really beside him. But the lovely visions became a nightmare...he awoke with a start, his breathing labored, perspiration pouring through his hairline, the tight constriction of his throat threatening to erupt into screams. Trembling, awakened by the reality of his nightmare, Morgan swung his feet to the floor and rested his head in his palms. Would he ever forget the horror, the disappointment, the hurt he had felt that afternoon?

The following morning, he stood at the rail of the *Gulf Princess*, sipping hot chicory coffee, regaining his composure and trying to clear his mind in the golden dawn of a new day. He hadn't shaved in two days, and brought his hand up to stroke the stubble of his chin. Then Graz approached, crossed his arms and stood silently beside him.

"You were assigned respectable quarters?" Morgan asked.

"Yes," the other man replied huskily. "Mr. Pettigrew treats Graz with respect, and he does appreciate it."

"Yes, I'm sure that he does." Absently, Morgan watched a dock crew loading large crates onto a tugboat. The docks were stirring to life. Barges floated on the tossing waves of the Mississippi, narrowly missing small fishing boats. Soon the finely dressed ladies and their indulgent husbands and courtiers would flock to the pier. They would view the exotic, brightly colored parrots gaining popularity among the elite that had been brought up from South America. They were to be exhibited in large iron aviaries on the east docks this morning.

Morgan watched a familiar, dark-clothed man walking slowly along the docks, stopping to ask directions of one of the workmen. He approached, stopped beside the plank leading to the *Gulf Princess,* stepped cautiously and began to ascend. Morgan leaned lazily against the rail, his eyes narrowed, following the footsteps of the man who thought his identity was well hidden beneath the brim of his hat. But Morgan knew who he was.

Morgan's body stiffened and, simultaneously, Graz stepped away from him. Across the immaculate whitewashed deck of the *Gulf Princess*, Wren Wellington looked at him critically. He straightened his coat and moved slowly in his direction.

Their eyes met. They had spoken only briefly in the past, yet there permeated a mutual dislike between the two men. "You're a long way from Hopewell," Morgan said.

"May we speak in private, Mr. York?"

Graz bowed perfunctorily. "Excuse me."

Only when Graz was out of hearing range did Morgan speak again. "What can you possibly have to discuss with me, Mr. Wellington?"

"I've come about. . ." He'd been about to speak Anna's name, but thought better of it. "Shadow Marsh."

Morgan turned sharply away. "Then we have nothing to discuss."

Wren took his arm, and his grip communicated a certain degree of threat. "You *will* talk to me, Mr. York–please."

Perhaps humoring him would release some of the boredom he had felt over the past few months. Morgan shook his arm free. "Come with me. I have a good bottle of rum in my cabin."

Wren entered the small, neatly kept cabin ahead of Morgan, standing aside while he entered. The door closed. Morgan took a bottle of rum from a small sea chest and opened it. Before he could make the offer, Wren said, "Too early for me." Wren had remembered the Shadow Marsh overseer as a quiet, gentle man. But he seemed curt, almost rude, now. Morgan poured rum into a clean glass and sat at the desk, bringing his booted foot up to his knee. "What has brought you to Natchez? How did you locate me, by the way?"

"Violet."

"So...the lady is not discreet as Madame Etienne assured me."

"The lady is my wife."

Morgan took a drink of the bitter liquid. "Congratulations...wedded bliss, every man's euphoria." The sarcasm could not be hidden. Gritting his teeth, Morgan came hastily to his feet. "Say what you have to say, so that you may be on your way, Mr. Wellington."

Wren had never seen so much bitterness in a man. He understood how he felt. "You have a son, Mr. York."

A short, bitter laugh erupted, even as he wanted to jump for joy inside. "Anna has a son–and she has Shadow Marsh legally. It is what she wanted." A thought came to Morgan and he turned, eyeing Wren Wellington critically. "You came all the way to Natchez to tell me I have a son? I would have learned soon enough from Louvenia, who is kept abreast of happenings at Shadow Marsh through your informative wife."

Wren creased his hat between his fingers. "Which would indicate to me, Sir, that you do care about Anna and the future of Shadow Marsh. For this reason, I ask you to consider returning with me."

"You ask," Morgan shot back vehemently. "What the hell

do you care about Shadow Marsh?" Again, Morgan laughed, but this time it was low and sarcastic. "You've wasted your time. I don't care what you have heard, but I did not desert my wife. My wife ordered me to leave and..." Morgan outstretched his hands, "Here I am, a bookkeeper for a riverboat line."

It had been a long, exhausting ride from Alexandria, taking three days' time, and Wren was too tired to argue. He wanted to blurt out that Anna might be dying but, on the spur of the moment, felt he had to know how much this man really loved her. He wanted him to return to Shadow Marsh because he was concerned for Anna–felt that Morgan York was the reason she had given up on life–and he did not want her to leave a young son to be cared for by servants. He wanted Morgan to return to his new son and the future of Shadow Marsh, not out of pity because his wife might be dying. He had to know if he truly deserved Anna. He knew that if he returned, Anna would want to live, and that was all he cared about.

"Sir, I have been entrusted with finding a qualified overseer for Shadow Marsh. I have spoken with Joby Cade, who has assumed the job for the time being, and who will accept training only under your guidance. I have been keeping the books for Shadow Marsh, but also keeping books for Hopewell, I am tired and over-worked. I have gathered enough information from the folks at Shadow Marsh to know that no one is better qualified than you. They respect you, and I would ask you to return."

"Anna does not want me there."

"Anna is being cared for at Hopewell. Your son is at Shadow Marsh for the time being with a wet nurse, but will soon be brought to Hopewell. You will no longer deal with Anna, but with me, Mr. York. As Violet's husband, and Anna's friend, I have been making managerial decisions for Shadow Marsh until you are willing to do so.

"I'm sorry. I can't go back there." Morgan turned away, hoping Wren Wellington might graciously leave. But it seemed that he had no intentions of doing so.

"I had thought you a sensitive man, Mr. York. I have my hands full with our own plantation. Shadow Marsh will suffer if placed in incompetent hands. If you'll forget your personal feelings–God, man! There is a child bearing your name. Think about him!"

Morgan swung back, his eyes spitting fury. "Don't you think I care about my son? Damn you! Why have you placed me in this situation? Of course I want to be near my son, to be a father to him–but Shadow Marsh belongs to Anna, and she does not want me! She has what she wants! Can you not understand that?"

Wren sat tiredly on the small cot, resting his hands across his knees. "If you love Anna and your child, you will return."

"You have an audacity to question my feelings for my wife and son. No one should be happier than you that I have been driven from Shadow Marsh. I am well aware of your feelings for Anna."

"Yes, I care for Anna, but I am married to Violet. I have a duty, while Anna is bedridden, to assume the responsibility for Shadow Marsh." Wren slowly rose, looking across the small, dark room at the man whose true identity he had only recently learned...the man Anna loved enough to die for, as she might possibly be doing now.

"Anna doesn't want me," Morgan stated again, flatly, finally, pouring another goblet of rum. "Does she know you're here?"

"Anna isn't up and about yet after giving birth to the child. She has no idea."

Despite the heated arguments between him and Wren, Morgan was filled with curiosity about his child. He had a thousand questions he wanted to ask. But he was stubborn; he didn't want Wren Wellington to know how much he cared. "What did she name the boy?" he asked after a moment.

"Michael George."

Morgan felt a sudden shortness of breath. The horror of that last afternoon, when Anna had degraded him, had called him a murderer, had said she'd never loved him and wanted only his child, whirled rapidly through his head. And yet, despite those hateful things she'd slung at him, she had named their son after him. He was pleased, but terribly confused. "I would thank you, Mr. Wellington, when you return to Shadow Marsh, not to tell Anna you have seen me. She won't wish to hear it."

"Are you telling me that you won't return with me?"

"Did you really expect that I would?"

"I had hoped you would, for your son's sake."

"My son..." A tremble settled in Morgan's throat as he thought he was forever cutting himself off from his son, "...is in good hands."

"I wish you'd reconsider."

Morgan stood. "We could sit here all day, Mr. Wellington, and get no better results. Let me sum it up for you–I married Anna St. Cyr, she accomplished her goal, married me, and gave birth to a legitimate son. That gave her legal ownership of Shadow Marsh. She asked me to clear out. I will always love her and my son, but in the same breath, I despise her, just as I despise you for making me think about her today. It is over. She and I have gone our separate ways, and I will thank you to leave me to my peace."

"I hadn't wanted to bring this up...Captain Fielding."

Morgan paled visibly. "You know who I am?"

"I know who you *were*, Mr. York." All Wren could think about was Anna–dear, lovely Anna, who had decided she had no reason to live. "Alistair St. Cyr claimed to have sent a telegraph message to the War Department. Rather than have someone come to arrest you, Anna chose to send you away the only way she knew how. I don't know what way she chose, but it was motivated by the greatest love a woman can have for a man. Were I to be loved like that, I would feel so blessed. In seven months' time no one of authority has arrived at Shadow Marsh to take you into custody, and we all question Alistair St. Cyr's motives in instigating these actions."

Morgan was quiet for a moment, and when he spoke, his voice was strangely controlled. "This is foolishness. Anna would have told me if her brother had found out who I was...we kept no secrets from one another."

"You kept many secrets, Mr. York...perhaps both of you."

Wren wanted to be rational, controlled...convincing, but he was quickly losing patience. "I don't know what you did to have a bounty on your head, Mr. York, and frankly, I don't care. I care only about Anna and Shadow Marsh and the fact that I cannot physically run two plantations. Please reconsider." Wren pulled the door open. "My horse is stabled on the bluffs, and I believe I saw your horse there. Please conclude your business here and I will await you at the livery. I will not take no for an answer."

Morgan was consumed with visions of his son, a tiny life that he had helped to create. He wanted nothing more than to hold him in his arms and that alone compelled him to accept Wren Wellington's offer. He had vowed never again to set foot on Shadow Marsh land, but...that was before he had a son. "Mr. Wellington..." Wren turned back. "Are you sure Anna does not know you have journeyed here?"

"She does not. She resides at Hopewell until she recovers her strength. Bea and a wet nurse are caring for your son at Shadow Marsh."

"Is Anna too ill to take care of our son?"

*She may be dying, sir.* "We thought it best that she not feel pressured to take care of the child until she has recovered completely."

Morgan knew he could refuse to return to Shadow Marsh, but he would be spiting no one but himself. More than anything in the world he wanted to see his new son. "My return will carry certain conditions."

"And what are they?"

"It is understood that I will remain at Shadow Marsh only until such time as Joby Cade is suitably trained to take over the position I held. The second is that I will be allowed to see my son at least once a day. I also want to spend time with Patrick. I felt like a father to him when Alistair rejected him. I also do not want Anna to be told I have returned. I wish to have no dealings with her."

"You will deal only with me, Mr. York. I accept your conditions. I will arrange to have Patrick and your son brought to you each evening. Anna need not know. Now–I will await you at the livery. You can saddle your own horse." With a light laugh, Wren added, "That painted devil scares the dickens out of me." The door quietly closed.

Morgan felt tension crawl through his shoulders. His fingers dug madly at his temples and he closed his eyes, to try to think, to sort things out. His mind was in a jumble. Anna had hurt him so deeply that he felt he could never forgive her. But she was the mother of his son. Why was he so confused and torn in his feelings? Why was he returning to Shadow Marsh, and could he believe Wren's explanation for why she sent him away?

During the next hour, Morgan gathered his personal belongings and straightened the desk, where he kept the *Gulf Princess* ledgers. At half past the hour of eight, he stepped out to the deck, a move that brought him face to face with Hiram Pettigrew.

"You're leaving me, are you, boy?"

"Yes," Morgan replied. "I am returning to Shadow Marsh and my new son."

Graz exited his cabin and approached, extending his hand to Morgan, which he took. "We will meet again one day, and you will be reluctant to take Graz's hand."

"I doubt it," Morgan replied. "I never decline the hand of a good man." He then took Hiram's hand. "Thank you for everything you've done for me. I am forever grateful...give Louvenia my love when again you see her."

Hiram Pettigrew turned away and cleared his throat, to choke back the emotion settling there. He had grown especially fond of Morgan. Then he said to Graz, "Come, let's go over the gaming rules." They quietly entered the gaming room and disappeared from Morgan's view."

He paused and looked out over the Mississippi River, at the loading docks and boats swaying back and forth on the rushing waves. The air was cool, the sky gray and overcast, and he thought he might miss this aspect of his life, at least for a little while. Tossing his saddle bags across his shoulder–all he had of personal possessions–Morgan quietly left the *Gulf Princess*.

He no longer felt the threat of his past. He was beyond

coherent reasoning. The Army could come for him if they wanted him so badly after all these years. He was tired of running, and he was tired of playing their game. From this moment forward, he would be grateful for every moment he was allowed to spend with his new son, Michael George...

Why would Anna, who had tossed him out of her life like so much rubbish, name their son after him?

# Seventeen

Violet was quite at odds with Wren over the subject of Anna. She had spent the last week, in his absence, brooding over his feelings for her. Wren had no right to interfere in the problems of the St. Cyr family just because she herself had been a St. Cyr before her marriage to him. On top of this, after harsh words with Anna on the day following the birth of her child, Alistair had packed everything he owned and had left Shadow Marsh, with a rashly spoken vow never to return. And now, grieving for the loss of a husband that she herself had sent away, Anna was recuperating at Hopewell, her son being cared for by the servants at Shadow Marsh. It sickened Violet that Anna was being pampered and petted and treated like royalty by Mrs. Wellington and the entire domestic staff at Hopewell.

Violet sat quietly on the veranda, sulking in her self-pity, hugging her cape to her, and feeling the chill of the November air against her flushed cheeks. She felt a pain in her throat, a lump of rage that had stuck menacingly there for the past week. She scarcely heard the foyer door open and Marigold approach her.

"Miz Wellington, she say you should come in from the cold, Miz Violet, befo' you catch yo' death."

"Death wouldn't dare touch me," she mumbled, almost intolerantly. "The house is too hot and stuffy."

Marigold had never been one to approach the family with caution. She knew the men, including the Wellingtons, enjoyed watching her dance, and somehow this knowledge left her feeling a cut above the other slaves. "Massa Wren, he won't be likin' you out like this," Marigold said after a moment, tucking her hands into the pockets of her apron.

Violet pressed her lips into a thin line. She simply hated it when a slave argued with her. "Massa Wren couldn't care less about me," she replied tonelessly. "Now, please, go on in,

Marigold. I wish to be alone." When Marigold faltered, Violet growled, "Now!"

Marigold turned, mumbled something Violet did not hear, and reentered the house. Across the bayou, two riders entered the clearing from the timberline–her sister-in-law, Sarah, bundled in a white rabbit fur cape, laughing pleasantly with Warren Fairgate. He was coming to Hopewell to see Anna about Shadow Marsh business, and also to spend time with the flirtatious Sarah. Rumors had circulated that there might be wedding plans in the future. Sarah had certainly set her caps for Warren, employing her feminine, yet crafty virtues as bait. Widowed three years in January, Warren was quite receptive to the charms and attentions of the much younger woman, which she had showered on him in nauseating abundance. Enraptured by her, he had turned a deaf ear to the rumors that every man east of the Mississippi had tasted the sweetness of various and sundry areas of her anatomy in various and sundry locations, including the hayloft. Sarah had filled an empty void for Warren, and he cared not a whit that she was loose with the men.

With Marigold's entreaties a dismal failure, Mrs. Wellington came out to the veranda to reason with Violet. She was a stern woman who always wore dark clothing, no matter the season, and she very seldom smiled. But she was a kind woman, and Violet got along somewhat well with her.

"I must insist that you come into the house, Violet."

"No," Violet answered flatly.

Mrs. Wellington prepared to argue further, but across the bayou another rider approached and drew their attentions. Both she and Violet immediately recognized Wren's sorrel gelding entering the wood bridge across the bayou. Wren spoke for a moment with his little sister and Warren Fairgate, and eased the horse into a canter over the narrow bridge leading to Hopewell. Violet, smiling and happy to see him, rushed toward the steps when he dismounted. But without looking her way, Wren drew his mother into his arms and hugged her warmly. Violet's smile faded into shock and dismay as he entered the house without acknowledging her presence.

Marigold met them in the foyer and Wren favored her with a warm smile. "How about a mug of your delicious hot chocolate when I return to the parlor?" he asked. "It's been a bitter cold journey." Then, "I would like to look in on Anna."

"Jes' made a fresh pot, Massa Wren."

When Marigold disappeared toward the kitchen, Wren asked his mother, "Has Anna improved at all? Has she asked about her son?" He still did not acknowledge Violet, who was standing in the doorway.

"She asks about him daily," Mrs. Wellington replied gloomily, shaking her head, "but has expressed no desire that he be brought to Hopewell that she might see him. She grieves deeply for the loss of her husband." Mrs. Wellington paused on the first stair and turned toward her son. Violet had entered the parlor, and she heard her throw herself rather dramatically onto the fainting couch. "Did you speak to Mr. York?" his mother asked.

"I did."

"And he has returned with you?"

Wren looked around to see where Violet was. He especially did not want her overhearing Morgan's name. She had caused enough trouble as it was, keeping her secrets. "I left him at the crossroads. He is going to Shadow Marsh to see his son, but does not want Anna to know. He's very bitter and says he doesn't plan to stay long."

Wren accompanied her up the stairs. "And how do you suppose we're going to keep it from her?" Mrs. Wellington reasoned. "If he did not return because of Anna's health, for what reason did he return? You told him that Anna was ill–that Alistair had threatened to expose his true identity?"

"I let him know that I knew who he was, and that Alistair also knew. He wouldn't believe it was the reason Anna sent him away. He'll believe nothing but that she despises him."

"He returned to Shadow Marsh simply for the child?"

They were outside Anna's closed door. Wren threw off his damp coat and loosened his jabot. "I told him Joby Cade was being pressured to assume a foreman's position at Shadow

Marsh and had suggested training under Morgan's guidance. He agreed to stay on as long as he's needed. While he's there, he does not want to see Anna nor have any business dealings with her. He does, however, wish to see his son and Patrick. Now—let us hush before Anna senses our conspiracy. I need to see her."

"Allow me to look in on her first." Mrs. Wellington's hand went to the doorknob, but she hesitated. She was staring absently at the floor, but lifted her eyes and quietly studied her son's face. "You still love Anna, don't you, son?"

"I will always love her," he replied without a moment's hesitation. "But she is Morgan's wife."

"And Violet?"

"She is my wife. I'll be a faithful husband, you needn't worry about that. But I will never love her—not after what she has done. And I will never share her bed again."

"Son, your vow is grounds for divorce. No Wellington has ever divorced."

"Violet said she would see Anna dead if it were in her hands. She made that plain enough. If she wishes a divorce, then so be it. I will not stand in her away."

Without further words, Mrs. Wellington eased into Anna's room. She was usually not one to interfere in the affairs of her children, but Wren's vow was a serious threat to the Wellington record. She would pray that there was something Violet could do to redeem herself and this latest Wellington marriage.

His mother's voice, and then Anna's sleepy one drew Wren into the room. "She wishes to see you," his mother said.

Wren entered the semi-dark chamber. Anna reclined against two satin pillows, a book of poetry resting beneath her hand. She looked quite lovely, her pale, ivory features surrounded by her thick, freshly washed tresses, and her satin bed jacket so light a shade of green as to appear white. Wren approached, sat on the bed beside her and took her hand in his. Her eyes opened and she smiled.

"How are you feeling?"

"A little better." Wren was surprised by her tone, free of the gloom that had been with her these past seven months. "Where have you been?"

"Away on business. Now–young lady. . ."

Anna eased her hand over his. "Before you scold me for not taking care of myself, I have something to say. You must promise that you won't interrupt me."

Wren was happy just to listen to her speak, with her voice vibrant and again with life "I promise."

Anna smiled, but it was a sad smile this time, filled with regret. "I've had a lot of time to think this past week, and I know I haven't been sensible. Nor have I been fair to little Michael...it is important, Wren, that you hear from *me* why I sent Morgan away..."

"That is your business, Anna...not mine."

"I must tell you...please listen."

"Very well."

Anna squeezed his hand reassuringly. It hurt very much to speak of Morgan, but she had made a lot of important decisions this past week. One of them was to stop punishing herself for hurting Morgan. She had done what was necessary. "You and I have always been close, Wren. I love you in a special way. I know it isn't what you want to hear, but I love you as a good and faithful friend I can count on in a pinch." Her eyes dropped and she rubbed Wren's hand very gently. "I love Morgan as a man and a husband. He was everything in the world I wanted. I made him my life and my reason for living, and when his life was endangered, I sent him away from me with cruel, vicious words. He will hate me forever for the things I said to him, but I would say them all again to save his life. When I watched Morgan ride away from Shadow Marsh, my heart went with him. Now I have a duty to our son."

"But suppose Morgan should return? He will eventually find out he has a son."

Anna's eyes widened in surprise and alarm. "He can never return. Never–you must understand–you know about the Army and who Morgan really is."

"Yes, but..."

"Then you must understand that he can never return." Anna

cocked her head to the side and looked at him as if he'd lost all reasoning.

Wren enjoyed the feel of Anna's warm hands between his own. How beautiful she was; the radiance of her youth, renewed by this new determination to meet the future and put the past behind her, beamed in her high cheekbones, the wisdom beyond her tender years reflecting in her green eyes, softened by the fond yet sad remembrances of the man she loved. Wren would always love her, and knowing she could never be his would always tear at his heart. But he had learned to accept what could not be changed.

Wren heard muted voices downstairs and immediately footsteps approached on the stairs. For a moment, he was annoyed that his attentions had been drawn from Anna. Then he saw a boot at the edge of the door, a very familiar boot, and felt the presence of the man standing quietly there without making himself known. So, Wren turned his attentions back to Anna.

"Let me get this straight, Anna. You sent Morgan away because Alistair knew he was this Captain Fielding who had been court-martialed and sentenced to death, and threatened to expose him. So you told him you did not love him and only wanted his child, when that was not the case at all. And—what would you tell him were you to come face to face with him now?"

Anna adjusted her position on the pillows, slowly eased her hand from Wren's, and a new brightness shone in her lovely eyes. Absently, she twisted her wedding ring, which she had never removed from her finger. Dreamily watching the shadows from the hearth flicker slowly across the ceiling, she collected her thoughts before she began to speak.

"If I were face to face with him this very minute...oh, Wren, my love for him would compel me to say those same awful things I said to him that day back in March, to spare him the awful deed Alistair had caused. But my heart would want only to tell him how much I loved him, to tell him that he gave purpose to my life when it had always been just outside my grasp. I would tell him that if just one wish were to be granted to me it would be to spend every moment of my existence with him, to love him and take care of him, and to know that he loved me in return." Tears filled her eyes, though she resolutely maintained her composure. "I would tell him that I would go to the ends of the earth with him and would always be beside him. But..." She looked to Wren now, "I will never get the chance to say these things to him. He is gone from me forever. Half my heart is with him, and the other half must stay here with our beautiful son."

The door slowly opened. Outlined against the light pouring from the corridor into the darkened chamber was the familiar form of the man who had not spoken. Wren rose and approached him, put his hand on his arm for a moment and slipped quietly past him.

Morgan had thought about it on the short ride to Shadow Marsh–their son there being cared for by the servants and Anna here at Hopewell. He had just needed to see her sleeping face without waking her–without her knowing he was there–and had turned his horse on the road to head back to Hopewell. He wasn't one to eavesdrop, but this one occasion, he was glad that he had.

Morgan approached Anna, looking at her for a long, silent moment before he sat on the bed beside her. He had never seen her so pale, so thin. In his mind ran the words she had spat at him last March...cruel, mocking, humiliating words that had driven him away so quickly he had not even bothered to collect his personal belongings. He remembered his pain–his heartbreak–his shock, and finally his hatred as strong as his love for her. He had vowed never to return to Shadow Marsh, and to forget that he had loved this beautiful, dark-haired child-woman who now looked at him with awe and disbelief.

Anna did not respond as Morgan sat beside her and drew her into his arms. Disoriented, she tried to shake away this painfully realistic illusion, to bring reality back into her world. She thought for a moment that she was dreaming the same tragic dream that had plagued her so many nights. She wanted Morgan so badly that she imagined he sat beside her this very minute, gently rocking her in his arms. Her trembling hands slipped cautiously around his shoulders, lest he disappear forever. She held him, her shock too deep to allow any other emotion.

Morgan had dreamed obsessively of her warmth, of the softness of her body against his. Despite the world of hurt she had dropped on his shoulders that afternoon, he had continued to love her just as much as he had hated her.

"It is you, Morgan. It really is," she whispered in disbelief, closing her eyes against his shoulder.

"In the flesh, Anna." A tremble settled in his throat. He had heard every word spoken to Wren Wellington just moments ago. He had come to Hopewell, wanting only to see her asleep from a distance, to see her sweet and innocent and dreaming her dreams. Now, all he wanted was to feel her in his arms. "You can tell me all those wonderful things you said you'd tell me. I want to hear them again, but spoken to me this time."

The warmth that had been missing from her life for so many months penetrated to her heart. Was she dreaming, even now? Oh, she didn't want to believe it. If he was a dream, destined to disappear forever with her awakening, then she did not want to awaken. Her arms tightened around him.

Anna realized it wasn't a dream...that he was holding her as gently as she'd dreamed a thousand times. But with her happiness came despair, as she remembered the reason she had sent him away to begin with.

"Morgan, you can't be here," she whispered harshly, only now finding her voice. "Oh, you shouldn't be here." A sob collected in her throat as she remembered Alistair's recklessly slung threat to expose him. "You can't stay...I would rather you hated me for all time than to see the Army take you from me...to know that they would kill you, for no crime other than your deepest compassion."

Morgan drew back, so that he could see her tearful eyes. "I will take my chances, Anna. From this moment forward, I will live one day at a time, and be grateful for every moment I am able to spend with you, my son, and with Patrick."

Anna held him close. "How you must have hated me..."

"I was hurt," he admitted. "But I never hated you. God, but

I tried. Now...will you return to Shadow Marsh with me?" He drew back and shook her very gently. "I will not have my wife neglecting our son."

Anna slipped her arms beneath his jacket, to his firm, muscular back covered by a thick cotton shirt. "Wren brought you back, didn't me?"

"Yes."

"How did he find you?"

"Don't worry about that. I am here, that's all that matters now."

"Will you ever forgive me for the things I said that day?"

"I have already forgiven you. Because I love you, Anna, and that's what people who love do."

"Morgan...Alistair left Shadow Marsh. It is just as well, because he was a threat to you."

"I am wondering if he was a threat at all, Anna. Seven months ago he is supposed to have informed the Army where I was. Have soldiers come to Shadow Marsh looking for me?" She shook her head against his shoulder. "So much could happen in twelve years, Anna. When plans were made to transfer me to Fort Scott to face the firing squad, my stepbrother, Jarred, had begun making appeals for leniency. How do I know the Army still considers me a fugitive? Perhaps I am a free man. So–I will not keep running. You are my wife, and we have a son...we have Patrick. I will stay with you as long as I am able. And...thank you for the greatest gift you could give this old man."

"Your son?"

"My son, indeed...and the name you gave him. Michael George."

Morgan cupped her face, his parted lips touching the softness of her forehead, her cheeks, her pert nose, moist lips which responded eagerly to his. She was the mother of his son, and the woman who had captured his heart.

He could not imagine life without her. He knew that, somewhere in the future, an escort of blue-uniformed soldiers might tear him away from her, but until that time, she was his woman...his wife. Every moment fate gave to him he would spend with her. Their union had been predestined.

Morgan and Anna held one another gently, renewed by the warmth, the spirit, the fire of their love. No foreseeable act of mortal man or harshly spoken words would come between them again.

Neither could imagine a force so great that it could tear them apart.

Love triumphed.

# Eighteen

Anna sat quietly on the veranda, putting the finishing touches on the lace collar she had made for her blue velvet gown. The boys, Michael and Patrick, sat by her skirts, talking to one another in their baby language, and taking turns stacking the brightly colored wooden blocks Joby Cade had carved and painted for them.

The traits of the boys were separate and distinct. Michael was bright, studious, and a bit of a snob, as he had well demonstrated at his recently celebrated second birthday gathering. Patrick wasn't as quick to catch on as Michael, despite seven months' seniority, but was friendly, affectionate and likeable. He had inherited none of the traits of his father, Alistair, whom Anna had not seen in two years.

In a cool, shaded corner of the veranda, little Bonnie, Morgan and Anna's four-month-old baby girl, played quietly with her now uncovered toes. She had managed to remove her white knitted booties and had thrown them to the veranda floor where Patrick's kitten now batted them playfully around.

It was warm for late September. Far upon the horizon, the sky was overcast, threatening rain for the first time in weeks. The lawns were looking blanched, and the fields were dry. A little rain would be refreshing.

The last two years had been wonderful for Morgan and Anna and had brought them oh, so much closer together. They had worked to build Shadow Marsh into the richest plantation in Louisiana, and Morgan had assumed Anna's chair in the Organization. This gave her more time with the account ledgers and supervising the development and moral guidance of the children.

Anna had felt free and happy these past two years. Morgan had been a kind, loving husband and father. Her dread of the

219

arrival of the blue-uniform had slowly faded. Strangers approaching the house were no longer viewed with suspicion, and Morgan had lately begun speaking enthusiastically of the future, something he had carefully avoided.

But now, Anna was again worried. She couldn't bear the thought of losing Morgan, and the threat of it always seemed to dangle over her head. She knew that Morgan was aware of her fears, but he quietly indulged them without argument.

The foyer door opened. Morgan walked out to the veranda, shirt unbuttoned and tan trousers tucked into his black boots. He stretched back his shoulders; he and the men had worked late in the cotton fields last evening, getting ready for the harvest, and he had slept in this morning. It was half-past seven, and way past time to be tending the day's obligations.

Groaning as he yawned, he approached the crib and put his head down to little Bonnie. "Want to pull Papa's hair?" he teased. Bonnie's bright golden eyes were lost in the rosebuds of her cheeks as she smiled. She quickly entwined her fingers tightly in Morgan's hair. It had become a game with them, seeing how long Bonnie could maintain her hold. "Ouch–you've got a grip there, little girl," he laughed, gently prying her fingers loose. Before he released them, he kissed them very gently on the tips. Again, Morgan yawned as he approached the table and sat across from Anna. Briefly, he touched the boys' hair. "Good morning, little men."

Deeply engaged in stacking the blocks, his own son ignored him. But Patrick looked up and smiled. "Morn', Pa," he said in a small, happy voice. Morgan winked, again tousling his hair.

"Would you care for tea, husband?" Anna asked. Her tone was impatient, almost rude, certainly without intention.

Morgan gave her a strange look. "A little would be nice, with honey in it this morning instead of sugar." Leaning across the table, Morgan took and held her hand while he spoke. "Have I told you lately how much I love you?"

Anna's smile did not linger. "Not a day goes by that you don't tell me, husband."

Morgan squeezed her fingers lightly. "And so it should be."

He watched as she gracefully poured the tea, added a touch of honey, and handed it to him. Then he felt a pressure against his leg and looked down. Patrick was standing beside him, handing one of the wooden blocks out to him.

"Mi don't want it." Patrick had not yet been able to pronounce Michael's name. "Hold me, Pa."

Morgan put the block on the table and drew Patrick to his knee. "I know what you want, little humbug–a sip of Pa's tea." Patrick smiled, nodding his head very enthusiastically. Morgan took a little of the tea in a spoon, blew on it for a moment, and offered it to Patrick.

"You spoil him," Anna reminded him for the thousandth time. Dropping her tatting, Anna looked quietly across the table to where Patrick eagerly awaited a second spoon to be brought to his mouth. It concerned her that Patrick referred to them as Mama and Pa, although it had seemed such a natural thing. She worried that Alistair might return one day, and that it would only deepen the trouble between them.

She had heard unreliable rumors that Alistair was running guns south of the Rio Grande, had gotten into trouble in Mexico City, and had spent several months in jail. These past two years he had not collected the three-hundred-dollar-a-month allowance provided by the stipulations of their father's will, a logical indication that he was engaged in nefarious and profitable schemes–and that he had completely turned his back on Shadow Marsh, his family, and his son. It was highly doubtful that he would return and cause trouble. Still, Anna worried.

Only now, with Morgan spoon-feeding Patrick the sweetened tea, did Michael decide to take notice. He rose to his feet, tugged on Patrick's shirt and angrily demanded, "My turn–down, Pat–down!"

Anna watched Morgan give the boys equal treatment. He was terribly patient, much more patient than she found herself being at times. She could tell by the face Michael made that he hadn't really wanted the tea. He simply wanted what Patrick had, and Patrick always gave willingly. Presently, Morgan drank down what remained of his tea, encouraged the boys to return to

221

their play, and arose. Anna quietly watched as he drew his hands to his hips and looked out over the lawns and Cabin Row.

Life stirred among the whitewashed cabins–Auntie Goose rocking on her front porch, the children playing a game of catch, and several women washing and hanging laundry. The men had left for the fields a few minutes ago, and Morgan felt it was way past time for him to join them.

The expression on Morgan's face as he looked across the veranda at his baby daughter pleased Anna. She, too, looked at their dark-haired daughter, and returned to Morgan almost instantly. His love for the children beamed in his every look. Yet, Anna couldn't help noticing that Morgan spent more time with Patrick, although it could be that it was because the freckled, auburn-haired boy was a tad older and much friendlier than Michael. He always seemed to take an interest in whatever Morgan was doing. Sometimes she felt that he favored Patrick over their children. Anna often wondered if Morgan shared her fear–that Alistair might return one day and take Patrick away from them.

Despite her happiness with the children, there were times when Anna wished for time alone with Morgan. They had so little of it now. It had been almost three years since their marriage, yet every moment with him was a new experience, a new challenge–a new passion fanned by the strong, masculine excitement of him.

But she imagined no pleasures greater than those Morgan gave her, and one of those treasures was his love for the children. With this thought in mind, she looked across at him, immediately concerned that instead of the serene, contented look she had expected, he appeared troubled. She wondered what was on his mind. He had crossed his arms and was looking across the lawns and the timberline along Bayou Bouef.

Morgan was remembering a conversation that had unwarily ensnared him at yesterday's meeting of the Organization, which had renewed his apprehensions about the future. Why did conversations among men inevitably lead to politics? Louisianans viewed the approaching presidential election, and the possible election of Abraham Lincoln, as a threat to their economic and social institutions, the most notable of which was slavery. Northern hostilities over the Kansas-Nebraska Bill, and the phenomenal growth of the Republican Party, which had pitted their controversial and moralistic Abraham Lincoln against the fiery orator, Stephen A. Douglas, had only served to enflame the fanaticism of Southern slaveholders. If elected, Lincoln had promised to work toward the abolition of slavery, an act that Congress had, a year ago, warned the southern states to expect.

Louisiana's current governor, Thomas Overton Moore, had gained popularity with his firm stand on Louisiana's rights, shared by other southern states, to determine their own social structure. The preceding March, the state Democratic convention had met in Baton Rouge, and had adopted a series of resolutions, one of which would allow Louisiana to meet in council with her sister slaveholding states to consult as to the means of future protection...should the Republican Party be successful in placing its candidate in the presidency. Rumors of the possibility of secession from the union had been circulating for months. Abraham Lincoln had stirred this apprehension. The simple country lawyer from Illinois was popular in the North. His victory–synonymous with civil strife, and possibly war–was imminent.

Morgan wasn't sure how long he'd stood against the veranda rail when Anna's arms slipped gently around his waist, her dark hair resting against his back. Only then was he aware of the absence of the children, although he vaguely recalled Bea coming out to the porch to bring them inside.

"What were you thinking?" Anna asked quietly.

Morgan turned and took her in his arms. He didn't want to bring up the subject of politics, or the tension crawling like ants between the North and the South. It was too beautiful a day. "I was thinking how happy I am, Anna. I was thinking that..." He took her by the shoulders and stood slightly away from her, "–that you might ride with me to Natchez to collect the new bull."

Anna was a bit taken aback. She had just been wistfully

223

thinking that a holiday was long past due for them. Now, in the very last words he had spoken, she sensed a conspiracy that excluded her from the business of Shadow Marsh. He had sworn that would *never* happen. "Bull? What bull, Morgan?"

"I didn't tell you?" Morgan wasn't really surprised that he'd forgotten to tell her about the bull. He'd been so concerned about the cotton getting picked before any heavy rains, and replacing the grain bin in the east field that had been struck by lightning. "Forgive me, Anna. I've had a lot on my mind. I want to build up a good herd for Shadow Marsh. I'd seen the bull at Jasper Falcon's Plantation when I was in Natchez this past June. It was an impressive animal and I asked him to give me first chance should he decide to sell. I got a note from Hiram that the bull was for sale and wrote back asking him to personally take my confirmation of purchase to Jasper...no one knows a lot of bull better than I do," he added in an attempt at humor.

But it did not work this time. "And how much is this *lot of bull* going to cost?"

"Fifteen hundred dollars."

Anna wasn't really sure why she felt so annoyed. Fifteen hundred dollars was certainly one of the smaller financial decisions Morgan had made without consulting her. She wanted to tell him it was all right, that the purchase was a good investment and she concurred. But she usually avoided giving in so easily, and that Morgan might even be disappointed if she did. And–she was worried about him again, and those blasted Army boys showing up. That always made her short-tempered.

Thus, she flung her wrists up as she prepared to enter the house, so that she might not be forced to tell him what really bothered her. "Go on...buy your bull, Morgan, and may the two of you be happy together." The door slammed soundly behind her, but she still heard the light echo of Morgan's laughter.

Alone now, Morgan stood with his hands drawn to his hips, staring out across the grounds of Shadow Marsh, and knowing in his heart what was really bothering his beloved Anna. It wasn't the bull or the fifteen hundred dollars. Wren Wellington had ridden to Shadow Marsh yesterday afternoon with the news that a company of federal troops was in Alexandria, preparing for a campaign on the Rio Grande. Mexican bandits had pillaged several American settlements, and several men had been killed. Morgan knew that Anna was short-tempered only because she was worried about him and her omnipresent anxiety over the possibility of federal troops taking him prisoner. Thus, he tucked his thumbs into the pockets of his trousers and entered the house.

Anna was not in the parlor where he had expected to find her. He made a search of the kitchens, stopped to taste a morsel of Bea's apple pie, and hurried upstairs to their bedchamber. He heard the children playing in the nursery down the hall, accompanied by Lovey's soft humming.

Their bedchamber door was closed. Morgan turned the knob and gently pushed it open. Anna was lying across the bed with a handkerchief drawn to her eyes. Morgan sat beside her, brushed back her long loose hair, and whispered, "Tell me what's wrong, Anna. I know you couldn't care less about the bull."

"Nothing...please, I just want to be alone for a little while."

Morgan was not prepared to let her weep in solitude, knowing full well that he was the reason for it. "Wren was here yesterday," he said after a moment. "He gave you news that has worried you."

She looked up now, sniffing back her tears. "Did Bea tell you he was here?"

"Bea said nothing. Wren rode through the fields where we were working after he left the house. I know about the federal troops in Alexandria." His hands went round her arms just above her elbows and pulled her to him. "I won't have you despairing every time you think I'm in danger. I am *not* in danger, Anna. We live a happy, contented life and nothing is going to spoil it for us—not federal troops—and not this gentle Republican scarecrow who wants to be president."

"Don't speak of him," Anna whispered. "If he's elected there will be a war. The newspapers are full of it. If that happens, you will leave me...leave me because you have grown to love Louisiana so much. I won't have to wait for those damned federal troops, because your loyalty to Louisiana will drag you away from me."

He couldn't deny that he would fight for Louisiana if the time came. Not slavery! But he would fight for Louisiana.

The last thing Morgan had wanted to think about when he had arisen this morning was war, but it had managed to fill his thoughts. These past three years he had considered himself a Southerner–a Louisianan–yet his heart was not with the primary southern cause–slavery. Rodney Wellington had already approached him about forming a military company in preparation of civil war. He had gone so far as to offer Morgan a major's commission and leadership of the first organized division of the Louisiana cavalry, with Wren Wellington his second in command.

"Yes, Louisiana is my home," he replied eventually, allowing the gloom of war to settle in him. "But we cannot worry about what may or may not happen. Lincoln could get defeated."

"Bull-pucky!"

Drawing her slightly away, Morgan favored her with a gentle smile. "By damn, that's it!"

"What's it?"

"Pucky...the name we'll give that fifteen-hundred-dollar bull!" Anna laughed outright. "Now–no more worries, all right, wife?"

"No more worries," she repeated quietly, "Until I see federal troops riding up the road toward Shadow Marsh."

Morgan rose, approached the door and slipped the lock.

Anna noticed at once that familiar look in his golden eyes. She had pulled the draperies when she'd entered the room a few minutes before, and it was now in semi-darkness. Without words, Morgan sat on the bed and took off his boots, unbuttoning and throwing his shirt aside. Seeing the humor in his wife's eyes, he said, "No, I am not coming back to bed...I am not sleepy–are you?"

She did not reply, but rose and quietly unfastened the stays of her gown, soon letting it fall to the floor. Morgan stood back and looked at her, at her body firm and unmarred by the usual signs of past pregnancies. She stepped into his embrace and moved gently against his body.

"Forgive me, Morgan?"

"For what?"

"For worrying about you, for letting it spoil our happiness. But I do worry...I worry myself sick at times. I really do."

Morgan eased her to the bed, to rest very gently over her. "I want you to hear everything I am going to say to you right now, and I will then ask for a promise. It has been almost three years since Alistair is supposed to have notified federal authorities of my whereabouts. No one came for me then, and no one will come for me now." When she started to speak, Morgan's finger gently touched her lips, to quiet her. "Alistair was bluffing. He wanted Shadow Marsh, and he knew it was beyond his reach. He wanted to hurt you, and he did. He left Shadow Marsh, and he will not be back. No federal troops will come for me–not after this great length of time. We have nothing else to worry about. Now–I want you to promise that you will never again worry about danger coming to me."

"You can ask almost anything of me, Morgan. To ask me to stop worrying about you is to ask me to stop loving you. As long as the danger of federal troops coming is possible, I am going to worry."

Her reasoning left him without a sensible argument. Thus, his lips touched hers and, drawn by the flutter of her thick, dark eyelashes, he gently kissed her brows.

"If you must worry about me, Anna, then worry about me. Don't do it in my presence, or in the presence of the children. I don't want them picking up on your constant worry and growing up to be worriers themselves. All right?" A familiar ache in his shoulders traveled the length of his back. He removed his trousers that he might feel the full, sensual length of her against his body, gently caressing, arousing the fire that leaped for freedom in his loins. He entwined his fingers through her hair and brought it to his lips. "Two old married people with children," he laughed against her hairline, "and the passion of

227

newlyweds." Easing her up on the bed, her dark, tangled hair spread on the satin pillow, like the skirts of a wild gypsy dancer. His mouth captured hers in a gentle, commanding kiss, his hands awakening her flesh with every caress. His legs were hard and muscular as they entwined among her smooth ones.

For many long, wonderful moments they were content to touch, to caress, to explore each other's bodies as if it were the first time. Anna wanted him as badly as he wanted her; pain grabbed her, commanding her body to rise against his own, and she felt the sudden, gentle fullness of him. His hands moved beneath her, to lift her to him that he might deepen his thrusts, to close the distance between their bodies. His passion was like fire, leaping at her, and wild need echoed deep within her, exploding in rapture against his nakedness. Her hands lifted, twining firmly through his hair, and coaxed his mouth down to hers. Her tiny moans whispered sporadically against his parted lips.

"Stay with me, Morgan..." she whispered. "Don't go to Natchez today."

But Morgan heard nothing but the sounds of their bodies bound together, working in unison in the smoldering passion of their mutual needs. As his body exploded in ecstasy within the sensual, burning heat of her, he held her tightly enough that he feared he might bruise her tender flesh. But he did not, and within moments, his breathing slowed and he propped himself above her.

"Look at us," he laughed after a moment. "Two old marrieds making love in the morning. Whatever would the neighbors think?" Then she laughed, too, and held him close for a long, long while.

While they were dressing, Morgan asked, "Will you go to Natchez with me to get that bull?"

He had apparently not heard her ask him to stay home. Considering what they were doing at the time, she couldn't be angry with him for failing to hear her plea. "I must attend a tea being given by the ladies of the parish for the d'Arcenault family who have just arrived from France."

228

"The fellow who purchased the Johnston Plantation?"

"Yes...Godawful rat-trap, isn't it?"

"You're Godawful," he replied, turning to take her in his arms. "Seducing me this time of morning. Now...when I return from Natchez, what shall I bring you? Anything your heart desires."

He always brought her a small treasure when he went away on a trip. "A rose bush," she replied. "White roses gently laced with crimson, to plant on the east side of the veranda."

Morgan softly chuckled. "My wife–I offer you anything your heart desires that is within my power to give you. And you ask for a rose bush."

She smiled, feeling the gentle, rhythmic movement of his chest against hers. "I will tend it forever, and when we are old and gray, its fragrance will remain as strong as when we planted it, just as will our love."

She held him gently for a long, long while, so that the warmth of him would penetrate deeply and remain with her for the week that he would be gone.

# Nineteen

Morgan had been gone from Shadow Marsh on his bull-buying trip for five days when Anna looked across her French writing desk in front of the parlor window and saw the approach of four uniformed men. Their horses were hot and lathered, and one of the men was using the gold bandanna from his neck to wipe his forehead.

All the horrid fears of three years now rose in Anna's heart, quickening its pace, then seemed to cease, as if her life had been unexpectedly terminated. Panic consumed her and she rushed through the parlor toward the foyer, where Bea was approaching to answer the knock at the door.

"I'll get it," Anna whispered harshly. "Tell the others they mustn't say anything about Mr. York. I can only say this once, Bea, so listen closely. I am a widow, my husband is dead, our overseer was dismissed a long time ago, and we haven't seen him since. It's very important–we cannot tell them about my husband."

Since she didn't even know who was at the door, Bea's brows pinched in confusion. "Overseer, he do be dismissed long time ago." She was thinking of Luther Brady. "But Miss Anna...sho' ain't no dead man been sittin' at the dinner table these past two years an' makin' you beam like a newlywed."

"Just, don't argue...please, Bea."

"Sho', Miss Anna...Mist' Morgan, he be dead–sho' 'nuf." Bea returned to the kitchens shaking her head, sure that Anna had completely lost her mind.

The knock at the door became louder and more persistent. Anna paused a moment, breathed deeply to still the tremble within her, and quietly opened the door. She stood there, waiting for the officer to speak.

Major Lane Canady had been giving orders to his men, but turned sharply when the door opened. Anna was caught by surprise by remarkably blue eyes embedded in bronze skin. He was a pleasant-looking man–but the blue and gold uniform, depressing and a threat to her security, forced a lump to rise in Anna's throat.

The officer removed his hat and managed a very tired smile. "Good day, madame. May I have a word with you?" Anna quietly nodded. Canady unrolled a document he was holding and then a flat metal object which he turned to show her.. "Have you seen this man?"

Anna felt her knees weaken. The daguerreotype of a stiff young West Point cadet stared back at her...a very young image of her husband. She might have fainted if all the determination in the world had not collected within her, giving her strength. "I really cannot tell, sir."

"It's an old likeness, ma'am," he continued. "His name is Michael George Fielding, and he is believed to be working on a plantation in this area. We have narrowed it down to *this* plantation." Canady looked back at his men before returning his attention to Anna. "My men are tired. May they water their horses and rest on your veranda?"

"Certainly, sir. I'll instruct Bea–our maid–to prepare lemonade for all of you."

There was a rather rugged detachment in the way the officer spoke. He turned to his men and announced, "We have been offered amenities. Water your horses and return to the veranda." The men dismounted and led their horses, including Canady's, to the trough down the lawns from the house. Seeing the question in Anna's eyes, Canady said, "I have orders from Washington. We've been checking on most of the plantations here, and your plantation is the best prospect so far for locating Captain Fielding."

Anna's legs again went limp and she sat in the nearest chair on the veranda. "Have you been to Hopewell?"

Canady removed a map from inside his jacket pocket and looked at it. "Hopewell is just up the bayou–next on our agenda."

Anna's thoughts raced at an incredible speed. If she denied

knowing the man, they would travel on to Hopewell. If they talked to Violet..."May I see his likeness again–this Captain Fielding?" Canady caught a smile, because he had never told her that he was a captain. He handed the daguerreotype to her. She took a moment to study the youthful features of her husband–so handsome, with smiling eyes and thick, curly hair so pale it appeared white in the photograph. How proud he looked in his uniform, gently holding his hat to his chest.

Bea entered the veranda with the tray of lemonade, distracting Anna from her thoughts. When she had set the tray down and departed, Anna looked to Canady. "If I'm not mistaken, this man may have been our overseer a few years ago. But he was very unsettled and didn't stay long."

"Do you recall the name he was using?"

"No," she lied. "I don't. My brother Alistair dealt with employment and he is not here."

"When will he return?"

"He isn't returning...he resides in Mexico now from what I have heard."

Canady looked around, at the evidence of wealth, five hundred acres of cotton that he could see ready to be picked, and a rich herd of cattle grazing in meadows knee-high in winter grass. "Your brother left such a place as this for the squalor of Mexico?" Canady questioned.

"My brother was not happy here," Anna replied. "I inherited the plantation on my father's death, and he was not happy about it."

Anna did not want to look up. She knew those cold blue eyes were quietly studying her. She wished the major and his men would water their horses, drink down their lemonade and leave Shadow Marsh. She could send one of the men to Hopewell to warn them before the soldiers arrived. She wished these men had never come to Louisiana...they had brought reality to a nightmare that had plagued her for three long years.

Little Bonnie's hungry cry echoed from the nursery. "I must attend my children," she announced, arising to enter the house.

"They don't have a nanny?" Canady asked.

Anna's fear for Morgan was replaced by annoyance. "Whether they have a nanny or not, I am still their mother." She immediately knew that showing hostility would not encourage this efficient officer to gather his men and leave, and might even draw suspicion. "Please do forgive me. It has been a hectic morning so far." She started to leave, but Canady's voice compelled her to turn back.

"May I speak to your husband, Mrs...?

"My husband is dead, Major."

Canady turned a little pink with embarrassment, even as he thought she was being untruthful. "I do apologize. How long?"

"Two years."

Instant surprise marked his pleasant features. "The child I just heard seems to be an infant, Ma'am. Long gestation, I presume? Or do other women reside here?"

His sarcasm overwhelmed her. She realized she had made her first mistake and her mind whirled, trying to grasp an answer. "I'm sorry, I meant two months. I'm not thinking clearly, Major."

Anna felt hopelessly entangled in a conversation that was not going to her liking. She was not a very good liar. She so wanted the major to leave, to take with him the three soldiers wandering through her parlor, mauling her delicate antiques and getting dirt on her oriental carpets.

"While you check on your children, may I question some of your servants?"

"I'd rather you didn't." Just at that moment, Bea appeared.

"Anything you need, Miss Anna?"

Canada turned toward her. "You! What is your name?"

Bea's eyes widened into white china saucers, her hand rising to her throat. "Me, sir? Name's Bea, sir."

"Do you know this man?"

Bea looked quickly at the picture, then back at Canada. "No, sir … Miss Anna, she a widow, an' the overseer, he be discharged three years ago."

"Who told you to say that?"

"Nobody, sir."

"Stop it ... stop harassing the poor woman!" Anna had raised her voice, infuriated by his thoughtless intimidation. "Bea, darlin', you may return to your duties." Bea hastily departed. "How dare you frighten that poor woman! How dare you! Why...you frightened her so badly she wasn't even aware of what she was saying!"

"Captain Fielding is here," he accused. "And I don't know why the hell you don't admit it."

"He is not here," she shot back. "He was the overseer and he was discharged."

"For what reason?"

"Incompetence, and he was terribly unfriendly. None of us liked him very much."

"Oh, I see..." Canady had heard that Captain Fielding had been a kind, sensitive man loved by all who knew him. *Why is she lying,* he wondered as he barked sharply at his men. "Wait outside for me. Lieutenant Ames, you'd best see to unsaddling the horses and getting some hay and sweet feed."

Anna gasped in surprise. "You're staying?"

Canada turned back. "Yes, ma'am. I've got reports from two plantations to the west that this man greatly resembles your husband. So I would kindly ask you to tell me where he is."

"My husband is dead," Anna replied again, hesitantly, scarcely able to put life into her voice. She sat and gathered her hands in the folds of her gown. "Wherever you have gotten these reports..."

"Will you show me your husband's grave?"

"No...I mean, I cannot. He died in St. Louis and was not brought home for burial."

Canady grunted rather rudely. "You are a most accomplished liar, Mrs. Fielding." Just at that moment, little Michael rushed into the parlor, with Lovey close behind, trying to catch him.

"Mama...Mama..." he cried, putting his arms up to her. Anna quickly picked him up and started toward Lovey.

"Just a minute, ma'am." Anna was beginning to hate the sound of Canady's voice. She did not turn. Canady held the daguerreotype up to the child, whose head rested on Anna's shoulder. "Who is this, little man?"

Unsmiling, Michael's plump fingers went toward the picture. "Papa..."

Anna's shoulders sank. She handed Michael to Lovey, gathered her wits and quickly turned back. Her eyes spat fury at Canady. "How dare you encourage my son to refer to a stranger as his father. I must order you to leave. Your presence is intrusive and intimidating."

"When will he be back?"

"Who?"

"I am not playing games, ma'am." Canady pointed across the room. "That's quite an expensive pair of men's boots thrown beneath your divan. Don't tell me they belong to one of your workers?"

Anna sat very still. It was all over for them. Morgan might ride through the gates any moment, unsuspecting of the danger awaiting him. The life drained from her. "Why do you want my husband? Why, after all these years?" she softly asked, raising her eyes to expose the deepest despair Canady had ever seen.

He turned away, the hard core of his military discipline momentarily dented by her despair. He was tired. He'd departed from his troops in Alexandria and would rejoin them in Texas when this mission had been accomplished. And he damned sure wasn't even sure what the mission was. Would he end up arresting Captain Fielding, or was he merely a messenger boy? "Please, forgive me, ma'am, but I must await his return. It would be a great assistance if you would tell me how long that wait will be."

Anna's young kitchen maid, Bess, entered the parlor. "Bea, she say to tell you dinner be on the table in 'bout half hour." Bess usually stayed in the kitchens. Her appearance made it quite evident that the officer had greatly upset Bea.

Anna's features were strangely void of emotion. "Thank you, Bess," she responded, looking toward Major Canady. Hating him would not change the circumstances. Being unkind to him would not ensure Morgan's safety. "Will you and your men take dinner at Shadow Marsh, Major? You must all be hungry."

Her offer surprised him. From the look in her eyes, it was evident that she wanted them as far away from Shadow Marsh as possible. She felt so threatened by him, and all he knew was that he'd been ordered to find Captain Fielding. He wished he knew more about him–about the circumstances–other than that he had been wanted by the Army for thirteen years. Perhaps he would understand the hostility of his wife. "Your offer is very kind," he replied in a more sensitive tone. "We're all dirty and smell like horses. We'll partake of our dinner out of doors, if you'll permit."

"There is no need. I'll summon one of the men who will escort you to a cabin where you can take baths and freshen up. I'll delay dinner by half an hour to give you time." She turned toward the foyer, but immediately turned back. "How long do you intend to stay at Shadow Marsh?"

"Until your husband returns."

"Why, Major...can you tell me that...why after all these years have you come for him?"

Canady gave her a long, thoughtful look. "Ma'am, I don't know what you think I'm doing here, but I was instructed to make a check of this area for Captain Fielding." Canady took a folded document from his pocket. "These papers," he slightly held out in his right hand, "I have been instructed to open when and if I find Captain Fielding. They are my further orders which are at present unknown to me. If I do not find him, I have been instructed to return these to Washington unopened."

"Can't you send it back and tell Washington he could not be located?"

"I'm sorry–no."

Tears shone in her emerald eyes. "You're not going to take him away, are you?"

"Until I open this, I don't know. Please–don't ask questions of me I cannot answer for you." Canady returned the envelope to his jacket pocket. "Can you give me some idea how long I will have to wait for Cap–for your husband?"

She didn't want to tell him anything. All she could think

236

about was Morgan returning to Shadow Marsh, unaware of the blue-uniformed men who had been a threat to his very existence. She felt a sick, sinking feeling in the pit of her stomach rise into nausea in the tight confines of her throat. "He'll possibly be home tomorrow," she replied hesitantly. "Oh, but she couldn't just sit back and allow this stranger to think the worst of her husband. "He's a very good man, Major Canady. What he did fifteen years ago has tormented him and he has paid dearly..."

"Ma'am, I have never been told what your husband did, and frankly I don't care. All I know is that I was given orders. Please don't ask me to compromise my position, and don't make me feel like a damned bully. Pardon my language." Lane Canady slightly bowed his head and moved toward the foyer.

* * *

Anna tried her best to be pleasant during dinner. She smiled dutifully when one of the men told a quite boring joke, and tried to look interested as they spoke of Army life. She accepted the gracious compliments that came readily her way, but Major Canady said very little. Once, Anna saw his hand go to the bulge in his jacket where the envelope was located and she wondered what he was thinking. Was he having second thoughts? Would he return the letter to Washington with the news that Captain Fielding could not be located?

But she looked at eyes hardened by the rough life of a soldier, eyes that had seen very few frills or luxuries. She wished that somewhere in the piece of granite the Army had made of his heart that there could be enough compassion to compel him to move on without accomplishing his mission.

Anna did not sleep that night but lay awake, considering the possibilities. Orders from Washington could only mean Morgan's arrest. She imagined his humiliation. She imagined him graciously accepting what could not be changed. She could already feel the tears rising within her. What would she do if they took him away? What would she tell her children when they were old enough to understand?

Pressing her eyes tightly, she prayed for sleep. But she could not sleep and by dawn had stood by the window of her

237

bedchamber for hours, plagued by a fear that eluded her self-discipline. She wished, foolishly, that Morgan had never returned to Shadow Marsh. But he had, and nothing could change that.

By midmorning as she forced herself through the regimen of her domestic duties, her dreaded anticipation became a dull, nonspecific, throbbing thing. She felt like a puppet, manipulated by the cruel tentacles of fate and circumstance.

But why was she letting herself be defeated so easily? She could send Joby Cade to intercept Morgan. Oh, but that was preposterous. Morgan could have taken any of a dozen routes back from Natchez, and he had made many friends along the way that he could have stopped to visit. The chances of intercepting him were next to impossible.

Anna sighed deeply. Morgan would return in spite of Major Canady and his men. He had made a vow never to flee again. Thus, Anna arose from her ledgers, walked slowly up the stairs and entered her bedchamber. Quietly closing the door, she threw herself across her bed. Patrick's kitten had crept in sometime during the morning, possibly to escape his rambunctious play, and was now napping at the foot of her bed. Anna's hand had fallen very near the kitten, which wrapped its paws around her wrist and buried its small head among her fingers. Anna absently stroked its head and its soft fur, feeling the gentle tremble in the kitten's throat as it purred happily against her fingers.

"Oh, Morgan," she whispered, fighting back her tears. "Will the uncertainty ever end? Will you return, only to be parted from us again?" Then she closed her eyes and forced sleep upon herself.

* * *

It was almost dusk. The last few miles the bull had lagged tiredly behind Morgan's horse and had begun to fight the rope looped through the halter beneath its chin. Morgan was also tired. He wanted to bathe and freshen up, hear the pleasant voice of his wife welcoming him home, and the squeals of the children delighted to see him. He wanted to hold the little ones and watch their happy faces as they opened the gifts he had brought for them from Natchez. He had spent a long, lonely night camped somewhere along the Atchafalaya River last evening and longed for the comfort of his own bed.

The moment he maneuvered the curve in the road toward Cabin Row he saw the blue-uniformed soldiers reclining lazily on the porch of the empty cabin. Halting his horse, he moved off into a clump of trees. So–his past had finally caught up to him, though his first thought was why it had taken so long. He had covered his tracks well in Mexico and Texas, so their only lead would have been through Alistair St. Cyr. But that had been two and a half years ago. What had happened to make catching him a priority to the Army?

A sick, empty feeling hit him. He imagined how Anna must feel knowing that they sat there awaiting him, and wondered what she expected him to do. Did she believe he would flee at the sight of them?

But he knew that was one thing he wouldn't do...he wouldn't run again. He didn't relish the idea of imprisonment– and possibly execution–but he'd had four wonderful years with Anna. He didn't want to give that up, but he was adamant in his decision not to run again. Thus, with this resolution firmly stuck inside him, he eased the stallion back onto the road.

One of the children of Cabin Row spied him and happily alerted the others with his joyful squeal, "Mist' Morgan, Mist' Morgan."

Morgan hopped down from his horse as the children swarmed around him. They went through the same ritual every time he returned from a journey. The children knew he'd have sweets for them in his saddle cases.

Young Lucie collected her treats first and begged, "Can I lead the big cow, Mist' Morgan?" and Morgan, laughing softly, handed over the rope.

But across the children's heads he watched the soldiers come to their feet and turn toward him. A tall man–he could tell by his epaulets that he was an officer–had crossed his arms. One of the children took the reins of Morgan's horse, leaving him free to walk ahead, toward the bronze-skinned officer. Morgan's eyes narrowed, studying him. He had seen military men like him before...disciplined and efficient. As he approached, the officer uncrossed his arms.

Morgan removed his hat and wiped his sweating brow, cutting off the officer when he started to speak. "Sir, I do hope whatever business you have with me can wait until I've seen my wife and children." Canady bowed perfunctorily. Morgan turned toward the children and continued with haste, "Lowey, make sure my horse is bedded down and fed, and Lucie, let Peter take the big cow out to the barn."

"The youngsters like you," Canady observed.

"They're friendly children," Morgan replied politely. He started toward the house, but immediately turned back when the officer spoke to him.

"Sir, when may we conduct our business?"

"Have you had supper?" Morgan asked.

"Mrs. Field–umm, York, has kindly offered us dinner at your table tonight."

Morgan returned his hat to his head and adjusted his saddle bags, which he'd thrown across his shoulder. "Very well, Major..."

"Canady–Lane Canady."

"Major Canady, dine with us. We can conclude our business with a brandy afterward." Morgan turned to resume his walk, but quickly turned back. "Do you wish to have one of your men accompany me?"

"I certainly can see no need, sir."

Lane Canady watched him walk away. There was dignity in the way he moved, and Lane easily imagined him in the immaculate dress of West Point's finest officers. He wondered again what he had done to deserve the death penalty. His hand rose to the envelope in his pocket. Maybe it would give him the answers he wanted. He prayed that whatever orders were contained within, he would not be forced to tear apart this happy, contented family.

He turned away only when the lady of the house exited, rushed quickly down the steps and threw herself into her

240

husband's arms.

"Morgan. Morgan," she whispered in despair, "They've come, they've finally come. Whatever are we to do?"

Morgan held her tightly and his lips brushed lightly against her cheek. Rather than reply, he asked, "Did you see that fine fifteen hundred dollar bull? We'll have a good herd next year."

Pulling away from his embrace, fear darkened her eyes. "Damn the bull, Morgan! There are four men out there..."

Morgan's fingers lightly touched her lips, silencing her. "And do you see me in chains? Do you see them watching my every move?" Morgan had looked out the corner of his eye, noticing none of the men in sight. "We'll find out what they want later. Right now, I want to spend time with you and see the children." She started to protest, but his eyes narrowed. Beneath the darkened gold of them, she saw fear being hidden. "Have you missed me?" he asked, resting his arm across her shoulder as they walked.

"Oh, terribly, Morgan...and yes, it's a fine bull, what I could see of him through the children."

"He is, indeed...and how are my little ones?"

"They've missed you. And they've taken advantage of your absence to be quite naughty."

Morgan laughed, but it was completely without humor. They were in the parlor, and he threw himself lazily onto the sofa. He was sick with worry, and trying very hard to hide it from Anna. "God, I'm tired!"

Anna sat beside him and gently traced her finger along the straight line of his nose. "I'm afraid, Morgan...afraid of what those men want with you."

"Don't be...I am just one life in billions that have existed since the dawn of time."

Anna was instantly annoyed by his nonchalant behavior. Those men could prove a valid threat to him, and he was treating it as a neighbor's visit. "And what does that have to do with anything? Sometimes I just hate you, Morgan."

"Really?"

"No, not really..." she answered quietly. "I love you and I'm

241

afraid of losing you. I don't want any of those other billions of people who have existed since the dawn of time. I want you."

Patting her back comfortingly, he arose. "I'm going to freshen up, we're going to have dinner with this Major Canady and his men, and he will tell me what he wants." He wanted to tell Anna that he had a good feeling, and certainly did not feel threatened by these Army soldiers. If Major Canady planned to take him as his prisoner, he would have taken him upon their first meeting. He certainly would not partake of his hospitality on the one hand, and chain him up on the other. Still, Morgan did not want to give Anna hope if there was none. "Let's go to the nursery and see our children. Then you can sit with me while I bathe, and..." Morgan's arm around her shoulder tightened. "We'll spend some time together before dinner, just you and me."

Drawing Anna into his arms, he held her, in the same moment watching Major Lane Canady through the parlor window talking with his men. What did they want, if not to take him prisoner? God! What did they want?

# Twenty

With Morgan's arm resting lightly across her shoulder, Anna accompanied him to the nursery to see the children. Michael would not hug him and grunted, as his excuse, "Dirty," but Patrick threw his arms around Morgan's neck and planted a wet kiss on his cheek. After he gave the boys the small gifts he had brought them from Natchez, he stood quietly beside little Bonnie's crib and felt her fingers grip tightly around his index finger for a few moments. There was sadness in the way he stood there, as if he feared it would be the very last moments he spent with his children.

When he and Anna stood in their bedchamber a few minutes later, Morgan closed the door and turned, his arms going out and gently coaxing her into his embrace. As he held her, Anna watched the delicate swirl of steam from the hot bath Lovey had drawn off in the small bathing alcove. Tears filled her eyes and, instinctively, her grip tightened around the steel-hard muscles of Morgan's shoulders. "I have a horrible fear," she eventually whispered, "that I am going to lose you."

Morgan drew back, held her shoulders gently in his strong hands, and favored her with a warm smile. "Bathe with me, Anna. Now, wouldn't that be more fun than worrying? I'll even let you scrub my back." Stepping away from her, he began to remove his clothing, which he threw to a pile where he had dropped his saddle case. "I brought you some French perfume," he said, sitting on the day bed to remove his boots. "A new silk scarf from China, and..." He rose to unbutton his trousers, but when he saw her standing there, unmoving, he quickly approached her. "Not going to bathe with me, huh?"

She'd been deep in thought. Startled, her eyes lifted, darting across his worried features as if she'd just seen them for the first time. "I'm sorry. My mind was elsewhere." Her fingers lifted to the stays of her gown. When Morgan saw them trembling, his fingers closed tightly over hers, easing them downward as he began unfastening her stays. As the smooth roundness of her breasts was exposed, he gently cupped them, his lips touching her cheek and moving slowly over the smooth contours of her neck.

Anna smothered the tears resting on her eyelids so that she might savor the gentleness of his touch. That these might be their last intimate moments together filled her with dread and uncertainty. Very soon, she wasn't really aware of their movements, as their naked bodies entwined and embraced. Anna didn't want any gloomy thoughts to possess her; she just wanted to enjoy being with Morgan and feeling the iron-hard muscles of his body against her soft one. But fear and dreaded anticipation cast a dark veil over her, and when their lips met, tears trickled slowly down her cheeks and mingled with their lingering kiss. Morgan's hands rose, gently cupping her face, and she felt the gentleness of his fingertips smoothing away the tears. She heard his gently whispered words, "*Poco novia*–little sweetheart. You are my friend, my confidante, my darling. You are my wife. How proud you have made me. Come. . ." His eyes lingered affectionately on hers, and he stepped away, took her hand and pulled her toward the large tub in the bathing alcove.

When they were snuggled comfortably against each other, feeling the water warm and soothing over their delicately entwined bodies, only then did Anna restrain her tears. She had not pinned up her hair, and it floated smoothly among the white bubbles forming around them.

But the omnipresent gloom caused by the presence of four armed soldiers just outside the window stuck with Anna. She trembled. Unconsciously, her grip tightened around Morgan's neck, relaxing only when he gently laughed.

"Anna...do you intend to choke me?" Peeling her arms from his neck, he kissed each of her palms, and rested them on his chest. His mouth sought and captured hers in a warm, lingering kiss.

"Oh, Morgan, we are...we..."

He refused to allow her to finish her statement, but pressed his mouth to hers–sweet, moist and trembling, as innocent as the first time he'd touched her lips. Had it been so long ago that he'd captured this wonderful treasure for the first time and held it possessively to his heart? It didn't seem possible.

Their lips met and conquered over and over again, and only too soon their common fears were lost in the wonderful ecstasy of mutual desire. The fear dissipated into nothingness, and there existed between them only an intense need. Somewhere in her movements, Anna had picked up the washcloth and held it to Morgan's back. When he felt it against him, he again favored her with a warm smile. "Wash my back for me, little sweetheart. I am dirty and do not deserve to touch you until I am clean."

Without warning, Morgan sank beneath the water, and when he rose, laughing, he shook his head, spraying her with a thousand droplets of water. "Oh, you!" She laughed, dunking him again beneath the water. "You're a monster and a rogue...and I so love you!" They laughed together for a moment, during which all their worries were forgotten. They cared only that they were together and that their bodies responded in mutual want for one another. They laughed, and their lips met in quick, playful, teasing kisses. The water splashed over the sides of the tub and onto the highly polished wood floor. "Bea is going to be furious!" Anna laughed.

But she cared not a whit about the floors. She cared only that she was with Morgan, her husband, her sweetheart, the man who had awakened her passion and kept it alive with his very nearness to her. How happy she was, and how wonderful was the touch of his hands on her body, traveling, teasing, exploring every inch of her flesh beneath the water's surface. She could never tire of his caresses, of his fingers magically awakening feelings that only he could give her.

As their lips touched, Anna eased her legs across his slender hips beneath the water and gently lowered herself to him, to be filled with the strength of his manhood.

"Little *chica*," Morgan half-groaned, nipping at her parted mouth and her gently closed eyes, "you are a delight...you make me delirious for you."

The delicate slush of the water over their tightly entwined bodies did something pleasant to Anna. They had never made love in the bath before, and it was a new and exciting experience. Her hips moved, easing the length of his manhood into the farthest depths of her body. Her muscles tightened with his own gentle movements.

Then, for a few moments, they clung together, unmoving, their bodies entwined beneath the warm, smooth surface of the water. Their silence was broken only by their even breathing. Anna felt Morgan's arms harden around her slender waist, and his lips parted and possessed hers once again.

"Promise me, Anna," he began softly, "that should we be parted..." She opened her mouth to protest, but his hand went to the back of her head and drew her closer, halting any words she might have spoken. "Promise me that you will stay here with the children and not follow me. Promise me. I ask so little of you."

Anna had thought that if they took him, she would travel as far as the ends of the earth to make pleas in his behalf. Although she did not want to make this promise, she spoke the words, "I will stay with our children," simply to make him happy. She would do whatever had to be done to save his life–if it came to that.

Morgan's hips began to move again. He sat forward, maintaining their union, and rocked gently against her body, smothering her to him in a long, almost desperate embrace. Swiftly, silently, their bodies rose in spontaneous union, driving hard against each other as that thrilling moment arrived for them. They clung together in continued silence, their breathing quick and erratic and warm against each other's cheek. Only when Morgan quickly touched his lips to hers did Anna move to his side. As if this were nothing more than an ordinary bath, she picked up the washcloth and began to scrub his shoulders.

"You'd best cooperate if you want me to scrub your back," she said with a small laugh. Morgan sat forward as Anna moved lower on his back with the washcloth. As the cloth slowly traced the line of one of the scars across his shoulder, she dropped her face against his back and burst into tears.

"Why these tears, Anna?" he asked, pulling her around to him.

"Forgive me...for eleven long years you traveled alone, despairing in your heart. You worked hard when given the chance, and you were so brutally mistreated. Then fate brought you to me, so that I could love you and care for you. We've had four wonderful, happy years and...now it might be over."

"We don't know that, Anna. Don't be so presumptive."

She drew back, and without strength her fist dropped to his chest as if to strike him in frustration. "Of course it is over! They're going to take you away and I will never see you again. They're..."

"They're what?"

"They're going to shoot you."

Morgan said nothing. Tears filled his eyes, not because the threat of death was a vague possibility, but because he would lose Anna. Thus, they held each other for a long, silent moment, until the water began to cool. Morgan rose then and coaxed her from the tub. The sun was setting, and through the parted draperies, Anna saw it sinking on the horizon across Bayou Bouef like a huge orange ball.

Morgan began to dress in one corner while Anna put on her underclothing. She sat at her dressing table to put a little powder and rouge on her face. He watched her sitting quietly at the mirror, her fingers absently rubbing the soft, loose powder between her fingers. She had pulled her hair up in ivory combs, and across the satin day bed she had laid out the dress she would wear at dinner this evening–the green chiffon that fit snugly to her slender frame. Around her neck she wore the gold locket Morgan had given her for their first Christmas together.

Completing his dressing, Morgan approached and put his hand out, waiting for hers to rest in it. "You will want Lovey to help you into your gown," he said. "I will leave you for a little while." Rising, stepping into his inviting embrace, Anna enjoyed his parting words, "Remember always that I love you, Anna."

"I love you more," she whispered.

"Not possible." Stepping away, Morgan favored her with a

smile laced with sadness and regret. "I will tuck in our sleepy, contented children while you dress. Then we shall open our home to our guests."

"Guests," Anna spat back, unthinking, "Butchers more than likely!" But when she saw the pain her words had evoked, she quickly apologized. "Forgive me. I am filled with bitterness."

Morgan dropped his hands across her slender shoulders and his forehead met hers. "Be a good hostess to Major Canady and his men. He is only doing his job, and I'm sure he feels as badly about it as we do. Now–I will send Lovey to assist you."

\* \* \*

Morgan was in the parlor with Major Canady and his men when Anna entered half an hour later. A fire had been lit in the hearth and the parlor was too warm. Anna began pushing the sleeves of her gown up from her elbows. A strange tension filled the parlor. Greetings were exchanged without feeling. Then dinner was announced and Anna, especially, was relieved.

She didn't want the men there...Canady with the slight bulge in his jacket where his orders awaited. Through the blue threads of his dreadful jacket, her eyes penetrated deeply to the core of his heart. What beat there where compassion should be? A sadistic sense of pleasure that this man and woman's future rested on the contents of the orders sealed in his pocket? Anna hadn't realized she'd been staring until her eyes lifted and met the narrowed eyes of Lane Canady. She blushed delicately.

During dinner, Morgan responded noncommittally to Canady's interrogation about his past fifteen years. The three young officers, caught once again in the spell of Anna's rare beauty, shared small talk with her, unaware that she was more concerned with the conversation of Major Canady and her husband. Yet, she easily offered her smiles and small gasps of surprise when a story was told of military life, and gave the appropriate responses to their own indelicate questioning. She scarcely touched the food on her plate, feeling queasy and nauseous and wanting only for the evening to be over.

After dinner, Morgan rose, stretching his hand out to Canady. "You and I, sir, can conduct our business while your men partake of desert." When Anna started to rise, Morgan continued with haste, "Please, be a good hostess until I return."

Hardly had the parlor door closed when Canady turned toward Morgan, removed the sealed envelope from his pocket and held it tightly in his hand. He said nothing as Morgan approached the liquor cabinet, poured two brandies and handed one to Canady. He hesitated to take it.

"Sir, this envelope contains my further orders."

"Yes, I know.... open it now."

"In just a few short hours I have observed a man whose past contrasts with his reputation. You have been kind and hospitable. You have a lovely wife who appears to love you very much." Canady held the envelope close to his jacket. "Merely instruct me, sir, to return these to my pocket and leave and I will do so. I am willing to return them to Washington with the news that you cannot be located."

"Did my wife not ask you to return your orders to Washington unopened?"

"She did, sir."

"Why will you now consent to do so?"

"A woman is blinded by love and will stand by a man no matter what he is. I did not know you then."

"And you know me now?"

"Well enough Sir that I will risk a reputation I have spent eighteen years nurturing to perfection."

Morgan looked at Canady for a long, silent moment, surprised at his offer. "And if they are returned to Washington, will someone else come in search of me?"

"Eventually, I would imagine."

"Then it is my wish that you carry through with your orders."

"They may be a warrant for your arrest."

"I will take that chance. If you have a warrant, I will pose you no problem, but will come peaceably."

"Are you sure this is what you want?"

Morgan swirled the brandy in his goblet, thinking of Anna and the children and the wonderful life he'd had with them. Had it not been for Canady's indirect reminder, and his very presence here, he would not be thinking about his past and the beloved stepbrother he had killed. He had put his past behind him, but now, Canady reminded him vividly of it. He had been happy as Morgan York. These past few years he had silently laid Captain Michael George Fielding to a peaceful rest. But now, he had been cruelly resurrected, and Morgan was forced to deal with him.

"Sir, Captain Fielding? What is your final answer?"

Tension crawled across Morgan's flesh. "Read your orders, Major Canady."

"You are sure?" Morgan merely nodded. Without cutting his eyes from Morgan's quiet gaze, Canady broke the seal of the envelope he'd carried with him for the past three weeks. Another sealed envelope, upon which was written "To Michael George Fielding" was inside, as well as a note folded in thirds. Canady opened it and his eyes darted over the words written there. He scarcely contained his smile as he finished reading, refolded the note and returned it to his jacket pocket. He handed the envelope to Morgan. "Sir, the men and horses are well rested. We will now depart for Alexandria and rejoin our troops."

When he started to leave, Morgan called him back. "Sir, what was contained in your orders?"

Canady turned to face him. "I am sure, Captain Fielding, that anything you want to know will be revealed in the documents I have given you. Good day."

Very quickly the booted feet of four men reverberated across the porch. Simultaneously, Anna's half-running footsteps approached, stopping short in the doorway of the parlor. Her face filled with relief and confusion, she said nothing, but the question was there in her eyes as she looked at him. "They're leaving, Morgan?"

When she approached, his arms slipped around her shoulders. "He read his orders and gave me this..." Stepping back, he held the sealed document out to her. "I don't know what to think."

"Open it, Morgan. I must know what was so important that

they went to all this trouble and then just left. It must be good news...it must be!"

Approaching the hearth, Morgan quietly broke the seal. There were three documents, and the one on top was a letter. Morgan quickly recognized the handwriting of his brother, Jarred, and quietly began to read: *My dear brother, Michael, It has been many years since last I saw you. Since that day, I have fought your battle in my own heart and with the labors of pen and paper. Three years ago I learned that you had made Louisiana your home and had changed your identity. I would have allowed you your new life, but just so much can be expected of a brother who has continued to love you. I pray you were informed that President Buchanan granted you a full pardon in November of eighteen-fifty-eight. There have been further endeavors to clear your good name, and your military record has been cleared. You have been recommissioned as a captain. You may, of course, deny the commission.*

*Our dear mother sends you her love. Father died three months ago. I enclose for you a copy of his will, in which you and I have together inherited half the shipping industry, with our dear mother to maintain ownership of the other half. Our father would not have made you an equal heir had he not loved you and forgiven you. I pray you will find consolation in his last wishes. I pray you are well, Michael. The carrier of these documents was given orders only to relay to me news of you and to leave my correspondence and enclosures with you. Should I not hear from you, I will understand. And I will be made aware by Major Canady of your well-being. That is all I ask. Remember that you are always welcome home to Tarrytown. Your loving brother, Major General Jarred Gunthar. P.S. I have a lovely wife and two fine children. I would like for you to meet them some day.*

Morgan dropped his head against the mantel. Tears moistened his eyes–tears both of joy and of sadness. Anna approached, putting her hand lightly on his arm. He raised his head, betraying his pain, his heartache...his relief. Then he drew her into his arms and held her for a long, long while.

251

"My stepfather died."

"I am sorry, Morgan."

"I was pardoned by the president and my commission was reinstated."

The weight of the world was lifted from Anna's shoulders. There would never again be the horrible watching over her shoulder for blue uniformed men. Morgan was free. They were free. "Do tell me that you will not accept the commission?

"I certainly will not. The Army has seen the last of Michael George Fielding. But..." Morgan held her slightly back so that he could meet her emerald gaze. "I must know, Anna, whether you want me to drop this façade, this identity I picked up on the Texas trails. Do you want Morgan York...or Michael George Fielding?"

Anna threw herself into his embrace. "Oh, but could I make love to a stranger–this Michael Fielding, when it is Morgan York I fell in love with?" But, at once, she realized she was being selfish. Morgan had once been proud of his family name–the name his parents had chosen for him. An instinctive fight for survival had thrust this new identity upon him, and there was no longer any need to watch over his shoulder, like a wary hare. "But that is a decision you must make, and I will accept whatever you decide."

"Morgan York. I am so accustomed to this fellow that I think I'll keep him around for a while. He hasn't been so bad, has he–this Morgan York?"

"He's been wonderful!" Anna laughed gently against him. "He has been a wonderful husband and lover."

"And the fellow you fell in love with?"

"Oh, yes indeed!" Anna's hands slipped round his arms and she swung round and round with him before the hearth, their moving bodies dancing in the delicate flicker of the flames. "I feel like a young girl again. Let's have a big celebration tomorrow, you and me and the children, and all our wonderful people. I'm so happy...so happy!" Then she threw her arms around him and wept with relief.

"Our worst fear is over," he spoke the tender words against

her dark tresses. "Nothing in this world will ever part us again. One day when the children are a little older we will journey to Tarrytown. I will be so proud to introduce you to my mother and my brother."

"Dear husband," Anna whispered in reply. "I will challenge with my every strength the force that tries to separate us again. You are everything in the world I want and need...the love of my life."

There were no more fears—no more cruel enemies lurking in the shadows of their future, waiting to tear them apart for all time.

Tonight was a new beginning.

# Twenty-one

Louisiana seceded from the union on January 26, 1861, a move that followed the secession of five of her sister states. Emotions in the South were enflamed by the election of Abraham Lincoln as President of the United States. Two days after the secession, the owners of the large plantations in central Louisiana met at Shadow Marsh to discuss this new state of affairs and the formation of a military company. The Union would not take secession lightly. War was inevitable.

Morgan sat quietly, listening to the pros and cons of secession and the heated, often jubilant cries of young hotheads who viewed secession as a new and better way of life for the South. But Morgan was troubled. Rodney Wellington had again brought up the subject of his assuming command of a cavalry unit, and Morgan had been unreceptive. Only too recently, he had promised Anna that nothing would ever part them again. And now, something as troublesome and unjust as slavery was destined to accomplish what neither of them wanted.

Morgan had sworn to say nothing to his neighbors, or rub his opinions into their noses. Most of the planters were aware of Morgan's sentiments regarding slavery and secession—both of which were bad for the country—and none, he was sure, would be rude enough to drag it out at a public meeting.

But he had made too hasty an assumption. There was always at least one troublemaker at gatherings like this, a role now readily assumed by the Frenchman, Andre d'Arcenaut "Tell me, Monsieur York, you being a man of West Point, how do you feel about our Louisiana seceding from her fatherland?"

This was not something he wanted to answer. "I am sure you don't want to hear my opinion," Morgan politely replied.

"Oh, but we do," Andre countered in his pedantic English.

Wren approached and calmly put his hand on Morgan's arm. He whispered to him, "My father and I have accepted your views and we are well aware they do not dampen your passion for Louisiana. There is no need to alienate these men."

"No...let him speak," Rodney Wellington argued. "Mr. d'Arcenault, I hardly believe you have not been made aware of Morgan's sentiments, and I resent you bringing it up at this time. But, Mr. York," he continued, turning to him, "Since you have agreed to command a military unit–somewhat reluctantly I must add–let us clear the air with these men so that this matter will never be dragged up again."

"Father, there is no need." Wren turned hotly toward Andre d'Arcenault "Damn you, Frenchman! You are not even one of *us*!"

Morgan raised his hands, quieting Wren. "Your father is right." He turned sharply, his arms crossing at his chest. "I sat here for two hours listening to your views. Perhaps I do have something to say." His eyes made a slow, fluid sweep of the men in the room. "Do you think Louisiana will be treated like a blushing bride embarking on a new way of life?" he began in an even tone. "My God–no! She will be viewed as a naughty, ungrateful child that has kicked its mother in the shin. How can you be so blind? Watch the thousands who will gather to defend the glory of Louisiana, as we all will. And when our powerful foe, the Union, has tired of indulging our fantasies, count the few who limp back, only to find remnants of what once was and can never be again. Yes–Louisiana seceded from the Union. Three cheers for Louisiana! She may well have driven a dagger into her heart. The results will be the same."

Andre de'Arcenault's eyes narrowed as they met Morgan's. "You gave Monsieur Wellington a commitment earlier in the day. Do you now say you will not take up arms with your neighbors against our enemies should it come to that? Tell us, monsieur..." Andre stretched out his arms. "I am sure we all want to know, once and for all, whether you stand for or against us. We will place our lives in the hands of our commanding officer–a position you have accepted–tell us if your loyalty is with the men you will command!"

Morgan drew up, set his goblet on the trestle table beside

him, and tucked his thumbs into the pockets of his trousers, flaring back his coat. "Every man in this room knows I will not fight for the right to own slaves. You all know I am not a born Louisianan–but hear my words now. I will fight for Louisiana as if she was my own, and I will die for her if I must. But God help us, I have a fear..." Morgan's palm rose to his forehead, quickly lowering. "I have a fear right here in my heart that some of us, should we ever take up arms against the Union, will never again meet in this world." The men gave him a strange, silent look that denoted fears of their own. Most of the men had sons joining Morgan's command. "Now," Morgan continued quietly, "I have offered half the horses we possess for the cavalry troop now forming. We will need ten times as many."

"Then you will begin training?" Rodney Wellington asked.

"The men will be fit for a king's brigade when I finish with them. But I cannot play God, and I cannot promise they will be returned to you when any conflict we might face is ended. That is the chance you are taking by offering them to me."

A man in the back of the room stated "No one has said secession will lead to war."

"That is true," Morgan replied. "But the possibility is great."

Andre d'Arcenault returned to the subject of sons contributed to the cause. Laughter echoed in his words. "I have no sons...only daughters. But they are fine stock and would fight well."

Not a single man saw humor in his words. Fire sparked between Andre and Morgan. "Keep your daughters at home," Morgan replied. "We will accept a contribution of all but three of your horses."

"In a bloody pig's eye!"

The two men started toward each other, but Wren stepped into their path. 'We are all very tired. The women are planning a big ball tonight to celebrate secession. Let us rest up for that."

"Bah," Morgan spat, only now turning his angry eyes from d'Arcenault "You speak of troops and drills and training in one breath, and speak of an elaborate ball to celebrate secession in the next. Secession is not worthy of a celebration. It is a disgrace!"

Wren feared a scene. He had not seen either Morgan or Andre so heated before. His arm went across Morgan's shoulder. But Morgan pulled away and immediately turned back to Andre. He started to say something but Anna knocked at the parlor door before entering. She approached, her hand going through the crook of Morgan's arm. It was as if she knew an unsalvageable moment had been reached.

"Gentlemen, dinner has been prepared for all of you. I would be pleased if you consent to take dinner with us."

Only half the men were able to stay to dinner, at which time Anna whispered to Morgan, "You do have a way of making friends, don't you, Husband?" He smiled but said nothing.

Through dinner, Anna noticed the lack of feeling in the smiles Morgan reluctantly bestowed on their guests. Anna knew that his heart was not with the southern cause. He abhorred slavery and had not hesitated to make his feelings known this afternoon. Yet, she knew that despite hell and damnation and fanatic secessionists, he would fight to the death for Louisiana.

Slavery was a bitter gall in his throat. Shadow Marsh had lived and thrived without it these past few years. Their people were free and happy and worked hard and willingly in the cotton fields for a home and an adequate wage. Incentive was the only true motivation–not brutality.

But the South, guided by her fanatic urges and passions, was determined to lead her young men into a fate worse than death. War...a cruel, needless war that would pit brother against brother.

* * *

It was April, 1861. Anna sat quietly in the shade of the veranda. Michael and Patrick played contentedly with their wooden soldiers at her skirts, while little Bonnie slept peacefully in her crib. The early morning air was cool and refreshing. Bea sat in the rocking chair beside Anna, her head back and her eyes closed in sleep. Anna looked around at the meadows tall with grass, at the overseer's empty cottage where the azaleas were in profuse bloom. Everything was lovely and green and colorful. She felt so at peace.

Morgan had assigned the bulk of Shadow Marsh's business responsibilities to Joby Cade, so that he would be free to train with the men forming the Second Louisiana Cavalry Division. Other units, over the past few months, had toyed with federal troops, who had not heeded warnings to vacate the state, but the skirmishes were merely aggravating thorns in Mr. Lincoln's sides. Anna prayed that the war everyone spoke almost proudly of was just a rumor carried on the wind by hotheaded fanatics. Lincoln had issued various ultimatums to Louisiana and her sister secessionists, but all had gone unheeded by the state legislatures. Louisiana was determined to remain a vital part of the newly formed Confederate States of America.

Anna caught sight of Wren Wellington, gouging the sides of his horse as he flew through the gates of Shadow Marsh, screaming at the top of his lungs. She came to her feet, knowing that whatever news he screamed was not good. By the time he arrived at the veranda, their people had rushed from the house and from Cabin Row to hear the news.

"What are you saying, Wren?" Anna rushed up to him as he dismounted.

Wren took her hands and held them lightly. "Our own General Beauregard has fired on Major Anderson at Fort Sumter. The federals would not withdraw from South Carolina territory and thus have been fired upon." Excitedly, Wren touched his lips to her fingers. "It is the beginning, Anna. War! We are at war with the United States!"

Anna hastily withdrew her fingers. "You don't have to be so jubilant about it, for mercy's sake! Where is Morgan?"

"He is just finishing up with the men. He'll be here shortly."

She'd seen it coming. As each of the eleven southern states had seceded, orders had been issued to the federals to surrender arsenals and forts within its borders. But the federals had been as stubborn as the secessionists calling on them to quit their territories, and had clung to their rights to deny secession. Now she knew where all this stubbornness was leading.

War!

Bea began to wail, "Lawd, Jesus, we'll be slaughtered like lambs at the altar," which made the children start to cry. Before Anna might chastise her, Bea descended the steps to be with her people, and they joined in a low, haunting hymn. Disgruntled, Anna gathered up her children to enter the house. "Go on about your business, Wren Wellington...you have stirred the passions of this plantation, and I am angry with you for it." Before he might respond, she entered the house with three crying children.

Tears rested on her eyelids. How could Wren be so happy? What were the sentiments of the other men training under Morgan's command? She knew how Morgan felt, and surely he had not been infected by the excitement and patriotic passions of his neighbors. Thank God for one rational man among the lot, Anna thought, pressing her lips into a thin line.

She did not want to think about the black cloud settling over the South. She wanted everything to be normal and sane again, and for men not to be taking to the fields to train for war. Yes, they looked splendid in their gray and gold uniforms made lovingly by doting mothers and wives. But how many of those uniforms would end up on the battlefields with lifeless bodies in them? Anna shuddered at the thought.

When the children had been taken to the nursery, Anna sat alone in the parlor, where she dropped her head into her hands and wept. Then Bea approached, gave her a clean handkerchief, and sat beside her. She said nothing, but merely shared the pain of her broken heart.

"Bea...Bea," Anna whispered. "Do you know what has happened?"

"Yas'sum, I do."

"Fort Sumter is the beginning of the end. The North and the South will settle their complex differences in the simplest and deadliest of ways."

"Yas'sum...war. That be men fo' ya."

As they comforted one another, the men rode up the lawns with jubilant war cries, waving banners in a wind created by their fast-moving horses. Anna rose and silently watched,

259

horrified. In the dust stirred by a dozen or more horses she could not see Morgan. Just the prospect that he might be among this fanatic crowd sent her angrily into the foyer where Wren awaited the other men. Andre d'Arcenault demanded one of the servants passing toward the kitchens to bring a bottle of whiskey to celebrate. Then several other dusty men rushed into the foyer.

"I wouldn't come into my house making demands," Anna snapped at d'Arcenault "Get out...get out all of you!" Anger flashed in her emerald eyes. Wren, astonished, quietly motioned the men outside.

"What troubles you?" he asked, approaching Anna, taking her arm rather roughly when she entered the stairs for a hasty departure. When she did not answer, but stood looking at him, he repeated, "What is wrong, Anna?"

"What is wrong?" she repeated, pulling her arm from his grip. "All you hotheaded, immature puppies...coming in here like a Titan army in your fancy uniforms, demanding whiskey!" She could not prevent her tears. "There is nothing to be proud of. War is a horrible thing and you make light of it as you would a casual dance or a Christmas party. I am sickened–sickened, do you hear?" Her voice became high-pitched and angry, and she could scarcely restrain the sob collecting in her throat. Morgan silently approached from the veranda, carrying his gray uniform hat. His jacket was unbuttoned, revealing his slim physique and the tight military pants tucked into highly polished black boots. The double row of brass buttons shone brilliantly in the light of the chandelier spilling in from the parlor. "And you," Anna screamed at Morgan, "Were you with that insane bunch?"

"No, Anna...I just rode up."

Sobbing now, scarcely aware that Wren had backed away and left the house, she moved into Morgan's arms. "Forgive me. Your days of playing soldier are over. It is for real now. Why– why must it be so?"

Morgan escorted her into the parlor and quickly shut the double doors. He sat beside her on the divan and took her hands in his. "There will be a ball tonight at Hopewell. We must attend, Anna. Tomorrow..." Morgan held her fingers between his warm hands and gently stroked them. "Tomorrow our company will depart for Baton Rouge to join other companies forming for the defense of our new Confederacy."

Anna threw herself against him and wept. "Tomorrow you will leave us?" She did not try to stop the tears dampening the shoulder of his uniform. She remembered not too long ago their sacred vow to each other that no force on earth would tear them apart. But they had not expected war–war within their own country, or what used to be their own country. "Damn this new Confederacy!" Anna had not realized she'd spoken the harsh words until she felt Morgan's arms tighten around her shoulders.

He drew back, favored her with a warm smile, and touched his fingertips to her tear-stained cheeks. "Dry your tears. Tonight wear your prettiest gown and show the other women had beautiful you are. Show your husband how courageous you are."

Again, Anna drew into his arms. "I am not courageous...I am frightened, more frightened than I have ever been. Every day I will watch for you, and every day I will fear that you'll never return to me."

Morgan said nothing, for in his heart was the same terrible fear. He could face dying, if that was the fate awaiting him. But at this moment, he could not bear the thought of death forever parting him from the woman he loved. Thus, he continued to say nothing, but contented himself to hold her in his arms, to feel the warmth of her penetrate his flesh, like a rapturous, wild gypsy wind. Then one of his lieutenants knocked and Morgan called out for him to enter. He approached, stood off a few feet and spoke only when Morgan looked to him.

"Colonel, the men await your further orders."

Morgan rose now, straightened his jacket, and put his hand on Anna's shoulder. Again he gave her a comforting smile. "I'll dismiss the men. You begin your dressing and I'll meet you in half an hour."

When she heard the dull thud of the men's boots disappear from the house, Anna rose and started toward the stairs. In the course of a few short minutes her life had turned topsy-turvy. The second future she had happily contemplated for herself and

Morgan was shattered beyond redemption. They would be parted by a vile, vicious war, and Morgan's life–the lives of many men–would dangle on the cords of fate.

Lovey helped her with her hoops and petticoats and swept her hair up in a high coiffeur into which she placed diamond and emerald-studded combs. As Lovey fastened the stays of her emerald satin gown, Anna quietly studied her reflection in the mirror. She was twenty-six years old, yet this morning she had felt like a naïve schoolgirl. Her gaze went beyond her pale ivory skin and black hair, and she saw the remnants of her youth slowly sag with defeat. She realized she was weeping only when Lovey's hands went fondly around her shoulders.

"Miss Anna, my good friend. Don't you worry none 'bout that man o' yours. He'll be comin' back to Shadow Marsh. This be his home, an' you his woman."

Anna patted her hand, trying to still the sob gathering anew in her throat. Turning to hug Lovey with a fierce desperation, she whispered, "Yes...yes, we must pray that all our men return." When Anna drew back to show Lovey that she could smile and be brave, she saw that Lovey, too, was weeping.

Lovey explained, "It's my man–Joby Cade–he be goin' off to war with Mist' Morgan."

Anna drew back in surprise. "But he can't. We need him here to run Shadow Marsh."

Lovey quietly shook her head. "Joby Cade, he be sayin' Shuckin' Sam got a good head. An' Joby Cade, he be sayin' with all the strappin' men here at Shadow Marsh, he can be spared to go with Mist' Morgan. Mist' Morgan, he say Joby Cade, he can't go with him, but Joby Cade, he remind Mist' Morgan he be a free man, and he do what he want to do."

Anna took Lovey's hand and started toward the door. "Come, we must talk sense into him."

Lovey held her back. "Miss Anna, you jes' let Joby Cade go with Mist' Morgan, if that what he want. The plantation men that take up the uniform, they be needin' a manservant to care fo' them."

Anna drew a quick breath, surprised at Lovey's suggestion.

"Morgan has never considered Joby Cade a manservant, Lovey! You know that!"

"An' Joby Cade, he know that, too. He be goin' as a friend, but he won't be sittin' 'round with idle hands. You let Joby Cade serve Mist' Morgan the way he want to. It ain't rightly none o' our business."

Anna was resolute. "Morgan will stop him."

Behind her tears, Lovey gave Anna a gentle smile. "Joby Cade, he done tol' Mist' Morgan it ain't none o' his business either. He a free man. Mist' Morgan, he tol' Joby it be his decision to go off to war with him."

Anna and Lovey embraced, both broken-hearted and both needing the comfort of the other. "My dear friend," Anna whispered. "What would I do without you?"

* * *

Morgan dropped to the ground against the trunk of the ancient cypress. He needed the solace of the special bayou clearing where he and Anna often went. It was quiet, serene; he enjoyed watching the herons roost along the bayou and turtles bask lazily on half-submerged logs. Occasionally, the dark eyes of an alligator would break the water's surface, quickly submerging again. The sweet, early spring smell of honeysuckle drifted into his senses. Far behind him, he heard the rumblings of Cabin Row and the neighing of horses being harnessed to carriages and wagons. He heard a high-pitched, possessive squeal–his own faithful Amigo–protesting the departure of the mares from his fields.

The happy, carefree life of the southern planter was at an end. The days ahead were destined to shatter the hopes and dreams of the Deep South. Morgan didn't relish the idea of going off to war and leaving Anna and the children alone. No matter what horrors he witnessed in the weeks and months to come, he prayed that war would never reach Shadow Marsh. He wanted only the arrival of the day when he would return to well-kept green meadows, herds of fat cattle, the lovely, untouched bayou clearing where he had dreamed many dreams–and to a dear wife, the mother of his children, who would await him with loving

263

arms.

A movement startled him and his body went rigid for a moment. Anna dropped to the ground, her hands coming up to gently rest around his shoulders. Her soft, clean hair touched his cheek. "I knew you would be here," she whispered. "It is our special place. When you are parted from me, I will come here to think my special thoughts of you, and pray for your speedy return."

"And what special thoughts will you think of me?"

"All of my thoughts of you are special. Oh, Morgan...do you have to go?"

"I must, Anna. I have made Louisiana my home and I owe her my allegiance."

"Men and their loyalties!" Then, "Please keep yourself safe for me."

"My sweet, sweet Anna...your lovely face embedded deeply in my heart will see me through the worst of times. You know I will return to you." Capturing her mouth in a gentle kiss, he whispered, "A man with a woman like you does not give her up easily...I *will* return," he promised again.

"I hold you to that promise, Husband."

Twilight fell and a million tiny stars gleamed like diamonds in the velvet sky. Nothing existed outside the circle binding them in the deep, possessive embrace that was a promise in itself.

# Twenty-two

The men had been gone scarcely three months when Anna took it upon herself to go to Hopewell and make amends with Violet. It had been more than two years since they'd spoken, and every moment of silence between them had taken its toll on Anna. They had once been like sisters. Anna wasn't really sure what had caused the rift between them, but she was sure it had something to do with Wren.

Bea intercepted her as she entered the foyer in her tan riding dress. "Where you think you goin'?" Bea asked, drawing her hands to her wide hips.

"Out riding," Anna replied casually, adjusting her riding gloves and calling Lowey across the veranda. "Lowey, ready my horse, will you?"

"You ain't leavin' the house," Bea argued. "What with riff-raff a-goin' back and forth on them roads, it ain't safe fo' you to be out there without a man beside you."

"Posh … I'll cut across our own fields. I'm going to visit Violet."

Bea chuckled beneath her breath. "Miss Violet be findin' a little corner to hide herself in when she sees you a-comin', Miss Anna. Now, don't be foolish! Stay here where you be safe."

Anna usually listened to Bea, but Violet's open antagonism toward her had gone on long enough. When Morgan had come home, he had often said that Violet would come around when she was ready. But Anna would no longer be put off. Their family had been divided by political hostilities, and it was time to put petty bickering behind them. Therefore, she stepped out to the veranda and waited for Lowey to bring her saddled horse. He wasn't as quick to accomplish his duties as their late groom, Quash, had been, and Anna was prepared for a longer wait. She sat down at the table and contemplated the morning's lemonade, which still stood there, diluted by the ice that had long since melted. Anna was reminded that she had yet to order that new hinges be installed on the ice house door, and made a mental note to mention it to Sam upon her return.

Absently, Anna stirred a little sugar into her lemonade. She was apprehensive about what would be her first meeting with Violet in over two years. She wondered how Violet would receive her, or if she would receive her at all.

When Lowey eventually appeared from the stables, Anna breathed a little sigh that denoted irritation. Not only had Lowey saddled the wrong horse, but he had used Violet's old side-saddle, with a stirrup that was much too short for her.

But, saying nothing, Anna favored the friendly boy with a smile and lifted herself into the saddle. She was not used to the quick movements of the gelding, which had unseated more than its share of riders. Adjusting her foot in the stirrup, she felt that her knee was all the way up to her chin. It wasn't, of course, but she felt more than a little awkward in the unfamiliar saddle.

When she entered the meadow toward the cotton fields separating Shadow Marsh from Hopewell, Morgan's painted stallion trotted up to her, expecting the lump of sugar she usually carried in her pocket for him. Laughing, Anna halted, gave Amigo his expected treat, and fondly patted the diamond of white hair between his eyes. "You miss your master, don't you, old boy?" Tears filled her eyes as she thought of Morgan, even as she smiled at the painted horse following them a little way down the meadow before returning to his herd of mares. They'd had quite a few painted foals these past few years that had shown the quality and breeding of their sire.

The morning was warm, the sun penetrating her blouse and burning hot against her skin. Sparrows tittered in the treetops, and overhead vultures circled the bayou. She heard the long, pained cry of a young heifer drifting through the woods and instinctively turned the gelding toward it.

As she exited the woods into the bayou clearing she saw the weak thrashing of a young calf stuck in the marsh, its mother circling from left to right. The calf dropped its head so that its chin scarcely rested above the sludge of mud entrapping it.

Quickly, Anna alighted her horse, surveyed the ground, and used her handkerchief to frighten the waiting mother off a few feet. She bent next to the exhausted calf, dug her arms into the mud up under its front legs and worked the calf up through the slush. When it was free and trotting toward its mother, Anna rose, approached the bayou and wet her handkerchief in the cool water. But it was useless in removing the thick mud covering her from her cheek to her skirt. She removed her blouse and dragged it back and forth through the water.

She had just pulled it back on and was fastening the buttons when she heard the wild vibration of what seemed to be a hundred horses galloping toward her. She turned on her knees and, against the bright glare of the sun, scarcely made out the shapes of half a dozen men who had formed a half circle around her. She was suddenly very frightened and her heart began to beat frantically. Gathering her wits, she made a move toward her horse. But one of the men, whose face she could not see, quickly jumped from his horse and held her firmly to him. As he laughed heartily, the others alighted and moved in.

"Let me go! You–you..."

A slim, bearded man approached her. "Quite a humane act," he sneered, "to mess up your fancy clothing to save a calf."

Anna recognized him only by his characteristic sarcasm. Her futile attempts to escape stilled. "Alistair?"

He circled her, and only when he stepped out of the sun did she clearly see the glittering brown eyes of her brother above odorous clothing and the brush of an unkempt beard. Alistair's fingers lifted to the dark, loose tresses of her hair. "Did I not tell you my sister is beautiful?" he said mockingly.

The men laughed, and one said something in Spanish mixed with inaudible broken English.

Anna had never seen maniacal cruelty such as she now saw reflected in her brother's eyes. Alistair took her arm firmly, causing her to cry out from the sudden pain, and dragged her toward him. "What do you want, Alistair?" she whispered harshly.

"Is that any way to greet a long lost brother?" he said,

laughing. "We want to be greeted with open arms, with a little food, a little wine, and the men are hungry for a beautiful woman." Oh, how often she had seen that sarcastic, half-cocked smile. "And I have promised them the most beautiful woman of all, dear sister … you!"

Alistair slung her into the midst of the men with a rude grunt and remounted his horse. "You will want some privacy I am sure, to entertain my friends. This..." his eyes moved over the peaceful, isolated bayou clearing, "will provide a romantic setting." Then he said something in Spanish to the men which made them laugh wickedly.

Anna's eyes grew wide and glazed with fear, and she saw the hand of one of the men lower and gently stroke his groin.

"Alistair," she screamed, slinging herself at his horse. "Don't leave me here. For God's sake, I am your sister!" But he merely gave her another of his wicked smiles, gripped her arm firmly, and pushed her toward the men. The filthy, vile bodies of seven men smothered her and she heard, through their deep, lust-filled grunts, the retreating hooves of Alistair's horse. She dropped to her knees and covered her ears with her hands.

"Senor St. Cyr say to treat you like the *elegante senora*," a black-mustachioed man said, digging his fingers into her hair. "You tell us if we hurt you, eh, *elegante senora*?"

Powerful arms circled and dragged her own tender arms back, and Anna felt herself being lowered to the ground. She gasped in horror as the hands of another man traveled the length of her thighs and brought her undergarments down. "Get your hands off me, you filth!" She screamed hysterically, feeling the greatest depths of fear she had ever felt.

Anna closed her eyes so that she would not have to witness this vile act upon her body. She wanted to die. She tried again to free her wrists and ankles, but the men were too strong for her.

Then across their heads she heard the single word, "No!" The man who had exposed himself, preparing to take Anna, turned on his knees toward Alistair.

"What you mean...no!"

"I mean leave her be. You have frightened her. That is all I wanted. There are other women at Shadow Marsh who will satisfy you just as well."

"You say, Senor St. Cyr..." the large man said, outstretching his hands, "that the *elegante senora*, your *hermana*, will be our *recompensa*, our reward."

A rifle clicked across the pommel of Alistair's saddle. "You touch her, Hernandez, and I'll leave a big hole where you pride once was. Now–move away from her."

Sobbing softly, Anna rose to her knees and held the remnants of her undergarments to her. "I hate you, Alistair! I swear, I'll see you dead!"

"Shut up, sister, or I'll change my mind about making you their prize." Alistair motioned his men away with a slow, fluid sweep of his rifle. "You–Hernandez." Alistair threw a short length of rope down to him. "Tie my sister to that tree over there. We cannot have her returning to Shadow Marsh until we have departed. She is damned good with a gun and might have one hidden somewhere."

Hernandez did not have to say anything to relay his feelings. The glimmer of disappointment, of unquenched lust, reflected in his small, beady eyes.

* * *

Alistair sat at the head of the bandits he had led for the past seven months. He had escaped from jail in Mexico City with the two Texans, and the others he had picked up along the way. One, Hernandez, he had taken from the hangman's noose after killing two federal soldiers.

Nudging his horse onto the road, Alistair and the men prepared to enter Cabin Row. Seeing the band of men sent the women and children scurrying to the indoors. Lovey, unaware of the approach of the strangers, stepped from her porch, humming a happy tune. Suddenly finding herself surrounded by the smiling, lecherous faces, she dropped the basket of corn she had been prepared to throw to the chickens.

"Take whatever you want, *amigos*," Alistair offered. "I'm going up to the house."

Screaming with wild abandon, the men charged into Cabin

Row, scattering chickens, tearing newly washed clothing off lines and trampling it into the dirt. Lovey picked up her skirts and ran back toward her cabin but was caught between two men, one of whom lifted her across his shoulder. As she screamed and beat at his back, he half ran toward the cabin with her.

Alistair dismounted at the porch just as Bea rushed from the house with a rifle, preparing to head toward Cabin Row to protect her family. She tried to dodge Alistair, but he caught her, snatched the rifle, breaking it against a marble column, and pushed her back toward the veranda. "Get to the kitchen, old woman. I'm hungry. In a while..." his head nodded imperceptibly toward Cabin Row, "my men will also be hungry for food. They are working up quite an appetite."

"Massa Alistair, what you be doin' back here?"

"I lived here once," he spat back, "And I want to see my boy!"

Bea shook her head, angry, and yet fearful of what might be happening at her daughter's cabin. "Ain't yo' boy, Massa Alistair. He be Miss Anna's boy. You give him to her. I heard it with my own ears."

Alistair ignored her outspoken reminder. "Where's York?"

"Gone off to war."

"Too bad," Alistair replied, entering the foyer. "I was going to kill him. Guess I'll have to kill that painted stallion of his instead."

"Why you kill that horse?" Bea thought quickly. She knew how much her beloved Anna's husband loved that horse, and to think that he might return to Shadow Marsh and learn that it had been killed for no good reason...Bea just couldn't bear the thought. She loved this family too much. "Mistah York, he give that horse to yo' son," she continued, her voice high-pitched with nerves, "an' the colts what come from him, when they sell, that money goes to yo' son fo' his education one day. If'n you have any decency at all, you won't be takin' that horse from yo' son!"

"Well...in that case, I'll let the beast live. In the meantime," he continued, pointing a finger at Bea. "If you leave this house I'll put a bullet through your head. Don't think I won't."

In the next few minutes, Alistair looted the house, taking what little cash was contained in Anna's cash box, and a few choice pieces of jewelry from her bedchamber. He then stopped by the nursery. Bea followed in his shadow as he marauded through the house, stealing what there was of value. But when he started to enter the nursery where Bess, one of the young women from Cabin Row, was tending the children, Bea tried to stop him. He pushed her violently out of the way. When she again tried to block his path, Alistair drew his pistol and pointed it at her head.

"You ready to die, old woman?"

Frightened, Bea stepped out of his path. Bess, when she had heard the screams of the other women in Cabin Row, had gathered the children to a dark corner. That was where Alistair found them.

He bent and picked up the oldest boy, who immediately began to cry. "I'm your daddy, little man," Alistair said in a soft, almost cordial tone. But Patrick saw only the dark, unkempt beard of a stranger who had dragged across the floor like a monster. He started to scream and thrash about so that Alistair could hardly restrain him. When Bea tried to take the boy from him, Alistair gathered Patrick in his left arm and his right fist swung back. Bea staggered from the brutal blow. Stunned, she lay across Anna's bed, a small gash in the right side of her face bleeding profusely.

Patrick continued to scream. Angered, Alistair merely threw him at the trembling nanny. "Take the damn brat," he hissed. "And I'm going to kill that damned horse!"

Bea raised her head only when she heard the door slam soundly. She rose, unwrapped her scarf and held it to her wound to stop the bleeding. "You take care of the young'uns," she said softly to Bess. "An' pray to God our Miss Anna don't get back till this heathen an' his outlaws done left."

Trembling with fear and dreaded anticipation, Bea prayed desperately that her daughter and the other women were not being hurt. She was powerless to do anything. All the weapons in the house, except the rifle Alistair had broken, were locked away in a cabinet and she didn't know where Anna kept the key.

* * *

Anna finally managed to free her wrists and remove the vile bit of cloth one of the men had forced between her teeth. She felt nauseous and could scarcely move without going to her knees. She'd heard a single gunshot some moments ago and fear filled her. The gelding had fled in the wake of the bandits who had attacked her, and she saw him down the meadow. Only when she tried to move did she realize she had turned her ankle. She limped toward the horse but, as she neared, it began a maneuver to keep constant distance between them.

Thus, Anna started back across the meadow toward Shadow Marsh. She felt her foot swelling inside her riding boot, and by the time she entered the meadow adjoining the house, pain wracked her every step. She saw a corner of the fence torn down, and realized that the panicked stallion and mares had broken through the fence and would have to be rounded up from the surrounding woods.

A few minutes later, as if existing in a terrible nightmare from which she could not awaken, she limped into Cabin Row. Dead chickens were strewn over the yards, furniture had been taken from the cabins and smashed against the sidewalls. She saw weeping, half-clothed women and heard the hysterical crying of the children. She stood in the midst of the horror and tried desperately to cover her ears.

But she could not succumb to hysteria. Thus, she moved as if hypnotized through Cabin Row, making a mental note of the damages, and comforting crying children and the women who had been viciously mauled and raped by the outlaws. The grounds of Cabin Row were in shambles.

And on the porch of Bea's cabin the worst sight of all. Bea sat in a great, sobbing heap, blood dripping from the side of her face and covering her shoulder as she rocked the tiny lifeless body of their dear Lovey against her own.

* * *

The sky was gray and overcast on the morning of Lovey's funeral. Gloom settled over Shadow Marsh and the mourners who gathered in the small clapboard church. The women cried openly and the men held their faces in large handkerchiefs and wept quietly. Anna was still in a state of shock. A few feet from her, Lovey's coffin sat among daisies gathered from the meadows by the children of Cabin Row. Anna had added roses from her gardens. She scarcely heard the solemn words of their own Reverend Ike, whose bony fingers tightly clutched the pulpit. Emotion had created a tight constriction in his throat.

"Weep not, my children, for our Lovey is not dead. She rests at the throne of the Almighty. Sons and daughters, weep not for your mother. She has gone to her heavenly home." Gradually, his voice faded into a silence that could not penetrate the small world in which Anna momentarily existed. She had tried these past two days to shut out the pain, the horror, the bitterness that rose within her, and the hatred that flooded her heart. Then her world of silence was shattered by the sudden, angry inflection reverberating in the reverend's voice. "Death took her up from the horror! But when she laid in his icy arms, Sister Lovey, she didn't feel no cold. Death rode to the evening star, into the wonderful light of glory, and on to the great white throne." Reverend Ike looked out over the mourners. "Weep not, children of the earth. Sister Lovey rests in the bosom of the Lord."

Less than an hour later, Lovey was buried alongside her daddy Mose in the quiet, peaceful little cemetery. The parish was horrified by what had happened at Shadow Marsh. Pop Gunter organized a posse of men who went in pursuit of the murderers, but they escaped into the jurisdiction of Mississippi and blended into the war consuming the South.

Now, Anna kept a loaded gun beside her. When the tears had dried and the pain inside had become a throbbing numbness, she swore that she would get even. There would be no remorse, no familial loyalty to breed even a moment's hesitation. She had never been so consumed by hatred.

Ironically, Alistair's devastation of Shadow Marsh brought Violet back to the fold. As Anna sat before her, feeling the gentle caress of Violet's fingers on her own, she listened to what she had to say and, at Violet's insistence, did not interrupt.

"I hated you, Anna," Violet whispered, ashamed. "You are beautiful and intelligent and witty and charming. You are everything I am not. Wren loved you, not me. When you were ill after giving birth to little Michael, I wished death upon you. For it, Wren turned me from his heart as he would a tenant from one of his farms. I hated you more then. Every time I saw the light in Wren's eyes at the very mention of your name, I wished death upon you." Tears filled Violet's eyes as she drew Anna to her in a fond embrace. "The night before our men left, I provoked Wren into slapping me. And when I wept, he drew me into his arms and tenderly held me. He came to my bed that night, Anna, for the first time in over two years. He still does not love me, but I have learned to accept."

Anna's arms slipped around Violet's shoulders. Bending forward brought pain to her still swollen ankle, and she winced. Violet did not notice. "Oh, dear Violet, don't you know that I have loved you as a sister? It has taken tragedy to bring you back to Shadow Marsh, and I hope that my deepest love for you will bring you back often. I never gave up, Violet. I always knew that we would hold each other again and share our sisterly secrets. Just you and me, like when we were happy, carefree children. I have missed you so."

"And I have missed you." Violet drew back and favored her with a shy smile. "I have a favor to ask, Anna...I am expecting Wren's child. May I come home to Shadow Marsh and be cared for by the ones I love?"

Anna drew her into her arms and laughed gently. "Oh, yes, yes, dear Violet. We will be so happy!"

But as she held Violet in another warm embrace, she knew she could never be happy, not as long as Morgan was involved somewhere beneath the fanatic veil of hostilities that covered their beloved South. *Dear Morgan*, she wondered, *where are you at this very moment?*

# Twenty-three

Morgan's division was camped near Chattanooga, Tennessee when news was received of the Confederate victory at Manassas, Virginia, in which two thousand of their men were either killed or wounded, as well as an equal number of federals. There was unrestrained jubilance among the troops over this early and decisive victory for the South, and the celebrating continued for days.

But Morgan did not celebrate. He was sick at heart. He had harbored hopes deep within him that sensible men would reach a sensible solution to the troubles between North and South, a dream not shared by some of the hotheaded young warmongers of his division.

Receiving the news of Manassas brought memories of his stepbrother, Jarred, and for the first time Morgan wondered what part he was playing in this war. He wondered if Jarred had been at Manassas on that fatal day. He wondered, despondently, if he could have been among the first federal casualties. Morgan drank away his sorrows in a bottle of good Scotch he'd carried in his saddle bag for days.

But with the news of victory for the Confederates came also the rumors of atrocities, one of which told of soldiers of Colonel Powell's Virginia cavalry mercilessly slaughtering Union soldiers who had crowded for safety in a field hospital after their defeat at Bull Run.

Sitting alone in the darkness of a great oak, Morgan listened to the sounds of night and the faraway chatter of the encampments of a thousand men. He thought of boys scarcely fifteen years of age throwing rifles over their shoulders in preparation for fighting for their new President, Jefferson Davis. They were dressed in a sundry assortment of Confederate uniforms made by wives and daughters, mothers and lovers, and speaking as lightly of war as they might a game of kick ball or marbles.

Morgan had left camp soon after receiving the news of Manassas, so that he might sit and reminisce and sort things out in his mind. A drizzling rain fell, but he made no attempt to protect himself from it. It had been several months since he'd seen his beloved Anna. The photograph of her and the children that he carried in a small brass and velvet frame had proven a great consolation in his loneliness. The photograph had been taken just days before their departure, and her slight smile indicated that, in a way, she had known they would soon be parted. There was sadness in her features, even as she'd tried to show only happiness for him.

Looking at the photograph for a long, long while, he felt assured that she was safe and far away from the hostilities quickly closing in on them. His division had not yet seen battle, but it was inevitable. They were now organizing for a move to Springfield, Missouri, where it was rumored several divisions of federal soldiers were now encamped.

He didn't want to think about that now. He wanted only to think of the cool spring days on which he and Anna had ridden horse back together over the meadows and fields. He wanted only to close his eyes and remember the warm, soft skin against his, and feel the thick, dark, rich hair that framed her delicate ivory features. He wanted only to hear in his mind her gentle laughter, and her words of love and adoration, which had flowed easily and often, capturing him in the spellbinding world of her gentle beauty.

*Anna...Anna*...he heard her name echo softly in his mind, bringing a smile to his lips and a deep, painful wanting that warmed his flesh and made his muscles quiver from the very thought of her. And it was her beauty that filled his mind when he was called to from the darkness of the timberline.

"Colonel?"

Startled, Morgan felt his muscles jump. His eyes narrowed, trying to penetrate the foggy darkness. Wren, his face in darkness beneath his canvas covering and untouched by the moonlight beaming through the oaks, knelt beside him. "What is the trouble, Wren? Has there been a movement of the federals?" He quickly returned the photograph to the inner pocket of his jacket, next to his heart.

"No–I am worried about you, Morgan."

"Me? I'm fit as a fiddle and ready to move on."

"Bull! You'd like nothing better than to return home...to Anna. A move I, too, would give my eye-teeth to make."

A frown pinched Morgan's features. Did Wren mean a move to home, or a move nearer to Anna?

Morgan mentally chastised himself for his doubts and settled back against the oak. He was well aware of Wren's feelings for Anna. "I'd be a fool not to want to go home," he eventually commented, "and a liar if I tried to deny that I did."

"Come back to camp with me. I wouldn't want to see you accidentally shot by our nervous sentry. Mabry is on duty."

"Heaven help us!" Morgan drew his knees up and rested his hands across them. Again he laughed. "I should have sent Mabry home the first time he shot the toes out of his boots. Now he has two boots without toes! Good thing they were too big for him or he'd have lost some toes too."

Wren, too, laughed. "Poor young fellow–the way he shakes he could churn butter just standing still."

Morgan suddenly grasped Wren's arm. These past two months their friendship had deepened into something special. They confided their feelings and their fears to each other, and there were times that Morgan wasn't sure what he'd do without him. "Thanks, good friend."

"For what?"

"For cheering me up. Now..." Morgan rose. "Let's return to camp and see what the hell the cook is stewing for us tonight. Hopefully, we won't end up with cramps in our bellies and half the unit pushing up daisies from eating the dastardly stuff."

They both laughed, yet there was no humor, just a strange, gentle sadness, and an understanding.

\* \* \*

In the weeks to come, Morgan saw atrocities he had not seen since the war with Mexico in '45. He saw fields so thick with corpses that a space did not exist to place one's foot. He wept silently to himself, even as he reflected a façade of strength and leadership that gained the immense respect of his men. Finally, in early August, Morgan joined forces with Colonel James McIntosh of the 3rd Louisiana Volunteers at Wilson's Creek in Missouri.

Their encampments were strung out for approximately two miles on either side of the road to Springfield. Many of the men had rigged open-air beds by heaping straw or leaves between two logs. During the day they engaged in scrubbing clothes, frying corn pones, and chopping firewood. After the day's duties were done, many engaged in letter writing, playing cards, and bouts of wrestling in which bets were placed. Many posed with comrades for photographs to be proudly sent home to wives and sweethearts. Toward midnight, in a moment of light fun, a few of Morgan's men chased down a goose that had wandered into camp. Rather than cook her as originally planned they named her Sally Dear, after the sweetheart of one of the men, and set her free in the woods.

In the night, as a light rain fell, federal troops under the command of Brigadier General Nathaniel Lyon took positions to move in on the Confederate encampments. Wilson's Creek curved west and south toward the James River, passing between steeply rising bluffs and tall hills cut by ravines. Lyon's forces approached from the west, over a high spur of land overlooking Morgan's encampment. The forces of Colonel Franz Sigel approached from the east.

By the time the Confederates were called to arms, a heavy rain obstructed vision. Confederate pickets and foragers had been placed under shelter at midnight to keep ammunition dry, which resulted in Sigel's flanking movements going undetected. Lyon's columns were not discovered until dawn.

General Lyon deployed his federal troops, threw out skirmishers, and advanced at the double up the northern slope of the spur, toward a plateau where a Confederate detachment awaited. Armed only with shotguns, the Confederates were forced back to the crest of the hill by the muskets of Lyon's troops.

Caught unaware by the advancing federal troops, Morgan mustered his men to arms. But, hopelessly surrounded by Lyon's troops, he ordered a retreat to Bloody Hill, a move that resulted in their being pinned against the bluffs above Wilson's Creek.

Morgan usually addressed Wren by his Christian name, but now, caught in the deadly crossfire of Yankee troops on either side of him, he called sharply, "Captain Wellington! Fall back to the timberline! For God's sake, fall back!"

Wren had taken a flesh wound in his upper arm that was more annoying than painful. He had lost a considerable amount of blood from the wound and scarcely saw Morgan through the maze of smoke filling the ravines. "Men, retreat," he eventually ordered, "Retreat yonder to the woods."

But it was too late. Federal troops moved to their rear. A small garrison of the New York 5th Cavalry and a unit of coloreds to the left and in front of them had trapped them on the hill.

"Cease fire, men," Morgan yelled, falling back against the earth wall of the ravine. The deafening roar of enemy cannon and of discharging rifles was silenced in the aftermath of Morgan's cease fire. He didn't know what to do. If they kept fighting, they would all die. He didn't want to ask his men to surrender, but he didn't want to see them dead either. His emotions fought one another. His all-consuming logic told him there was no other way but surrender. Then, as the smoke cleared, Morgan saw the struggles of a colored Yankee cavalryman, whose leg was caught beneath the weight of his dead horse.

Andre d'Arcenault fell to the earth wall beside Morgan. "Shall I kill the Yank, Colonel?"

Morgan grabbed the front of d'Arcenault's jacket. "No, you damned hotheaded Frenchman! We're soldiers–not butchers!" Morgan released him with a disgusted groan, and took a handkerchief from his jacket pocket, which he tied around the barrel of his rifle.

Wren looked across the ravine at him. "Surrender,

Colonel?"

"We'll discuss that later. I will not engage in fire with our enemy as long as that man lies helplessly there. Now..." Morgan's eyes made a slow sweep over his men. "Any of you have an objection to me helping that man?"

"I'll go," Joby Cade offered.

Morgan's hand fell to Joby's arm when he started to rise. "No, you won't. You'll remain here with the men. Damn..." He'd been about to remind Joby Cade for the hundredth time that he hadn't wanted him to leave Shadow Marsh, but all the harsh words in the world would not penetrate his stubborn determination. Morgan gave Joby an affectionate pat on the shoulder as he rose to his knees against the earth wall of the ravine.

The white handkerchief coming up from the ravine was immediately detected by Captain Tobias Peckinpah of the 1st New York Volunteers. He raised his hand, ordering that the cease fire of his men continue. Morgan rose, walking into the clearing between the two opposing armies. Peckinpah cautiously approached.

"Are you surrendering your troops, sir?" Peckinpah asked. He was a small man whose eyes appeared large and distorted through the lenses of his wire-rimmed spectacles.

"Not at this time, sir," Morgan replied politely. "A Yank– umm, Union soldier is trapped beneath his horse over there. This cease fire will allow him to be freed and seen safely behind your own lines."

Peckinpah did not attempt to halt his surprised look. He took a moment to study the tall, distinguished rebel officer, whose eyes were bright and golden above a neatly trimmed beard. "You halt a battle, sir, to save your enemy?"

"I halt a battle, sir, to save a man," Morgan countered, lowering his rifle. "If you will send out one of your strongest men, I will assist him in freeing your soldier."

Peckinpah snapped his fingers. "Sergeant Moody!"

A tall, burly sergeant approached, spat a wad of tobacco on the ground, certainly meant as an offense toward Morgan, and moved with him toward the grounded cavalryman. Morgan knelt and put his palm beneath the man's face to lift it. Startled, he ceased his movements at once. Staring back at him was the one blue eye that had watched him in amusement across their tightly entwined fists when they'd arm-wrestled aboard a Natchez whore-barge. Recovering his moment of surprise, Morgan gave Graz a weak smile that received only a contemptuous look.

The horse was too heavy for the two men. Morgan called to Peckinpah, "Send another of your men and some tree limbs, anything that can be used as a lever." Moments later, the Yankee soldiers had lifted the dead horse enough that Morgan could pull Graz out from beneath its weight. But Graz refused to take Morgan's hand and his good eye continued to hold him with contempt. Very quietly, Morgan said, "The last thing you said to me was that one day we would meet and I would be reluctant to take your hand. Now look at you–reluctant to take mine." He bent close and whispered, "I offer my hand as a friend, not as your enemy."

The softly spoken words elicited the smallest smile as Graz took Morgan's hand. When he was free and standing on his own two feet, Graz asked, "Why, Mr. York, do you take up arms for slavery? I thought you were a decent man."

"I do not take up arms for slavery, Graz...I take up arms for the South and for Louisiana, which I have made my home."

It was an explanation that Graz seemed willing to accept. When he staggered as if he might fall, the burly sergeant and the private supported him between them back to their own ranks. Morgan approached Peckinpah. "You may resume the battle, sir," he said dryly, retrieving his rifle, "when I am safely behind my lines."

"Sir." Morgan turned back. "You are outnumbered and surrounded. We have cannons–you do not. Save your life and the lives of your men by surrendering before another shot is fired. You and your men will be treated with the utmost dignity."

Morgan's eyes narrowed as he contemplated his offer. "I will discuss it with my men."

"I will allow you five minutes."

Moments later, Morgan sank against the earth wall, his silence summoning to him the few men he had left. He, Captain Wellington, Lieutenant d'Arcenault, Joby Cade, and twenty-seven other men had been separated from the main body of their division. Two of those men lay dead half a dozen yards away. "I guess you heard the Yank ask for our surrender."

"What are your sentiments, Colonel?" The question came from Wren Wellington.

"That we surrender. I can see no reason to sacrifice these men."

"Very well, we..."

Wren was not given a chance to complete his statement. Andre d'Arcenault rose to his feet and in a deep, throaty voice yelled at them, "No–*dieu damne*–surrender is a dishonorable thing! In France, true soldiers fight to the death!" Then, before anyone could stop him, he pointed his weapon across the earth bank and fired at the waiting federal troops. The responding shots echoed tenfold.

"You fool," Morgan growled. "You have sealed our fate. I would court-martial you for this, but there won't be anything left of us!"

In the course of the following hour, Morgan watched helplessly as the young men of his unit were cut down. D'Arcenault stood his ground like a madman, firing as fast as he could reload his weapon. Then, through the dense smoke, Morgan watched him drop his weapon and turn, a look of shock below the neat hole in the center of his forehead. He was dead before he hit the ground.

Morgan and the remaining seven men were able to hold off the advancing Yankees by sheer force of will. Morgan felt a penetrating sting in his shoulder–a bullet exiting through his back. For two hours more, as he tried to stop the steady flow of blood, the Yanks slowly closed in on them. Then the rifles of Morgan's men fell silent.

It took only a few minutes for Peckinpah to realize that the fire of his troops was not being returned. He raised his hand. "Hold your fire, men." The smoke was too dense to see beyond a few feet. Peckinpah called toward the enemy lines, "Rebel...Rebel colonel!" But he received no reply. He waited another half hour, discharging his rifle several times and waiting for return fire that never came. "Moody, accompany me." Cautiously, Peckinpah and the sergeant moved into the dense smoke. Bloodied, gray-clad bodies were strewn the length of the ravine. One young soldier had been decapitated by a cannon ball.

Peckinpah felt sick as he moved over the corpses, nudging them to see if any man was left alive. Hearing a movement, he brought his rifle to a ready position. A burly black man sat against the earth bank, Morgan drawn against his half-reclining body. The chest of the rebel colonel was covered with blood, and no movement could be detected.

"Don't kill 'em, Yank," Joby Cade softly pleaded.

"Is he your master?" Peckinpah asked with a note of compassion.

"No...he's my friend."

Sergeant Moody found only two other men still alive. Wren Wellington had taken another shot in his leg and had applied a tourniquet just above his knee. He willingly surrendered his weapon to the Yankee sergeant.

Peckinpah knelt and opened Morgan's shirt. He had taken bullets in his shoulder and the right side of his chest. Peckinpah felt for a pulse in his neck. Such a shame, he thought, shaking his head. He had never witnessed such an unselfish act of humanity as the one performed just hours ago by this rebel officer.

Another Yankee officer approached. "Sir, a courier has just brought news of General Lyon's death in the field. Our troops are retreating in the face of overwhelming rebel movements."

"And what am I supposed to do with these men?" Peckinpah asked, outstretching his hand.

"Colonel Gunthar has ordered that prisoners be taken and the rebel dead left where they fell."

Peckinpah sighed deeply. "Send the courier back to Colonel Gunthar that we will retreat as ordered." Tobias Peckinpah looked into Joby Cade's dark, glistening eyes. He didn't know what to say, or what to do. He didn't know whether this man so tenderly holding the rebel officer would be receptive to words of sympathy, so he said nothing.

"He's dead, ain't he?" Joby Cade hesitantly asked.

Peckinpah looked at Joby and the gray-clad officer for a long, silent moment. How long would this merciless slaughter continue? "I am sorry..."

Joby Cade held Morgan tenderly, his hand rising to brush the hair back from his still face. "Promised Miss Anna," he said softly against Morgan's hairline. "Promised her Joby'd keep you safe. How can I go home now, Mist' Morgan, an' break Miss Anna's heart?" Tear's traced a path down Joby's face. "Like ol' Joby's heart be broke right now."

Holding his dead friend, Joby's mind flew back over the good times...their hard work in the fields mixed with the light moments and laughing together–he remembered their trips to Natchez and Natchitoches, and Morgan never failing to introduce him to the men he did business with. He remembered the time in Natchez when Morgan had refused to dine at a restaurant because the proprietor had said Joby would have to eat in the kitchens. He remembered their iron-hard bodies locked in combat, as Morgan had tried to knock him off his feet in a rigorous but friendly bout of wrestling.

Remembering the good times that were forever gone, Joby held Morgan close and wept without shame.

# Twenty-four

*November, 1861*

Every morning for the past three months Anna had awakened with a terrible sense of doom. It was an intuition she could not recognize, a feeling that something had happened that would change the course of her life. She'd found herself fretting too often over menial things, and showing irritation when she would normally have reflected only patience. She often went for long rides along the bayou. But since the day Alistair and his outlaws had snaked through Shadow Marsh, pillaging and murdering, she kept a loaded rifle in the sheath of her saddle. Sam had spent a very patient week not too long ago teaching her how to use it more proficiently, and she could probably shoot the center out of an oak leaf at a hundred paces.

This morning she awakened drenched in a cold, clammy sweat that had nothing to do with the unusual warmth of the day. She had retired the evening before with a migraine and now, startled from her sleep by a terrible nightmare, she felt the beginnings of the migraine anew in the right side of her head.

She had tried to explain to Tylas last evening that laudanum would make her sleep too heavily, a condition that invariably caused the headaches to worsen. But he had not listened and had stated in a brisk tone that *I am the doctor and know what is best for you*! He had, therefore, left a large bottle of the potion by the wash stand with instructions that she should take it every four to six hours. Violet, enthusiastically sprung into action by an intense need to make amends for her past behavior, had indelicately coaxed her to take regular doses during the course of the evening and morning.

Anna swung her feet to the floor, approached the washstand and, frustrated by her illness when she had so much to be done, threw the bottle to a dark corner of her bedchamber. She hated it when drugs hampered her senses, made her eyes hollow and dark and left her skin with a sick, pasty hue.

Sitting on the edge of her bed, Anna wasn't sure why tears filled her eyes. She felt that strange, nagging emptiness she had felt for weeks now, and a dread that clung to her with vicious pincers. It had been seven months since Morgan had dutifully–and hesitantly–gone off to war, and in that time she had received only one letter from him, written five months ago. She wondered how many others he had written that she had not received. The mails were terrible these days. Oftentimes she imagined his warmth beside her, and heard, far in the back of her mind, the words of love and adoration he had often spoken against her cheek.

Oh, how she missed him! How she longed to see him riding up the drive toward Shadow Marsh, to feel him taking her in his arms and hear him swear–swear with all his heart and soul–that nothing would ever part them again. She tried to smile when she thought of him but, too often, found herself brooding in her loneliness and embittered by the war that had separated them. She despised Mr. Jefferson Davis and the fanatic passions of the South. She hated the horrid emptiness when she thought of Morgan fighting for a cause as despicable as slavery–though she knew he fought only for the State of Louisiana–and wanting only to be home at Shadow Marsh. Sometimes Anna felt they would never meet again.

She was about to return to her bed, despite the late morning hour, when Violet burst upon her. Anna quickly flicked the tears from her cheeks so that Violet would not see them. "Anna, arise quickly! A group of peckerwoods and field slaves is downstairs asking to see you! *Oof*! How awful they smell! And one of the rotters is wearing the uniform of our dear Confederacy!"

Anna did not like to hear the poor whites referred to as peckerwoods. Her disdain for the expression was evident in the way she returned Violet's wide-eyed look. "What do they want?"

"The one in uniform said something about requisitioning the signal bells from all plantations to be melted down for cannons. He is also asking for one good field wagon and a team of horses from each plantation. He has an order signed by

Lieutenant Colonel Charles Bramton of Baton Rouge."

"A mandatory order?" Anna questioned.

"It would seem so."

Annoyed by being dragged downstairs to deal with a summons that Violet could have handled herself, Anna brought her hand to her forehead and sat for a moment in silence. "If it is for our Confederacy, give them whatever they want. I would ask that they leave the signal bell at the house and take only those in the fields. You may summon Sam to escort them to their locations and to personally choose the wagon and horses he believes we can spare."

Violet stamped her foot in a childish fashion. "We need the bells in the fields," she argued, turning from Anna, "and Shadow Marsh has already donated half its horses. It won't look decent, Anna, if we end up on foot like the peckerwoods."

Anna didn't like that Violet's old, argumentative ways were returning. "Think of Wren," she responded sensibly. "Remember that he is off fighting for our Confederacy and perhaps the bells and wagons and horses donated by Shadow Marsh today might benefit him in some small way tomorrow."

Violet's cheeks suddenly grew pink with shame. "I hadn't looked at it that way." Kneeling beside Anna and tenderly resting her head in Anna's lap, she entreated, "Forgive me. Sometimes I don't know what comes over me. Of course I would do anything to help our men. Really I would."

In just four months Violet would be a mother. Anna hoped she would learn tact and kindness before she held a precious infant to her bosom. She did not want a child—especially a girl—growing up with the tart tongue of her mother. She patted Violet's shoulder, sorry that she'd gotten cross with her. Perhaps she should try to be more indulgent, and more understanding. "Of course, you would. Come. . ." Anna's hand went to Violet's shoulder and coaxed her up. "Relay our compliance to the servants of the Confederacy and send for Sam. Go on—be good for your cousin."

As Violet rose, she took Anna's hand and enveloped it between her own. "Thank you for being so patient with me, dear

Anna. Sometimes I don't know why you are. I can be such a vicious girl!"

"We are family. Now, run on. And be careful on the stairs going down."

When Violet left, Anna attempted to get a few more minutes of rest. But memories of Morgan filled her with an intense need she somehow felt would never again be quenched...and a sadness she could not explain.

* * *

Later in the afternoon, Anna accompanied Violet on her weekly visit to Hopewell to see Mrs. Wellington and hear news of the war. The Wellingtons had only their servants now that Sarah had married Warren Fairgate and moved to Alexandria to be with him. Despite a lack of family feeling for Violet, Mrs. Wellington was always glad to see her. She was, after all, carrying her first grandchild. Sam drove Violet in the buggy, and Anna rode her own mare side-saddle beside them. She enjoyed the ride along the bayou and through the mile-long carriage-way leading to Hopewell, which was shaded by trees festooned with Spanish moss.

It was Tuesday, the day Mr. Pyree, the only literate tenant farmer at Hopewell, made his weekly trip to the printing office in Alexandria to read the news of the war and pick up a list of the casualties. It was always with a still heart that Mr. Pyree was invited to sit in the Hopewell parlor and read the list to the representatives of each family along Bayou Bouef who flocked to Hopewell, praying that a familiar name would not be listed among the dead and wounded.

Mrs. Wellington was especially pleased to see Anna and spent a few minutes showing her the pansies she had planted in window boxes along the veranda. Violet sat alone in the parlor, sipping hot chocolate, staring around the massive, elegantly furnished room at the generations of Wellington portraits in gold-gilted frames. She sighed deeply and did not hear Marigold approach.

"More chocolate, Miss Violet?" There was always the slightest note of sarcasm in Marigold's voice when she spoke to

Violet.

"Mrs. Wellington," Violet snapped. "Whenever will you learn some manners, girl?"

"When you moved out of yo' husband's house, *Miss Violet*," Marigold responded, unsmiling, "you gave up the right to his name."

Violet sprang to her feet, enraged by Marigold's impertinence. "How dare you take that tone with me! You evil girl–how dare you!"

Her purse clutched tightly between her fingers, Violet started around the trestle table toward Marigold, more than likely her intent to slap her with it. But gentle laughter became louder in its approach from the foyer and Violet turned back, immediately regaining her composure. Pleased and smiling to herself, Marigold returned to the kitchens, leaving Violet to face Mrs. Wellington.

Faced with the angry flush of Violet's thin features, Anna's laughter became a questioning gaze. "Oh, it's that girl," Violet snapped, flipping her wrist. "She just–just twists my guts so that I'd like to slap her face. The little bitch!"

Mrs. Wellington gasped. She'd never heard Violet use such language.

Anna responded, "You don't need to be getting in a state, Violet, not in your condition."

Violet shrugged and threw herself back to the divan.

After a light lunch and tea, Mrs. Wellington prepared the parlor to receive their regular Tuesday visitors. By two o'clock the ladies had not arrived. At half-past two, Anna watched Mr. Pyree's wagon slowly pull up to the front veranda. He handed something to James, the Hopewell butler, and drove off at a much quicker pace. It was very unnerving, the way Mr. Pyree had departed and the ladies of the neighboring plantations failing to show up for their regular gathering. Like an all-consuming fog, Anna's worst fears became a dark, empty void, where she could not even detect her own heartbeat. There was nothing in the world that could empty a room like the imminence of dreadful news.

James entered the parlor. "Mist' Pyree, he leave the list, Miz Wellington." There was a distinct sadness in his eyes, and hesitancy in his voice. Anna felt a sudden urge to flee before the terrible, dreaded truth could be heard. But her need to know outweighed the dread that had settled upon her.

Mrs. Wellington cleared the tremble in her tightly constricted throat. "Read the names on the list, James, of people that we know." She arose, approaching the window to look out. She was visibly trembling.

Slowly, James began to read the names on the list that he recognized, and that he knew would be known to Mrs. Wellington and Mrs. York. Lieutenant Andre' d'Arcenault, killed at Wilson's Creek, Missouri...Luther Brady's son, Clem, wounded at Wilson's Creek. Both sons of Hopewell tenant farmer, Mr. Johnson, killed at Manassas. James had just completed reading through the letter S when he looked up. "Please, ma'am...do I have to do this?"

Violet brought her trembling fingers to her mouth, and her eyes were wide with fear and dreaded anticipation. Mrs. Wellington released a nervous "*Hrumph*," and replied, "Yes, James, you do."

James looked back down, hesitating ever so slightly. "Cap'n Wren Wellington, Second Louisiana Cavalry—wounded and taken prisoner at Wilson's Creek, Missouri."

Violet cried in relief, "Thank God...thank God he is not killed," and clasped her hands firmly together.

There was no need for James to continue. Anna easily read his thin, gaunt features, and the world of sadness that gathered in his dark eyes as he looked at her. "Colonel Morgan York, Second Louisiana Cavalry..." Anna felt that sick, sinking feeling in the pit of her stomach. Dread consumed her. The world's noises became a dull, nonexistent thing that could not penetrate the void surrounding her, crushing in on her like a huge rock. She wanted to die. She wanted to crawl away somewhere so that the dreadful pain of knowing could not reach her. Then—slowly—the world's noises returned, and through the dreadful fog of her worst nightmare, she felt rather than heard the thundering echo of James's softly spoken words: "Killed at Wilson's Creek, Missouri, August Fifth, Eighteen-Sixty-One."

Anna sat unmoving, no emotion readable in her still, wan features. She scarcely felt Mrs. Wellington's hand fall to her shoulder, or heard Violet's softly spoken words of condolence. She had known all along that something dreadful had happened. She'd felt it for weeks now—an emptiness that had once been filled with the power of his love...Morgan's love that could defy the barriers of time and distance...the love of the man who was her husband and one of the most wonderful reasons in the world she had for living.

Slowly, silently, Anna rose and allowed her feet to take her where they would, out to the veranda where, in a matter of moments, her sorrel mare thundered across the meadows of Hopewell Plantation toward the bayou clearing. She and her beloved had spent so many, many happy, intimate moments there, embracing, caressing, and assuring each other of their love. But now, the most brutal barrier of all had forever separated them.

With the crisp November wind rustling through her thick hair and turning her tears to bits of ice, Anna cared about nothing—nothing but escape from the horror that fell upon her tender shoulders that had reached deeply into her heart and wrenched it until there was nothing left...not even a heartbeat.

She didn't remember the long, fierce ride along the bayou. She didn't remember dismounting from the mare at the bend in the bayou where she and Morgan had spent their happiest moments together. She knew only that her whole world had been shattered. Repeating his name over and over, she hoped that it would make the terrible news she had received go away. She screamed a loud, groaning scream and buried her long, well-groomed fingernails deeply into the soft bank of the bayou. Soon, her screams became broken, erratic sobs, and her sobs became quick, exhausted breaths that wracked her body. Then, a dull, throbbing numbness enveloped her.

Anna's face gently touched the cool earth thickly blanketed in oak leaves. Her senses caught in the pungent smell of rotting leaves, in the early winter smell of the bayou, she slowly, slowly drifted away, leaving an empty void where consciousness once had been.

* * *

There was nothing wrong with Anna that time would not mend somehow. For several weeks, she confined herself between her bedchamber and the nursery. She temporarily turned the plantation ledgers over to an accountant in Alexandria and spent as much time as she could with the children. They often looked at her in confusion, because she was always so sad and they were accustomed to seeing her only in the early morning, when they took their meals, and when she heard their prayers at night. During that last few minutes together, they would each receive a hug and a kiss.

It was at this last visit of the day that her memories of Morgan were so strong. He had always been beside her to hear the children's prayers. But he was gone now, his life snuffed out by a vicious war–a war whose early months had left Anna angry and resentful and bitter. At first she had wept brokenly when she thought of Morgan, but now, there was only a cold, empty numbness. She frequently rode down to the bayou clearing, oftentimes taking no protection against the winter, which was colder this year than it had been any other year that she could remember. She would sit against the cypress trunk and feel the icy fingers of the winter eve sting her delicate skin and turn her cheeks a bright crimson. Sometimes, if she sat long enough in solitude, she would begin to wonder if there was any reason to live.

Then she would think of the children and the answer was always right there within her grasp. Her broken heart and the loneliness that filled her with a dull, throbbing pain would have to take second place to the needs of the children. She was the only parent they had left now.

Tonight Anna wrapped herself in her rabbit fur cape and walked slowly toward the bayou clearing. Christmas would be upon them shortly, and she had promised the children gay festivities and a big party, as in the past. Bea had not been herself since Lovey's death and had, in quite definite words, refused to lend her assistance at any such gathering. But Anna was not annoyed with her. Bea's own outspoken bitterness was Anna's silent bitterness.

Sitting against the cypress trunk and hugging her cape closely to her, Anna thought of the children, whom she had put to bed within the last hour. She could still feel the tightness of their little arms around her neck. They had stopped asking about Papa long ago, yet there was always a question gleaming in their eyes as they looked at her. She had not told the boys that their papa was dead. They were too young to understand the finality of it, and would ask questions Anna would be unable to answer.

Anna looked across the bare, bleak timberline of Bayou Bouef. Winter, like the culmination of a battle, had a way of silencing the world's noises. The sky was a clear, purple-black, twinkling with a thousand stars. A quarter moon met her silent gaze. Strangely, Anna's mind was devoid of thought. It was as if she were asleep, staring at the stars in the velvet sky, cleansing her mind of all that had troubled her and made her despair.

Suddenly, a twig snapped behind her. Remembering how unexpectedly Alistair and his outlaws had come upon her some months ago Anna came forward from her relaxed position. But half hidden in the shadows was the gangly form of Bea's grandson, Lowey, who stood back looking at Anna. He'd brooded deeply over the loss of his mother...and now his father, Joby Cade, was gone, too.

"Lowey?"

The young boy stepped forward. "Yes, Miss Anna?"

Anna outstretched her hand. "Come–sit beside me."

Lowey dropped to the ground beside Anna and sat Indiana style. He said nothing for a while, nor did Anna, but both watched the stars and the moon on its lazy perch above the timberline.

"Miss Anna?" Lowey's hesitation to speak echoed in his softly spoken words. "You reckon the Yankees took my pappy?"

Anna really didn't know what to say. She was so at a loss for words. So, she let a moment pass before responding, "Well–I wouldn't think so, Lowey. The Yankees are fighting for the freedom of your people. He isn't a soldier, so I don't think they'll take him prisoner."

Lowey shrugged. "Then where he be?"

"He's probably on his way home, Lowey. Missouri is a long way. It'll take him time to get home. But–you'll see..." Hope rose in Anna's voice, born of her desire to comfort this innocent child who could not understand the ways and reasons of war. "One day, you'll see him walking around the bend toward Cabin Row. You'll see..."

She thought at once of Morgan. She would not see him coming around the bend. His arms would never again open to her, nor would she feel the warm, tender embrace that had comforted her so many, many times. His silent, golden gaze would never meet hers, nor would she feel his gently whispered breath against her cheek. She would not feel the tenderness of his mouth claiming hers in a long, lingering kiss. Oh, if only she could have returned him to Shadow Marsh for a proper burial...but war would not allow that.

Tears rose within her, a painful lump choking in her throat. She managed only to say to Lowey, "Better get home before Bea misses you," and watched him disappear through the woods before she succumbed, sobbing brokenheartedly. She loved Morgan so deeply. Could death break the strength of her love? Could she just forget what they'd had together? Was she expected to be so emotionless that she could go on with her life without longing for him, wishing for him, and praying that she could be with him once again?

Another sound–almost a thrash–reached her from the timberline and she immediately composed herself. "Lowey, you must go to your mammy," she insisted without turning. When the boy did not answer, she looked around, preparing to scold him further. There, leaning against a tree, hardly visible in the dark, was the form of a man. She could see only his torso covered by a limp, dirty brown jacket. Her heart almost ceased to beat as she rose to her feet and started to run back toward the house. But she had gotten no more than a step or two when she heard her name spoken ever so gently.

"Anna..." She spun back just as the man slid heavily down the length of the tree and the moonlight caught his bearded, unkempt face. "Anna, help me. Please, help me."

Anna approached cautiously. There was huskiness in the familiar voice that made it impossible for her to identify it. Yet she felt no danger posed by the figure separated from her only by a few feet of darkness. Then the moonlight shone through the timberline and caught the gleam in those oh, so familiar doleful eyes. "Wren?" Anna sat beside him and cupped his ragged face between her hands. A pair of crudely made crutches had fallen to the ground, and there was an empty space where Wren's left leg had once been. She drew him into her arms and felt his hands slowly slip around her waist beneath the fur cape.

"I'm home, Anna...I'm home. I thought I'd never see Hopewell again."

"You're at Shadow Marsh, Wren."

"Shadow Marsh?" he echoed weakly. "Yes–yes, I should have known. Violet wrote some time ago that she would be here until the baby–"

"She's here, Wren." Anna eased from him so that she might help him up. "Come–we must get you into dry clothing and into bed. We must summon Tylas..."

"Private Jenkins and I escaped near Chattanooga...he died about forty miles from here. I couldn't even bury him, Anna. I just covered him with pine straw and left him in the woods."

"Shh...you had no choice."

Anna helped him rise, supporting his body against her own. "I'm sorry about Morgan," Wren half whispered. "He was a fine man...he kept your picture next to his heart. He loved you, Anna."

Right now, Anna could not answer. Tears were behind every movement she made and every word she uttered. Bitterness pressed her lips into a thin line. Damn this war!

Morgan was dead, and Wren had returned home to Bayou Bouef. Anna's only wish was that the quirk of fate that had brought Wren home to Violet might also have brought Morgan home to her.

# Twenty-five

Wren collapsed in exhaustion halfway to Cabin Row. As they had moved farther out of the shadows of the timberline his emaciation and extreme illness became more evident to Anna and she was shocked to tears. She remembered only his good nature and sharp wit...his wonderful tendency to be a bit of a bore when he had so frequently confessed his feelings for her. She remembered a tall, slim frame and lazy gait, and smiles that had frequently warmed her heart. She remembered that he had loved her.

And now, in her arms, was a maimed, emaciated man who was more dead than alive. He had said very little since leaving the bayou clearing, and the little he had said made no sense at all. Anna was at odds wondering what to do. She did not want to leave him alone, yet she knew she had to get help. Half-conscious, yet perceptive of her plight, Wren refused to be coaxed from his half-reclining position against a fallen log.

"Get some help, Anna," he mumbled weakly. "I'll be all right." But as he uttered the last words, darkness folded around him and his head fell limply to the side.

Anna frantically shook his shoulders. "Wren...Wren! For Heaven's sake, don't die now! Not now!"

Get...help...Anna..." Despite the bitter cold, sweat broke out on his brow.

Anna rose and rushed through the orchard toward Cabin Row. Winter-barren limbs snapped at her face and her cape half slid from her shoulders. She lost her footing in the mud and slipped once, but rose with only one thought in mind–getting help for Wren. He was clad only in a wet, tattered shirt and trousers with his foot covered only by bits of rag. He probably hadn't eaten in days. Then she saw Shucking Sam putting out scraps for his hunting dogs and released a huge sigh of relief.

"Sam! Sam!"

Startled, Sam dropped the wooden bowl. "Miss Anna—what you be doin' out yonder this time o' night?"

Anna's lungs burst with icy pain and she could not speak for a moment. The wind had numbed her face and her throat felt like it, too, had turned to ice. She finally forced herself to gasp, "Wren—Wren Wellington...he's out there," and pointed with a trembling finger.

"Massa Wellington, Miss Anna? You sayin' he's out yonder?"

"Yes—in the orchard."

Sam jumped immediately into action, calling to his eldest son, and both men disappeared into the orchard. Anna leaned against the support post of Sam's cabin porch for a moment, accepting the cup of hot coffee Sam's wife, Lizzie, handed to her. But her hands were shaking so that she could only take a sip or two without spilling it. She handed the cup back to Lizzie.

"Better come on in by the fire, Miss Anna," Lizzie coaxed with concern.

"Can't—must wait for the men to bring Wren." Then she saw their dark forms appear from the shadows of the orchard. Sam was carrying the unconscious Wren.

By the time they reached the Big House, Shadow Marsh was in turmoil. Servants ran to and fro, Shucking Sam went for the doctor, and Bea quickly heated water to bathe Wren's ice-cold skin and revive his circulation. Violet, drawn by the commotion in the parlor where Wren had been laid on the divan, entered rubbing her sleepy eyes. Then she saw the prostrate form and the familiar features half hidden beneath the dirty, unkempt beard and rushed to him. The blanket Bea had thrown across him hid the loss of his leg.

"Wren—Wren..." she sobbed, in relief that he was alive and in pain at seeing him so thin and malnourished.

Weakly, Wren's hand came up to her shoulder, lightly brushing his fingertips against her warm cheek. "Forgive me, Violet...for not being a good husband to you."

A weeping Violet drew him into her arms. "You are a good husband, Wren. Things will get better. You'll see—you'll see..."

"Forgive me."

"Shh..."

* * *

In the days to follow, surrounded by loved ones, Wren regained his strength and was able to be moved back to Hopewell. Violet took the amputation of his leg surprisingly well. While she still possessed certain undesirable flaws in her character, Anna saw the great desire within her to change. And she was changing. Every day Anna admired her more for her spirit and determination.

With Wren and Violet gone from Shadow Marsh, Anna found more time to think, and to brood over the loss of her own dear husband. Whenever she looked into the eyes of her little son, she saw Morgan. Michael looked back at her with the warm, golden eyes of his father. Although Michael, unlike his father, tended by nature to be a little shy of affection, she still had this wonderful reminder of her love for Morgan, along with their precious little Bonnie, to keep him forever alive in her heart.

Rumors had been circulating for weeks that New Orleans expected to be invaded by the federals. Governor Thomas Overton Moore had mustered men to arms in preparation for the invasion, possibly by sea, and had asked for heavy artillery from the Confederacy. So far, masts of federal ships had not been seen on the horizon, and heavy artillery had been denied him. President Jefferson Davis boldly voiced his opinion that the federals had more important goals in mind than taking New Orleans. And, of course, Governor Moore, a proud Louisianan, was furious.

Anna had harbored ideas of visiting Louvenia Etienne in New Orleans for a few weeks, to relax away from Shadow Marsh, but had been discouraged by the rumors of invasion and the concerns of her people. Thus, she contented herself to return to the boring drudgeries of managing Shadow Marsh. She tried to put her pain to the farthest corner of her heart, although she frequently found herself thinking of Morgan for long periods of time. She took extended rides through the fields to see where

299

expansions in planting could be made in the spring, and often rode to Hopewell to visit Violet and Wren. He was ecstatic over the imminent birth of his child.

Anna stayed longer at Hopewell today, laughing for the first time in weeks. Wren's and Violet's newfound happiness was her own happiness, and she departed with a strange sense of well-being. But as she rode along the bayou and saw all the favorite places where she and Morgan had often gone together on horseback, her sense of well-being was replaced by the omnipresent gloom that had been with her since that fated day she had learned of his death.

Coaxing her mare into a fast gallop, she flew onto the grounds of Shadow Marsh as if all of hell was behind her. Bea was waiting on the veranda when she climbed down from her horse. Normally, she might have berated Anna for her recklessness on horseback, but today she did not. She had come out to the veranda for a reason when she'd seen her crossing the meadow, and so got right to the point. "Messenger, he rode in this mornin' with a letter fo' you," Bea said dryly. The happiness that had once been so evident in every word she spoke was missing. She still had not gotten over Lovey's death and the senselessness of it.

"For me?" Anna asked.

"No...fo' Abraham Lincoln," came Bea's sarcastic reply. "O'course fo' you, Why you think I'm tellin' you about it? It from N'Awleans."

Lowey appeared from the stables and took the reins of Anna's horse.

Aunt Louvenia! Anna rushed into the house and to the mantel where Bea customarily placed letters that came for her. But it was not Louvenia Etienne's scratched handwriting, it was– my God! What would he have to say to her that he had not said before? Trembling, Anna broke the seal of the letter dated Christmas Day and unfolded it.

*My dear sister,*

*I am well aware of your feelings for me and harbor no ill feelings in return...*

And so you shouldn't! Anna thought, briefly lifting her eyes from the paper.

*I have done things in the past that have placed your forgiveness far beyond my reach. I need you now, Anna, more than I have ever needed anyone before. On the 14th of December, 1861, I found Sudie living with a wealthy gentleman, her new husband, on Chartres Street. In his presence, and the presence of a new baby daughter, with no other thought in mind but her deception in our marriage, I shot her dead. I have no regrets. She deserved to die.*

*I have been condemned to hang on January 10th, 1862 unless Governor Moore grants me a reprieve. The woman was a whore. No man should be condemned for killing a whore. I beg of you, Anna, to journey in my behalf to Governor Moore and to plead for my life. If for no other reason, do it because I am your brother.*

The letter was signed simply *Alistair*. Anna held it between her fingers and read the words again. She felt nothing inside. He was her brother, yet she felt no remorse over the prospect of his death. All her memories of him were brutal and unhappy. He had been the main source of all evil since her earliest recollection, and she remembered, with horror, the last time she had seen him...the way he had callously sat astride his horse while seven foul-smelling men prepared to rape her in the bayou clearing. She had hated him then and had wanted to see him dead. He had left a path of death and destruction through Shadow Marsh and had broken the hearts of them all by allowing his men to murder Lovey. He was a weak, sniveling coward who truly deserved to die.

But here in her hand was a hastily written plea for his life. The gall of him to think she would care enough...the audacity! She clenched her teeth so tightly that she felt pain. Turning to the hearth where a warm fire burned, she rested her arm on the mantel and dropped her head. All manner of thought rushed frantically through her mind.

No matter what he had done he was still her brother. And she knew she would do whatever was in her power to save his life. His abominations mattered not; neither his hatred of her nor the fact that he had forced her to drive away from Shadow Marsh the only man she would ever love. Nothing could overshadow the fact that he was tied to her by blood. It mattered only that he was her brother and he was in trouble.

She would have to make plans for the trip. Should she go by carriage or by train? How many changes of clothing would she need? Should she send the children to Hopewell, or leave them at Shadow Marsh to be cared for by Bea and Bess? Should she confide her plans–her dilemma–to Wren and Violet?

She began to worry about things beyond her control. Suppose she was to be caught in New Orleans in the midst of an enemy invasion? Would Governor Moore grant her an audience? Would she arrive in time to plead for Alistair's life before the date set for his hanging?

January 10$^{th}$ was only eight days away...eight days to try to save the life of a brother who had spent a lifetime earning her hatred. What Sudie had done was vicious and deceptive and wicked, but she hadn't deserved to be killed. How long had he carried his plan for vengeance inside of him? Did his obsession to punish her give him no other recourse?

Did he hate his son the way he had hated his son's mother? Anna didn't want to think so. He had left him unharmed when he'd come through Shadow Marsh some months ago. Did he, after all, have a soft spot in his heart for the boy? Anna wanted to think so. It somehow made her feel better about what she had to do.

Bea's hand suddenly fell to Anna's arm. Startled, her body went rigid, and color returned to her ashen features. "Chile, what be's in that letter what's made you all white as a ghost."

Hurriedly, Anna gave Bea the details and watched her features for some sign of emotion. But there was none, not even anger. A world of hurt reflected in Bea's eyes, even as she knew she would not want Anna to do anything but try to save her brother. Kin was kin, and that's all there was to it.

"What should I do, Bea?"

Bea turned slightly away from her, the words she spoke

soft and polite. "From the look in yo' eyes, Bea knows what y'all be doin'. He kil't my girl jes' sure as if he thrust the knife hisself—but Miss Anna, he yo' brother...if'n he be my brother, I'd do what I could to save 'em. Jes' don't be askin' fo' Bea's blessin'." Then she quietly left the room.

\* \* \*

They decided to take a wagon rather than the carriage, so that they could pick up needed supplies at the St. Cyr warehouse on the Algiers dock. Shucking Sam drove the wagon, because he had kinfolk living near the docks that would put him up during their stay. Five days later, after a bitter cold journey, the lights of the Crescent City came into view across the marshland. It had rained heavily during the afternoon, and far across the horizon a plain of swiftly moving storm clouds was parted from the timberline only by a narrow strip of pale crimson.

A quiet tension permeated the usually bustling New Orleans. Visitors were viewed with suspicion since the institution of the governor's order to report all persons suspected of being unpatriotic to the new Confederacy. Neighbors had reported the actions of neighbors, sons of fathers, fathers of sons, and so on and so on until one was not sure who could be trusted. It was not safe to travel the streets of New Orleans. Martial law was in effect, and Anna instructed Shucking Sam to take her directly to the St. Charles and then to go straightaway to the docks and his kinfolk, where he would be safe.

Five days away from the children and she was already anxious to return to Shadow Marsh.

After taking her suite at the St. Charles, Anna freshened up, changed into a new dress, and touched a little powder to her nose, which had reddened in the five days of cold weather. She pulled on her white wrist gloves, locked her suite, and walked toward Louvenia Etienne's door, knocking hesitantly, the fear foremost in her mind that Louvenia would ask about Morgan. She had never been able to bring herself to write and tell her about his death.

Beyond the doors, Anna heard Louvenia's husky voice, like an echo, interlaced with the quiet voice of her maid. Then the attractive, neatly dressed slave girl named Theodora opened the door. She beamed when she saw Anna standing there, hastily took her hand and drew her into the warm, lighted alcove. "Miss Louvie–look who's come a-callin' on you. My, my..." Theodora drew her hands to her hips and smiled widely at Anna. "You do get handsomer ever' time I see you, Miss Anna."

Louvenia entered the alcove, strangely attired in a brocade robe that might once have been draperies, its yards and yards of hem edged in thick white fur.

"Anna, dear Anna..." Affection slipped into the husky voice. "What brings you to N'Awleans, with the Yankees expected any day? Or is it that nasty business our Alistair has gotten himself into."

A lump gathered in Anna's slender throat, but she managed to force it down with a weak smile. She sat in one of the matching Queen Anne chairs before the hearth where a warm fire blazed, and they discussed the plight of Alistair. She was surprised that Louvenia had not asked about Morgan, but it might have been, in her deteriorating state of mind, that she didn't even remember he existed.

"Alistair wants me to make a plea to the governor, Aunt Louvie," she ended on a quiet note. "I don't know the governor...do you know him?"

"I know him very well," she replied, sipping the tea that Theodora had served while they spoke. Anna had not touched hers. "I have kept abreast of Alistair's ways through dear Violet," Louvenia continued, "How is she, by the way?"

"Doing wonderfully. She and Wren are expecting their first child."

"Louvenia's hand tenderly covered Anna's. "And how are you holding up since the loss of your dear husband?"

"You know about it?" Louvenia nodded sadly, and Anna suspected that Violet had sent the news. "Well, I'm holding up as best I can."

Louvenia knew not to press the subject of Anna's husband. Setting her cup on the silver tray, she lightly slapped her knees. "Now–what do you expect our illustrious Governor Moore to do on behalf of Alistair?"

"I am hoping for a reprieve."

"Bah! As if that rascal deserves it!"

Theodora approached. "More tea, Miss Louvie?" Louvenia impatiently flicked her wrist, meaning nothing impolite by it. She adored the girl, and knew Theodora was long past taking offense at her brisk mannerisms.

"I wouldn't count on Governor Moore, Anna," Louvenia continued. "I have already talked to him, being that Alistair is, unfortunately, my nephew. Even for me he said there was nothing he could do. Alistair killed the woman in cold blood, and I understand he was responsible for the death of a negress at Shadow Marsh."

That Louvenia's own plea had been denied was dreadful news. Suddenly, it occurred to Anna how gruesome–how final–hanging was. She sat back, her hands suddenly moist and cool, her eyes almost a deep, empty void. "Yes, he was responsible for our Lovey's death, though he didn't actually wield the knife that killed her."

"Ah, but he did actually wield the gun that killed Sudella Hoskins. And that is the crime for which he will be hanged."

Despair filled Anna, even as she wanted to remain detached, to keep in mind that Alistair's fate was of his own making. "Will you come to the governor's mansion with me, that I may make my own plea?"

Louvenia Etienne laughed gently. "You are much prettier than this old hag, and a plea by you might be more receptive to our lecherous old governor," she replied, the moment of humor fading at once. She loved Anna like her own daughter, and would do anything for her. But she despised Anna's brother, who was cruel and relentless. She hated to see Anna waste her efforts on him. "There is no need to make the trip, dear," she replied. "The governor will dine with Mr. Pettigrew and me tomorrow evening. I'll be pleased to have you join us. And..." Louvenia shook her head as if to scold her, "what you say to the governor in confidence is up to you. Make a plea for your brother, if that is what you want. Despite your beauty, my dear girl, I wouldn't hold out any hope." Louvenia reached across and firmly patted Anna's hand. "Go on to your suite and get some rest. Tomorrow we shall take lunch together and I'll take you to a nice little place on Conti Street where they sell the most delicious hats."

"I will see Alistair tomorrow. At least let him know I'm trying."

* * *

Throughout the night, alone in her large, ornately decorated suite, Anna thought obsessively of Alistair. Perhaps it was a way of forgetting Morgan for a little while. She wondered what Alistair would do with his life if she managed to get him reprieved from the gallows? She wondered if he would grow old in prison if given a life term? Anna was in conflict with herself. She hated Alistair in her heart, yet her soul cried out in love for a brother who had fought her at every turn. Most of her heartaches had been of his doing.

He was cruel and without feeling. He had no conscience. He had caused the death of her father, had denied his son, had marauded through Shadow Marsh raping and killing, and had murdered the mother of his son. He had forced her to send her husband away from Shadow Marsh with cruel, vicious threats that had broken her heart.

And now, Morgan was dead. In three days' time her brother might also be. Anna paced back and forth in the warm glow of a single lamp on the mantel. The fire in the hearth had burned down hours ago, and she silently watched the glowing embers of wood until there was nothing left but ashes.

She had once vowed to see Alistair dead. Now, because he was her brother, the thought was repulsive to her. That his death was just a step beyond the threshold filled her with a familial loyalty she could not deny, even for the sake of her dear friend whose death he had caused.

Simply put, Alistair was her brother. All his horrid acts would not change that. Thus, with the first light of dawn, Anna freshened, donned her white fur cape, and prepared to leave her suite. When she reached the service desk, she asked that a carriage be rented. Half an hour later, she stepped out into the cold January morning and stood for a while, feeling the chill gently crawl across her flushed features. The weather was dark and gloomy, and a somber cloud overspread the face of the sky. Angry flashes of lightning lit the scene with short, lurid shots of flame. In the distance, the dull, rolling echo of thunder tore away the barrier of early morning silence.

Soon a carriage pulled up to the walkway and a friendly driver identified himself as Jackson. He alighted and stood quietly by, awaiting her instructions. Anna straightened her drooping shoulders. "To the Parish Prison, Jackson." He opened the door for her, securing it after she had settled comfortably into the plush interior.

The Parish Prison consisted of two brick buildings three stories high between St. Ann and Orleans Streets. They arrived there after a short ride, during which Anna sat numbly by the window of the carriage. They pulled up to the main entrance on Orleans Street, which was closed by heavy iron doors.

Anna did not await Jackson's assistance in opening the door. Before he had left his seat, she was standing on the walkway, staring up at the huge, ugly building. Pulling her gloves up, she gathered her inner strength and sharply rapped at the door. Anna was sure an hour had passed rather than the few minutes before a burly, dark-clothed man pulled open the door. He was carrying a large ring on which dangled a hundred or more keys. When Anna lifted her eyes and saw the pockmarked face and deep, searching eyes, she was momentarily at a loss for words. He smiled, betraying black spaces where there had once been teeth.

"I wish to see my brother who is incarcerated here."

The jailer maintained his smile. "And who might your brother be, Miss?"

"Alistair St. Cyr."

Oh–him! I'll have to ask the warden."

Before she could ask how long it would take, the heavy iron doors closed in her face. Anna turned to Jackson, who was stroking the patch of white fur between the eyes of the harness mare. "Well, what do you think about that, Jackson?"

"Don't rightly know, Miss. I be thinkin' you shouldn't come to a place like this, you bein' a lady an' all."

Anna crossed her arms beneath the warmth of her cape and paced back and forth. A few minutes later, the door opened again. "The warden says you can stay ten minutes. I'll need to make sure you ain't got no weapons."

Throwing off her cape at once, Anna raised her arms, revealing the tight bodice of her gown. "Do you wish to search me?"

The guard's face turned crimson. "No, ma'am. You look trustworthy."

Her cape returned to her shoulders, she turned to Jackson and said, "Wait for me?"

"Be mighty unsociable, Miss, if Jackson jus' drove off."

Anna was taken into a corridor where the jailer's apartments and offices were located, and to wide stairs rising to platforms. They turned and rose again until, exhausted, she had risen to the third floor of the prison. There she was taken to the condemned man's cell. The jailer took his time finding the right key and when the door eventually opened, Anna narrowed her eyes to see into the darkened interior. She was surprised, under the circumstances, to see Alistair–the ugly, unkempt beard shaved and his clothing clean.

Expecting another bland meal, Alistair did not look up but continued to sit with his forehead resting on his palms. Then, through the muskiness and the odor of unwashed bodies that seemed capable of penetrating the walls, the delicate aroma of familiar lilac perfume drifted into his senses. Lifting his eyes, he saw Anna standing there, and relief swept over him. He came to his feet and moved slowly toward her. He did not see her pinched, emotionless features...he saw only hope, salvation...a sister who had defied the hatred in her heart to come to him in his hour of need. When his arms slipped around her, she made no move to respond.

"Thank you, Anna, for coming. Here..." With his arm around her shoulder, he escorted her to the small cot on which he had been sitting. "Tell me–have you seen the governor?"

"No...I'll see him this evening."

"With your looks..." Alistair's fingers flicked gently across Anna's flushed cheek. "You could squeeze a reprieve out of Genghis Khan."

Anna's cool, moist lips became an angry line. "Is that why I'm here, Alistair? Because you think I can get a reprieve for you simply because you think I'm pretty?" With that bold arrogance she remembered only too well, Alistair met her silent gaze. "I may as well tell you, Alistair, that Louvenia has already spoken to the governor about a reprieve and he said absolutely no."

"Louvenia looks like an old crow," Alistair countered. "How is she, by the way?"

"Twittering, as usual...defying the gravity of time."

"And..." Alistair forced himself to say it, ". . . your husband?"

Thinking of Morgan always brought immense pain, followed by a bitterness that left her without words. She allowed a moment of silence to follow before answering. "He died in Missouri five months ago."

Beneath the emotionless façade of Alistair St. Cyr lurked a twisted grin that spoke so eloquently of his immense pleasure. It was a look Anna had often seen, and a look that never ceased to stir the quiet rage within her. Still, the moment and the tragedy were Alistair's, and she would not allow him to dampen her spirit and her duty to do whatever she could to help him.

Rising, she prepared to leave before he said something to anger her. "I wanted to see how you were, Alistair. I wanted to see if you were worth this trip I have made, and the fool I will make of myself this evening when I broach the subject of your reprieve to Governor Moore."

Alistair, too, rose. "And am I worth it?"

"As a man–no. As a friend–no. As my brother–yes. I despise you for what you are, what you have been, and what you have done. But nothing changes the fact that you are my brother. I will humble myself in your behalf, Alistair. Should I fail, you will go to the gallows knowing that I tried." Anna was astounded at the lack of emotion she felt She had thought that, perhaps, affinity might stir something within her when she saw him here in prison. But there was only a cold, empty numbness gently laced with dispassion. As she prepared to leave, she added, "That is the way of it, Alistair. But before I speak to the governor I want to know what has become of the men who were with you."

"I shot and killed the one who bragged about killing one of the women at Cabin Row–from the description he gave of her I assume it was Lovey...sorry, I know how special she was to you."

Anna was not prepared to accept his apology. "Go on...the others?"

"Two were killed in a dock fight in Natchez, one was lynched on the Atchafalaya for stealing a horse...the others were shot trying to rob a bank in Georgia.

Anna turned now to knock at the door, signaling to the jailer that she wished to leave.

"Anna?" She turned without looking at him. If I hang, may I be buried at Shadow Marsh?"

Only now did a lump rise in Anna's throat, filling her with an immense guilt that for her brother she had no feeling, not even a kind word–or a word of hope. She had spoken to him as she might a stranger. Turning, betraying a world of hurt in her tear-moistened eyes, she replied, "Oh, Alistair, of course." He arose and closed her into his arms. Neither spoke for a moment, his body trembling against hers. "You're dreadful," Anna continued quietly, "A wretched coward–but still my brother. Whatever you have done, whatever you have been, I love you."

The door came open. Quickly, Anna broke away from him, for she didn't want him to see her cry.

\* \* \*

The governor, with all his charms and chivalry, and the wit of a thousand court jesters, made the evening meal one of the most pleasant Anna could remember. He was interesting and informative, and quite surprised that a woman as pretty as Anna could hold her end in a conversation that revolved around politics, skillful battle maneuvers, and the state of world affairs

# Twenty-six

Morgan York was alive only through sheer determination and a strange, unnatural separation of physical and mental entities. On a warm morning in late September, Morgan had looked up into the blurred, indistinguishable features of a Union doctor bending slightly over his cot. It was the first sign of life he had displayed in over seven weeks. Morgan felt as weak as a kitten, and disoriented as to time and place. He tried to raise his arm, but it seemed intent on remaining next to his body, like a lead weight. Bandages with spots of dried blood were bound tightly around his chest and held his right arm firmly in place. He tried to free it, but pain intensified through his chest and shoulder. He looked around at the prostrated forms in the field hospital that had been set up in a stable north of Springfield. The small cot on which he lay was separated from the federal wounded by only a few feet of floor space.

"Do you hear my voice?" The words of the Union doctor drifted slowly toward him, as if he were far, far away, across a wide, misty meadow. The only thing he could distinguish of the man speaking to him was the dark, curled moustache stiffened by grease.

Morgan's brows pinched, betraying the moment of pain as he had tried to shift his body. Presently, he replied, "I do." Immediately, the federal wounded that were able began to cheer and clap their hands.

The Union doctor managed a half-cocked, humorless smile. "You have gained widespread notoriety among your enemy, Colonel, by your humane act at Wilson's Creek.

"I'm sorry—I don't know what you're talking about. How long have I been here?"

"Seven weeks."

Seven weeks out of his lifetime forever lost to him. There were questions Morgan wanted to ask, yet he had not enough strength to ask them. He looked around, expecting to see Joby Cade, who had not been very far from his side since their departure from Shadow Marsh. He opened his mouth to ask about him, but the words were too slow to form.

Captain Lawrence had tended Morgan's wounds these past seven weeks, ever since a Union grave crew had found him alive just moments before he would have been placed in a shallow grave. Lawrence had seen men die with minor flesh wounds that had become gangrenous. Given the extent of this man's wounds, he certainly hadn't expected him to live. "You're quite a fortunate man, Colonel York."

Gradually, the slur began to leave Morgan's voice. "How is that?"

Captain Lawrence pulled up a stool beside Morgan's cot. "You were left for dead at Wilson's Creek, even by your own troops who swept through after our retreat and who did not have the decency to stop long enough to bury their own dead. Had it not been for Tobias Peckinpah, you'd have died right there."

"Who?"

"You really don't remember, do you?"

"Remember what?" Morgan asked weakly.

"Stopping a battle, Colonel York, to save the life of one of our cavalrymen."

Morgan shook his head. "No, I'm afraid I don't."

Lawrence sat forward now. "Colonel, you're not a born Southerner, are you?"

Morgan wanted to deny it—to fervently claim Louisiana as his home since birth—but in fifteen years he had not been able to shake his northern accent. He wanted to claim to be a true Southerner and passionately swear his allegiance to its cause. But he could not. So, he replied shortly, "No."

"May I ask where you grew up?"

"Tarrytown, New York." Morgan became aware of the stench of death and decay, of ethers and alcohol and unwashed bodies, some of which scarcely seemed to be alive. He felt nauseous and breathed deeply, dispelling the moment of weakness that came upon him. "Sir," he said to Captain

Lawrence, "Don't waste your time with me when you have your own men to care for."

Lawrence had been in deep thought these past few moments. *Strange...Tarrytown.* He was thinking of Colonel Jarred Gunthar, also of Tarrytown, for whom this rebel officer, who'd had the good graces to live, was to be exchanged. An irony, he thought, mentally shrugging. "You'll be hungry, sir. I'll have a tray sent to you. You should rebuild your strength before being moved. I will do what I can to delay your transfer."

"Where will I be moved?"

"To a prison facility nearby, then you will be exchanged for one of our officers being held by your troops. I should inform you, Colonel York, that it has become standard that a term of your exchange will be that you sign a pledge to resign from active service in your Confederacy and to bear no further arms against the Union."

Morgan had not wanted to fight this war. But he did not like the decision being taken out of his hands like this. It would be with great reluctance that he signed such a pledge, although he would stand honor bound to it. And—he sighed with relief—he could return home to his wife and children.

"Will the officer for whom I am to be exchanged also be expected to sign such a pledge?"

"Of course not, Sir. He is an American, and his mission is in behalf of the United States. Secessionists are considered traitors, as you very well know." Captain Lawrence moved away from him, preparing to resume his duties. He turned back when Morgan spoke.

"May I be brought pen and paper that I might write to my wife?"

Lawrence nodded. "The chance that it will reach her is highly unlikely."

"I must try." Then, "When will the prisoner exchange take place?"

"When you are strong enough," Lawrence replied.

"Why me? Why not a higher ranking officer?"

"Because..." Lawrence paused, ". . . of what you did at

Wilson's Creek."

"Oh, I see." Morgan felt almost too weak to talk further. But he had to know. "There was a black man with me the last I remember–by the name of Joby Cade. Do you know where he is?"

"Left a few minutes ago to get something to eat at the mess tent. Your friend has not been far from your side these past seven weeks."

"And a captain in my unit–Wren Wellington?"

"I don't know. I'd imagine if he's still alive that he's been sent to Fort Douglas, Illinois."

"He had a leg wound..."

"Ah, yes–Wellington, Second Louisiana Cavalry, your unit. He was sent to Fort Douglas." Lawrence remembered only because they'd taken very few officers prisoner at Wilson's Creek, and only one who'd required amputation. Recalling his critical condition, he thought it highly unlikely that he had survived the move.

As the effects of his long, delirious sleep began to wear off, slowly, Morgan's mind filled with questions that needed answers and concerns that weighed heavily on him. He shuddered to think that Anna might even now think him to be dead. It tore at him, like the treacherous claws of a wild beast, until he felt a deep, agonizing pain slowly replace his loneliness for her. He was almost glad of the wounded Union soldier a few feet from him who called, "Rebel colonel," and diverted him from his lonely thoughts. Morgan turned his head. "Rebel–I was at Wilson's Creek. I saw what you did. Sir, you seemed to know the man who had been trapped beneath his dead horse."

"What was his name? Do you recall?"

"Corporal Graz–no first name–or no last, whichever."

Morgan smiled hesitantly. "Yes, I knew him some years ago. In Natchez."

"Sir...what is it like in the South?"

Morgan smiled sadly, the chance to speak warmly of the South filling him with a new strength. "Warm days and honeysuckle growing along the bayou, filling a man's senses

316

with an ethereal joy that does not exist anywhere else on earth. It is a wonderful place to call home." Thinking of the South–and home–continued to give Morgan strength that made his heart beat fiercely with longing. "And beautiful women," he added softly. "Beautiful women like my wife, Anna."

A burly sergeant on the other side of the talkative young soldier spat a wad of tobacco on the floor. "Talkin' to the damn rebel, boy, ain't goin' to win you no friends here."

The young soldier settled against his hard cot and gave the sergeant a look that did not match his youthful looks. "Friends like you, Sergeant Potts, I can do without."

The sergeant cursed beneath his breath, and turned his back on them both.

The door of the infirmary creaked. Morgan turned his head, narrowing his eyes as the familiar form of Joby Cade came into view against the light of morning. Joby said nothing as he approached the cot where Morgan lay. He was twisting the rim of his hat between his fingers.

The shadows left his face and he was enveloped within the soft light of the lantern on the desk where Captain Lawrence sat. Joby looked at Morgan as if he couldn't believe he was really alert and back among the living. A Union soldier had come just moments ago to the mess tent to tell him the rebel colonel–his friend–had awakened.

When Joby said nothing, Morgan gave him a weak smile. "So, my friend, you have stayed with me?"

A grin lit Joby's face and he went to one knee beside Morgan to firmly pat his arm. "Lawd, Jesus, Mist' Morgan–ain't you a sight fo' ol' Joby's eyes!" He could not restrain his joy. "Miss Anna, she'll be a might pleased!"

"Hey, colored boy..." The smile left Joby's face as he looked across at the belligerent Yankee sergeant. "He'd take away your right to freedom. What you bein' his friend for?"

Morgan's grip on his hand tightened, indicating that he would prefer he not respond. Joby understood and nodded ever so slightly. "Joby–I know you've stayed with me through thick and thin, but now you must return to Shadow Marsh."

"Not without you, Mist' Morgan."

"Do it because I am your friend, and because I asked you to. You must let Anna know I'm being exchanged for a Union officer and will be home in a few weeks–at most a couple of months or so."

"Let me wait with you, Mist' Morgan."

"They're sending me to a prison...I don't want you there." Morgan sighed deeply. "You have not seen Lovey and your children in a long time. You don't know how I've felt about that. Please–go home to Shadow Marsh and tell Anna I will be home in time for the spring planting."

"But, Mist' Morgan–"

"Don't be an argumentative ass, Joby. Don't you think I can make it alone in the world?"

"Reckon so, Mist' Morgan."

"Then you'll go home to Shadow Marsh?"

"Reckon so, Mist' Morgan...but don't like it one bit–not one li'l bit!"

Two days later, on the morning of Joby's departure, Morgan gave him the four twenty-dollar gold pieces Captain Lawrence had returned to him from his property, with orders to buy a good horse. He also gave him instructions on how to retain ownership of the horse and how to avoid the Confederate and Union encampments, settlements, towns and, most important, troops in movement. "And don't be brash and arrogant, Joby, to the rebels. Humble yourself if you have to and get home safely."

"I ain't never been brash an' arrogant, Mist' Morgan."

"Bull!" And both men laughed.

"God, it sho' is good to have you back, Mist' Morgan." Joby departed, hoping to the last minute that Morgan would change his mind and let him stay.

Morgan felt a strange sense of isolation without him nearby. The friendly Union soldier gave Morgan some reading material from the North–magazines and books of poetry and a two-month-old newspaper from Philadelphia that gave a rather distorted view of the rebellion.

Each day, Morgan grew stronger and was able to stand for

318

longer periods of time. On a brisk October morning, Captain Lawrence brought him the news that he wouldn't be moved to their prison facility, but would be exchanged for the Union officer the following afternoon.

The following morning, Morgan was given a shirt and his freshly laundered uniform trousers. His jacket had been discarded, and he was given a dark green coat and his own boots which had stood beneath his cot for the seven weeks he had lain in semi-consciousness. He arose in a good humor–a humor that turned immediately to embarrassment when Captain Lawrence discreetly handed him a twenty-dollar gold piece to assist in his journey home.

"I saw you give your friend what was left of your money," Lawrence admitted quietly. "You'll need this for meals. Louisiana is a far piece to walk."

Before he left the field hospital with an escort of two Union officers, Morgan spent a few minutes with Private Johnson, who had lent him the books. He offered them back, but the lad refused to take them. "They're small enough to tuck into a pocket, so you keep them, sir. They'll help on those lonely nights when you're camped beneath the stars."

Soon, Morgan walked out to a wind-cooled October morning. He was still a little weak as he breathed deeply of the first fresh air he'd smelled in months. The two officers of the Connecticut 1st Infantry and a small troop of men were waiting to escort him. Because of his weakened condition, he had to be helped into the saddle of a waiting horse.

A young officer nearby offered the information, "We'll meet at the bridge crossing at Reilly's Creek, Sir. Are you well enough to ride?"

"I am," Morgan replied, thinking only of Anna and being able to return to her.

On the seven-mile trip, Morgan saw forests turning gold and bronze with the coming of fall, cool, clear streams breaking the monotony of pine-covered grounds speckled with beauty. He thought of home and the azaleas that would bloom in the spring, perhaps about the same time he was able to make it home. He thought of high rushes of white cumulus clouds parting the horizon from the blue sky above Bayou Bouef and the small clearing that was his and Anna's favorite place. How he missed his dear Anna, whose warm green eyes had held him with unfettered love, whose willing arms had opened and welcomed him into their warm embrace. He thought of her clean, powder-softened skin against the iron hardness of his body, a body that was now pale and malnourished from his long illness. He heard Anna's softly whispered words expressing undying love. He was so lonely for her that, gradually, all the noises of the forest surrounding him became a dull, gentle lulling beyond the *clickity-clack* of wagon wheels and the rhythmic plodding of half a dozen horses.

Then with a sharply repeated, "Sir!" he was snapped back from his wonderful thoughts of Anna.

"We have reached the place of exchange. Are you prepared?"

Morgan was scarcely aware of the time that had passed. They had left the forest behind them and had entered a long clearing beside a river over which extended a narrow wooden bridge. On the other side of the water he saw a group of gray-clad men and one dark-clothed man. Morgan was apprehensive. He had long nurtured an instinct that cautioned him to be wary of all strangers, even strangers who wore the same uniform as he.

He got down from his horse, stood for a moment, and impatiently flicked the dust of travel from the heavy green coat. He felt a sudden chill and shivered, bringing his balled hands to his mouth to blow lightly on them. When the blue-uniformed men moved to either side of him, he began to walk briskly toward the bridge across which the Confederates had gathered.

For a moment he studied the narrow bridge and the small platforms halfway across just inches above the water where two small boats were docked. The Union officer waiting for exchange paced nervously, tucking his thumbs into the waist of his trousers, untucking them, and tucking them again. Something clicked far back in Morgan's mind, as if he had seen this done many times before.

"Colonel York!" Startled, Morgan turned. The Union officer held several documents. "Sir, you must sign these pledging that in exchange for your freedom you will not bear arms against the United States for the duration of the conflict. It is standard."

"Is it, indeed!" Sarcasm laced Morgan's sharp words. "And my service to the Confederacy is also expected to discontinue?"

"You may serve the cause as you see fit, sir...but don't serve it with a weapon in your hand." The officer handed him the documents, and his aide brought a small wooden lap desk, out of which he took a pen and bottle of ink. The pen was dipped and handed to Morgan.

Morgan hastily read the document, signing both copies beneath the signature of a Union officer whose name he could not read. He handed the documents back to the officer. When both copies had been blotted, one was handed back to him. "You will instruct the Confederate officer who receives you to also sign this document. It will ensure your passage home through both ranks, without intimidation, and you should keep it on you at all times." The officer's eyes narrowed with certain defiance, studying the pale, wan features of the Confederate officer. He turned and called across the bridge to the waiting Confederates. "We are prepared. Our men shall meet halfway."

The officer reluctantly offered Morgan his hand, which Morgan just as reluctantly accepted. "Good luck, Colonel York, on your journey home. You may rejoin your comrades now."

Morgan stood for a moment, regaining his strength. As he stepped down to the bridge, he felt isolated and alone. At the same moment, the Union officer across the bridge slowly began walking toward him.

Morgan's eyes narrowed, watching the almost brisk approach of the Union officer–that stature, the quick, military steps, the way he held his left arm straight while tucking his right thumb into the waist of his trousers. Boots–polished to a high gleam–familiar...so familiar.

*My God!* Morgan reached the middle of the bridge and

ceased to move. His heart beat fiercely in his chest, reverberating through his body like a mindless echo. He had never imagined they would meet like this...Jarred in the immaculate blue uniform of the United States, and he himself in what remained of a Confederate uniform, with a mismatched green canvas coat hanging to his knees.

They stood before each other for a moment in utter silence, golden eyes held transfixed to hazel eyes–all the conflicts of the world forgotten. Slowly, as if reality had just returned from some deep, dark, sinister void, Morgan warmly embraced his brother.

"My God, Michael," Jarred uttered in disbelief, "What has brought you to bear arms against your own country?"

"My own country," Morgan reminded him, his voice choked with emotion, "put me in front of a firing squad."

Jarred did not respond to this truth, but was content to feel the warmth of his long lost brother against him. He had easily detected the bitterness that lingered even after this long passage of time. Fifteen years, parted from a stepbrother he had loved and who had loved him in return–a lifetime obsessed with clearing Michael's name, not even knowing if he were dead or alive. But, for the moment, all that was forgotten. Nothing mattered but that, by the grace of God, they were reunited for oh, so short a while.

Jarred became aware of the mutterings of the Union soldiers awaiting him on the east side of the river, and those of the Confederate officers who had just released him. But he had waited fifteen years for this moment, and he would not be rushed through it by impatient men. He pulled back and firmly gripped Morgan's shoulders, betraying the emotion in his eyes. "Come, Michael." He motioned him to the boat platform. "To hell with this damned war and those impatient men. You and I have a lot of catching up to do." They sat together on the wide steps, and Jarred drew his knee up.

Morgan was still in a mild state of shock at encountering his brother in this exchange. "I can't believe we have met like this. It is ironic, Jarred–you in the blue uniform and I in the gray...brother against brother."

There was nothing Jarred could graciously say in response to this comment. "You received my letter?"

"I did."

"I was surprised you didn't come home after getting news of your pardon. Your–our mother was hoping that you would."

"I have a wife, a son, and a daughter–another child, my nephew, has been like my own. My wife and I are raising him." Morgan took the photograph of his family from his waistcoat pocket and proudly showed it to Jarred. "This is my wife, Anna, my son–sons, Michael and Patrick, and my little girl, Bonnie."

"A beautiful family," Jarred reflected thoughtfully. "You are doing well for yourself then?"

"We have built my wife's plantation up to be one of the richest in Louisiana."

Jarred gently folded the brass and velvet case containing the photograph and handed it back to Michael. "But for how long, Michael? If the secessionists continue with this rebellion, the South will be gutted. There will remain no semblance of what you know and love."

"There will always be Anna and the children," Morgan countered politely. "And the land will always be there." Morgan favored his stepbrother with a warm smile. "Anna and I are very much in love. That makes material possessions and wealth unimportant."

"You have our father's inheritance, Michael, whenever you want or need it."

Morgan looked toward the water breaking against the bridge supports, at tiny minnows darting back and forth, like indistinct shadows. "I am happy as Morgan York. I want nothing of my past–except you–and my mother."

"And what of Michael George Fielding?"

"He died years ago."

"Did he, indeed?" Jarred understood how his brother felt, but he was not willing to accept. "You can never destroy Michael. As long as I draw breath, you will be Michael. Despite the color of your uniform, and whatever loyalties may move in

323

your heart, you will always be my brother—"

"Your stepbrother, Jarred."

"No...my brother. You and me and John. We were brothers then. John is gone now. You and I are brothers, just as surely as if we'd been born of the same parents."

A lump rose in Morgan's throat. He brought his trembling hand to his bearded chin in a moment of thoughtful silence. So much was going through his mind that he felt dizzy. "So—how about your family?" he asked as a pleasant diversion. "How are they?"

"My wife, Rebecca, is expecting our third child, any day now, actually. My son, George, and my daughter, Selma, have both expressed a desire to meet you one day. Perhaps when this conflict has ended, you and your family will come to Tarrytown for a long visit?"

"Perhaps," Morgan replied softly, but he really didn't think so.

Jarred became aware of the nervous pacing of a Union officer in the group awaiting him. The man took his watch from his pocket, looked at it, paced a few more minutes, then removed it and looked again at the time. Jarred very much resented that they would rush him through this reunion with his brother. In a moment of silence, Jarred began to think. Morgan absently tossed small stones he'd picked up from the fishing platform into the gently swirling waves of the river.

With the possibility that he and Morgan might never meet again, Jarred had questions he wanted answers to. "Michael—when you were being moved to Fort Scott in the Kansas Territory, how is it that you were the only survivor of the convoy?"

"By the grace of one of our biggest enemies...a very compassionate Indian named Lone Bear." It was the first time in many years Morgan had spoken of that time in his life.

"There were rumors that whoever had escaped from the wagon—you or the other prisoner—could possibly have killed the others."

"That's not true." Defense rose in Morgan's voice. It had

324

never crossed his mind that murder might have been suspected. "If the convoy was found, I am sure there was no evidence of foul play. The harsh elements killed those men...and they might have killed me."

"You're right–there was no suspicious evidence. I thought in defense of yourself, you might tell me the story.

Morgan's brows pinched in a thoughtful frown. "There's not really much to tell. As you will recall, the day we left Fort Marcy a late winter storm was settling in. We had traveled three days when one of the horses collapsed and died. Two days later we came across a covered wagon. A man and woman and three young girls had been brutally slaughtered and scalped by Indians. The guards buried them. We thereafter took a diversion off the Santa Fe Trail to avoid war parties and were trapped beneath the buttes by the storm. The horses died over the course of a single day. One of the guards left the convoy to get help at Fort Marcy. We never saw him again. One at a time, the guards died, then the other prisoner." The horrible memory made Morgan tremble. "For two days I worked with freezing hands trying to break the lock on the wagon. Just a few feet out of my reach, the keys dangled from the belt of a dead guard. I used the dead prisoner's clothing and belt to try to snag them but never could. Eventually I became too weak to move and sat there, waiting to die, as they had. Then days later I awoke beside a warm fire in a teepee, being nursed back to health by an Indiana woman. Lone Bear and his renegades had come across us and because I was chained and apparently an enemy of the white man, Lone Bear decided that I should not be killed. I stayed with them for two years and moved on." Morgan laughed, without humor. "So, now you know. And look..." Morgan motioned toward their waiting troops on either side. "Our men are wondering what the hell we're doing down here, chatting like old friends."

"They will have to wait. There is so much I have to know about you, Mich–would you prefer Morgan?"

"I would."

"Morgan, then–it will take some getting used to. I want to

know everything you did after you were rescued by the Indians."

"A good story to tell your children one day, eh?"

"Why do you think I'm asking? Now—come on, be a good sport."

"Well, I traveled through the Southwest and Mexico, took odd jobs working on ranches and cattle drives—got myself in a bit of trouble but won't go into that—and even tried my hand at serving tequila in a tavern in Mexico. But I never did anything I was ashamed of. I was instilled with a great sense of morals at a very early age, as were you and John, and no matter the injuries I felt I had suffered, I tried to live by those morals—except once..." He was thinking about *Amigo*, but he had deserved the horse after not being paid for his work. "I'm sorry that everything happened the way it did. I lost my own identity, and I lost my family in Tarrytown—"

"You would have had a brilliant career in the military."

That was something Morgan did not want to discuss. Presently, his hand fell affectionately to Jarred's arm. "I have missed you very much these past fifteen years. I have missed talking my troubles over with you. I have missed the laughter and the good times..." He didn't want to show emotion, even as tears moistened his eyes. "I have missed Mother. When you return home, tell her that I asked about her and send my love. Assure her that one day we might meet again. Tell her that never a day has passed that I didn't think about her."

"I will—of course." Jarred embraced him warmly and rose to his feet. "Now!" He clapped his hands. "We must conclude this exchange of officers before our troops decide the deal is off." Laughing together, they moved back up to the bridge. "Will you have a horse awaiting you?"

"I wouldn't imagine."

"Do you have any money?"

"A few dollars a good Union doctor gave to me. But—not to worry, brother, I will make do on my natural charms."

Jarred took several gold coins from his jacket pocket. "Here, an advance on your inheritance. It should help you get home." He started toward his own ranks. "Don't leave yet,

Mich–Morgan. I'll be right back."

As Jarred stepped into his own ranks, his waiting aide-de-camp started to ask questions. Jarred cut him off. "Not now, Brinkley...Soldier," he barked at the men standing behind Brinkley. "One of you bring me a good horse." Immediately a high stepping bay gelding was brought to Jarred. He took the reins and started back across the bridge."

"Sir–sir, that is my horse!" Jarred turned and glared at the young, wide-eyed lieutenant. "But you may take him, if you wish."

Jarred returned to Morgan and handed him the reins. "My compliments, Morgan, and I curse any man who tries to take him from you. Now...go home to your wife and family." Jarred favored him with a warm, yet sad smile. "Perhaps we'll meet again soon."

Jarred turned away, immediately turning back to embrace Morgan, who was reminded of the morning on the parade ground when he and Jarred had briefly spoken. He remembered the isolation that had followed, as he had waited for twelve rifles to end his life. He didn't want to release Jarred and see him walk away.

"I will pray for you, Morgan." Emotion choked within him. These past fifteen years he had hardened himself, adapted to a strict military regimen, but he felt now like a frightened schoolboy, torn for the first time from his mother's apron. "Answer me one question, Morgan, before we part...do you approve of slavery?"

"No–my wife and I own no slaves."

His answer pleased Jarred. He gave him one last firm embrace and turned to walk briskly away. Morgan watched until he was lost among the waiting men.

# Twenty-seven

A gentle wind swept along Bayou Bouef, among the cattails and the new leaves of oak trees pale green with the arrival of spring. Far off in the meadow, the bellowing of a cow hinted at new life coming forth. Hundreds of birds twittered back and forth in the treetops, beneath puffs of white clouds perched motionless in the sky, like cotton ready to be picked.

But Anna saw only death. She walked slowly among the tombstones in the St. Cyr cemetery, briefly touching her fingertips to the generations of inscriptions that had gracefully weathered the passage of time. When she reached the tall, commanding gravestone of her father, she stood silently before it with her arms crossed and her feet slightly apart. She remembered a time when she had come to the cemetery every Sunday to visit him. But this was her first visit in many months. She hadn't even stopped to tell him they had buried Alistair very nearby, but she would remedy that today.

"Father, it has been a long time since I visited you." Her voice was a quiet, toneless whisper. "So much has happened since last we talked. We're in the midst of a terrible war. Alistair lies just over there–killed not by the war but by his own selfish greed. You always said he would go that way. Mose is gone now...and so is my sweet Lovey. Auntie Goose–you remember how she cared for the children of Cabin Row for forty years...she became part of the earth only last week. I have two children now, Papa, my own little Michael and little Bonnie, and I am mother to Alistair's son, Patrick–yes, we named him after you. Violet has a new baby daughter named Martha. And Wren came home early from the war. He lost his leg at Wilson's Creek, Missouri. The South considered Wilson's Creek a victory, but it was a tragedy nonetheless." Anna became silent for a moment, breathing deeply of the clean, fresh air of early spring. The faint aroma of honeysuckle drifted among the oaks, mixed with that of new pine, filling her senses with the beauty of the season. Yet she was unhappy. Things had not gone well. Spring planting had been delayed by heavy rains, and lightning had burned several hundred acres of Shadow Marsh woodland.

Returning her quiet gaze to the grave marker, she tenderly touched her fingertips to her father's inscribed name. "I wish you could have met my husband. He was a kind, sensitive, wonderful man–the kind of man you would have wanted me to marry. Oh, Papa..." She smiled sadly, "If you only knew how angry the provisions of your will made me. How dare you try to control my life from the grave? I was going to defy you. I was determined not to marry, to remain a bitter old spinster sticking her nose into other people's business. But I met Morgan, and loved him from the first moment we met. Seeing him in the water trough after Alistair had bashed his head with a length of board...oh, you might have laughed at that! I wish you could have known him. Perhaps you *have* met. He died at Wilson's Creek last August, and with him died a very big part of my heart. The rest I reserve for the children and our good people here."

For the first time in weeks, bitter tears touched Anna's cheeks. Although she knew she would never fully recover from Morgan's death, she had tried to throw up a façade of strength and had devoted her attention to the war her people had begun with the Union a year ago this month by firing on Fort Sumter. She had kept up with the battles, the skirmishes, the casualties...oh yes, the casualties. She had kept abreast of the movements of the federals who had invaded New Orleans and occupied the city. But all her attention to the war could not prevent her private thoughts from returning to Morgan, her love– her one and only love. She was embittered by the cause that had cut him down, and it was the anger within her that so frequently moved her to tears.

"Before this war is over, Papa, how many of our friends will be gone? How many of our men will die in battle? Tylas Miller's eldest boy, Thomas, has assumed command of what is left of my husband's unit. Last we heard they were in Florida, but the mails aren't running well these days. And often, by the time we learn they are in one place, we receive news they are in another. It's hard to keep up with them."

"Miss Anna?"

Startled, Anna turned sharply toward Bea. "Oh, my." She could find no excuses for standing in the midst of the cemetery, spilling her heart to her dead father.

Aware of her melancholy, Bea's hand slipped round Anna's shoulder and she touched her head to hers. "Child, it sometimes takes the burden off yo' heart to talk to the departed ones. Bea knows. Why Bea, she talks to her Mose an' her Lovey pert near ever' week–an' you know, chile, sometime Bea's sho' they talk back. I can hear them–like chimes in the night wind–tellin' me not to worry.

Tears again moistened Anna's emerald eyes. "How dear you are to me. How would I have ever survived without you?"

"How'd we have survived," Bea lovingly amended, "without each other? Folks need other folks, and when those folks love you and cherish you, why, it's a whole lot easier to get by. God made love to share with other people. That's what makes life worthwhile."

Anna turned and embraced her friend. "Thank you...thank you, Bea."

Brusquely, Bea pulled away, her own dark eyes moist with tears. "Now, come on to the house, chile. Miss Violet's brought that precious baby girl to see you. An' Massa Wren be wantin' to show off his new wood leg Doc Tylas brought him from Houston."

"All right, dear." Anna patted her hand affectionately. "Has Sam departed with the supplies for the Alexandria warehouse?"

"Sho' did, but they's talk, missy, that if'n the Yanks move up this way, they's goin' to be burnin' people's houses. Ain't it a shame? Reckon that'll be happenin' here, chile?"

"Pray it doesn't, Bea. And if it does, we'll make do. Don't you worry about it."

"Oh..." Bea sighed wearily, annoyed with herself for forgetting one of the reasons she'd come up to the cemetery.

"Massa Grogan—you know, his boy organized the Moore Guards, he'll be callin' at Shadow Marsh this afternoon."

Anna was delighted at the prospect of company, and very glad to know Violet and Wren were waiting for her at the house. Mr. Grogan was always jovial, and the children of Cabin Row were always happy to see him...Anna suspected it was because she always asked Bea to make apple tarts when he was going to visit...and extras for the children. Before she could say anything, Bea waved a hand as she turned, "Yas'sum, Bea'll make them apple tarts." Then, "Massa Grogan, I hear, he makin' an appeal fo' mo' cotton to be sent over to England in the fall. He's wantin' pledges from all the Rapides crops. England, she's a'goin' to pay top price."

"If the Yankee patrollers don't intercept our ships and confiscate our cargo," Anna replied. "If that happens, all the planters will be ruined. Come—let's not talk about this silly old war and cotton and ships and Yankees. Let's go up to the house and see Wren and Violet and that new baby girl."

"I'd tell you where we should stick them Yankees," Bea mumbled, "But it'll be mighty uncomfortable for them to be a-walkin'..."

\* \* \*

The visit with Wren and Violet was pleasant, as was the visit with Mr. Grogan, who stated he would stop by again after visiting Hopewell, since those apple tarts had not been ready. Thereafter, Anna departed for her daily ride along the bayou and through the fields, stopping beside the work crew in the east field, where she spoke to Sam. He showed her the areas where new planting was being done, and pointed out a few of the horses that had gotten out of the pasture with their new foals. He promised to round them up after the fields were worked.

The ride took Anna's mind off the problems of running Shadow Marsh and the loneliness that often ate at her. It was nice to get away from the constant demands of the children for a while, also. Bea's grandson, Lowey, was teaching the boys how to ride their new ponies, and, to pacify little Bonnie's jealousy, he had carved a jointed wooden doll for her, for which Bea had

331

sewn several suits of brightly colored dresses. They were such good children–Anna often felt guilty that she sometimes liked to get away from Shadow Marsh.

But she did enjoy her solitude, nudging her mare into a fast gallop and flying like the wind across the meadows. She enjoyed the gentle breeze that rustled her loose, dark hair, and imagining that, just behind and out of her line of sight, Morgan was fast approaching. She remembered a time he had swept her from her horse and into his arms, and captured her mouth in a long, lingering kiss before releasing her to the ground. Of course her horse was long gone, and they had to ride double back to Shadow Marsh. She fussed at him for hours about that.

She missed him so much. Why did this horrible, vicious war have to come upon them? Why did it have to destroy her world so completely? Inevitably, Anna's ride ended at the bayou clearing. She sat against the cypress trunk and picked up a twig, which she began stabbing into the dirt. The play of the children in Cabin Row echoed hauntingly–very distantly–toward her, and the loud, commanding crow of Bea's favorite old rooster, followed immediately by the frightened squeal of one of the children whose leg it must have pecked.

With sadness filling her heart, Anna released a small sigh. Thus far the war had not affected Shadow Marsh as it had other areas of the South. They had plenty to eat, clothing to wear, their crops had brought good prices at the markets, and the supply wagons had managed to get through from Texas. There was nothing they didn't have...except their men. Some were already dead, as was her Morgan, and others were waiting to die in some distant battle. War was an ugly way to settle differences between men.

Across the far distance Anna heard the voices of the children raise in excitement. Someone must have ridden into Cabin Row; she was sure she heard the galloping of a horse. Then through the timberline she thought she heard, "Mist' Morgan...Mist' Morgan..."

Stunned, disbelieving, her heart ceased to beat. But in the same moment that hope rose in her, she collected her senses and realized that the children could not be chanting, "Mist' Morgan," but were probably, in their peculiar language that scarcely resembled English at times, chanting, "Massa Grogan." He must have returned for Bea's delicious apple tarts.

Anna hated herself for clinging to every thread of hope when there was none to cling to. Why couldn't she accept and go on with her life? Why must she constantly, continually punish herself? Damn! Damn! Again, Anna settled against the tree trunk, picked up a rock and threw it with a vengeance, far out into the middle of the bayou. She needed these moments of solitude, so that she could wallow in her misery, and nurture the bitterness and anger that had stayed with her these long months. She wanted to hate, an emotion so nearly alien to her that it was like two separate worlds tugging at her heart.

She needed to return to Shadow Marsh but could not find the motivation to rise and mount her horse. She wondered if Mr. Grogan needed to speak to her again about the pledge of this year's crops for England?

A gentle breeze rustled the timberline. Puffs of white clouds moved imperceptibly across the blue sky, occasionally blocking out the sun that shone boldly down on her. The light rays filtered like gold dust through the new leaves of the mighty oaks and gently touched Anna's ivory skin. It felt soothing and relaxing. Turtles basked lazily on half-submerged logs and when a heron took to flight, quickly darted beneath the water's surface.

This place was such a great comfort to her. Here she and Morgan had embraced, they had made love in their boldest, happiest moments, and had spent many wonderful hours confessing their deepest, darkest secrets, and comforting each other with assurances of their everlasting love.

A movement behind startled her. Anna sat forward and from the corner of her eye she saw a scurrying rabbit. Her startled gasp became a gentle laugh of relief. She guarded against every movement these days, even though at times she no longer cared what happened to her. Then she would feel guilty, because of the children.

She was thinking of Morgan again, wanting to be with him,

imagining she could detect the pleasant, masculine smell of him, imagining she could hear his footsteps approaching her. She closed her eyes and envisioned him as he had once been, tall and proud and reserved in his immaculate gray and gold uniform, his golden eyes discreetly holding her gaze, adoring her, his lips wanting to seek hers, to capture and possess them for a moment that became an eternity when they gently met.

* * *

Morgan stood back in the shadows of the timberline. His emerald-eyed Anna sat quietly against the tree trunk, her dark skirts spread over the soft ground, her hand absently flicking a twig back and forth through a small pile of stones. He wanted to rush to her, draw her into his arms, and capture her mouth in a long, lingering kiss. He imagined that she wouldn't even care that he smelled like an unwashed horse.

But he didn't want to shock her. From what he had just learned in his short talk with one of the women of Cabin Row, Joby Cade had not returned to Shadow Marsh. Anna had received the false news of his death, and at this moment knew no different. To appear suddenly before her, alive and well, might be too great a shock for her.

Morgan was at odds, quietly trying to figure the best way to approach her. All his inner instincts compelled him to rush to her, to lift her into his embrace. Yet, he knew how he would feel if, for half a year, he had believed Anna, his only love, to be dead. He knew how he would feel if, believing this, she were suddenly to stand before him, the ghost of the woman he had loved with all his heart and soul. With that understanding, he stepped quietly out of the shadows, prepared with every emotion that was his to assure her he was very much alive.

"Anna?" He saw her body stiffen, yet she made no other visible movement. "Anna?"

She spun rapidly on her knees when her name was spoken the second time. Her eyes lifted to the bearded, unkempt face, and the familiar golden eyes caught by a shimmering ray of sunlight. Horrified by the vision of her lost love–a vision born of her immense need to see him once again–Anna slowly rose to her feet. Convinced she had finally driven herself mad by her obsession for him, Anna slowly began to speak. "No...no...you're not real. You're dead." Closing her eyes tightly, she simultaneously shook her head until the black thunderclouds of her hair tossed madly about her shoulders.

Morgan's heart broke to see her like this. Instinctively, wanting only to reassure her that he was very much alive, he approached her. "Anna, I am not dead."

Before he could pull her into his embrace, her eyes flung open, spitting green fire at him, and she flayed out at him with her right hand. "No...no, you're dead...and I'm going mad!" She clutched at her temples and turned away, unable to prevent the tears that traced burning rivers down her flushed cheeks. "I am going mad...I truly am."

When he approached her, she again flung out her hand, but it touched his solid weight and she drew back, stunned and disoriented, believing only that her obsession for him had destroyed what remained of her sanity–had even given solid form to the ghost of him. She slowly, tearfully, sank to her knees on the soft ground.

His hands moved beneath her arms and drew her toward him. She did not fight, but succumbed quietly to her madness and the warm, willing comfort of the ghost who stood before her. Her senses were filled with the strong, masculine smell of him–oh, he did so need a bath!–and her fingers hesitantly rose, to touch the dirt-stiffened threads of his uniform shirt and, beneath, to the soft, matted fur of his chest, which pulsated with life.

Emerald eyes lifted to reassuring golden ones. Her fingers rose to the long blond waves of his hair, to his cheek, which moved to enjoy the brief tenderness of her touch. She saw the shimmering moisture in his eyes and, hesitantly, with a deep-rooted fear that he might disappear forever from her memories, she spoke his name, "Morgan?"

He folded her within his embrace, his hand rising to the back of her head and his fingers entwining firmly through her hair. "My little *chica*..." he whispered against her hairline, "How

I have missed you–how I have wanted to be with you."

She heard only his intimate, softly whispered words. All other sounds became nonexistent. The only thought in Anna's mind was that she would share her secret little world, lost somewhere between reality and madness, with the man she loved. A slow, billowing fog slowly enveloped her, veiling the bayou clearing until it was a gray sheet of nothingness beyond their entwined bodies.

She sank, unconscious, into the arms of Morgan's ghost.

* * *

Anna knew she was in her bedchamber and felt coolness on her forehead and sounds slowly gained clarity all around her...soothing, everyday sounds, like her children playing in the wide corridor that echoed their every laugh, Bea's delicate breathing beside her, and Bess humming a happy tune as she filled the tub in the bathing alcove with hot, steaming water. Anna did not want to open her eyes and was compelled to do so only by Bea's low, coaxing words as she gently rubbed her hand.

"Come on now, chile."

The past few moments rushed back at her...the sensual reality of Morgan lovingly holding her, speaking her name, and picking her up in his strong arms to carry her to the house. Yet she knew this could not have happened, but could not remember getting back on her horse. She knew she had imagined Morgan, and the twinkle in his golden eyes, and the matted fur of his chest. She had shared a dream with him, and a few short, brief moments beyond the realms of reality. Meeting Bea's pinched, worried features she threw herself forward into her arms. "Oh, Bea...I'm going mad. I thought I was with Morgan."

Roughly, Bea put her slightly away and a wide smile lit her pleasant features. "Then Bea, she be sharin' yo' madness," she replied, rising, motioning to Bess, who slipped past her and into the corridor. With another beaming smile, Bea pulled the door closed behind her.

Anna's hand darted out toward the closing door. "Don't leave me alone, Bea...don't..."

"You are not alone, Anna." Morgan stepped from the

336

shadows and was encircled by the soft glow of the lamp on the mantel.

Anna removed the cool cloth Bea had placed on her forehead, her eyes holding Morgan with fascination and a tiny, lingering twinge of disbelief. Yet she knew he was there...that he was alive and looking at her with love and adoration. She had felt warm flesh against her own, and had felt his delicate breathing against her cheek.

"Morgan..." Hesitating ever so slightly she held her hand out to him. When his fingers slipped between hers, she drew his hand against her mouth and tenderly kissed it. "You are real, not a ghost at all." Her hopes and dreams had come true. Still, she was afraid to believe, lest she had been made the victim of the cruelest of jokes.

Morgan drew her close. "I am not a ghost, Anna...God, I have missed you!"

Anna wanted to show only joy at being with him, at knowing he was alive and in her arms. But more alive in her mind were the months of pain and loneliness—the tears—she had suffered believing him to be dead. "How could such a mistake have occurred?" she asked in what seemed to him an angry whisper. "Why was your death reported? My heart was more broken than it has ever been and never will be again. Can you ever understand how deeply I grieved for you?"

Morgan rose, pulled her from the bed and into his arms. "Come, little *chica*—I will tell you the long, grueling story while I bathe and make myself deserving of my family."

As he slowly undressed, Anna cringed from his wan appearance, at how much weight he had lost and the long, jagged scar down his chest that had been left by a surgeon's scalpel. Only now did she realize the seriousness of the injuries he had received, and how such a mistake might have been made.

Morgan told her everything and she sat spellbound...how he and a small unit of his men had been trapped in the ravines at Wilson's Creek, how all had been killed but himself, Joby Cade, Wren Wellington, and two enlisted men. He told her how Joby Cade had faithfully remained with him when the federals retreated and the Confederates came through, of the federal gravediggers burying corpses of their own dead and finding him still alive, resting against Joby Cade's body. Proudly, he told her of the irony of his reunion with Jarred, his stepbrother...what were the chances?

"I am so happy for you, Morgan," she replied, absorbing every word he spoke. Still she harbored a silent fear inside her that she might awaken and find she had been dreaming all along.

"And I am happy for us, little *chica*. Here..." Morgan handed her the soap and a brush. "Wash my back for me?" he asked, leaning forward. "I didn't see Amigo in the meadows."

"The mares are foaling...Sam confined him to the back pasture. I'm surprised you didn't hear him complaining. Morgan...last June Alistair returned to Shadow Marsh with six terrible men he'd picked up along his travels from Mexico. They marauded through Shadow Marsh, stealing and raping the women and..."

"You, Anna?" Fear and outrage trembled in his throat. Anna could not meet his eyes.

"No, they spared me at Alistair's command. But the women of Cabin Row were assaulted in the vilest of ways. Lovey was. . ." Anna forced herself to complete the sentence, "killed by those men."

Hatred darkened Morgan's features. "The bastard! I'll kill him if ever I see him again!"

"It has already been done. This past January he was hanged at the Parish Prison in New Orleans for the murder of Sudie."

"Forgive me, Anna, for feeling no remorse."

Anna picked up the brush and soap and began scrubbing his back and shoulders with renewed gaiety. "I am tired of all this talk, husband. The water is cooling...climb out so that I can pamper you." She didn't want to be away from him for even a minute, but arose and stepped away, so that he would have room to step from the tub. As he did so, he swept her into his arms without drying off, and carried her to the bed. He cared not about the warm, soapy water clinging to his body; he cared only that they were together, and time and space existed only for them and for their love. He cared only that he was alive and home at Shadow Marsh with his beloved. He cared only that they were alone in their warm, cozy bedchamber where they had often raised their love for each other to the highest planes of passion and desire. He continued to hold her, to caress her, possess her willing mouth, her damp, warm cheeks and closed eyes, which fluttered against his taut features.

The sinewy muscles of his arms hardened as he gently held her close, refusing to release her for even a minute. He was alive and strong and virile, only because she made him feel that way. He was gentle and commanding–because he loved her so–and he wanted only to awaken her passions with his very nearness.

Soon, Morgan fell to the bed with her and slowly, methodically, unfastened the buttons of her blouse. As her garments slipped down the length of her body beneath his gentle hands, Anna eased slightly off the bed so that her clothing could be discarded to the floor.

Anna savored every tender move...his mouth lingering over each kiss, his hands exploring and awakening every vulnerable spot that fired her passion and sent it pulsing through every vein in her body. Her flesh quivered beneath his caressing hands, and her lips parted to accept his soft, exploring tongue. As the flames raced through her thighs and her hips, she took small gasps that turned immediately into kittenish moans and playful, teasing nips as their mouths explored and searched each other, to claim and to possess.

She had missed that look in his eyes–the love and adoration–the desire that could not be hidden and that now twinkled in a moment of humor.

"Do you still think I am dead, my *chica*?" he asked softly.

"I feel only life, my love. I feel only the wonderful gentleness of the man I have missed so deeply. You did break my heart, Morgan, but..." her parted lips rose to brush his smiling ones, "you are with me now. And I will never, ever let you get away from me again. But..." she laughed, "we might see tomorrow about doing away with the fuzzy chin."

Morgan looked at her in feigned, humored surprise. "You

don't like bearded men?"

"Only if the man is old and his hands shake so that the act of shaving might prove fatal. Besides—it tickles terribly."

He just smiled, his soft, sensual lips touching each of her eyelids in turn, her cheeks, her willing mouth that responded without hesitation, lowering to the small, delicate pulse of her neck, and to the soft, round flesh and pink buds that hungered for his caresses. As his hands moved to her long, firm thighs, she felt a flood of warm waves sweep across the flat plane of her abdomen. As they were joined, she matched his rhythm and pace, slow and methodical at first, and quickening with each passing moment. She had almost forgotten the commanding gentleness of him, and the way his hands could, themselves, tap the vast reservoir of desire that burst within her.

"You are alive," she gasped, "If I doubted it a minute ago, I do not doubt it now."

His lips captured her softly whispered words, feeding a world of liquid passion into his throbbing veins. Morgan felt that gnawing, grabbing, wonderful moment of pain that meant fulfillment and his hips closed commandingly against her tender flesh until he could stand it no more. He did not move from the soft, warm pillow of her hair beneath his face, but remained one with her as his hands slipped beneath her shoulders.

"If I am ever defeated," he responded after a moment, "it will not be in battle, but by one woman. You have made a whimpering puppy of my heart, Anna Rose..."

Anna's arms slipped around his shoulders and drew him close. "I may never sleep again, for when I awaken I might find your returning to Shadow Marsh is just a long sad dream. I couldn't bear it—not to lose you again."

Morgan gently chuckled. "If my death could not part us, Anna...nothing can."

She had hesitated to ask, possibly because she did not want to hear the answer. But she had to know what the immediate future held for them. "Will you have to rejoin your company?"

Morgan eased to her side and drew her to him. "I will not leave Shadow Marsh. Before returning here I went to see

Governor Moore. Since the federal occupation, he has moved his offices to Opelousas. The governor and I..."

"You went to the governor, Morgan, before returning to let me know you were alive?" She was quite surprised that he had done so.

"You must remember, Anna, that I expected Joby Cade to precede me home. I have no idea where he is–but I will do my best to find out. As I was saying, the governor and I..."

Only now did Anna allow herself the smallest laugh. "The governor and I! That does sound so intimate!"

"The governor and I..." Morgan began again, touching his lips to her pertly lifted nose, "have agreed that I will honor the conditions of my release. I will not hold a weapon in my hand or carry one on my person. But beginning next month..." Morgan rolled to his back and linked his fingers beneath his head. "I will train small companies of men here at Shadow Marsh and get them battle ready."

"I am not sure I want the children exposed to military training, Morgan."

"I will conduct all training exercises in the meadows out of sight of the house. I promise you that. Now...do you have any more objections?"

"I suppose not–since my dear husband has had the common decency to return to me alive." Then she snuggled against him, and with a soft, cooing sound, closed her eyes against his bare chest.

Her family was complete, and life was perfectly wonderful once again.

# Twenty-eight

All day long Anna had felt a frenzy of nerves that made it impossible for her to sit still for even a moment. She couldn't work on the ledgers without finding herself sitting with her chin propped on her palm, idly tapping her fingers against her temple and gazing out the window. The warm summer day seemed to beckon her away from the drudgeries of her daily duties. Morgan kept a hectic schedule since he'd started training troops the week after his return home, and Anna saw little of him. He spent long hours with the men, boosting their morale, and attempting to instill in each and every one an instinct for survival that would take them safely through the worst of battles. And–true to his pledge when he was released–he did not hold a weapon or wear one at his waist.

Unable to restrain her nerves, Anna requested that her horse be saddled, and she took a long ride along the bayou and through the cotton fields. The weather had been kind thus far, and the cotton was green and full. The rich, fertile soil of Shadow Marsh would surely yield a fine crop this year. Getting it to market would be a dilemma in itself.

Before returning to the Big House Anna galloped her horse across the back fields and sat for a few moments behind one of the silos, watching Morgan work with the latest of his untrained men. Most weren't much older than school boys, and others appeared old enough to be Anna's father. As Morgan related to her, some exhibited strong leadership qualities, and others couldn't pull on their boots without help. One, a towheaded boy sent by a doting father believing that he had the ambitions to become a general, had been heard to weep into his pillow at night. And Morgan, while frustration was frequently reflected in his voice and in his golden eyes, continued to display the patience of Job. With the keen and disciplined eye of a West Point man, Morgan easily recognized the flaws, weaknesses and strengths in the men who would become soldiers in the Confederacy.

As far as the war was concerned, Anna had decided to adopt a wait-and-see attitude. She had kept up with the accounts of battle and the published casualty lists, which were longer and longer and more closely followed the last. Both North and South had expected to triumph early in the war, and as casualties mounted and each side suffered one setback after another, spirits continued to fall.

In the parlor of Shadow Marsh that evening, Morgan sat before the cold hearth with his tired feet drawn up to a stool. He had eaten very little super and had not bothered to remove his dusty uniform jacket. He had spent the long, grueling day drilling the men and was almost too exhausted to retire to bed.

Anna sat quietly across from him, reading the latest issue of *The Daily Picayune* that Shucking Sam had brought to her, along with yard goods, lamp oil and other needed supplies from their private warehouse at the Algiers docks in New Orleans. Sam had also returned with shocking stories of the federal occupation of that dear city, and the submission of its inhabitants, who were living under the martial law imposed by Union General Nathaniel Butler. One New Orleans citizen, a Mr. William Mumford, had been hanged for tearing down the flag of the United States of America, which had been raised over the Mint. This vile act–the hanging–was just one of many that was making the name of Butler hated throughout the South.

On this comfortable June evening in 1862, with her beloved husband contentedly resting beside her and the children engaged in a quiet game beneath the large dining room table where they often played, Anna couldn't imagine anything capable of inflaming her temper. She'd spent a relaxing afternoon on horseback, enjoying her solitude and sorting things out in her mind. She had even taken a quiet moment to be thankful for the millionth time that Morgan had come home to her. Nothing in the world could disturb the peace that had settled within her.

Suddenly, though, her eyes caught sight of a bold headline in the newspaper and a spark of emerald fire replaced her absent gaze. "*Ohh*," she groaned indelicately. Startled by her unexpected outburst, Morgan lurched forward from his slumped position. "Listen to this, Morgan." Had he not been in a mood to listen to the distressing news apparently contained in the paper she was reading, he would have been powerless to stop her, for she continued in haste, "Listen to this outrageous order issued by that Yankee no-good general who controls New Orleans...that despicable General Butler! The outrage!"

Morgan did not want to betray his moment of humor, lest he anger her, so he gathered a world of patience and replied, "You've roused my curiosity, Anna. Read me what it is that has made the blood boil in your veins."

Pertly, Anna lifted her nose. "Apparently the ladies of New Orleans protested the attention of those damned Yankees, for their Mr. Butler, who considers himself a general, has issued this proclamation." Anna sniffed, relaying her disdain, and prepared to read: *No lady will take any notice of a strange gentleman, and, a fortiori of any stranger, in such a form as to attract attention. Common women do. Therefore, whatever woman, lady, or mistress, gentle or simple, who by gesture, look or word insults, shows contempt for (thus attracting the notice of) my officers and soldiers, will be deemed to act as becomes her vocation as a common woman, and will be liable to be treated accordingly. This was most fully explained to you at my office. I shall not abate, as I have not abated, a single word of that order. It was well considered. If obeyed, it will protect the true and modest woman from all possible insult. The others will take care of themselves...*" Anna's eyes lifted, filled with fiery resistance against this unseen suppressor. "How dare that warring cur dog consider decent southern women cheap and common...like his Yankee women?" Anna stopped speaking, and the way she looked at Morgan clearly indicated that she expected a degree of outrage similar to her own.

Morgan could not prevent a soft chuckle. He rose, knelt beside her and drew her close to him. His love and adoration flowed across her flesh, like a gentle wave. "My sweet Anna, my flustered little *chica* will stick up for the rights of all people, and especially your own gentle breed. How pretty you are when you are fired up like this." He smiled a wide, humorous smile. Renewed by the passion, the spirit, the beauty of her, he forgot how tired he was.

Anna cocked her head to the side and gentleness touched her features. "You're making fun of me," she pouted, drawing her hands to his strong, waiting shoulders.

"No..." Morgan nestled his head against the ruffles of her silk blouse. "I am loving you, Anna." Then, "Let us retire for the evening."

"It is only seven-thirty," she responded, smiling, aware of his thoughts and the true reason he was willing to retire so early.

"We'll have more time to cuddle, and discuss this outrageous proclamation of that warring cur dog in New Orleans."

Smiling, Anna placed her hand in his and started to rise, but swiftly moving horse's hooves suddenly echoed across the lawns of Shadow Marsh, breaking an almost haunting stillness that had settled in with the night. Morgan rose immediately and started toward the foyer. Anna merely leaped from her chair.

The door burst open and Violet stood there, her eyes wide with fear and her face flushed by her long hard ride from Hopewell, Relief at seeing Morgan temporarily erased the fear from her eyes. "Morgan, Morgan, you must flee from Shadow Marsh!"

"What has happened, Violet?" Anna interrupted.

"Federals...the federals in New Orleans are sending a company of men to arrest Morgan!"

Strangely, Morgan's features remained impassive, as if his mind could not digest this news. "What are the charges?" If he was at all surprised, he brilliantly hid it behind a look of strength and dignity quickly summoned for the moment.

"My father-in-law has just returned from visiting Governor Moore in Opelousas. He would have come himself but has taken a fever. The governor's intelligence department has learned of an order issued by General Butler to arrest you for subversion and treason against the United States."

"Subversion and treason–preposterous! I'm not sure what I did to warrant these charges...why would the governor send me this fair warning?"

"That you are both loyal men of the Confederacy should be reason enough," Violet replied with certain indignation. "The truth is that the governor remembers a time when he was not willing to save Anna's brother from the gallows, and to make amends, he is willing to save her husband."

"Christ Allmighty." Only now did a note of fear creep into Morgan's voice. He felt that sense of self-discipline he had tried to instill in other men slowly crumbling within him.

"It was the training, Morgan...training the Confederate troops here at Shadow Marsh," Violet offered. "Butler considers it an open act of treason against the United States."

"I was told when I signed that stupid pledge that I could serve the Confederacy any way I chose, except with a weapon in my hand. I have not touched a weapon since I returned to Shadow Marsh."

"Have you any idea how the federals found out, Violet?" Anna wasn't sure where she found the strength to speak. She was filled with a familiar fear...of another time...another group of blue-uniformed soldiers coming to Shadow Marsh.

A pained look came to Violet. "I don't know that part at all, and I don't know how reliable the information is either, but..." Violet looked to both Anna and Morgan, in turn. She didn't expect either to believe what she was about to tell them. "Some federal officer, knowing of her connection to the family, told Aunt Louvenia, and Aunt Louvenia, of course, sent word to Governor Moore so that he could get word to you much quicker than she could."

"What federal officer?" Anna asked.

"I don't know."

"And neither do I," Morgan interjected. "The only federal officer who would have done this is my brother, Jarred. If he was in New Orleans, he would have found a way to let me know. No–it is not Jarred."

"Then who?" Anna queried, sitting on the edge of the divan

to think about this startling development.

"The governor wasn't told his name," Violet replied. "Louvenia would say nothing to jeopardize the Yankee's life."

Morgan cleared his throat. "We cannot concern ourselves with the identity of our mysterious protector. We need to decide what to do."

Violet's eyes filled with tears. There was almost prettiness in her thin features as she looked at Morgan. "Governor Moore indicates that in addition to the federals taking you prisoner, it is rumored that Shadow Marsh may be..." Her voice trailed off into an inaudible whisper.

"May be what, Violet?" Anna's voice rose in intensity–and fear.

Frightened by the inflection in her mother's voice, Bonnie began to cry, and the boys looked at their parents with confusion and worry. Bess appeared from the foyer, gathered the children up, and with comforting words moved with them toward the stairs and the nursery.

Anna raced back through her mind to remember what Violet had said. "You were going to say something about Shadow Marsh."

Momentarily distracted by the retreat of Bess and the children, Violet looked toward Anna. "Shadow Marsh will be burned, Anna–burned," she repeated with more vehemence. "It is the Yankees' way of dealing with traitors!"

"I am not a traitor," Morgan said quietly.

"I know that. I didn't mean to imply that you were."

Morgan gave Violet an apologetic smile, and slowly walked back into the parlor, standing for a moment before the window. He looked out into the peaceful gray evening and watched gold shimmer across the timberline with calm deliberateness. Thoughts raced through his head. He heard Anna's hesitant approach and without speaking opened an inviting arm to her.

Anna didn't know what to say or do. She knew only that she could not bear to be parted from Morgan again. There had been too many partings, and each one had thoroughly broken her heart. "When you leave, Morgan, the children and I will leave with you."

"I don't know if I will allow myself to be driven away by this injustice," he said thoughtfully. "I don't understand...I am not the only exchanged Confederate officer in the South training men for battle."

"You must not allow yourself to be taken. That's all there is to it."

Morgan turned and met her silent, expectant gaze. She was right, of course. It would be suicidal. "I will not allow myself to be taken prisoner, Anna, but running will not save Shadow Marsh from being needlessly torched," he reasoned. "I need a moment to think this out–to decide what to do."

"Whenever you decide that you must leave, the children and I *will* go with you."

"Yes, I know that you will, Anna...but that's not what worries me right now. It's Shadow Marsh–the home your great-grandfather built for his family–for you and the generations to come after you. I will not see what is yours destroyed because of me."

"Shadow Marsh is *ours...ours!*" Anna's dark head rested against his chest. "The house is not important, for I would live in a tent with you. Our togetherness, our love–our children–that is all I care about."

"I will not see Shadow Marsh destroyed because of me," he repeated with more emotion.

Violet, who had waited nearby and had heard every word exchanged between them, slowly approached. "Morgan...about Shadow Marsh–my father-in-law had a suggestion that might work. He suggested that you take Anna and the children and flee to Mexico until the war has ended. The people of Cabin Row are the salvation of Shadow Marsh," Violet continued. "It is their race the Yankees fight to free from slavery. If their families occupy Shadow Marsh–this house–if this roof shelters what the Yankees consider the South's suppressed people, perhaps it will not be burned.

"I will not ask the people at Shadow Marsh to save a luxury

for us that is not also their luxury."

Hope at Violet's suggestion had leaped into Anna's heart. "And how do you think they would feel, Morgan, to hear you say that?"

"What do you mean?"

"These people don't just work for Shadow Marsh, Morgan. They are our friends–our family. Their children grow with our children and learn from each other. Their tears are our tears, and their happiness ours. How can you even think they would resent helping us in this way?" Anna quickly closed the distance between them. "Morgan, we share a close bond with our people..."

They hadn't heard her approach, but now, Bea stood behind them. "Mist' Morgan, you too proud to be askin' us for help?"

A delicate crimson brushed Morgan's features."No, Bea, of course not."

"Then Bea's folks–they do what they can, Mist' Morgan."

Morgan turned, his eyes warming as they looked toward the solemn Bea. He approached and put his hand lightly on her shoulders. "Forgive me. I just sometimes don't look at things in the same light as everyone else. Gather our people together, Bea. And send Sam out to the encampment to rouse the soldiers. I think we all need to talk."

When Bea had left, Morgan again put an inviting arm out to Anna. He lifted a hand to Violet, who was quietly leaving. His heart was quietly breaking, and he could tell, by her gentle tremble against his body, that Anna's heart was breaking, too.

* * *

Nathaniel Butler sat back in his chair and drew his booted feet up to the polished desk. He was digging at his immaculate fingernails with a pocket knife and trying very hard to suppress a sigh of boredom. He was well aware of his immense unpopularity, both among his own officers and among the people of New Orleans because of his hanging of Mr. Mumford. He had never tried to deny that he was an unlikable, pompous lout, and that he derived great pleasure from the impression he made on other people.

The officer who sat before him had gained the popularity in New Orleans that Nathaniel Butler had not. While Major Lane Canady was a strictly disciplined man, there was also a deep awareness and understanding in him that was easily detected by the citizens of New Orleans–an understanding that went far beyond the realms of this pompous general's consciousness.

"What were we discussing, Canady?" Butler asked.

"You were asking me, sir," Canady reminded him, "how the Louisiana governor learned of the arrest warrant for Colonel York."

"And can you enlighten me?"

Sweat broke beneath Lane Canady's collar. He wondered, worriedly, if Butler already knew from where the information had leaked. "A network of spies," Canady replied cautiously. "Every war is plagued by them. And you know, being a loyal Southerner, Moore has already informed Colonel York of the warrant. I simply cannot see the necessity of risking the lives of even one of our men to attempt to act on such a warrant."

"Do you know precisely who took the news to Moore?" Butler was watching him intently, aware of his sudden nervousness–and a waterfall of perspiration easing down his neck.

Canady would never have relayed the news of the warrant to Louvenia Etienne had he felt it was justified. York's activities had been relayed to Butler by a vicious, vindictive man bent on revenge–a man named Luther Brady. "I do not."

"Would you tell me if you did?"

"Probably not, sir," Canady replied truthfully.

Butler came forward angrily, banging his fists on his desk. "If I find out I'll hang the bastard, you can be sure of that! And I've a good mind to hang you, too, Canady, for your insolence!" Nathaniel Butler was well aware that Lane Canady was not an easily intimidated man. There was a quiet dignity about him that the general envied. "You're saying then that this rebel officer has probably already fled?"

Canady had not taken Butler's threat to hang him seriously. He had made the same threat against his manservant several weeks ago when a rat had gotten into his water closet. Aware, now, of the general's stern glare, he raced back through his mind to remember what he had been asked. "York—yes, I believe he has already fled."

"You condone what he is doing?"

"I do not, sir," Canady replied wearily. "But other exchanged southern officers are training troops on their home ground and you have not issued warrants for their arrests. I am left cold trying to figure why you singled York out."

Butler raised his finger and lightly shook it. "None of those others are West Point officers. They are untrained nincompoops! But this York—he is a well-trained, well-disciplined West Point man. He could put some good rebel soldiers in the field."

"You have singled him out because he's a West Point man?"

"Partly..." Butler absently flipped his wrist. "And to be rid of this insipid man who came to me about his activities. Since you are so sure York may already have fled, we will hold the warrant in abeyance."

"For how long, sir?"

"A day and a half longer than forever," Butler replied sarcastically. "Take half a dozen men to this man's home and burn it to the ground."

Canady rose immediately. "I have heard you were going to take this action, general, but didn't want to believe it. The house does not belong to Colonel York, but is the ancestral home of his wife and her children. They have done nothing wrong!"

"The woman harbored the rebel."

"The woman harbored her husband!"

Butler was a little surprised both by Canady's insolent tone and his knowledge of the rebel colonel whose activities had pinched such a nerve within him. "And how is it that you know so much of York?"

"I met the family some years ago," Canady admitted. "They're decent people." Canady drew his fingers to his clean-shaven chin. Since meeting Morgan three years ago, he had gone out of his way to learn as much about him as possible.

Everything he had learned had only served to enhance the respect he had felt for him that warm September evening. "Sir, could I tell you what I know of Colonel York?"

Linking his fingers, Butler again settled back and gave Canady a crisp look across the desktop. "In an attempt to change my mind?"

"Perhaps."

Butler was willing to entertain Canady's gentle entreaties to save the home of this traitor to the honor of West Point. He had been bored with the day, and perhaps Canady could humor him. "Very well, continue, Major."

In the next few minutes, Canady told General Butler about how Morgan–or Captain Michael George Fielding–an honor graduate of West Point Military Academy, had tearfully killed his mortally wounded brother after battle with Mexicans...how he had been sentenced to death, and of a compassionate firing squad who had refused to execute him. He told him of the move to Fort Scott that had resulted in the intervention of providence and Morgan's miraculous survival in sub-freezing weather that had claimed the lives of five other men. He told him everything he had learned of the man and how his travels had ultimately led him to Shadow Marsh and the woman who was now his wife. He told him of his loving children, and the orphaned son of his wife's brother he had accepted as his own.

Although Butler seemed to listen attentively, he made no immediate reply. He returned to the chore of picking at his nails, then cleared his throat, looked across the desk at Canady and favored him with a half-smile. "You are asking for compassion, Major?"

"Yes," Canady replied.

"You know I am not a compassionate man."

"I am aware of it, sir, but I thought you might have a heart for Colonel's York's plight–that it might move some emotion in you."

"You feel you have justified his betrayal of the United States?"

"If you call it betrayal–then yes, I feel I have, sir."

Butler threw his head back and laughed heartily. "I like you, Canady. You're an open, straight-forward man. I don't always like what I hear, but, by damn, you're no coward." The front legs of Butler's chair hit the floor with an alarming thud and, immediately, dark anger replaced the crimson of humor. "I am not a compassionate man...regardless of the true ownership of Shadow Marsh, the grounds have been used to train rebel troops. This Colonel York is a traitor and since it is your belief he may have fled, I'll make sure he has no home to return to. Destroy Shadow Marsh." A world of rage swelled with the deeply drawn breath Lane Canady took. He quietly rose, preparing to leave. "Canady?" He turned back when General Butler spoke. "Take Jackson and three reliable men with you. You might be sensible to engage in this mission as a civilian–all of you." Butler gave him a look that denoted threat. "If Shadow Marsh is not burned, I'll personally conduct your court-martial."

"Please be more specific as to what you want destroyed."

"Everything, Canady...every manmade structure except those that house the suppressed people."

"The Negroes?"

"Yes." Butler again leaned back. "Residences, stables, barns, etcetera and etcetera. I think you have the picture." Just before Canady stepped out into the corridor of Butler's headquarters office, Butler added with a glint of malice, "Tell me, Canady, did you yourself pass the information about York on to a rebel sympathizer?" Butler did not detect the long, deep breath trembling down Canady's throat.

"I resent your interrogation, sir. If you believe that I did, you can take me out right now and hang me."

From the narrow, thoughtful look crossing Butler's face, Canady wondered if he was contemplating it. But a moment later Butler said, "Do have a safe trip, Canady. You're a fine officer. I depend on your loyalty to the Union. And...take plenty of matches with you."

The door quietly closed.

* * *

Morgan sat quietly in the front pew of the small clapboard

353

church. The hour was late, and a haunting stillness closed out all sounds of night–the faraway clatter and clangor of weapons and accoutrements being packed up by the men as they prepared to depart from Shadow Marsh, the melancholic humming of a young woman sitting quietly in Cabin Row, rocking a child, perhaps, or just trying to put this terrible thing that was happening out of her mind. The emotion Morgan had felt as he'd spoken to the people of Shadow Marsh, and the soldiers entrusted to his care was still a tight knot in his throat. Here, in this simple little church, he could release all the pain growing inside him.

Would there ever be a day that he could be happy and contented–a time that no evil force lurked just beyond the horizon to threaten his happiness and his world? At times like this he wished the firing squad he had faced those many years ago had not been sympathetic. Every happy moment in his life since that fated day had been ultimately spoiled by some unforeseeable injustice.

He watched the delicate swirl of satin skirts and heard, through the fog of his emotions, the soft, even breathing of his dear Anna Rose. He put his hand out to her and, without rising, gently drew the hand she placed in his to his lips to kiss it. She sat beside him and filled his arms with her softness. Her hair was long and loose, the way he liked it, and his fingers absently entwined in the thick, dark tresses.

"That was the hardest thing I have ever done," Morgan said quietly. "Dismissing the soldiers and telling our people we would have to leave Shadow Marsh. I've never felt so much pain, and so much bitterness."

"I know, Morgan...but Shadow Marsh will be here when we return. Even if the house is no longer standing, the land will be here for us. Our people will be here for us."

Gently pulling her head back, that her eyes might meet his, he said, "I have sat here, Anna, thinking about everything. My decision was made in a rash moment in which I considered the safety of only one person–myself." His hand withdrew from the softness of her hair and he stood away from her. "I won't leave,

Anna...I won't be driven away like this."

"You will–damn you, Morgan, you will," she replied, wide eyed with shock and refusing to believe this was her sensible Morgan speaking. "Put away your pride for a while and think of your family. Don't do this to us."

"You don't understand." Morgan tiredly rubbed his eyes. "If I run away, I am admitting guilt–guilt of these charges of subversion and treason."

Anna leaped to her feet, her fingers locked firmly around Morgan's wrists. "Guilt–guilt, Morgan! Are you saying that when you fled into Mexico after you put your stepbrother out of his misery that you were indeed guilty of murder?"

"No..." Anna's words shocked him, leaving him almost speechless. "My God, no, it wasn't murder."

"There!" Anna gently caressed his wrists, and took his hands to hold them. "And you're not guilty of subversion and treason either. Sam is polishing up a carriage, checking over harnesses and grooming two of our best horses. Bea is packing for our departure in the morning. And we'll leave with only one thought in mind...returning as a family to Shadow Marsh and the people we love. Returning together, Morgan–you and me and the children. Now, come..." Anna coaxed him up. "Let us sleep, for tomorrow will be a day of many decisions."

When they stepped out to the star-studded night, Morgan paused, pulling her back into his embrace. "Thank you, Anna, for being my sensible, loving wife. How would I live my life without you?"

Anna rose to her tiptoes, touching her cheek to his. "I wouldn't want you to try, Morgan. It is not your life or my life...but our life. And as long as we remember that, nothing will ever come between us."

Slowly, together, they walked toward the Big House outlined against the purple of the approaching midnight hour. Yes–tomorrow would be a day of many decisions.

# Twenty-nine

Morgan and Anna walked slowly back toward Shadow Marsh, where a stir of activity had replaced the usual quiet of the late hour. Only when they entered the house and the aroma of ham and sugared yams drifted from the kitchens did Anna remember that she'd eaten very little supper.

"Are you hungry, Morgan?"

His brows pinched, as if he needed a moment to contemplate it. Actually, his mind was a million miles away, his thoughts in turmoil in his bitterness over another forced move. "No–I couldn't eat a thing. If you're hungry go ahead and eat. I'll retire for the night." He didn't even await her response, but disappeared toward the stairs. Anna stood in the wide foyer until the sound of his boot steps disappeared behind a closing door. Suddenly, she wasn't hungry either. In the short walk from the bayou clearing, she had felt Morgan abandon the tender words he had spoken to her and mentally put distance between them. It reminded her of when they had first met, and he had viewed everyone with suspicion. It pained her that, at a time when togetherness and trust were so important, he would even think about shutting her out.

As she moved slowly in the direction of her bedchamber, she felt the weight of defeat on her shoulders. As she traversed the stairs, her eyes moved from one St. Cyr portrait to another, the grim, silent faces, the smiling, happy ones–her poor mother, Dora, who had managed to look dour even with her mouth turned ever so slightly into a smile. They were all there, hiding behind the shadow of her slow moving form. Her eyes dimmed with tears as she wondered if Shadow Marsh would be burned, despite all their efforts, and if these family portraits would be lost forever, to remain only a faint memory in her mind.

No–she would not let that happen. They would hide the portraits before their departure from Shadow Marsh. If the house burned, they would still have the faces of her family to return to.

Anna looked in on her sleeping children, kissed each one on the forehead without waking them, and quietly closed the door. She entered her own bedchamber and stood for a moment, watching Morgan's still form, his broad, naked back, and his hands drawn up and tucked beneath his face. His eyes were closed, but she knew he wasn't sleeping. She knew, when he did not acknowledge her that he had, indeed, put distance between them at a time when they needed to be close.

Anna slipped out of her clothes and into a loose fitting bed gown, easing beneath the sheets beside him. Normally Morgan would have turned and drawn her to him, but not so much as a muscle jumped when she got into bed. Yet she could see how rigid he lay, as if he were deliberately trying to fool her. Slowly, hesitantly, Anna drew close to him and her arm went across his back. She felt his flesh recoil from her touch. Although it surprised her, she did not withdraw from him.

"Don't shut me out now, Husband."

"I am not shutting you out." Anger sharpened his voice. She felt his muscles again harden beneath her touch.

"Yes, you are..."

Morgan turned, propped himself on one elbow and coldly looked at her. "What do you want of me, Anna?"

She had never seen such a look, almost as if he hated her. "A commitment."

"I gave you that when we married."

"Not that kind of commitment." Frustrated by his moroseness, Anna moved, slipped her arms around his neck and drew close to him. He relaxed against his pillow, and his hand slipped around her shoulder. "I want a commitment, Morgan, that you will make no decisions alone. I don't want to be part of your life only when things go smoothly. Let me be part of your life when you're in trouble."

Morgan made no response, but his hand traced her slender curves, her soft shoulder, her back, and the delicate rise of her slim hips. The silky gown shifted as his hand moved. Anna knew he was deep in thought and that his mind was far away from the soft, willing flesh he so absently touched. Frustrated to tears, she drew away and slipped quietly out of the bed. Standing in silhouette against the darkened window, Morgan saw the grace and beauty of her femininity gently wracked by sobs. Quickly he rose from bed and drew her into his arms.

"Forgive me, Anna–I was thinking only of myself. Feeling sorry for myself again, and when I do that, it seems I take it out on you."

"Sometimes I don't know what to do. When you put this distance between us, I feel that I can't reach you. Will you ever completely open your heart to me?"

"Come, let us return to bed," he replied, entwining his fingers in her hair. And the look in his eyes clearly told her what he wanted.

Suddenly, Anna was moved to anger. When he started to take her hand, she pulled violently away, and her melancholy was shattered by anger that came from deep within. "That's your answer to everything, Morgan! Every time I want to talk, every time I want you to talk to me, you think flopping beneath the sheets will shut me up! Not this time...talk to me, Morgan!"

Her ire could not have matched the emotions that suddenly turned his eyes to deep, dark wells. He stared at her for a moment, his eyes narrowed and hateful, and with a brief, sarcastic quirk to his mouth, turned, pulled on his trousers and boots, grabbed his shirt from the back of a chair, and hastily left their bedchamber. She stood there, stunned by his sudden departure, hearing a door slam soundly at the front of the house. They had exchanged angry words before, but he had never walked out on her like this, not in their worst of moments.

Anna rushed from the darkened house, her only thought to be with Morgan. She needed to mend this tense moment that had risen between them, to seal the bonds of a union that should keep their hearts open to each other. She thought he would have gone to the bayou clearing, but as she passed the overseer's cottage, she noticed the sudden glow of a lamp being lit in the parlor. The cottage had been vacant for two years, and she knew Morgan was seeking solitude there.

Tiptoeing across the wide porch, she opened the door and stood for a moment. He was sitting at the table, absently, angrily, arranging the chess pieces on the board. He had not pulled on his shirt but had thrown it to the divan. Morgan did not look up as she approached. He did not acknowledge her but continued picking at the board.

"Why didn't you ever bring that up to the house?" Anna asked after a moment. There was lightness in her voice–lightness she hoped might mend the harsh words that had risen between them.

"Just never did," he replied shortly. "What do you want, Anna?"

Anna knelt and a world of hurt in her eyes was betrayed to him. "Morgan, I am so sorry. I love you very much and cannot bear this pain you're feeling. Please–I'll ask no more questions of you. You needn't say anything. Just let me be with you. Please, let me into your heart, and I will be silently yours for all time."

Taking his eyes from the chess pieces, his fingers moved toward her warm, flushed cheek, to the deep, rich masses of her hair falling across her shoulders. Tears dulled his eyes as they looked at her, and his body tensed. "Anna–dear Anna–will there ever come a day I don't disrupt your life? I love you too much to constantly put you through the torment of my problems."

He cried out to her from the very depths of his soul–a deep cry for understanding and love. And, as natural for her as was breathing, Anna's heart opened and welcomed him in. Her eyes alone were the mirrors that solicited a tiny, knowing smile and a return of the sparkle to his golden eyes. Dropping the silver chess piece he held tightly between his fingers, he drew her to him. Gently, releasing a world of hurt, enraptured by the unselfish love that flowed so naturally from her, he allowed to fall the tears he had restrained for sixteen long years, feeling them wet the rich waves of her hair.

"Don't ever leave me, Anna."

"Never," she replied, closing the breath of space that existed between them.

All noises ceased, and they entered a magical world

swirling with bright, happy colors, a world where their flesh soared as one on the wings of ecstasy, higher, higher, until they no longer controlled their own bodies. Something powerful and wonderful drew the passion from their embracing forms and blended it together, into one vast, whirling vortex of joy and wonder. Their mouths met, and the heat of desire lifted them, lifted Anna into the iron-hard, willing arms of the man she loved. He moved toward the large bed in the sleeping alcove, gently cradling her in his arms.

Her soft body beneath his hard one, Morgan smothered any words she might have spoken with a long, lingering kiss. His hands lowered and eased the loose gown up and over her body, leaving her naked beneath him. After he had shed his clothing he lay motionless, touching her, awakening every tiny cell of her body until each tingled with wondrous pain. The very depths of her were filled with the power and strength of him, and his gentle, conquering hand moved from her slender waist to the warm, moist flesh of her thighs. With a breathless gasp of anticipation and wonder, she felt the weight of his body lift for the slightest moment. As she was filled with the power of him, her legs entwined around his, and she matched his pace. As Anna was lifted to the stars by the ecstatic union of their bodies, Morgan was with her, sharing the joy and the ultimate pleasure of their mutual love for each other. As their breathing slowed in unison, Morgan eased to her side and drew her to him.

In the smallest whisper, she pledged, "I love you, Morgan, now and for all time."

Morgan gently caressed her shoulder, putting her a little away from him so that she could meet his gaze. "You have erased all my troubled thoughts, little *chica*. We will awaken in the morning and begin a new day, a new life that will ultimately return us to Shadow Marsh. This ridiculous charge of treason and subversion will not defeat us."

"Do you promise, Morgan?

"With all my heart and all my soul ... yes, I promise."

Caught in the wonderful light of his promise and the weariness of the late night, Anna drifted off to sleep in his strong arms. But Morgan lay awake, his mind filled with the worries that he had tried to convince himself would mend in time. The truth was that a deep bitterness tore at the very depths of his heart. He felt the agony in his soul that had once, a long, long time ago, set him on a very lonely path.

Morgan and Anna awakened simultaneously with the dawn. The house was already engrossed in activity and last-minute details. Anna returned to her bedchamber to bathe and change into traveling clothes, while Morgan gave various instructions to Sam. He was just returning to the house when Wren and Violet drove up in their carriage. Violet alighted and entered the house, and Morgan sat in the carriage beside Wren so that they could talk. Wren could not have arrived at a more opportune moment.

"While we're gone, Wren, I would be grateful if you'd supervise the running of Shadow Marsh. When Joby Cade returns..."

"Joby Cade probably will not return," Wren cut him off. "You should get that through your head. He's been gone too long."

"He *will* come home."

Wren settled back. He was not wearing his wooden leg and his empty trouser leg was tucked into his waistline. "Perhaps he will," he offered reluctantly. "As for Shadow Marsh, you know I will do what I can. Who controls the plantation accounts?"

"What is left of our funds is in the Alexandria Bank. You might see Anna's accountant and explain to him that you will be running things for a while. Funds are low, I understand. Our last shipments for England were confiscated by Yankee gunboats. We're fortunate to be able to sneak some supplies for the plantation from our warehouse in New Orleans, but when Butler gets wind of that, we'll lose access to the warehouse."

"Have you exchanged your notes for Confederate bills?"

Morgan shrugged. "I haven't. I believe Anna may have, but only at the insistence of the accountant."

"I do hope she didn't. It would be a grave mistake."

"And a grave mistake, I'm afraid, made by many southerners. I will not blame Anna for that. She is a passionate southern woman."

Anna exited the house with Bess and the children. Bea and Violet followed close behind, talking together in hushed tones. Both looked admonishing, a normal state for two women who had never really gotten along. Violet had always been a little envious of Bea's favoritism for Anna.

"Morgan, you'd best prepare for our departure," Anna suggested. "Children, sit and have some breakfast...and keep clean."

As Morgan hopped down from the carriage, Violet settled in. Just before they departed, she gave Anna a long hug. She did not see Anna wave goodbye because she didn't want to betray the tears she shed. Anna might have viewed such an emotion as highly suspicious. Anna sat quietly on the veranda with the children, who were morose, as though they were aware of the new life beginning for them—a new life that was breaking their parents' hearts.

"Why are we leaving, Mama?" Patrick asked, picking absently at his biscuit.

Anna leaned across the table and took his small hand in hers. "Because there are some terrible men who would put your papa in prison. We must leave so that will not happen."

"Is Papa a bad man?"

"Papa is a very good man. He has done nothing wrong. Now—don't you worry."

"Where we going, Mama?" Michael asked.

At ages three and four, the boys were very aware of the trials tugging at Anna's heart. She felt tears dim her eyes, even as she answered, "We don't know yet. We'll decide when we get a few miles away. We may even..." Anna forced a smile, "follow our hearts to the nearest rainbow—wouldn't that be fun?"

Morgan exited the house and stood for a moment, fondly looking at his family. Anna turned and, as she looked at him, was reminded of a time before their marriage, when he had been the overseer of Shadow Marsh and had dressed as he was now dressed—in dark brown trousers carefully tucked into high black boots, a white shirt, and a tan jacket. She rose when he opened

362

an inviting arm to her–to his family–and stepped into his waiting embrace.

"Are we ready?" Morgan asked, forcing back the lump in his throat.

"We are, Papa!" Patrick threw himself excitedly into Morgan's waiting arms. "Mama said we're going to visit a rainbow."

"A rainbow, eh?" Morgan approached the table to pick up Bonnie. "And does my little girl also want to visit a rainbow?"

Dimples burrowed into Bonnie's crimson cheeks as she smiled, hugging her father tightly.

Sam appeared from the carriage house with their finest carriage and pulled up to the veranda. He loaded up the bags Bea and Bess had put on the steps. The two faithful servants stood silently by, waiting for that terrible moment when the family they loved would have to leave Shadow Marsh.

Before Morgan could help Anna into the carriage with the children, a swiftly moving surrey appeared on the roadway, its occupants indistinguishable through the mass of dust stirred up by the wheels. Then the surrey pulled up to the veranda behind their carriage, and the dust settled away from the lined, smiling features of Louvenia Etienne. She climbed down with more agility than one would have expected of an eighty-year-old woman, and moved quickly toward Anna.

"Child, thank the Lord I have caught you."

A cold fear crept into Anna's voice. "Aunt Louvenia, what has happened?"

"Happened? Why nothing's happened–yet!" The old woman drew hastily away. I was afraid you'd leave without me!" Louvenie turned and barked at the hired driver, "Put my bags in this carriage. And be quick about it!"

Confusion reigned. Morgan approached and put his arm gently around Anna's shoulder. "What are you saying, Louvenia?"

Louvenia released a throaty laugh. "Just where do you think you're going with those precious children?"

"I don't really know yet," Morgan replied.

"Haa! Just as I imagined. Well–I know where I'm going, and y'all are going with me! I'm tired of being a lonely old woman with too much money. And I..." Louvenia proudly brought a withered hand to her chest, "did not exchange my gold for that worthless Confederate currency!"

"But your home is in New Orleans," Anna replied. "We can't go there."

"Child, I had four other husbands beside your Uncle Lester. Do you think my house in N'Awleans is the only one I have? No, indeed...now, come, let's depart before those damn Yankees arrive."

"But where to?" Anna asked.

"I'll tell you when we're a few days out. Right now, we wouldn't want anything to slip to the Yanks, now, would we?" Louvenia stood beside the carriage, and gave Morgan an annoyed look. "Come, come, young man–help me up! Where are your manners?"

Morgan and Anna shared a look, and sharing the same warm feeling for this blunt old woman, gave each other knowing smiles.

With Louvenia and the children settled into the carriage, Morgan and Anna said goodbye to the servants who had gathered. Morgan remained firm and spoke very little, lest he betray his emotions, but Anna broke down and wept in Bea's arms.

"Do take care, my friend," Anna whispered, "We'll be home in no time. Oh, I promise, we will come home." Then, so that no one but Bea could hear, "Do not jeopardize any of your people. If the Yanks want to burn Shadow Marsh, remember...it is just a house. We can build a new one." Sam and some of the men had already taken their family portraits out to the shed at the edge of the hidden pasture. They would be safe there.

A tearful Bea said nothing, but firmly patted Anna's shoulder and retreated quickly toward the house.

Morgan settled in the driver's seat and flicked the reins at the team. They drove slowly through Cabin Row, allowing the children to walk beside them, allowing weeping faces to bring tears to their own eyes. Then the carriage entered the curve in the bayou road. Through tear-dimmed eyes Anna watched the massive structure of Shadow Marsh–their happy and loving home–slowly disappear beyond the timberline. She wondered how long it would be before the Yankees came. She wondered if Shadow Marsh would still be there when they returned.

\* \* \*

For four days, Lane Canady had been trying to figure a way he could leave Shadow Marsh standing and still obey his orders. He hated Nathaniel Butler for sending him on this unjust mission. Yet he would rather have been sent himself than a less compassionate officer. He and the three civilians with him stopped somewhere along Bayou Bouef to make camp for the night and ate a silent meal of dried beef and cold biscuits. Afterwards, Lane took a few leisurely moments to smoke his pipe and look over his map. Shadow Marsh was about eight miles northwest.

Because he was in civilian clothes and looking very southern, Lane and his men had traveled unmolested through the Louisiana wilderness along the Atchafalaya and eventually to Bayou Bouef. They had spent a comfortable night in the warm hayloft of a plantation to the south the night before and had been fed a good breakfast of ham and eggs.

Looking at his pocket watch he saw that it was a quarter before the hour of eleven, the hands of his watch reflected in the light of the moon. The other men were asleep. Eventually Lane nestled down in his sleeping roll and crossed his arms at his chest. If they rose and began their journey at four in the morning, they should reach Shadow Marsh by dawn.

\* \* \*

Shucking Sam and the men had already loaded the wagon with provisions for the fields when the dust of approaching riders caught their attentions. Sam immediately sent one of the men scurrying for the Big House. "Bea! Bea!" Wiping her hands on a huge apron, Bea appeared at the veranda. "Men–men is a-comin'."

Bea drew a deep, trembling breath. "Lawd Jesus!" She

stood her ground firmly as the riders approached, and the tallest of the four dismounted his horse.

Lane Canady removed his hat, taking a paper from his jacket pocket, which he unfolded. "Please take this warrant to Colonel York and tell him we await him. He is being arrested."

Bea would not take the paper. "The colonel and his family, they done left. They ain't comin' back."

Lane Canady actually breathed a sigh of relief. He had expected as much. Producing another paper from his pocket, he announced, "Lady, these are my orders to burn every structure at Shadow Marsh that is not occupied by your people..." Bea felt faint. When she swayed, Lane Canady was instantly at her side, helping her to a chair. A moment later Bess and her two children, and Lizzie and her children exited the house. Lane approached. "What are you people doing in this house? Don't you live out there?" he continued, pointing to Cabin Row.

"Why we should live out there," Bea said firmly, "When we got this big ol' house? My family–family of Shuckin' Sam–and seven other families–we live in this house."

And for what reason are you living here?"

An impertinent scowl touched Bess's face. She was usually so quiet, and her sudden bravado surprised even Bea. "The white folks, they's gone. Why shouldn't we live here?"

Lane Canady turned with an imperceptible smile, watching a tall, willowy boy come out of the stable. "Boy," he called to him. Lowey approached. "Do you live in that barn?"

"Naw, suh."

"Do you ever sleep there tending sick stock?"

"Sometimes, suh."

"Then you live there, way I see it." Canady returned his attentions to Bea. "That structure out by the road–what's in it?"

"Supplies, hay...some of Miss Anna's old furniture."

"Any of your people live there?"

"Sir?" Through her fearful eyes, sudden recognition came to Bea. She remembered meeting this man a long time ago. She had served him at their dinner table and, strangely, remembered his compassion and the results of his last visit. Bea knew what he was getting at. "Yes, sir, they's lots o' folks livin' here and jes' a few cabins. They's folks livin' out yonder in that warehouse."

"Those silos–any grain kept there?"

"Naw. . ." Bea shook her head. "Run down. Miss Anna, she was goin' to have 'em torn down one day."

The other three men dismounted and the man named Jackson approached. "What the hell are you doin', Canady?"

Lane Canady turned and walked around the veranda. "I'm obeying my orders." He gave Jackson a narrow look. "You and Shopps go out there and burn those three old silos–not the new one–Wiggins, you come with me."

Bea gasped breathlessly. "You goin' to burn the house, Yank?"

"Your people live here, don't they?"

"Yes, sir."

"My orders are to burn every structure not occupied by your people. As I see it, that leaves those three old silos in the field. You did say you have a man living in that new silo, didn't you?" Bea merely nodded. "I'll burn the old ones and be on my way."

Jackson immediately took Canady's arm, swinging him around. "The general said burn everything–goddamn it, sir, if you don't burn that house, I'll report your actions to Butler."

Canady tore his arm from Jackson. Fury sparked between the two men. "I am obeying my orders, Jackson. Now–the two of you get back there and burn those silos!"

Jackson bristled up to argue. "The major is obeying orders," Shopps interjected, "the way I see it. Butler said to burn any structure that did not house the darkies. And that's what the major's doin'."

Disgruntled, Jackson took matches and a torch from his saddle case. As he started across the lawn, he said, "This ain't the end of it, Canady." He mumbled curses beneath his breath that Canady and Wiggins did not hear. When they were a few feet from the first of the silos, Jackson ordered, "You, Shopps, burn those two. And me–I'll burn this big bastard to the ground." With the energy of a madman, Jackson entered the small side door of the silo, pushing his way through fallen debris. The interior was dark. The nauseating smell of damp, rotting grain in a corner filled his senses. When he struck a match and lit the torch, a hundred rats scurried through the rotting grain to escape this unknown menace. With a mighty yelp, Jackson, as he tried to hastily retreat, hit his head on a board that had fallen across the doorway. The torch fell, and immediately the dry grain and lumber that had not been dampened by rainfall burst into flames around his body.

Shopps heard only the loud, terrified scream of Jackson as his flaming body walked a few feet across the meadow and collapsed, setting the grass around him on fire. None of the men had liked Jackson, but–what a way to die!

An hour later, the three silos were nothing but rubble in the meadows of Shadow Marsh, and the men of Cabin Row stood around with shovels, keeping the fires from spreading. What remained of Jackson was buried where he fell, and one of the men made a remark about Jackson taking no tales to General Butler.

At a quarter before the hour of ten, Canady and his men sat astride their horses, preparing to depart. Canady tipped his hat to Bea. "I can't say the house is safe tomorrow–but it is safe today...good day. Tell Mrs. York when again you see her that I'm sorry about the silos." Lane turned his horse, but paused and looked again at Bea. "Would you tell me how long they've been gone?"

"Fo' days," Bea replied.

"And to where have they gone?"

"Don't rightly know, Mr. Yank–an' wouldn't tell you if I did." There was no disrespect in her voice.

"You folks can keep Jackson's horse." Again Lane Canady tipped his hat and nudged his horse into a slow canter.

When the three riders had disappeared around the curve, Bea turned to Bess and Lizzie. "Now–you two–git all them young'uns out'n this house. Ain't goin' to have it messed up befo' Miss Anna and Mist' Morgan return."

Standing alone, Bea looked out over the wide green lawns

of Shadow Marsh with an emptiness in her heart. A tear touched her cheek. It was lonely without Anna and Morgan and the children. "When this ugly war is over, you'll be comin' home," she whispered. "I jus' know you will. An' Shadow Marsh will be here fo' you. Bea promises you that."

She entered the silent, lonely house whose happiness had fled with the family she missed with all her heart and all her soul. She lived only for the day she would see their warm, happy faces once again.

# Epilogue

When General Lee surrendered his troops to Ulysses S. Grant at Appomattox Courthouse on April 9, 1865, a new way of life began for the defeated South that bore little resemblance to the society of days long past. The life of the rich southern aristocracy was ended. Destroyed by the passion that had inflamed them were the often pompous chivalry of her gentlemen and the flirtatious blushes of wealthy southern daughters vying for their attentions. With the influx of federal troops to restore order to the South came the graft-ridden carpetbaggers. And behind them came the tax collectors.

Shadow Marsh and her sister plantations along Bayou Bouef had been overlooked in the burning of Alexandria by federal troops the year before. Three years later, a more lethal blight plagued the plantation that had been reluctantly abandoned by its owners for five long years. In addition to twenty-thousand dollars in debts that had not been paid to creditors, half that amount in taxes was levied against all properties of Shadow Marsh. One day, at the temporary parish courthouse in Alexandria, Luther Brady, carrying graft money provided by wealthy northern industrialists to buy debt-ridden plantations, waited patiently for the properties to go on the block. And he wanted Shadow Marsh with a vengeance.

It was a hot, humid July day. Sweating profusely, both from the heat and from too much whiskey flowing through his veins, Luther Brady took a dirty handkerchief from his pocket and wiped his neck and forehead. Small parcels of land had been put up and sold, and he was anxious to get his hands on Shadow Marsh. His first order of business would be to evict all residents of Cabin Row, and to bring in his own people from the North.

The auction was announced ended. With surprise bordering closely on panic, Luther Brady gruffly yelled, "Shadow Marsh is on the list for today!"

The town marshal looked briefly at Luther Brady, then at his list. "Shadow Marsh, sir?"

"Yeah–Shadow Marsh." Luther spat tobacco juice on the step, narrowly missing the shoes of a well-dressed city gentleman.

An imperceptible grin touched the normally stern features of the auctioneer. "Shadow Marsh, sir, was redeemed yesterday afternoon and taken off the list."

Luther Brady's knees weakened. Beneath the unkempt beard, a purple rage slowly flooded his thin, dry face. Nine years he had waited for vengeance, and it had been taken from him in the blink of an eye. "By who, dammit?"

"A bank draft was received, sir, from a reputable gentleman in Tarrytown, New York."

Hysteria rose in the cruel little man obsessed with taking Shadow Marsh from the uppity woman who had discharged him. "How, dammit–how did this *gentleman* learn of the tax sale?"

"I wrote him about it."

Luther Brady spun swiftly toward the deep, familiar voice several feet behind him. He might have leaped at the man, but the latter had twice his size and strength.

The three years he'd spent in an Arkansas prison, sentenced by rebel fanatics as a runaway slave, had left Joby Cade with a cold indifference and a strange, overpowering fearlessness that sensible men both avoided and respected. This past year since the war had ended the thing Joby Cade had cared most about was that one day Morgan and Anna should return to their home. He wanted Shadow Marsh to be there for them, virtually as they had left it.

"You–you damned interfering buck!" Luther's gruff, angry words drew a small crowd of men who had lingered after the sale. One taunted Luther Brady, who had become the town drunk.

"Gonna let the boy outsmart you, eh, Luther?"

With a torrent of mumbled curses, Luther took a bottle of whiskey from his jacket pocket and started toward the levee of the Red River.

Joby Cade picked up his new wife at the mercantile where she was purchasing needed supplies and, at Joby's request, sweets for the children of Cabin Row. Joby loaded the wagon, and with Marigold sitting silently beside him, headed slowly back toward Shadow Marsh, fourteen miles away.

Joby was learning to love the feisty Marigold, but he would never forget his gentle Lovey. He remembered with a deep pain her easily offered smiles, and warm, pleasant features–now characterized in the face of their young daughter. He remembered his shock at returning home and finding that she had been dead four long years. He remembered, in an insane rage, taking up an axe and hacking at Alistair St. Cyr's tombstone until it was just a pile of broken marble at his feet. He remembered the bitter, angry sobs as he had dropped to his knees on the rain-dampened earth and felt Bea's gentle, comforting hand drop to his shoulder.

He would never forget his Lovey. They'd shared something very special–something that would not come easily with another wife. But Joby had needed someone, both for himself and his children, and Marigold had filled that special need. Mentally, Joby Cade smiled. If he hadn't gotten Marigold away from Hopewell and Miss Violet, there was a pretty good chance the two women would have eventually ended up at each other's throats, like warring cats.

The trip was long and silent. Joby was glad to see the small settlement at Jude's Landing come into view and a few miles further on along Bayou Bouef, the large, familiar oaks that shrouded the wide roadway leading to Shadow Marsh. When the wagon entered the shaded common of Cabin Row, the children swarmed around them, waiting to see what treasures had been brought from Alexandria. By the veranda of the Big House, Joby saw an unfamiliar carriage with rich burgundy leather seats gleaming in the late afternoon sun.

"Got visitors, young'uns?" he asked, alighting. "Not them damn carpetbaggers, huh?"

Bess ran excitedly from her cabin. "Joby! Joby–Mist' Morgan and Miss Anna–they's come home."

For Joby, all else was forgotten. He did not stop to help Marigold down from the wagon, but left the job to Shucking Sam. He walked mechanically toward the Big House, mentally berating himself for the weakness he felt flood through him–and the disbelief draining the color from his face. When he reached the veranda, Morgan appeared from the foyer and, like old times past, flew off the porch with a mighty yell and locked himself in a firm bear hug with his friend.

"Mist' Morgan–God! It's good to see you!" Joby could not prevent the tears that moistened his eyes.

Morgan drew back, softly laughing. "My good friend, I thought you were lost. I thought I'd never see you again. When they told me you'd returned–damn! It's good to see you."

Joby grinned. "You ain't changed a bit, Mist' Morgan, 'cept fo' a few pounds maybe."

Morgan laughed. "I'm getting old, Joby." Then, "We have a lot to talk about, you and I."

Anna appeared from the foyer, followed closely by the boys and Bonnie. Joby greeted Anna warmly. "I was real sorry to hear about yo' Aunt Louvenia, Miss Anna," Joby said after a moment. "When Bea got yo' letter, she was real sorrowful."

"We had three wonderful years with her, Joby. And I like to think that our family made her last days happy."

"Yes, ma'am." Joby offered his hand to the children, who briefly and politely shook it. Momentarily, and with a great feeling of guilt, Joby had felt a renewed tinge of loathing for Alistair St. Cyr when he had gazed into the features of his son. But the smiling boy bore no resemblance to his father, and he knew that nothing more of Alistair St. Cyr resided there. Patrick was Morgan's son.

Michael bubbled forth, "Can we go down there, Mama..." he pointed to Cabin Row, "to meet all the children?"

"You certainly may," Anna replied, smiling at their enthusiasm. "Hold Bonnie's hand and don't let her fall." Then to Joby Cade, "We are so happy to return home to Shadow Marsh and find you here."

Joby smiled. "Got some stories to tell you when you got the

time, Miss Anna."

Morgan firmly gripped Joby's shoulder. "And we have some stories to tell you, Joby. Come, let's saddle a couple of horses and ride out to the fields." Morgan turned to Anna and gave her a brief smile. "Would you like to ride with us?"

"After all those miles of travel? No, indeed! Go on, you two—Bea and I have a world of catching up to do."

Half an hour later, Morgan and Joby crested the hill in the eastern meadow, which was green and thick with clover. Half a dozen cows with young calves and three mares with foals, grazed down the meadow. Then Morgan heard a familiar whinny, and from the far pasture, he saw Amigo straining against the fence. Then the stallion stepped back and began trotting up and down the fence, its tail high and flying in the summer wind, its nostrils flaring as it caught the human scent of them. Breathlessly, Morgan watched as Amigo reared on his haunches and his front legs sliced the air with more power than he had seen in any other horse.

"Kept him safe fo' ya," Joby said. "'Cause I know ya love 'em so." He had waited two long years for Morgan to see how strong and healthy he had kept his favorite horse and also through an almost fatal bout of colic last winter. He had lain down in the barn for seven nights with the horse while he had worked through the sickness.

Emotion was a hard, painful lump in Morgan's throat. Quietly he watched Amigo trot up to them as they entered his pasture, and nudge him for the lump of sugar Morgan had always kept for him. Joby discreetly produced a few lumps from the pocket of his trousers, which Morgan gave to him. "Thank you for keeping him safe. This horse and I have been through a lot together."

They rode for two long hours, seeing everything...the healthy, green cotton covering a thousand acres–the rice fields and the corn that was shoulder high. Joby showed him the herd of cows he'd purchased these past two years with money he'd earned working on other plantations on the weekends. And there, among the small, healthy herd, was Morgan's fifteen-hundred-dollar bull.

"Strange he wasn't taken by the federals," Morgan reflected.

"Shuckin' Sam, he hid that beast out in the swamp down 'round Beaver Creek. Ain't nobody but a snake could'a found him."

They shared reminiscences of long-past moments, then rode by Hopewell for a happy reunion with Wren and Violet, leaving with Violet's promise that she wouldn't tell Anna they'd come by. The visit next day of the family was supposed to be a surprise. They were coaxed home only by the late hour and the dinner that would be waiting to fill their empty stomachs.

After dinner, with the excitement of the day settled and exhausted children carted off to their bedchambers by a doting Bess, Morgan and Anna walked together to the veranda of Shadow Marsh. There they spent a few happy moments looking out over their beloved homeland.

It had been a long five years since they'd fled in haste with the children. But they had stayed together, and that was all that was important. They had spent a year in San Francisco, where the only evidence of war was newspaper accounts and swarms of both federal and confederate deserters fleeing to the west. Then at Aunt Louvenia's insistence, they had vacationed with her in Paris, where she had died just before Lee's surrender reached the Paris newspapers.

While Morgan had tried to show happiness, he had silently brooded over yet the latest injustice inflicted on him and had carried a constant, bitter anger in his heart. Succumbing to Anna's gentle coaxing, they had finally journeyed to Tarrytown, where Morgan was reunited with the mother he had not seen in nineteen years. Once again, through the endeavors of his stepbrother of whom he had asked assistance, the intervention of a President of the United States–this time President Andrew Johnson–the charges of subversion and treason lodged against him by General Nathaniel Butler in 1862 were personally dismissed as an insane whim of an insane man.

During the past twenty years Morgan had learned many

valuable lessons. He had learned to forgive and to respect the United States of America, no matter the sting of injustice he had felt He had learned that to ask help of another man was not a sign of weakness, but of strength. He had learned that the bitterness a man carried in his heart hurt no one but himself. He had learned, above all, that a warm, compassionate woman was the greatest treasure of all.

Anna, too, had learned many lessons. She had learned to trust, to share her problems with Morgan, and to quietly accept his judgment. She had learned that man and woman–husband and wife–should keep no secrets that might one day dampen their love for each other. She had learned, above all, that a gentle, warm-hearted man was the greatest treasure of all.

Morgan opened his arm and invited Anna into his warm embrace. He was happy to be home at Shadow Marsh. "Come, little *chica*, I am anxious to visit our favorite place, to see if it is as we left it."

Together, in silence, they strolled across the wide, green lawns of Shadow Marsh and toward the bayou clearing where they had shared their happiest moments. Not a twig or a leaf appeared different from the day they had reluctantly left their sanctuary.

Mingled with the soothing, faraway sounds of the quickly approaching night, Anna heard the soft, even breathing of a contented man. Morgan drew her into his arms and his mouth captured hers in the gentlest of kisses. "My Anna–my wild southern rose–how is it possible for a man to be so happy?" Anna merely cooed against him.

Content in each other's arms, Morgan and Anna watched the night settle upon the timberline of Shadow Marsh, boldly outlining the dormered roof of their home against the golden sunset of another day ended–and the beginning of a life renewed by the spirit of a love that time and distance would never destroy.

They were home at Shadow Marsh. They were Louisianans–and Americans. The future lay ahead of them like a long golden path to be walked hand in hand, and heart to heart.

As they stood there, the last gentle rays of the setting sun, slanting through the moss-shrouded cypress of Bayou Bouef, caught their passions for each other and scattered them among the stars.

**Caroline Bourne** was born in Southampton, England to an American father and an English mother. Spending only seven months in England, she grew up in the small southern town of Lecompte, Louisiana, in between transfers to Army posts in Texas and Arkansas with her Army father. She was an avid horse lover and spent many hours on horseback, riding with a group of friends on weekends. Graduating from Lecompte High School in 1965 she went on to spend two years in the United States Marine Corps, being honorably discharged as a Corporal E-4 in 1967. Returning to Louisiana, she went to work for a local newspaper, the Alexandria Daily Town Talk, eventually married and had two daughters, Kristen and Kimberly. Her first novel was published in 1984 by Kensington and 12 others, plus a co-authorship and two contributions to anthologies followed. As the years passed, she worked for lawyers and judges, and eventually moved to Indiana to be near her sister. For the past fourteen years she has worked for a Southern Indiana police department. Today, she is the grandmother of six granddaughters and one great-grandson.